Mr
CASSINI

To my mother, Mary,
My sister, Eurwen,
And my brother, Dafydd.

Mr
CASSINI

Lloyd Jones

seren

Seren is the book imprint of
Poetry Wales Press Ltd
57 Nolton Street, Bridgend, CF31 3AE, Wales
www.seren-books.com

ISBN 1-85411-425-5

A CIP record for this title is available from
the British Library.

The publisher works with the financial assistance
of the Welsh Books Council.

Printed in Plantin by CPD (Wales), Ebbw Vale

The spirit of any age is captured by the way it dances, and by the way it describes magic.

Cassini – *The Dexter Propensity.*

Is motion the only reality?

Theroux – *The Primary Colors.*

I wish to thank Academi, whose grant made it possible for me to write this book.

INTRODUCTION

IT was a time of ice and emptiness. A time of hunger, too. He had gone to the island in winter, and he had freed lapwings and redwings frozen to the white ground, glued into place as if they were living postage stamps.

He had stood on the ice to hear it crack. He had found echoes in the cliffs around him, and his voice had resounded from towers and steeples of uncontaminated white.

He had thrown stones on the frozen lakes, and they had zinged in the way that railway lines zing when a train is travelling down the line.

He had been to other islands, this man who wore gloves on his island of glass. He had been to one of the loneliest islands in the world, further away from the teeming continents than almost anywhere else on Earth – a speck in the South Atlantic. He had gone there to learn about a failed adventurer, hideously disfigured, who had hidden himself away for a very long time.

The adventurer was called Fernando Lopez, a Portuguese nobleman, who had been among a cadre of soldiers which had gone native while their commander left Goa to fetch more conquistadors. Shackled and maimed as a punishment for adopting the free-and-easy lifestyle of the Moslems, Lopez lost his right hand, his left thumb, his ears and his nose; also his hair, beard and eyebrows were plucked out in a practice known as *scaling the fish*. On his way back to Portugal in 1515, returning to his wife and children, Lopez was overcome by qualms when his ship anchored at St Helena to take on water. He fled ashore and hid in the forest. The crew left him a tinderbox and a saucepan, a barrel of biscuits and some dried meat. He was the island's first inhabitant, and his strange exile lasted for 30 years, until his death. In all those years, living so far from the mass of men, he slept on a straw bed in a grotto which he'd hewn himself. It became the still point of his life, far away from society's slow obsessions. As the years went by, Lopez showed himself to visiting sailors, who regarded him as a saint. Taking pity on him, they gave him whatever they had to offer, including seeds and tree cuttings such as palm, banana, lemon, orange, lime and pomegranate. They gave him ducks, hens, peacocks and turkeys; also cats and dogs, and farmyard animals. Labouring incessantly, he planted orchards and vine-yards, extravagant gardens and prosperous vegetable plots: his mini-paradise became legendary, and the story of his Lear-like kingship over a perfect, uncivilised dominion was eventually heard by the monarchy in his homeland. They summoned him to their palace and, once he had made his reticent appearance at court, he was allowed to go to Rome where he gained absolution for his sins. Then, overcome again by humanity, he returned to his island home and went into hiding until he secured a promise that he would never have to leave it again.

Our traveller – this man who wore gloves on his island of glass – had been to other islands too, many of them. He had been to Galapagos and to the Islands of the Colour-Blind. He had been to the Hebrides, to the island of Jura, where he'd heard the rockfall of Orwell's typewriter as his great futuristic novel *Nineteen Eighty-Four* took shape. He had listened to Orwell's consumptive cough as the dreadful winter of 1947 tightened his chest and took him ever-closer to death; he had seen new words etched in crystal ice on Orwell's windowpanes: *Newspeak, Doublespeak,* and *Big Brother.*

To learn something about this man who wears gloves, always, even in his sleep, we must go back in time. He was very ill once, in a hospital, and he felt very weak. As they tested his body he had time to reflect on his life. We must go back to one particular night, an important night in his life. It was New Year's Eve, and he was sitting alone in a hospital side room, fighting the forces of darkness as they gathered around him, and listening to fireworks going off in the nearby town, watching them streak the sky with silver and many brilliant colours. As Big Ben began its preamble to midnight a doctor summoned him, with a finger, to his bed. So, as midnight struck, he was being examined again and he was trying hard not to scream.

It was then, in the first minute of the new year, that he decided on a course of action. Tired of feeling neither dead nor alive, a zombie in fact, he had made a pact with himself: if he was to live he would *live*. If he was to die he would die, and quickly.

That night, as he sat in the hall of mirrors which is death's antechamber, a strange incident took place. He may have been semi-conscious, but he certainly wasn't asleep when he experienced a brief but intense vision. Quite suddenly he was in a small, roofless room which was perfectly white. He was sitting on a low bench, made of something like white plastic. In front of him were two unmarked doors, which could have been virtual doors because they had no handles. He knew without being told that one door led to life, the other to death. Our traveller took the one which led to life, and he is still with us today. What is remarkable is that during the six months following that miraculous escape through the white door, the world seemed more brilliant and beautiful than he had ever seen it: nature was more resplendent and exciting, Wales more lovely, colours more scintillating, experiences more resonant than at any other time in his life. That is what he told people whom he met walking in the snow.

Many people have had similar experiences – by using drugs, or by starving themselves, or by suffering some form of mental collapse. That's all by the by.

There came a time, many years later, when our traveller wanted to revisit that little white room so that he could step out of it again and see all those brilliant sights anew – but he wanted to do so without mescaline, or cocaine, or deprivation. He read about the subject. He rounded up all the usual suspects: Huxley peering through the doors of perception, Castaneda fooling with *peyote* in the Mexican desert; the sorcerer-saint Milarepa gaining the holy grail of all mystics in his Tibetan cave – mastery over his own self, and the power to change his body into any shape he wished, to fly across the sky like a bird.

But our traveller – let us call him by his nickname, Duxie – could see no way of returning to that white room. Then one day he came across the story of an eighteenth-century prince from Nigeria who'd been kidnapped by slavers. The prince, Olaudah Equiano, eventually settled in England after an adventurous life and wrote his memoirs. One particular passage made a great impression on Duxie:

> However, all my alarms began to subside when we got sight of land; and at last the ship reached Falmouth, after a passage of thirteen weeks. Every heart on board seemed gladdened on our reaching the

shore, and none more than mine. The captain immediately went on shore, and sent on board some fresh provisions, which we wanted very much: we made good use of them, and our famine soon turned into feasting, almost without ending. It was about the beginning of spring 1757, when I arrived in England, and I was nearly twelve years of age at that time. I was very much struck with the buildings and the pavement of the streets in Falmouth; and, indeed, every object I saw filled me with fresh surprise.

One morning, when I got up on deck, I perceived it covered all over with the snow that fell overnight. As I had never seen any thing of the kind before, I thought it was salt; so I immediately ran down to the mate and desired him, as well as I could, to come and see how somebody in the night had thrown salt all over the deck. He, knowing what it was, desired me to bring some of it down to him: accordingly I took up a handful of it, which I found very cold indeed; and when I bought it to him he desired me to taste it. I did so, and was surprised above measure. I then asked him what it was; he told me it was snow; but I could not by any means understand him. He asked me if we had no such thing in our country; I told him "No." I then asked him the use of it, and who made it: he told me a great man in the heavens, called God; but here again I was to all intents and purposes at a loss to understand him; and the more so, when a little after I saw the air filled with it, in a heavy shower, which fell down on the same day.

Our traveller, Duxie, felt sure that this passage had provided him with the means to describe those few seconds in his white room. Soon, he decided on a course of action. Shortly after Christmas he hired a boat to take him out to the least well known of the Welsh islands, Ynysvitrain as the English call it, together with sufficient food supplies to last him for a while. He obtained permission from the naturalists' trust, which owns a cabin on the island, to use it as a den, in return for a suitable donation towards the upkeep of his temporary home. He took with him pen and paper as well as a good supply of warm clothing. His gloves were a curio: he found them among his father's belongings, cleared from his house when he died. They fitted him perfectly, after he'd removed the cobwebbed dust-lace from their insides. They were of tight-fitting brown leather, fur-lined, with black press-studs at the wrist.

Duxie waited for the first snows of winter to fall, and then he started to write an account of the time leading up to his experience in the white room. He wrote the entire story wearing gloves, and, when he was too tired to write, he wandered around the island, which is also known as the island of glass because its many surfaces become a real-life Narnia when the cold sets in. He took with him, also, a telescope with which to study the skies and the natural world around him; finally, since all island castaways are allowed one book, he took a volume called *The Book of Snow*, written by an Inuit called Ootek. He was amazed to discover that every snowflake, though sharing the same six-sided shape, has its own individual pattern (though no one knows how this fact was established).

Which brings us to the main reason for his sojourn in the snow, on the Island of Ynysvitrain, in a wooden hut which harboured a dead ghost moth, silky white, in the barrel of its door-lock – *Wonderment*.

This everyday life of ours is rather short of it, don't you think? *True* wonderment – at the cosmos around us and within us – rather than at man's folly and madness. So he waited for the snow with a growing sense of anticipation: he was awed by the beauty of Ynysvitrain, by the beauty of the stars, and by the beauty of words, even Ootek's weird and wonderful Inuit words for snow:

anniu – falling snow
api – ground snow
siqoq – smoky, drifting snow
upsik – wind-beaten snow

and so on; Ootek also described ice – frazil ice, porridge ice, pancake ice – and the snows of Nunavut, tinted by fungi in marvellous shades of red, green, blue and black.

Sometimes our traveller imagines himself at the third pole – the Pole of Relative Inaccessibility, the furthest point from any land in the Arctic Circle. He sees birds moving in whitebait flocks, shimmering silently below the sun. He watches wax form in soft yellow tears on the candle in his hut, his lair of shadows. And so he trains his telescope on Saturn. As the north wind blows, as the snows gather, he examines the dark and divisive circle which cleaves the Rings of Saturn. That black hoop is known as Cassini's Ring: he must pass through its darkness before he can re-enter his white room. This is his story, as he tells it to strangers in the snow.

DUXIE'S PROLOGUE

OF all days, this must be the day. I have looked to all points of the mind's compass, and I know that this is the day.

Do you believe in signs, signals?

I have never done so... omens and auguries are the stuff of dreams.

And yet I cannot ignore these portents.

I awoke to a rainbow of mesmerising intensity, arched low over the swell of the land. Troubled by its message, I tried to remove its sedulous curve with my finger by smearing its seven colours in the condensation of my night-breath on the window pane. But it blazed, flooded into a brilliant bow.

And then, flying along the far-off rim of the sea, came the swans – seven in line, glittering under the sun. What could it all mean? Why did they pass through the rainbow in such silence, those paper birds – their mechanical wings pulled up and down, slowly, by the taut thread of the horizon?

There was a message there, surely. Seven colours, seven white birds...

You must understand that I am not superstitious; those birds were not a warning sent to me from heaven knows where, I know that. But when the swans entered that rainbow a key turned in the vaults of my memory.

The time has come, then, to tell you what happened. Perhaps I should have told you sooner. But too many people had been hurt; feelings were still raw. So I kept all those memories to myself, re-igniting them sometimes by looking at the black and white photographs, faded and creased, which I keep in an old toffee tin in my bedroom. The tin is rusty and musty, a stale reminder of the years which have passed. When I open the lid I smell a deep, acrid tang: and I yearn for the past, sniffing my own nostalgia as an addict smells Methadone. Each photograph, with its white border – its edging of surf – becomes an atoll of memory.

I must act now, before my next winter is an old man's winter: before I start to hoard time, before I become sleepy and watchful, frugal with heat and oxygen – an adventist waiting for the coming of his last spring-child. Even now the willows line the waysides in their winter orange, stooping to remind me.

The people in my story: you will get to know them well. My name is...

My name is loaded with associations. All names are. My name is so heavily marked with the stains of the past that I would rather keep it to myself for now; so let us start afresh – please use my nickname, Duxie. Let's forget about the physical details. They always get in the way, don't they. You wonder about my eyes? No, they're fine. It's the snow – it was like a flashbulb going off in my face, too close... the insides of my eyes are still white, all the detail has gone.

The people in my story, I will tell you about them. There's a young and beautiful woman – Olly. And there in the background, always, is Mr Cassini.

Seven days in a man's life: how can I possibly convey the importance of that week – among the countless weeks in my existence? No doubt you too can remember a decisive time in your life: an episode which shaped the person you've become, made you the human being you are today.

Duxie and Olly. Both of us have a past. When I say *a past* I think we all know what I mean by that. People who don't talk about their past tend to accumulate a certain air of mystery, do they not? Olly didn't do it deliberately, I assure you. But having closed the door on her previous life she kept it locked; the past was an archive or a fiction, and she was tired of its warped messages.

I think you already know that she disappeared once, quite some time ago now, when she was a young woman. Perhaps *went missing* would be a better way of putting it.

People were concerned; yes, there was a lot of worry, but foul play was never suspected. After all, she left a note. At the end of her brief message she'd scrawled something by a long-ago poet called Li Yu – a couple of lines I'd taught her while we watched boats on the river:

> A paddle in spring's breeze, a leaf-like boat,
> In the myriad ripples I attain freedom.

I'd felt close to her that day: we'd shared a giggle because one of the boats was called *Cirrhosis of the River*. And she'd compared the yachts lying on their sides in the estuary mud to fat white nudists, sleeping on their bellies in the sun.

That note – she left a solitary sentence at the end, a footnote from which I alone could draw any meaning:

Come to eat sweets and cry.

Nowadays there would be a huge drama no doubt: police cars with flashing lights, television appeals, counselling. But things were different then. I'm not saying better – just different. Also, everyone had a pretty strong feeling that Olly was somewhere safe, that everything would turn out OK. And, since she's very much alive and well today, I don't have to tell you that she was found again, all in one piece (if not particularly well). What you don't know, I suspect, is that something very important happened to *both* of us that week. Is that a shock to you?

I'll tell you all about it.

I want to go back – to the year she went missing. I will return to one particular day, a Sunday in February. She and I had arranged to go on an outing: a picnic, if the weather allowed. We were lucky – sandwiched among a pile of damp and mouldy days we found a bright, mostly sunny morning with spring-like bursts of promise. It was her turn to choose our destination. I was surprised, therefore, when the car turned eastwards. I remarked on this, since I couldn't remember a time when she'd turned to the east. She always went west, to Snowdonia or Anglesey. She smiled, but gave no clues. Although our friendship was relatively new we had slipped into an easy companionship and neither of us felt much need to talk as we motored on. She turned off at St Asaph, skirted the city, and drove a few miles into the country-side. After leaving the car on a deep bed of leaf-mould in a shallow lay-by, we walked along a rough track, between a huddle of houses, and headed for a field. At the topmost edge of this field, below a sombre, leafless wood, I could see a ruin. It looked ecclesiastical, and soon I was standing in the roofless chapel which is attached to an ancient well known as Ffynnon Fair. I sat on the star-shaped rim of the well, watching dreamy bubbles drifting to the surface, as if they were escaping from an antediluvian mudfish buried in the fine brown sediment below the water.

Apparently this well – used as a bathing pool, and famous for its healing powers – had a canopy resting on ornamental pillars long ago. It fell into disrepair after Henry VIII took his revenge on the Church. The ruin is in a pleasant, almost enchanted dingle, with butterbur and bamboo growing around a stumble of fallen stones, damp and mossy. As the sun played among the bubbles I trailed my fingers in the soft, lime-rich water and, such was the old-world feel of the place, I imagined I was in a realm of water-nymphs and dryads. You may condemn my description as fey, but I am merely trying to describe the nature of that particular day.

Olly had been silent for long periods. Had I been more observant I might have noticed the sag in her shoulders, the droop of her head. But I hadn't. As we ate the first of our sandwiches (ham, coleslaw and Branston Pickle on rye bread) and pored over children's prayers which had been written on scraps of paper – now mouldering – and placed in a hole in the chapel wall, I had no idea that Olly was being oppressed by an inner turmoil. I was serene and contented under my feeble winter sun, and totally impervious to her personal unhappiness. You needn't chide me. I have reproached myself often enough. So when I turned to talk to her, only to see tears running down her cheeks, I was shocked. For a moment I sat with my hand frozen in mid-air, clutching half a sandwich. My mouth was already open, ready to take a bite from the bread; I put it down immediately and moved closer to her. I put my arm around her, and we sat like that for a few minutes. She felt very slender, very vulnerable, and her body's little judders and spasms travelled down my arm, into my heart. She cried sound-lessly, and then stopped, sniffed, wiped her nose with her sleeve, and stood up. She smiled, and said sorry. Neither of us had a tissue so I handed her some of the kitchen towel lining the bottom of the sandwich box. Reddish patches spread around her eyes and nose.

'Sorry,' she said again. 'I don't know what's wrong – I keep breaking into tears unexpectedly, without any reason. It happened in Bangor High Street yesterday. Quite embarrassing. I was just walking along... '

She smiled again, and started packing the picnic into her rucksack.

'Come on,' she said. 'Let's find the caves.'

As I trudged behind her I wondered what I should do. Let it pass? Press her for more information? Something told me to bide my time. She'd said only a few words – but they were enough to trouble me considerably. We moved upwards slowly through a hanger of ash trees and holly, with the River Elwy glinting below us. Eventually we came to a clearing, a dome-like knoll overlooking the valley. We sat on two soft green tussock-stools and admired the view. Directly opposite was a hanging valley which cupped an emerald-green field and a smoking farmhouse. Curtains of rain drifted down the cwm in white pillars which toppled slowly onto the floor of the valley in slow-motion, silently, as if drifts of talcum powder were falling onto the floor of a bathroom, or flour was being sifted through a sieve. Inexplicably, we were left dry.

'Come on,' she said with a hint of mock gaiety. 'Let's explore.'

She led me down a steep, overgrown path. Soon we were among a plethora of limestone caves. A few years ago one of them had yielded a haul of ancient bones: bear, rhinoceros, wolf, leopard, deer and bison – and the earliest human bones ever found in Wales, from an early form of Neanderthal Man (with a large, powerful jaw and heavy eyebrows) who lived here a quarter of a million years ago.

She led me into a cave, using a key-ring torch, but when the cave narrowed sharply, forcing me to wriggle through a constriction, I lost my nerve and headed straight back to the entrance. Yes me, Superman, captain of the Welsh football team not so very long ago. Mr Nerves of Steel himself.

'Not very good in tight holes – claustrophobia,' I shouted back into the cave.

She followed me out, and led me to the mouth of another cave. This time I was better prepared, so I followed her along a longish stretch of tunnel which snaked through the rock. When we emerged into the sunlight, I realised quickly that we were back where I'd stood panting and palpitating after my earlier, aborted attempt – the two caves were linked. I looked sheepish, but she didn't tease me. So we wandered in and out of caves and caverns, pointing to striations and red-ochre tinges in the limestone. I made silly noises in the caverns so that I could enjoy the echoes. Childish, I know. But although it was February, a black winter month, nature's sudden burst of optimism had warmed my bones.

Then we headed back towards the car, along the valley floor, through a calm, reposeful meadow. On our way home, thrumming along the expressway, she revealed more to me about her state of mind. She'd been feeling very low. Sleeping badly. Lately, each day had been a challenge. She had felt estranged from society, and there had been physical symptoms: tiredness, and a flu-like sensitivity of the skin. She often felt like crying, suddenly and without warning. She was clearly stressed, or seriously depressed. I knew that she was due to be married in the spring. Was she worried about the wedding?

No.

Health?

She was checking that out.

Something to do with college?

Yes, in part. She'd fallen behind with her essays.

I asked her why, since she was always in the library when I went there.

A long pause. A squall hit the car and a few hailstones slithered down the windscreen – a tetchy reminder that winter was still with us.

'Can I ask you a favour?' she asked.

'Yes, of course.'

She flicked the wipers onto double speed.

'I need to take my mother to Glasgow next weekend, and I could do with some company on the way back. It's a long way to drive alone. And since you know about the crying... (pause)... I'm also having panic attacks.'

'Sure I'll come. No problem.'

I wondered what her boyfriend was doing. Had they fallen out? All the girls at college were mad about him. He was the best-looking man around.

I didn't pursue the topic.

On the white of her arm I noticed two circular Elastoplasts, wheat-coloured, which reminded me faintly of crop circles. I imagined a tiny alien craft landing on her arm in the night, leaving an exotic pattern in the soft, almost invisible down. I felt an urge to lean over and tease the sticky edge of the Elastoplast where it clung to the flat warm plain of her forearm, in the way we all want to pick at fresh Elastoplasts.

'Did you hurt yourself?' I asked her.

'Pardon?'

'Your arm – the plasters.'

'Blood tests,' she said, with a hint of annoyance. 'I'm not completely bloody helpless – I can just about get myself to a doctor, you know.'

And that was Olly all over – calm and composed one second, but a coil of barbed wire the next if you stepped on her.

Again, I let sleeping dogs lie. We drove to my home, where she dropped me off.

'See you in college tomorrow,' she said after refusing my offer of coffee.

Indoors, I sat in silence for a while, pondering the day's events. I had a smoke, too – it always helps me to relax.

I had never seen Olly in that state before. Normally she was reserved, quick-witted and funny in a droll sort of way. She experienced every single botheration suffered by the very beautiful: midge-clouds of men, and a continuous need to walk everywhere with the shield of her intelligence held up in front of her, to protect her from the regiments of fools who besieged her body.

Why she turned to me I have no idea. One of her friends – another woman – might have made better sense of it all. But it was me she chose, and the unravelling took me on a vertigo ride to the North and the South, to the East and the West. There was something the matter with Olly. I would have to wait some time before I found out what it was.

That night, the winter returned with a vengeance.

I would like to tell you the whole story. I want to tell you about my dreams and my daydreams too. I want to tell you about the snow. I want to tell you about love and the opposite of love, which isn't always hate.

Perhaps I should talk about everyday matters, but I don't want to now. I want a change. I want to talk about the big things... about whales, because they mourn, and about polar bears, because they're left-handed – southpaws – all of them. I want to talk about little things too – about iceworms and wormholes. I want to describe spiders, hanging in their nets like fallen acrobats. I want to describe silence, that sheet of glass on which the universe is painted.

I will have to tell you about Mr Cassini too. It was not my wish to include him in this story but he's a stubborn man who won't take no for an answer. He is obdurate. He won't go away. Sometimes he bangs about at night and keeps me awake. He calls at inconvenient times and takes up hours of my time. He refuses to leave until I give in to his demands. Mr Cassini has forced his way into my account. When I told him he was in my story he rubbed his hands and smiled.

In this world so large I have a little room. I will sit here and tell you what happened. You may want to know, for instance, why I have a telescope in my sea-facing window, pointing at the sky. If you ask me about my telescope, I will focus all the lenses in my mind and I will look into the past: I will go back four hundred years, to a town in Holland, where an obscure spectacle-maker called Hans Lippershey is sitting in his room, watching two small children at play. They are amusing themselves... they put two of his lenses together and they peer at a church tower in the distance. They see it wonderfully magnified. They laugh and they giggle... the telescope is born.

I will look again into the past. Not far away from Hans Lippershey, some of the most important discoveries in the history of biology have already been made by a tradesman called Antonie van Leeuwenhoek. Working alone in his room, driven by boundless curiosity, he has fashioned a microscope with skill and diligence; he has discovered bacteria, sperm cells, blood cells, and much else. He has discovered a world of microscopic life. How marvellous it would be if we could view ourselves, see ourselves squirming and darting on the glass plate of the past.

My own telescope helps me to look at what has happened already in the universe; after all, every single telescope trained on the stars is looking into the past. Take Saturn. When I focus on the planet's stupendous rings I am looking at something which happened up to 84 minutes ago.

The cosmos swirling around us in its incalculable vastness, the miniature cosmos under our fingernails: is there anything left to be discovered by the common man, sitting in his room? Or are we reduced to discovering a few small things about ourselves, of no import to anyone else: and if so, is the spirit of discovery dead?

Is that why we worry about weeds and wallpaper?

There is a point to all this pondering. I am about to go on a small personal voyage of discovery, and I must use every tool and artifice available to me. For instance, if I cannot actually be inside the Cassini spacecraft as it circles Saturn (a planet with seven main rings) following a voyage of seven years through space, then there are ways of simulating the experience. I am not referring to drugs alone, but they have their place of course. Paul Theroux went to South America to retrace William Burroughs' notorious trip to the rainforests in search of the holy grail of psychotropics, the final fix – *yage*:

> ... vine of the soul, secret nectar of the Amazon, the shaman's holy drink, the ultimate poison, a miracle cure. More generally known as ayahuasca, a word I found bewitching, it was said to make its users prescient if not telepathic. Rocket fuel is another active ingredient: in an ayahuasca trance, many users have testified, you travel to distant planets, you meet extraterrestials and moon goddesses.
>
> "Yage is space time travel," Burroughs said.

With or without drugs I will go on a journey through time and space. I assure you that I was free of any hallucinogenic when the swans passed through the rainbow. But since the number seven is my number, as they say; since I seem to choose it before all other numbers in draws and lotteries, I will use it too in my quest for personal discovery. There are no more than seven basic plots to the human story, according to some, and every tale ever told fits one of seven categories. Maybe this fable of mine is the eighth – my own. Now is the time, surely, for me to mix my own colours. What do painters say? Start with black and then move, shade by shade, towards the light. If you want to make white whiter, add a little blue.

In the harbour a fishing boat waits for me, placid in the pancake ice – its wooden hull, a bright new shade of powder blue, is dreamy and distorted in the water. A plume of diesel blue drifts from its exhaust. A million mirrors dangle from the sky.

I have seen such scenes in lonely fjords. But this is Wales, and I am leaving for the island. Something is happening inside me. I want to go back, to where the sum went wrong. My memories have been eaten away, moths plucked from the air by a night owl. My life is an ending without a story. They say the human body undergoes a complete change of cells every seven years. And this is it – a change is happening. I can feel it.

Lime-green catkins ooze from the trees like toothpaste escaping in fine whorls from cracks in the tube. The past is about to ooze out of me too.

This is my year of magic.

Part 1

Dreams

Part I

1
THE TIDE GOES OUT

The journey begins

I SLAMMED the boot lid, hard, and the car rocked.

Then I noticed something – a head, nodding rhythmically in the back seat.

A wig... my mind imagined... was that a wig? The hair was ash blonde and coarse.

There was something slightly unnatural about it. And I wasn't expecting anyone else to be with us.

My eyes moved from the wig to Olly's face.

Standing by the driver's door, with the keys in her right hand, she watched me with bemused eyes; smile lines were forming, delicately, at the corners of her eyes.

Her mouth parted and she laughed softly, looked down, and I heard a soft blip as she disabled the central locking system. There was a scrunch of chippings as she got in. Walking towards the passenger side, I glanced sideways at the person sitting in the back of the car.

Then I eased myself into my seat and belted myself in.

The interior of the car was cold and impassive: left to stand alone in an unpeopled landscape, I imagined it would guard itself, defend its own squat metal kennel for a thousand years. I sensed a foreboding – this box, trimmed in factory grey, had something about it that day which hinted at a cold, robotic future.

Her body was suddenly next to me, close. My stomach muscles tensed slightly as she swished her belt across her midriff. This accentuated her breasts, and I averted my eyes courteously. I was aware of small currents of air, sent by her movements, brushing coolly against my skin. As she leant towards me, head down, looking for the belt-snap, a swathe of hair fell from behind her right ear and curtained her face; it swayed in a graceful curve and my biology admired its rich cascade. There was a slight hint of shampoo; I thought of the shoulder underneath her hair, white, unclothed.

'Ready?'

I nodded, and our eyes locked momentarily. I had to look up slightly – she was higher in her seat than I expected. Then she started the car and we began our long journey north, the roads salty and white. Indicating, she steered us towards the expressway's churning, dyspeptic canal. My mind flitted from subject to subject.

Why was I needed now, yet again? Just when I was getting some peace and quiet – at last. I was so fed up with being needed all the time. People are so needy. Can't they ever sort out their own problems? Their voices gnaw at me: on my mobile, through the letterbox. Pleading. And I'm not getting any younger. Sometimes I feel as if I'm walking in a glass corridor, a circular tube of memories, walking round and round, getting tired...

'*You're* very quiet today,' she said.

'Just thinking.'

She was a fast driver, I noticed. But good. An easy, experienced competence. For a while, as we overtook in the fast lane, we were level with a car full of youngish men, uber-chavs in baseball caps. They studied her, dispassionately: an ordnance party, measuring her topography in trigs and chains. One of them said something and they all laughed. She was unaware of their interest; I shifted my eyes away from them.

'Something bothering you?' she asked.

'Oh, not really.'

Small clouds, greyed by the windscreen, travelled in a ghost-train of reflections across her face. The sky was a Brillo factory, puffing out small neat cloud-parcels on the horizon's conveyor belt. Above us, on the pockmarked cheek of the hill, gorse erupted in zit clusters.

'Are you absolutely sure you want to do this?' she asked in a carefully controlled voice.

'For God's sake yes, absolutely. I really want to – I promise.'

'I just thought then, for a moment, you were having second thoughts.'

'No, absolutely not. I'm looking forward to it, really. Life was getting far too boring. I need a new challenge.'

Liar. New challenge? Christ, hadn't I dealt with enough challenges – solved enough problems?

I snuggled into my seat and closed my eyes. The soporific hum of the engine eased me towards sleep. I needed to recharge, to recover. My toast had landed butter-side up whenever I'd tripped up in life, mostly. But I was getting older, I needed more rest. Stupefied, my body lay on a coned-off stretch of the human highway – like so many fortysomething people – recovering after my first big collision with mortality. I was time-fodder like everyone else; I was aware of death, in the corner of my eye, sitting in his dodgem, tattooed and fresh from the pub, singling me out and laughing a little too loudly as he prepared to ram me again, from behind. Someone famous said that middle age is when you stop running away from your past. Correction. Middle age is when you stop running away from your past and start running away from your future. But before I run I want to rest awhile, on the hard shoulder... waiting for my future.

I decided, after a while, to tell her. I wanted to begin with a clean slate – with nothing to hide. And I thought we could trade secrets, perhaps. If I told her a little about my inner life then she might tell me more about the demons running around inside her. It was worth a try.

'I'm trying to write about it... to tell the whole story – everything that's happened,' I said after a while.

'Really!' She was excited. 'That's incredible! I'm really glad.'

I knew she meant it.

She flicked us back into the slow lane.

'It's a great story... your fans'll be well happy!'

She was young enough to say *well* happy.

That word – *well*. There it was again. Perhaps our jaunt to Ffynnon Fair had triggered a recurring association. Everywhere I turned there seemed to be wells. I had even encountered a well in my front room while I stood waiting for Olly to pick me up. Standing in the bay window, listening for her car, I'd grabbed the nearest book on the top shelf of an old oak bookcase close to hand. My fingers had alighted on a dog-eared, cloth-covered *ex libris* edition of Knud Holmboe's *Desert Encounter* – and I'd thumbed through it, looking for a passage which had made a big impression on me many years previously. Holmboe, a Dane born in the early 1900s, had converted to Islam and had gone on a dangerous adventure in North Africa. It cost him his life – at the age of just 29 he was murdered by Arab brigands a few miles south of Akaba, but not before recording his fascinating story: a journey through the desert... and there I found it, the passage I'd wanted to read again. Travelling by car through the sands, with a leaky radiator, he had come across an old *marabout* – a sorcerer prophet as Holmboe describes him – who had refused a lift, despite being literally in the middle of nowhere. Having no urgent business elsewhere, or perhaps no business at all, anywhere in the world, he was content to walk all day, alone, in the searing heat. And then, after breaking down, Holmboe and his party had been saved by desert cave-dwellers, who gave them water and gypsum with which to repair their radiator. It had been a close run thing. My heart had been wrenched by a passage describing how the Italians had blocked up the Bedouin wells with concrete, condemning them to a slow death, in retribution for a Bedouin rebellion against the European occupation of their homeland.

'I've made a tentative start,' I said. 'Of course, I'll have to change it all later on. But you have to start somewhere... '

She glanced at me.

'Let me guess,' she said. 'I'm trying to guess where you'll start the story.'

I was almost asleep by the time she came up with anything. When I heard her voice I dipped out of the fog seeping around my brain.

'It's a place. I'm fairly sure it's a place, not a person, at the start of your story,' she said. 'The Millennium Stadium perhaps, after the final whistle... '

'Wrong,' I replied, laughing lightly. 'It's a place, sure, but there are people too. It's certainly not the Millennium Stadium. It's a place where nothing ever moves, nothing ever happens.'

'What do you mean?'

'I'm having to work from photos. That's all I have to go on.'

'You're writing about old photos?'

'Yes, in a way. It's a part of my life which I can't remember anything about, so I'm trying to work out what happened.'

'So there's no one in the photos?'

'There are people, yes.'

She waited for me to continue.

'But the people never move,' I added lamely. 'They're frozen – I can't remember them ever moving, or laughing, or saying anything. They're like cardboard cut-outs.'

'Nothing strange about that,' she said. 'Same with all pictures from the past – those people have gone... they might as well have been dead for a thousand years, in a way.'

I murmured something, purposefully indistinct, to fill in some time. I closed my eyes again. I was weary: after all, the whole country was a vast winter dormitory; millions of animals were snoozing contentedly while humanity ranged the land, a crazed squirrel looking for its nuts.

'You can't leave it at that,' she said, prodding me on again. She couldn't leave me alone, like the rest of them.

I told her: 'Nothing at all happens – there's a big gap in my memory. For ten years of my life, nothing at all happened. I can't remember a single thing. There's no footage – no film clips, no video to run. Blank. Just one big empty black hole.'

She looked towards me, through that smoky curl sweeping across her face.

'When was this?'

'Up to the age of ten. Absolutely nothing. And whenever I try to remember, a feeling comes over me... '

I hesitated, again.

'Go on... '

'It's like a numb feeling, but there's another feeling as well... a sort of prickly pre-excitement; the sort you get before doing a bungee jump.'

'Never done one.'

'Neither have I, actually. You know what I mean, though... '

'Butterflies, you mean?'

'Yeah, something like butterflies, but not quite – the dream equivalent of butterflies. The sort you get in your sleep and you wake up feeling edgy, wound up. As if someone had been chasing you, and you were glad to be awake... '

'How often do you go to this nothing place of yours?'

'Oh, every now and again. I don't go there often because I've a feeling it's too dangerous... that there's something in that hole which I don't want to know about, yet I'm drawn towards it, like a kid near a pond. I get a sort of vertigo, if you know what I mean... '

I relaxed against the head-rest and closed my eyes. Could shards of memory rise slowly to the surface – was it possible? When I was young I'd been too busy running around; now, perhaps, I had time to kneel and comb the soil with my fingers, gather all the pieces and reconstruct a vessel to hold my past.

I left her alone, to think for a while. I hoped there would be a trade-off – that she would reveal something about her problems. I wanted her to tell me why she was hurting inside – why she cried suddenly in unexpected places. It became a wink-joke between us: she would start to cry, silently, and I would hand her a sweet. Almost Pavlovian – but it was the only response I could come up with, except for hugging her, which wasn't always appropriate. Not when she was driving, anyway. Today she stayed silent, flicking the sweet I'd given her from cheek to cheek. I could hear it rolling against her teeth occasionally and I thought of river boulders clunking downstream in a storm. I tried something new every day almost, but she liked the fruit gums best. Hated Liquorice Allsorts, spat them out. Slowly, I got to know her likes and dislikes. Her mannerisms too: the way she twanged her bra straps when she was bored, and blew out her fringe, her lips sounding like a muffled road drill, when she was exasperated. Strange quirks, too: she had a thing about the moon, knew all its phases; she liked French cinema but listened to country and western. Christ.

Then we needed petrol, she noticed, and we started looking for stations. We were running on empty, and a niggling worry entered the car space.

'You're going to tell everything then,' she said. 'Is it going to be kiss and tell or cry and tell, if you know what I mean?'

'Haven't decided yet.'

I was getting concerned.

'Have you got any petrol in a can?' I asked.

'No.'

I mulled, fatalistically, as we motored on.

'Anyway,' I said, 'how are you getting on at the moment? Are you still behind with your course work?'

'Yes, still trying to catch up.'

'What's the problem?'

She gathered a strand of hair curling across her eyes and tucked it behind her left ear. I admired its flow, the dynamic of its sidewinder snake-life. Also her nose, her mouth – everything about her was in the right quantity and proportion.

'I'm having trouble with history.'

'History?'

'Yep. I can't finish one of my essays.'

'What's it about?'

'John Dee.'

'I had trouble with him too. Very peculiar man.'

'Powerful, strange.'

'Yes, very. What's the problem – all that Harry Potter stuff, his dark arts?'

'No, nothing like that.'

'All that cabala and alchemy getting to you?'

'No, I'm fine with all that.'

'Well, what is it then?'

The strand of hair loosened and she tucked it back into place again; she rubbed her nose with her sleeve, sniffed, looked at me and smiled.

That was a lovely smile.

'You won't believe me, anyway.'

'Try me.'

'Do you believe in angels?'

'And fairies too, and Father Christmas... '

'Don't be nasty to me.'

I made sooth-a-baby noises.

'All right then – do you believe in the opposite of angels? Whatever the opposite of an angel is called. Incubus, is that right?'

'Something like that.'

'I think so. Incubus is male isn't it? A nasty man who comes to you in the night. Something like that, anyway.'

'Succubus.'

'Pardon?'

'Succubus is the female equivalent.'

'Oh.'

And I thought of Meridiana the Succubus – a beautiful tenth century demon who helped the first French Pope, Sylvester II, to gain power and riches – or so the story goes. A fabled scholar with an incredible knowledge of many subjects including Arab astronomy, Sylvester also studied magic and astrology. A myth arose that he was a sorcerer, in league with the Devil. He was forced to flee after 'stealing' a book of spells from an Arab philosopher who pursued him, tracing him by the stars. Sylvester hid by hanging from a wooden bridge, where, suspended between heaven and earth, he was invisible to the magician. Some say that Sylvester fashioned a bronze head which answered *yes* or *no* to his questions.

My mind returned to the present, and the reason for our journey. There was something the matter with Olly. She was out of sorts. She was caught in a fast spin cycle.

'I've been howling at the moon again,' she said as we drove through one of the tunnels.

'Pardon?'

'Howling at the moon.'

'You mean howling, literally?'

'No. Phoning my friends late at night when I'm drunk.'

She still had a sense of humour. That was a good sign. I liked the way she lobbed her mind at me like a grenade then watched, bemused, as I scanned it desperately to see if she'd removed the pin.

Out of the tunnel, a few miles further on, I said: 'Sleeping OK?'

She rubbed her nose with her sleeve again.

'No, not really... I've been having lots of bad dreams. Every night – feels like that, anyway.'

I wondered what she was dreaming about.

A half-sucked sweet peeped out between her lips, sickly-green, and she wiggled it about for a while with her tongue.

'For ages now... mostly about a war. It starts with a statue coming down, and I'm underneath it, trying to get out of the way.'

I gave her time to follow this up, but she was silent for a mile or so. I thought perhaps she wanted to shrug it off.

She told me eventually. The statue toppled down on her every night. Then she was on the run, in derelict buildings or in lonely places. She was always in a war, and it was really frightening. She told me about the jets screaming down on her.

'How could I imagine it? I've never seen anything like that – but it's so realistic,' she said. 'As if I'm there when it's happening.'

I was really fascinated now. Involved. I wanted to know what was going on.

An Orwellian nightmare was taking place in Iraq, but the British public had gone back to sleep, engorged on fantasy. I started to rant about it, one of those middle-aged loop tapes you slot in and then off you go, knowing that everyone else has a vast collection of their own too, gathering dust, re-played on long walks or during sleepless nights. The very last station on the line for an old British freight train called *free speech*; where lost commuters rant to antique gods on darkened platforms in the middle of nowhere, somewhere like Cilmeri or Adlestrop. Perhaps I ranted too long, too hard, because at some stage I stopped suddenly, as if a fox had heard a twig snap.

She turned and tried to give me an encouraging smile, but it wasn't the right sort of smile: it turned down at the edges, into a snarl almost. Again, I sensed that vulnerability in her, the white-ness of her neck under the sidewinder curl.

Then her shoulders sagged a bit, and I knew I'd hurt her. Reminded her of something, or someone. Ranting. The last thing she wanted was a fool like me talking shit. She'd made a simple child-like sign, a gesture of futility... I shut up straight away. I sensed she was on the edge. Maybe her mind was bending with fatigue, or worse – about to wander off the edge of reason.

I adjusted my position in the seat, lifting the seat belt off my chest with my left thumb so that I could stretch and squirm, faff about until I was comfortable again.

She detected my thoughts, and in a second she flared up.

'Don't bother your little brain with it,' she said hotly. 'I don't need any Ladybird Book of Psychology stuff from you, OK? And for the record I'm completely sane – a whole lot saner than you'll ever be.'

I didn't even try to rescue the situation. I just sat still and waited. This made matters worse.

'You think I'm cracking up or something?'

'No,' I whimpered.

Worse again. She hit me, quite hard, across my chest, with her left arm. And again. The car wobbled twice as she did so.

'No?' she said, and again: 'Don't believe me? No?'

She shoved the side of my head, roughly – on the wrong side

of playful. I was really surprised; I just sat there, feeling shocked.

'Think I'm making this up?' she said, but less aggressively this time. There was a wobble in her voice. Bloody hell. What had I let myself in for? A loony female, a loony mission. I was tangled up in a web already, ready for the white coats to come for us both.

'Well you *are* acting a bit strange,' I said as reasonably as possible. 'And you *are* battering me. You're not exactly behaving normally, are you?'

She let that rest for a while.

'These dreams,' she said. 'Please try to understand. They won't go away. And now they've moved into my life.'

I know how creatures of the mind take on a life of their own. It's the dream-work. Your subconscious and all that.

A few miles later she said: 'Sorry about hitting you... really. I'm sorry.'

She sounded a bit emotional.

'I've got some anger in there.'

'A helluva lot of anger if you ask me.'

'Yeah, well.'

I tell her more about my story. This story I'm about to write: I've decided to start it at the edge of the world, on the seashore. I don't feel as if I'm on dry land – but I'm not on water either. An in-between place. That's how I feel at the moment. Between one life and another: I feel as though I have to decide, soon, whether to head inland or whether to get in a boat and head off to another existence, completely different. Meanwhile, I'm walking along the shore, beachcombing my life for clues. Which way will I go? I simply don't know yet. Living on the edge of a country you get waves from both directions.

Olly was quiet for a long time; I left her alone with her thoughts... big grey thoughts which evaded me, made me think of a family of elephants retiring grumpily into their enclosure at the zoo and brooding heavily just out of sight, in the corner of their concrete bunker – everyone knew they were there but no one could see anything. Maddening.

After a while, she said:

'Where's it going, this story of ours – where will you take it?'

Suddenly the story was ours.

'Is this story *ours*?' I asked her.

She turned to look at me, for a little too long: I began to drive for her, staring at the road ahead in a meaningful way.

Then it happened. The car began to stutter and lose power. I realised what was happening and a wave of irritation – mixed with some anger – washed over me.

'You better get over onto the hard shoulder,' I said.

She looked taut, guilty, suddenly tired.

'Bugger. Why am I so stupid... '

I merely said: 'Don't worry, we've all done it.' As it happens, I never have.

So we rested there, on the hard shoulder, and passing cars took on a strange aggression. Not until you stop do you realise how really aggressive motorway traffic is – unforgiving, hostile even.

'I wonder what the police'll make of *her* if they come along,' I said.

She raised her eyebrows, quizzically.

I gestured behind me.

'Oh, the mannequin.'

She laughed, but her body was braced and her hands still grasped the steering wheel firmly.

'My mother,' she began, then she wafted air onto her face, using her hand as a fan: the gesture was girlish and appealing. Now I noticed, she was quite flushed.

'My mother's making me a wedding dress.' Pointing backwards over her shoulder, she added: 'That thing is supposed to be exactly the same size as me – that's what they said at college, anyway. It means mum can make the dress in her own time, when I'm not there.'

'You got it at college?'

'Yes – fashion department. Going spare. I've got to return it sometime.'

I turned and stared at the inanimate in the back seat. It looked straight ahead, lifeless. Mannequins I find spooky. They freak me a bit. Also those life-sized cartoon characters you get, like Mickey Mouse or Donald Duck, at Disneyland. I can't stand too close to them.

This mannequin was dressed in a simple floral dress made of a light, almost diaphanous material, and she was wearing an ash blonde wig and shades. She had regulation cone-shaped breasts swelling sexlessly under large print marigolds. Her legs were pressed neatly together and her hands were clasped in front of her virginally; she could have been an unmarried aunt being driven to church.

I looked at my watch: it was nine o'clock.

'What time is it?'

'Nine.'

She fiddled with the radio, and the news filtered in. I took little notice. News is seldom fresh: it's a soup made from very old bones. As I began a sentence she said *shush*! and turned up the volume.

The first item was freaky. Identical twin sisters in their seventies had walked into the sea near Porthcawl... suicide pact.

The next item was also strange: a small girl had fallen down a well... emergency services massing... four fire engines... old, disused... narrow, crumbling... child still alive... faint sounds from below...

Olly stooped down suddenly, turned it off. Perhaps I imagined it, but a shiver seemed to run through her body.

In the distance I could see an emergency telephone point.

'Are you in the AA? RAC?'

'No.'

'This is going to be fun, isn't it,' I said as I opened the door.

I sat for a while, one foot out of the car, working up some energy.

As I waited for impetus a rainbow formed, indistinctly, arching high over the emergency telephone but framing it perfectly, as though giving me a sign. We looked at it, emboldening now, its colours clarifying against the grey of the cloud-mass behind it. Something occurred to me. When we're children we're all told about the crock of gold but no one ever tells us how to find it. Isn't that life though?

'A rainbow,' she said, smiling. 'That means we're going to be all right – safe.'

I turned to look at her, quizzically.

'Arc of the covenant,' she said. 'No more floods. God says so. A promise.'

'Everything's going to be all right then,' I said, cynically.

'I promise,' she said. 'Cross my heart and hope to die.'

And she smiled that sweet smile of hers.

As I'm about to get out she lays her left hand on my sleeve and says:
'Listen.'

I sit quietly, but the only sounds I hear are traffic noises.

Then there's a lull, a brief respite in the cacophony, and I listen astutely.

She points to her left ear and waggles a finger in the direction of the sea, which gleams and sparkles through the trees alongside us.

She smiles.

'Can you hear the waves?'

And yes, I can hear the sound of the waves, coming to us somehow through the febrile air, sent to this strip of madness from the old world.

I nod, and then I start walking towards the telephone.

Other people's dreams are usually boring, aren't they? People say *I had this dream last night* and you switch off almost straight away. But dreams are central to our story, so I've got to include them. The truth is that I started remembering my dreams too, as if Olly's revelations had set off a recording device in my brain. They were bad dreams, nasty dreams. Dreams from long ago, from somewhere deep inside me. Our night lives had similar threads; my own dreams seemed to shadow Olly's dreams sympathetically – as if we were dreaming in syncopation. Maybe we were dreaming about the same things: the same old monsters in different clothing. Those dreams of mine came from a seemingly bottomless well within me, a ceaseless subconscious spring not unlike the bubbling outflow we'd visited at Ffynnon Fair. Dreams as stories... I wonder if there are seven basic dreams, as there are seven basic human stories. In Italo Calvino's masterpiece *If on a Winter's Night a Traveller* there is a fable about

an old Indian known as the Father of Stories, a man of immemorial age, blind and illiterate, who uninterruptedly tells stories that take place in countries and in times completely unknown to him. The phenomenon has brought expeditions of anthropologists and parapsychologists; it has been determined that many novels published by famous authors had been recited word for word by the wheezing voice of the Father of Stories several years before their appearance. The old Indian, according to some, is the universal source of narrative material, the primordial magma from which the individual manifestations of each writer develop; according to others, a seer who, thanks to his consumption of hallucinatory mushrooms, manages to establish communication with the inner world of the strongest visionary temperaments and pick up their psychic waves; according to still others he is the reincarnation of Homer, of the storyteller of the *Arabian Nights*, of the author of the Popol Vuh, as well as of Alexandre Dumas and James Joyce...

I will tell you about the man in my dreams, the man who rubs his hands and smiles.

He has become real to me, as real as Olly's parallel creation is to her. You might accuse me of using all the tired tricks of the symbolist, but I refute the charge: this is how it was, and I am telling you what happened as truthfully as I can. As she said – sad, lovely Olly – there's something deep inside all of us, firing away all the time, something like an old boiler-house in a museum cellar, heating up all the rooms inside our heads, the rooms of the past, so that we can walk through them now and again on rainy days. Olly's dream-rooms were a bit scary. Haunted, you might say.

When I think of antique gods I imagine large men, but not massive, well-muscled but beyond the first bloom, gold-skinned, with violet eyes I can barely look into. My antique god is sinuous, spare, silent, wise, and simply robed in blue, the rarest colour in nature: the blue worn by villains, supernatural creatures, ghosts and friends in Japanese theatre. I fear this antique god of mine.
We create, we imagine our own gods and monsters. The Ancients believed in two-headed monsters, and during the Middle Ages monsters were seen as forebodings or agents of wrath – half-human creatures spawned by bestiality. They ate and drank with both their mouths simultaneously – malefic signs of God's anger, symbols of nature's raw power.

Renaissance man also described *prodigies*, such as the monstrous head 'discovered' in an egg in 1569, with the face of a man and a beard and hair made of small living serpents... monstrosities such as this were portrayed on public display boards, or *broadsides*, around which crowds gathered to view fantastical illustrations and to hear the monster's story told aloud. And what of *Frankenstein*'s creator Mary Shelley – wasn't she responding to all those nineteenth-century attempts to engineer monstrous deformities in living organisms, in the name of science?

Olly's monster was a dream monster. Mine, too, rose sympathetically from an ancient bed to trouble my sleeping hours. I will tell you about my first dream. I will tell you about Mr Cassini and his friend the policeman.

Sometimes truth doesn't tell the truth as well as fiction does. Sometimes the truth needs telling in diverse ways. Butterflies taste with their feet. Did you know that? Sometimes we must use our senses in unexpected ways.

Flip the switch, douse the light. We're in our own cinema of the night. Some of the film is in colour, some in black and white.

2
THE TIDE COMES IN

Scenes from a dream:
the policeman's confession

Scene 1 – at a police station

It was a foul and dismal morning in February, and PC 66 was tired and irritable. He hadn't slept well, though his bed was comfortable enough. A dog had howled all night under his window. He'd put too much paprika in his stew the previous evening, and all through the night he'd had to drink water, constantly, from the carafe by his bedside at the police station. Then, in the dead shade of night, the heavy black clouds streaming past his grimy window had made him think of tarantulas scuttling across a body. Towards morning he was woken by a loud knocking. Rising quickly, guiltily, he unbolted the door and opened it to a huge man swathed in a black cape made of thick rubber; it left pools of rainwater on the tiles in the hallway. The huge man slumped into a chair while PC 66 made coffee in two dirty mugs, both cracked and stained a deep earthy brown. Afterwards, as the coffee sent coils of steam into the gloomy air, PC 66 stood at the main window, with his mug held low in his right hand, looking out towards the sea – though he saw nothing except a stunted rose bush by the window, since a ghostly mist had descended onto the garden. The shadows seemed to gather round him, and as he peered into the mist a sinister segment of his dreams returned to him from the depths of his sleep; in fact he was grateful that the night had passed, fitfully, into history. Out there on the sands he had heard a child running eastwards into the white of a sea mist: with each footbeat the child seemed to come closer. He'd heard cries of laughter and exultation; and then the child had moved away from him, westwards. He'd heard someone weep in the dolorous marshes beyond Little Bay.

Although he'd been awake for an hour now, PC 66 remained agitated: his mind was still troubled by the dreadful puppets of his dreams. And now, with daylight breaking, starving owls – unable to find food at night – were being mobbed by other birds. Silently, he addressed an imaginary jury on the other side of the window. Once or twice his lips moved to the flow of his confession. For he had a confession to make...

Scene 2 – PC 66 begins his confession to the invisible jury in the white mist outside his window. This is what he said:
I think you have a right to know what happened, right from the start. I'm almost excited about it – as if I were about to go through customs. I've got too much baggage. All those memories you leave in boxes all over the place, with your friends. In all the houses you've left behind. Bits and bobs in dusty attics everywhere. I have a declaration to make about my past. No, that's not strictly true. I have *many* things to declare about my past. It's time to get it all off my chest. I'd like that. Maybe I could relax a bit afterwards. That calm, drugged feeling you get when an ordeal is over. Actually, I was thinking about it yesterday, on the beach, walking along aimlessly. Daydreaming, really. It's an old daydream of mine. I imagine the seawater all gone, just for a day, so that I can walk along the bottom of the sea looking at what's there. Little hills and valleys I never knew about – wrecks, skeletons, whatever. I'd wander about all day, I'd walk all the way round the island and back; maybe I'd look over my shoulder now and again, fearful in case the sea came roaring back to swallow me up, but I'd really enjoy that day. I'd go on my own perhaps, and maybe I would meet other people wandering along the bottom of the sea bed and we'd laugh and say *did you see this* and *did you see that*. Maybe I'd take a camera, maybe not. Cameras make your memory lazy. I would remember it all for ever, after the sea's allowed back in. I want to start with a clean slate. I'll tell you all about it. Don't rush me though – I want to figure it all out first. I want to know exactly how and why I did it.
[The end of the admission]

PC 66 turned to the huge man in the chair and studied him, although his ravaged features were barely visible in the half-light.

Mr Cassini – yes, the story started with Mr Cassini, really. A gigantic man he was, nearly seven feet tall, he seemed that tall anyway, and immensely strong. A saturnine man, sitting in the gloom hatching vain empires, the sort of man who stole wild birds' eggs. Such a big laugh on him too, a big male noise coming out of his mouth, a bull-roar in a cavern; his teeth were bats hanging in a cave full of sound. Mr Cassini – with his ancient, fish-like smell – was the key to it all. Mad, yes, he was certainly mad. But PC 66 loved that man. And he hated him too. Was that possible? There were just a few people you could love and hate at the same time. Mr Cassini was just such a man, there was no doubt about that. So where did he start? He turned to face the courtroom…

Scene 3 – a courtroom: PC 66 is in the witness box
In your own time PC 66, could you please tell us when you first met Mr Cassini?
I think it was during the trial of Lady Violet Charlesworth.
You mean *Miss* Violet Charlesworth. She was certainly no *lady* [laughter].
You're right, she was no lady.
Can you tell us your first impressions?
It was a strange case. Miss Charlesworth…
No, your first impressions of Mr Cassini.
I'm sorry. Mr Cassini – a very big man, physically. Charismatic. Very powerful. I think everyone was rather afraid of him. We were in awe of him, all of us. He was very clever, he knew a lot about the world. And he was very funny at times. I remember the time when…
Thank you PC 66, there's no need for you to continue with your little story [titters from the gallery]. Ladies and gentlemen of the jury, I would like you to examine Specimen A – an essay on local history [the jury reads]:

The story of a bogus 'heiress', who cheated the young doctor who loved her and left a trail of debts before faking her own death, gripped Britain as the year 1909 dawned on a troubled country.

When she was finally brought to justice it became clear that Violet Charlesworth, who took on the trappings of great wealth – including mansions in Wiltshire and Scotland, a fleet of cars and chauffeurs, expensive dogs and fine clothes, had drawn her whole family into a web of deceit.

The sensational case of Lady Violet, as she became known, starts on the coast road between Conwy and Bangor. Nowadays it teems with traffic; in 1909 it was virtually deserted. On a spur of rock high above the sea Lady Violet started a trail of mystery which was to lead detectives all over Britain.

The *North Wales Weekly News* was absorbed in domestic matters: negligent parents were being taken to court by the NSPCC; abandoned wives were suing their husbands; young women, disappointed in love, were gaining compensation for breach of promise. Suffragettes were causing chaotic scenes everywhere, including the beach at Colwyn Bay. But the biggest story by far in the edition of January 8 was headlined:

MOTOR CAR MYSTERY
Young Lady's Supposed Terrible Death
Full Story of an Extraordinary Accident

It seems a terrible fate had befallen a young lady named Miss Violet Charlesworth of St Asaph. According to her travelling companions, one of them her sister, the other the chauffeur, Miss Charlesworth had been pitched out of the car after colliding with a wall, and had fallen fifty feet down a cliff into the sea. Her body had not been recovered. Reports of the tragedy had caused a thrill of horror to be experienced throughout the country.

The previous Saturday had been a fine day. Violet and her sister Lilian had decided to go for a short run in their car, a Minerva Landaulette, driven by their chauffeur Albert Watts. But the weather was so pleasant they extended their trip to Bangor, where they had tea at a prominent hotel. It was Violet, apparently, who took the wheel on the return journey. As she negotiated a dangerous bend the car apparently hit a stone, swerved to the left, and sped – out of control – into an opening in the boundary wall, coming to rest a few inches from the cliff edge. Violet was 'thrown' through the windscreen into the sea. Her sister Lilian ran, in a state of frenzy, to a nearby inn to get help. In the search that followed a lady's motoring cap and a notebook were found on the cliffs. But there were doubts from the outset. Witnesses said there was little or no water near the base of the rocks below when they searched for Violet's body – so how could she have been swept away? Violet had supposedly been the driver, yet the windscreen through which she'd been propelled was smashed on the passenger side.

The *Weekly News* delved briefly into Violet's colourful history.

It seemed she was very fond of motoring and employed two chauffeurs. Recently she had rented a house at Calne in Wiltshire and another at Fortrose in Ross-shire for seven years at an annual rent of £250. She had refurbished the Fortrose mansion in Highland fashion. There were three or four cars in the garage. She loved night driving and dogs.

Heavily in debt, she was traced to Oban in Scotland and then her name hit the headlines everywhere. In the following weeks she appeared at various music halls – though her reception 'did not encourage her to make many appearances' – and a film was made of her escapade, on location, starring Violet Charlesworth as herself. In the meantime, she was declared bankrupt.

Then came a huge surprise. Whilst probing her acquisition of various expensive rugs made of tiger, polar bear and leopard skins, police discovered that she had defrauded a Rhyl doctor – who had fallen in love with her – by pretending she was due to inherit a fortune from an old friend in Melbourne, Australia. By July, coach owners in Rhyl were making a feature of drives to her former home at St Asaph.

On February 11, 1910, eight days before Manchester United played their first league game at their new ground, Old Trafford, the newspaper reported 'the sensational arrest' of Miss Violet Charlesworth and her mother, to face charges of fraudulently obtaining large sums of money from the doctor and a widow from Derby. Dressed in a bright green coat lined with white satin, a large black hat trimmed with ostrich feathers, and a white stole, Violet looked extremely pale and her mother sobbed bitterly during the trial. Both mother and daughter, it appears, were initially sentenced to five years' penal servitude but their sentences were reduced to three years apiece because of ameliorating circumstances. And so ended the sensational case of 'Lady' Violet Charlesworth.

PC 66, have you read the evidence?
Yes I have.
Is it a fair representation of the case?
It is.
Does it shed any light on Mr Cassini's arrival in this part of the world?
What exactly do you mean?
Is it not true that Miss Charlesworth had two chauffeurs in her employ when she lived in this region?
I believe so.
One of them called Albert Watts, I believe, and the other was called Mr Cassini. Is that true?
That is what I've been told. Mr Cassini revealed to me one day that his father had been one of the chauffeurs who had accompanied

Lady Violet, I mean Miss Charlesworth, to Wales. Mr Cassini senior fell in love with the region. When he lost his employment with Lady Violet he decided to stay, and got a job as a bread van driver.

I have no further questions for the present.

Scene 4 – at the police station again

PC 66 gave up his daydream and turned to his guest. He offered him another drink, but the man refused. He had some urgent business in hand. He was there merely to remind PC 66 of their conversation the previous evening. But PC 66 would never forget that conversation, as long as he lived, since he'd made a promise which weighed on him as heavily as an anvil tied to his neck. Mr Cassini departed and PC 66 turned to the window again. The mist was clearing and, in the distance, he could see faint masses looming to the east and west, great haggard promontories which glowered over the two crescent bays down below him. It was on one of these jutting headlands that Violet Charlesworth had feigned her own death. Those headlands were dangerous to women. In 1631 a gentleman called Sir John Bramston had journeyed over one of the passes in the company of a lady. She became so frightened she had to be taken off her horse and led backwards along the steepest part of the track. There had been many accidents. In 1762 a rector, with a midwife behind him, had fallen with his horse down the steepest part of the cliff. The midwife and the horse were killed. The rector survived, rescued his saddle, and marched off *exulting at his preservation.*

Scene 5 – PC 66's first deposition

I am a policeman and this is my beat. I live in fantastical, dangerous times. Only a handful of the older townspeople know my real name. Everyone, however, knows my number, which is 66. Almost everyone calls me PC 66, but a few of the scumboys call me PC 99, referring to a notorious incident when I was held upside-down by one of them and subjected to various demeaning acts. They will be punished in the great courtroom in the sky.

Scene 6 – the rainbow messengers

At this point a rainbow appeared and PC 66 was visited by seven mental apparitions, each of them bearing a message…

As PC 66 was about to turn away from the window a rainbow began to form down below him, bridging the river which divided Big Bay from Little Bay. He watched it take shape against the intangible sea. The colours clarified, then burst into their full glory. He was amazed and touched by the rainbow's beauty as it flickered into life, emblazoning a world of insipid, washed-out nothingness. As he stood there, watching, the colours seemed to beam into his brain, activating a strange sequence of thoughts – as if the seven colours had triggered seven synaptic messengers who came dashing towards him along the runnels of his mind, all bearing messages. As each of them approached him he felt as though they were sticking Post-it notes to his forehead, one by one. This is what they said to him:

First messenger: Listen to me PC 66: when the past is ready to be revisited you must be ready to come in the beat of a single pulse. And today is the day. My friend, listen to me well. So that this story can be told in a satisfactory way we have been allocated:

Seven days, or the duration of fourteen tides.

Second messenger: We are required to employ the following symbols:

A hill
A stone
A palace
A seat
A tree
A well
A fire.

Third messenger: We are granted the following accoutrements:

The uniform of a serving police officer
A police station
A book entitled *The Dexter Propensity*
A book entitled *Water-Divining in the Foothills of Paradise*
Twelve mannequins
A car
An onion.

Fourth messenger: We are granted the presence, real or imagined, of the following:

> The astrologer, alchemist and magician John Dee
> The Wizards of Cwrt-y-Cadno
> The Caerleon writer Arthur Machen and his
> story *The White People*
> Four Welsh eccentrics meeting on the summit of
> Pumlumon Arwystli as they cross Wales in four
> different directions
> Merlin – stricken by madness
> The psychoanalyst and writer Adam Phillips from
> Cardiff
> Freud's biographer, Ernest Jones from the Gower,
> whose sister died laughing.

Fifth messenger: Fortune will smile on us if we include:

> Four apple trees and four pigs
> Four inundations
> Four tears which change the course of someone's
> life
> Seven descriptions of Mr Cassini's nose
> Seven descriptions of Mr Cassini's eyes
> Seven descriptions of Mr Cassini's ears
> Seven descriptions of Mr Cassini's mouth.

Sixth messenger: We will be required to mention:

> Four battlegrounds or forests in Scotland, Ireland,
> Wales and England
> Four motorway service stations or cafes
> A reputable psychiatrist
> Big Bay
> Little Bay
> A football field
> The island in the centre of the lake known as
> Llyn-y-Dywarchen near Beddgelert.

Seventh messenger: The tale must be told by two people. You, PC 66, will recount the story as the tide comes in and Duxie, the celebrated former captain of the Welsh football team, will recite the story as the tide goes out. Do you understand?

Did he understand? Of course he didn't understand. PC 66 stuttered a few words, wanting clarification, but the messengers moved away from him swiftly as soon as the seventh had finished speaking. He shouted WAIT… but they'd gone. As far as he knew they were already running other errands in the hot blancmange of his brain, even as he spoke. He hoped they hadn't been put to death, as messengers so often were. In an ideal world they might have been allowed to spend a few hours with him, chatting around a table, poring over maps, looking at relevant photographs. But they were clearly agitated; they wanted to impart their messages and be off. PC 66 felt rather vulnerable. Seven messengers had assailed his mind with a barrage of strange commands.

Scene 7 – a strange incident involving PC 66 and one of the rainbow messengers. Shortly after the seventh messenger departed, PC 66 followed him and dropped him with a standard tackle somewhere deep inside his own cerebellum. This is PC 66's description of the arrest, recorded in his regulation police notebook:
Both of us still panting, I pushed him up against the side of a filthy, graffiti-strewn underpass (it was as commonplace as any piss-stained underpass in any brain). I held him against the concrete, hard, but he seemed strangely unperturbed as he waited for my next move. I gained the impression that he'd suffered this sort of indignity many times before. I looked into a finely creased, weather-beaten face, which was as shiny as an apple skin. His cheeks were healthy and ruddy, with tiny deltas of capillaries near the surface. I was reminded of a farmer in the Hiraethog Moors, warming himself by the fire after rescuing a sheep from the snowdrifts. His eyes were sharp and grey under tightly-curled, close-cropped hair greying at the temples. I put him at roughly my age, about forty. About my size too. With a deep pang in my heart, I realised that his clothes were quite exceptional, and from another age. His left shoulder, nearest my nose, smelt of moss and cowslips. He saw my wonderment, and looked down proudly at his brocaded silk tunic, and at the buskins on his feet, made of new cordwain with buckles of gold on the instep to fasten them.

He regarded me, solemnly, as if awaiting a response.

I was speechless.

'You don't recognise me, do you?'

I had absolutely no idea who he was. A figment? Someone I'd put behind bars, many years ago?

'I'm from *The Lady of the Fountain*,' he said proudly. 'Medieval romance. Remember reading it?'

'No.'

'You were still young – only nineteen. Sunday morning, very early. Very depressed. Sian Roberts had just run off with a rugby player.'

I barely remembered her, never mind *The Lady of the Fountain*. He put his hand on my shoulder, gently.

'Let us go from here,' he said. 'No man should loiter in a place like this.'

And side by side, amiably, we walked from that filthy hole and sought out a springy green bank in a glade where we lay on our backs in total silence for quite some time, looking into the treetops and tracing a troupe of mistle thrushes as they tadpoled a clear blue sky. I relaxed and almost forgot we were living in a state of emergency. After a while the realisation crept up on me that I recognised the glade we lay in – it was a place from my childhood.

'The underpass in your cerebellum,' said the seventh messenger in a lazy, sleepy voice. 'You do realise that I'll have to report it?'

'Yes.'

'It's a particularly disgusting underpass – I feel dirty all over.'

'Don't blame me – I didn't put it there. I just happened to walk through it one day, in Llandudno Junction as it happens.'

Rolling over, he cupped a flower to his nose and sniffed it expressively.

'I would really like to get rid of it,' I said. 'Llandudno Junction isn't the sort of place you're anxious to remember.'

He released the flower and made tutting noises.

'I certainly can't get it wiped from your memory, but I *will* ask for it to be dimmed. Perhaps you'll remember it occasionally, every ten years or so. That would be an improvement, wouldn't it?'

I made appreciative noises, and closed my eyes so that I could better enjoy the wavering drone of a bee rifling the drawers of a nearby foxglove.

'A strange phenomenon,' he said enigmatically by my side. 'A dirty stinky underpass in your brain. Stuck inside there for ever.'

I felt an urge to smell him again, so I rolled over onto my left side and put my face close to his tunic. Woven into that brocade were old sounds too: an orchestra of reedy sadness under the immense shadow of a greenwood tree – a shawm, a viol, a psaltery and a rebeck intoning a forgotten hymn to Cernunnos, lord of nature; in the strains of that music I saw a green sea of baby bracken springing in graceful swans' necks from the acrid belly of the soil, warming on a spring morning long ago.

The seventh messenger snapped his fingers, startling me.

'Of course,' he said, propping himself on his right elbow and gazing at me. His face was dappled with leaf shadows, reminding me of the flecks which speckled his own irises.

'The first messenger withheld some information which might interest you.'

'Yes?'

He chewed on a stem of grass, ruminatively.

'I'll make a deal with you,' he said, finally.

'Pardon?'

'Are you interested in doing a trade-off?'

Quite unused to being visited by seven messengers in one day, and slightly wary by now, I said:

'Depends.'

He guffawed. 'Once a policeman…'

'It's nothing to do with that.'

'Hah! So why be so suspicious?'

I claimed my right to silence, and he fell onto his back again.

'It's only a little favour I'm asking,' he said. 'And you'll get a rather valuable snippet of information in return. How about it?'

Since I was already caught up in a mad hatter's tea party, I went along with it all.

He continued: 'Only I was up in one of the more remote regions of your brain yesterday, just bowling along, minding my own business, when I thought of a neat little metaphor – which I'd like you to use. You're always going on about water, anyway, so it's quite relevant.'

'Is that all you're asking for?'

'It means quite a lot to me, as a matter of fact.'

I told him to spit it out.

'I was thinking about waves,' he said, 'and I realised that they remind me of the roar inside your body when all those micro-scopic beads of pleasure swarm to the surface of your skin during a love-storm.'

'Old hat,' I said wearily. 'Jaded old metaphors, worn away with use. Next you'll be comparing raindrops to the beads of sweat on my father's skin in the tiny moment he made me…'

He looked hurt.

'All right then. I'll try again. How about waves as… the spray-burst tang of an after-dinner mint, a white torrent spilling from the sea's dark, chocolate promise.'

'Christ,' I said, 'you sound like a wine bar hack who's spent all his life working for an advertising agency.'

'You're bloody hard to please today, aren't you?'

'Go on,' I said. 'How about waves as pianola keys played by a ghostly pair of hands or an old man's false teeth flapping inside the sea's foam-crazed mouth.'

He fell silent, and I fell to musing over his ridiculous symbols, and all those images presented to me by the seven messengers – outmoded, old-fashioned…

I felt depressed, suddenly, by the seven messengers and their archaic symbols. I'm a product of the twentieth century; surely the messengers could have come up with something newer, more scientific, more challenging.

'What's with all this antiquated stuff you've given me?' I asked querulously. 'Can't we be more modern? Why isn't there a motherboard or an interface in there?'

He shrugged his shoulders.

'Search me. I'm only the messenger. You'll have to have a word with your brain about that.'

So we left it at that. As he said, there was no point talking to him about it. But I was puzzled, and a bit angry. I felt more up-to-date than wells and rainbows and seven times bloody seven. I skulked, broodily, in a plantation of dark thoughts.

'You've forgotten already, haven't you,' he said.

Forgotten what?'

'The deal we made – I have to tell you something about the first messenger, remember?'

'God yes,' I cried, clapping my hand to my head melodramatically.

'There's no need to be sarcastic.'

'Sorry.'

I urged him, politely, to continue.

'Every seventh wave is larger than the others. And the fourteenth tide is the highest tide of all. Be careful that day. You must leave the seashore and head inland. Do you understand me?'

Understand him? Of course I didn't understand him.

'I understand you perfectly,' I said.

When I awoke the seventh messenger had gone and I was back in my own little bed. My first thoughts were of Lady Violet's car, see-sawing perilously on a cliff-edge, high above the sea-rocks, and I sat up quickly. Then I remembered that all this had happened in my mind. Next, I remembered my idyll in the glade with the seventh messenger.

A coldness came over me, and I buried myself in the bedclothes again. I felt rather sad.

The end of the dream.

3

THE TIDE GOES OUT

The journey to Dumbarton Rock

It's a February morning in Wales. The ground is white with hoar frost and the air is vestry-cold. Tinged with early morning red, the broken clouds which fill the sky are the sort of crimson-grey cobbles seen by a king moments before a Parisian guillotine sliced off his head. They're menacing – they're clouds with *altitude*.

February 2, marking the old pagan sabbat of Imbolc, has just passed and an embryonic spring is stirring in the Earth's womb. February 2 is also Groundhog Day; more importantly, it's the day after Charlie Bucket's life-changing trip to the chocolate factory. The milky air of winter smokes around us and we are drugged bees in a hive.

I'm on the road with Olly and we're sharing dreams. Both of us have a monster running around in our night brains – a fenodyree, a fetch, a fachan or a sluagh… one of the unforgiving dead – a man-beast who occupies our minds when we've finally fallen asleep in chairs and the TV gleam is moonlight, ghostly and white… when the night switchboards of the brain hum and glow.

That was one helluva weird dream she says after I've introduced her to Mr Cassini and PC 66. *You don't get much weirder than that.* A guilty copper, a huge man in a cape, a vanishing lady, seven rainbow messengers… full marks to you, she says, ten out of ten. But she's been taken over too, by Mr Cassini's *doppelganger*.

I have other dreams too – nagging dreams, insistent dreams. I'm needed somewhere. There are children in the background, I hear their voices. They're my own children and I'm torn in two; I want to go to them, but part of me wants to stay in the dream.

Anyway, back to the present, back to reality. The two of us are on the road and we've run out of petrol. As I walk towards the orange emergency telephone, I have time to tell you a little about myself.

I am Duxie, once the doyen of Welsh footballers and captain of the national team. Fallen into disrepute now. Tarnished image. *News of the World*, as usual. The sex, yes, I'll admit to that – but the drugs, no way. Looking back, I could have been many things, but, like most people, I took the easy route. In my case, the physical route. In the Cup Final between body and soul we all know which side usually wins.

I became a professional footballer.

High point: Captain of Wales. Low point: the final year, as player-manager of Carmarthen Town in the League of Wales. I wrote a book about it – you may have come across it: *Tales for Wales*.

> He strings sentences together quite professionally – what a pity his team never managed to string any passes together – *Western Mail*.

> Wales' answer to Thierry Henri: the only footballer in Wales who can think without dribbling – *The Sun*.

I've retired now, but I'm still good on my feet. I play in goal for a local pub in the Sunday League – a very enjoyable black joke, and it keeps me in shape. Which is why I break into a jog on my way to the emergency telephone. I try to keep fit – it's something that stays with you: it's a way of life for ever. You see ex-Army blokes and you know straight away, they're still immaculate. Skies and windows, another world shining in their shiny shoes.

I looked back at her when I reached the telephone. By now she was sitting on the rising bank by the edge of the expressway: a little girl lost in the yellow grass, in that familiar pose of hers with her legs tucked up, her chin on her knees and her arms hugging her shins.

Footballers don't like that word – shins. My own shins are old torch-barrels holding furred-over batteries of pain; at worst I get high-voltage jabs, at best a steady, humming ache. Shins... the only tenderness you'll ever experience on the pitch. And shins never let you forget their countless couplings with the stud. Shins of the father.

Anyway, as I messed with the phone, with a finger in my right ear trying to block out the traffic-roar, I noticed the fuzz arriving.

They parked behind her car, lights flashing, so I ambled back.

They both recognise me straight away, as usual. You get tired of it. Fame's a friggin' nuisance after a while.

'It's Duxie,' says one, all smarmy-faced and jolly-me-lad.

'Duxie!' simpers the other. 'Not going to score here, are you mate?'

He looks at the dummy in the back seat and then at Olly, still sitting on the grass. 'But then again...'

The other copper grins.

'You can't beat a nice little threesome, can you Duxie.'

The motorway traffic sucks me and blows me.

In the old days people used to stop, but chivalry is dead. Here I am, with a couple of upstarts and they're taking the piss. I mustn't complain however. Fortunately for me I was kind to Copper No 1 on a touchline once, when he was a kid, so he helps me out with a can of petrol. Not the normal procedure, but seeing as it's me...

'What'ya doing these days, Duxie?' asks Copper No 2.

Petrol fumes spread around us in the air. The smell of car-blood.

I offer some money for the petrol, but they wave me away.

'Student,' I reply, and they laugh soft and low, the way people do when they've spent too much time making jigsaws out of human parts.

I thank them and they go, quietly; back to the ant-run.

There's a rat-a-tat on my brain-window. It's Duxie the student, books tucked under his arm, leaving the library.

'Ahem,' he says, looking at me through the glass, with a faint gleam of contempt in his eye. 'For fuck's sake don't tell people – *especially* policemen – that you're a student. They'll take the piss, for ever. OK?'

I look away.

We're on the move again, thank God. I look at her surreptitiously. Her mouth is set in a hard, determined line. *I won't ever do that again*, she seems to be thinking.

I settle back in my seat and drift into dreamtime. The A55... it's tidal, I've noticed. Tyres hum a dawn chorus on the tarmac and then the morning tide sucks out thousands of human sand-grains, most of them dragged eastwards by a monetary moon.

Some of them are swept far away by the currents, as far as Manchester and Cheshire. They return on the evening flood, all used up, thousands of popped corks swept in on a tired tide, wave after wave flooding the Welsh shoreline. Civilisation is bad for your mental health. Freud said that, not me.

We swirl through tunnels, leaving the twin headlands behind us, and dive into the Conwy Tunnel, below the river; we're snug in our steel corpuscle, speeding through a tangle of artificial veins inserted under Wales' ageing, liver-spotted skin. The fans in the tunnel emit a tortured sci-fi hum and suddenly I'm in the belly of a space freighter, on the lookout for aliens. I look for the Elastoplasts on her arm: they're still there.

'What are you thinking about?'

I delay my response until we emerge from our underwater burrow, popping to the surface on the English side of the river. The Conwy is still one of the north's ancient delimiters. As we thud along the coast I scan the horizon for a phantom boat, the Ghost Ship of Abergele, which has its own web site (if nowhere else) to sail in.

I tell Olly about my wells and my sunken holes as we cruise through the red-roofed urban belt around Colwyn Bay. The glades around the Dingle have gone, demystified under English vernacular.

Am I starting to whinge?

No, merely comparing. I admire the contrasts, actually. Incidentally, a house destroyed in a dream signifies *grief*. One of the James Bonds was born in a house demolished to make way for this motorway. Timothy Dalton, I think. Green eyes, a cleft chin and a Martini (shaken not stirred) were enough to get him outta here. Also Terry Jones of Monty Python fame and Paula Yates. They all got out the superhuman way. And what do you need to get *into* Colwyn Bay nowadays?

A grand's worth of hash and a bootful of Es should do it.

A few explanations.

I am Duxie, former professional footballer, wing-clipped angel of the Astroturf, now a student at one of the local FE colleges. It's one of those sumps created by Maggie Thatcher to drain away the dole kids so they wouldn't appear in the figures; nowadays a reservoir for all sorts of people: kids avoiding the sixth form in a haze of spliffery and angsty wail-sounds, beleaguered single mothers hanging from the breadline, and small town self-improvers like me.

Official subjects: Psychology, Eng Lit, Welsh Lit, History and Media Studies.

Real subjects: The ghosts running around on that moonlit field in my head now the floodlights have been switched off and the gates are locked.

She is Olwen – Olly to her friends, fairest of all maidens on my psychology course (the one with the fewest spots) and generally fucked-up damosel. I am the father figure she needs for now; she talks to me as a daughter would, I imagine, but our coffee break chats are humid with sexuality. One day I sidled up to her in the caff after a lecture on Freud and changed a big round chocolaty O left by a mug-ring on the cover of her notebook into: *Will you be my Oedi-pal?*

She thought that was OK.

Large dimensions, regular good looks and childish humour have got me into plenty of beds. This one's different though. We both want to keep it clean, don't ask me why.

Olly comes to college every day, even when she has no lectures. She hates it at home.

She's a restless, unpredictable talker.

'Why do you always wear a suit?' she asked me soon after we met.

'Habit. I used to be a professional footballer, they sort of expect you to be an ambassador off the pitch.'

One day she turned to me and said: 'You're ideal for my big psychology essay this term. I'll call it *Courtship and the Offside Rule*. Do you mind?'

'Explain,' I said.

'In courtship you always need to be ahead of the game while appearing to be behind it.'

I smiled and said: 'True'.

Playing cat and mouse with defences... I've done plenty of that, on and off the pitch.

'Don't call it *The Goalkeeper's Fear of the Penalty*,' I added.

'That's been done, hasn't it?'

'Yes. Usual story, men fiddling around with their balls.'

She brought her mug down on my fingers, playfully but a bit too hard. She really was quite physical, this girl.

'Don't ever crack jokes like that again,' she said.

'OK,' I mumbled as I sucked an injured knuckle.

'Well, will you help me?'

I said I'd think about it, but I helped her; that way I could look at the nape of her neck when she was bent over the table, writing about me with a chewed-up biro. When you've glutted on flesh it's nice to sit and watch it sometimes. You can't really admire flesh when you're trying to nail a climax onto it.

By the way – my big essay will be on Holes (please, don't go all Freudian on me).

I started thinking about holes when I got tangled up in a goal-net one day. I realised I'd spent a lot of time aiming a ball – itself full of nothing – at a nylon web full of little nothings.

> He found holes in the defence as a sheep finds holes in a fence: one minute he was with the flock, the next he was clear, running for the wide open spaces, and he left the keeper bleating for help – *Caernarfon & Denbigh Herald*.

I found cunning little quotes:

> A net is a collection of holes tied together with string
> – Julian Barnes.

So I got interested in holes – black holes and white holes, empty holes and filled-in holes. Idle holes and busy holes: pits, quarries, mines, shafts, adits, caves, burrows, tunnels... and holes with a dark past.

> Emptiness is defined by the shape that will fill it – Adam Phillips.

Wales has about 7,000 holes and shafts left over from mining. I especially like holes with water in them: ponds, lakes, inland seas, wells...

> What is it that makes a pond so fascinating in a field, and land so amazing from the sea? – Lisa St Aubin de Teran.

I became interested in this Welsh guy, Llwyd ap Llwyd, who was born in the same county as me. He tinkered with words a bit.

> Holes, by their presence, imply an absence – ap Llwyd.

Two of his polemics have survived – one entitled *A Defence of Sheep* and the other bearing the enigmatic title *(sic)*. His first and only book, *Water-Divining in the Foothills of Paradise*, disappeared without trace – I believe I have the sole remaining copy.

We turned off the A55 and drove into Holywell, to pick up Olly's mother. This was the reason for our journey to Scotland. I didn't know the details, but her parents were splitting up, apparently. Olly was wordless about it. The usual dark secrets I surmised. There was an overall atmosphere of tension, fear perhaps, which triggered my early warning system. The kids had grown up… it was a late separation, maybe. A surprise to everyone except the cloven pair. I imagined a long, tired deception – a yellow, brittle parchment of dead love-skin stretched thin over the mummified corpse of their marriage; many years of passing each other silently on loveless landings. Those imagined scenes of tendresse which had intrigued or revolted the children had simply never taken place. But before loading her mother we stopped at St Winefride's Well.

History of a hole: Probably the most famous healing well in Britain. Nowadays a perpendicular gothic affair sleeps by a rather tired cistern of frothy water decked with flotillas of used cartons and sweet wrappers. Viewing this spot, it's difficult to imagine the busyness of the scene in medieval times, when hordes flocked to their British Lourdes. St Winefride's story was among the first to be printed. According to William Caxton's 1485 *Life of St Winefride*:

> … after the hede of the Vyrgyne was cut of and touchyd the ground,
> as we afore have said, sprang up a welle of spryngyng water largely
> endurying unto this day, which heleth al langours and sekenesses as
> well in men as in bestes…

She was the daughter of a local prince. One day a chieftain, Caradog, tried to seduce her. She resisted, but the bastard sliced her head off. A spring erupted where it landed. Well-side virgins often lost their heads, reflecting a sacrificial rite from prehistory. Reunited with her head, Winefride became a nun and had a white scar around her neck for the rest of her life. Her well was signposted from as far away as Northumberland and Norfolk. Henry V made a 45-mile pilgrimage on foot from Shrewsbury to St Winefride's to give thanks for his victory at Agincourt. Scandalised,

Dr Johnson complained in 1774 that *the bath is completely and inde-
cently open: a woman bathed while we all looked on.*

Some interesting facts about wells: People with maladies
bathed their wounds or diseased areas with rags which they tied
to a tree near the well (hoping the disease would stay on the rag).
Warty people pierced their warts with pins which were thrown in
the well to carry away the warts. Throughout history, up to
present-day Lourdes, pilgrims have gone to water to be cured.
The strongest of all Christian rituals, baptism, is very old – wells
were popular with pagans too. Prehistoric people clearly believed
that water was magical, and they worshipped it. What made it
move? A sacred power? *Flowing water is a magician's hinge, the
passage between two worlds,* says Iain Sinclair. Water rituals may
have been associated with the sun and the weather; magic may
have been used to prevent rain and flooding. Water can be light
and scintillating one day, dark and dangerous the next. It sustains
life and destroys it.

Invalids went to a certain Welsh well after sunset, made an
offering of fourpence and walked around it three times, reciting
the Lord's Prayer each time. Men offered a cockerel, women a
hen. They slept under the altar until dawn, using the Bible as a
pillow and a communion cloth as a coverlet. Finally, they made
an offering of sixpence and left their fowl as a gift. If the bird died
it was assumed the disease has been transferred to it.

A couple of times in my life I've opened a door and the room
behind it has been full of water, right up to the ceiling.

I sat by the well and tried to focus on the past, on the lost years
of my childhood. I seem to be the opposite of the Memory Man.
All I saw in that hole was melancholia. The water stared back at
me, unresponsive, a border guard waiting for a bribe.

Had I got myself into a tangle? My heart was sinking fast. I'd
been accidentally locked in the dressing rooms once after a particularly miserable home defeat; the memory of that dismal Saturday
evening crept greyly into my psyche now; the musky smell of
failure – male sweat, liniment and mud. Looking up, I saw Olly's
mannequin sitting in the back seat, staring ahead, impassively. I
had read recently about a German artist called Oscar Schlemmer
– one of the Bauhaus School – who'd fallen desperately in love

with Mahler's widow, Alma. She'd rejected him; his response had been to craft a life-sized doll which looked exactly like Alma: this doll had sat beside Schlemmer every day as he drove his car around Vienna. I'd been intrigued by his actions: they bordered on madness, certainly, but I thought I saw a certain viability there too. I seemed to be surrounded by bloody lunatics. I had other things to think about right now. My psychology course had confronted me with a difficult question: if my body was a small country ruled by chemicals, was I living in a chemical tyranny or a chemical democracy? Did I have any say in the way I operated, or was I merely following orders, slavishly, from cradle to grave? I thought the issue was important: if I was living in a democracy I could reason with it maybe – but if it was a tyranny I might have to deceive it, or wheedle with it, or even go underground... I would have to join an emotional resistance movement scuttling through the night-tunnels of my heart; a Maquis cell with an illicit radio in my cavernous sub-conscious, concerting an assault on the fascist overlord who ruled me with an iron fist. Me.

We nosed into a street of terraced houses and stopped. Olly got out and rapped on a door. My eyes may have deceived me, but I thought the door-knocker was in the shape of a pig's head. The house looked ragged, and a pane in one of the upstairs windows had been broken: a piece of cardboard had been stuffed into the aperture to keep out draughts.

A woman emerged suddenly from the house, with a battered suitcase in her left hand. She slammed the door behind her, pre-empting any attempt by Olly to go into the house; in fact she pushed Olly away, towards the car. She was dumpy, stolid, forbidding in her gestures. She wore tatty blue shoes and a long beige coat, done up to the top button – typical charity shop stuff. Her face, puffy and pasty, was almost obscured by a cheap pair of dark glasses. Oddly, she also seemed to be wearing a wig, making her look very much like the mannequin in the seat behind me. I got out of the car quickly and dropped my seat so that she could get into the back, which she did with alacrity. Olly was left on the pavement, looking at the downstairs window, hesitating, as if she should do something, or as if she expected something to happen. Then she got in and we drove off. No one said anything, until I broke the ice.

It was strange, I thought, how Olly had turned away from the house without wanting to say hello to her father. Her face was set, emotionless. Her mother said nothing, for mile after mile. I thought maybe she was ill, so I left her alone after the initial greetings. A long journey lay ahead of us: it would take up to five hours to get to Glasgow, where a sister lived.

We joined the M6 and my spirits fell. Entering England is always depressing, and that's not the way it should be: it's still a beautiful country, but its main portals – the heavy-duty motorways – are so grim. There's a foretaste as we leave Wales, at Deeside, with its straggly urban jumble and its deflowered verges, sickly trees. On the way we talk, Olly and me, but her mother stays quiet. After a while I forget her and the mannequin, sitting in the back. We talk about college, because we're still skating around each other, and my eyes are still having to spend too much time doing their biological chores, sweeping along the white corridors of her body.

I shift the conversation to our writing projects. Having started an essay on Dr John Dee, the Welsh-born mathematical genius and alchemist, a strange thing has happened – I've allowed Mr Cassini and PC 66 to invade my story. She doesn't believe me, she thinks I'm taking the piss, or writing a weak parable about Bush and Blair. But I'm not bullshitting her. This is really going on.

I look at her beside me and I feel guilty. Why the hell am I bothering her with all this, when she's so low? I have a pretty good idea what's upsetting her. In a way, I suppose, something has been wrong since I first got to know her. Looking back, I think there was a change in her mood right at the beginning, when I first met her, as if something bad was happening in her life; she became pensive, broody, preoccupied; she may have started to lose weight even then, as far back as a term ago. I began feeling protective towards her; after all, mental tyrants can be almost as troubling as real ones. Which do I fear most: the manager on the touchline or the manager in my head, shaking me awake every morning?

In the car I begin talking to her, and I notice her eyes flicking towards the rear-view mirror, checking what's happening behind her. But she's not looking at the traffic – she's looking at her mother.

Putting a finger to her lips, she says 'Shh!' and I look back. But the old dear is asleep.

'Whisper,' says Olly. 'I don't want her to know about this.'

So we talk in undertones.

'This character Mr Cassini reminds me of someone,' she says. 'Have you ever heard of Bluebeard?'

'No.'

She tells me a version of the story. Bluebeard's wife Judith demands the keys to their castle's seven locked doors, but her search for knowledge turns into a nightmare. The first five rooms are covered in blood and the sixth contains a lake of tears. Overcome by terror, she accuses Bluebeard of murdering all his wives – only to find them all in the seventh room, alive. As a punishment for her curiosity and doubt she is locked up with the others wives. Bluebeard is destroyed – he descends into his own dark world.

I'm silent for a while as I consider the story.

'Is that all a fiction, all made up?' I ask, checking the mirror.

'I think so,' she answers. She tells me about Gilles de Rais, executed by the Inquisition for heresy, sacrilege and offences against nature in 1440. He confessed to molesting and murdering nearly 150 children. It was rumoured he'd killed his wife when she discovered his terrible crimes. It was also rumoured that the Devil – appalled by his acts – turned his beard blue to distinguish him from other men.

So there were four of us in a car, heading north. Good feeling for me – I remember a couple of good wins at Hampden Park, and there's that old camaraderie with the Scots. But our passage became a journey into darkness. Even as we entered England the sky thickened; I felt as though we were being trapped under the damp, dirty underbelly of a gargantuan rabbit and the crowding nimbus clouds were its clogged fur, pressing down on us, muffling our mouths. It got to me; the world scraped its finger-nails on the car window. Every colour was sucked out of the landscape and the grey hurt my eyeballs; at one stage I touched my eyes, wondering if they were furring over with that fine downy mould which grows on rotting fruit. This was now a ride through a gun-barrel, and I could smell the nitric under-arm of the looming rain clouds. Holes and pits proliferated on either side of the motorway's swishing gloom; some were deserted, others offered their entrails to scavenging hi-macs and JCBs. I thought of ruined, peasant-abandoned commonwealths churned up by retreating armies, pitted with shell-holes and trenches, running with rats and dark crimson mud. This landscape had the ruination of a vast allotment, or a beach after a ragworm dig. My spirits plummeted; I sank, quickly, into a tundra twilight. We were travelling with no hope of arriving.

'She's dribbling,' said Olly. 'Look, she's dribbling.'

And she was too, her head skewed on the mannequin's left shoulder. They looked quite cosy.

'She doesn't feel anything on her face,' said Olly.

She meant her mother, presumably.

'Your mother?'

'Yes, her face is completely numb.'

Silence for a while.

'Why's that?'

'It's numb, that's all there is to it. Neurological, probably.'

'Really?'

'Really.'

'Why's that?'

'Don't honestly know. It's been like that for ages. For as long as I can remember.'

Again, I fell into a reverie. In the distance a jasmine tree in a long grey hedge reminded me of a yellow-adorned capital at the start of a line in the *Book of Kells*.

I was in strange territory here.

After a while, Olly asked me: 'What are you thinking about?'

'I…'

I was thinking mainly about the pubic clumps of down-curled, blackened hawthorns huddled in dark, pigmy clusters along the hard shoulder, and of an Afro-Caribbean girl in Bute Street – but I couldn't say that, could I?

'I was thinking… what's up with your ma?'

Again, that strong pause.

'It's family stuff – don't bother yourself with it.'

'Only she looks rather poorly, and the wig – has she had cancer or something?'

'Drop it for now. I'll explain sometime – promise.'

'OK.'

I let it be.

A splatter of rain hit the car, and I watched sperm-trails of water wriggling down the window. Against the darkened sky they were beads of sweat; my mind returned to the girl in Bute Street, and sex. Millions of ova and spermatozoon passing each other on this motorway every minute, sensing each other from our interiors, wondering if they would ever meet again in the incomprehensible roulette of mating.

By now the gloom was making a point of being gloomy. The cars floated around us in shoals, manta ray shadows on a deep-down ocean floor; the mist pressed onto my corneas: I felt as if I was going blind slowly; my eyeballs were being overgrown by a glaucous, grape-skin yeast bloom.

And then we were in the Scottish uplands, north of Carlisle. The country opened out, absorbing the dreich into blotting-paper blotches above the faraway shapes – the oystershell middens – of White Coomb, Hart Fell, Saddle Yoke and Ettrick Pen. The wind whistled in my window and now we were micro-fauna, lost in a fungal desert of greens and duns, rolling along the expanses of the Atlantic seaboard, the Scottish hills swelling around us as we shimmied between the goosebumps on a giant's back. I saw a Celtic cross by the roadside but the landscape offered no succour – to be lost in these rippling folds was to be lost for ever, I suspected.

'Anyway, I've got an appointment with Bond,' I say cryptically.

'James Bond? Of course, Connery was born in Glasgow. You know him then?'

'No, I mean Derek Bond.'

'Who's he then?'

'He's a man who walked out into the snow once.'

'For Christ's sakes, explain yourself man.'

She's getting tetchy again. So I explain it all in detail.

As part of my media studies course I'm making a short film, about five minutes long. I've already started it. Title: *Picnic in the Snow*. Five film characters meet in a snowscape, spread a cloth on the ground, have a picnic together. Don't ask me why. So my first shot shows one of those famous moments in history – Captain Oates walking out into the snow, saying his immortal words to Scott: *I am just going outside and may be some time.* I tell her all about it.

'Jesus, that's strange,' she says. 'I wouldn't like to see inside *your* head. But what's this Bond geezer got to do with it?'

'Actor born in Glasgow,' I reply. 'He played Captain Oates in the 1948 version of *Scott of the Antarctic*, with John Mills. James Robertson Justice played Edgar 'Taffy' Evans, chosen for his superhuman strength… he's buried in the churchyard at Rhossili.'

'But you can't get Bond to do it all over again, just for you.'

'No, you're right there. I use a clip from the film, the bit where he walks into the snow, then I've filmed one of the students walking through a blizzard. I'll do the same sort of thing with four other films, and then I'll arrange for them all to meet in the snow for a picnic. Got it now?'

She has a good think about it.

'Sounds OK, bit loopy. Can I be in it? You need a woman.'

'Yes, sure, if you can think of a relevant film.'

'Fine, I'll think of something.'

Another long pause.

'Why this snow thing, anyway?'

It's my turn to pause and think.

'I just love snow, that's all. I like the feel of it and all that… I even like snow language. Did you know that icebergs *calve* when smaller icebergs drop away? Floes, icebergs, avalanches… it's a different world. And it's so clean.'

'So you start off with Oates. Who next?'

'Haven't decided yet.'

But I have, really. I decided a long time ago who'd be walking out into the snow.

Olly's mum wakes up and calls for a toilet stop; we need a break anyway, so we put in at the Abington service station, one of those modern motorway bazaars which claw money from your hand any way they can. After fighting my way through the trinkets I sit down in the eating area; on the next table two jovial Scottish Asians are talking in a weird but attractive mixed dialect. One of them is worried because his sister is adding custard powder to her baby's milk to make the kid stronger. They're friendly and lively. I'm relaxing with a fag and studying the menu when a face catches my eye, two tables away. I study it, surreptitiously. It *must* be him – Adam Phillips. Cardiff boy, expert on Freud, psychoanalyst, writer… one of the best brains in Britain. That craggy face reminds me more than ever of a reconstruction on *Meet the Ancestor*, a noble skull brought to life again with modelling clay and horsehair.

'You're staring again,' says Olly.

'It's Adam Phillips,' I hiss. 'You know – the man who said *a couple is a conspiracy in search of a crime. Sex is often the closest they can get.*'

She glowers at me.

'Hope you're not getting any ideas about *us*.'

'No! It really is him – look!'

She peeks, then shrugs.

'Dunno. It *could* be him.'

'I'm not hungry,' says Olly's mum. 'I'll just have a cup of tea.'

Olly goes to order and I eavesdrop. Phillips is talking to someone, and I catch a few words. Christ! He's telling that story about the mullah and the tiger.

'Listen!' I say to Olly's mum. She never seems to do anything else anyway. She's hardly spoken.

We listen to the story. Mullah Nasrudin is standing in the yard outside his home one morning, throwing corn on the ground. A passer-by stops and says in a puzzled voice: 'Why are you throwing corn on the ground, Mullah Nasrudin?'

'To keep the tigers away,' he replies.

'But there aren't any tigers here,' says the passer-by.

'Well it works then, doesn't it?' says the Mullah.

Adam Phillips asks his friend: Had there been tigers in the Mullah's life, which he'd warded off with corn? Was it a symbolic ritual passed down through the generations? Or had the Mullah dreamt up this ploy in response to a threat from tigers in the past – a ploy which had co-incidentally worked?

It's all about personal fears. We know very little about the actual things we fear. It's like raising an arm instinctively to protect your face, not knowing how or when you'll be struck, or who'll hit you.

Olly returned and we drank our tea. The milk and sugar were in tiny cartons which were difficult to open; by the time we finished there was a mound of torn sachets and battered cartons on our tray. The clutter seemed to speak for the state of the world. Nonsensical and messy. But clutter is essential, according to Adam Phillips. By searching through the clutter of our lives we may find, often accidentally, what we're looking for. It's the searching that's important, usually, not the finding.

I tried to catch Adam Phillips' attention, but he was standing with his back to us, preparing to leave. We left too when the old dear had finished her brew, and headed for the car. As she got into the back she caught her shades on the doorjamb and dislodged them, so that they rested skew-whiff on her nose. It was then that I first saw the bruises around her eyes. I realised, immediately, what was going on, and I was silent all the way to Glasgow.

So that's the game, I thought. That's what I've been caught up in.

A chill crept towards me along the Scottish landscape.

Enormous blocks of flats lumbered towards us over the Motherwell skyline, and we were out of the country, slap bang in an urban bestiary – and the Motherwell beasts were magnificent, Star Wars impressive. We curled around the centre of Glasgow, and the sheer torrent of concrete was bigger than any aesthetic could grasp; it was just *there*, and that was it – my brain became small and asthmatic as it tried to cope with the size of this higgledy-piggledy asteroidal honeycomb.

And then we entered the city's small intestines, sweeping off the M8 onto the old Dumbarton Road through Clydebank. Saturday afternoon – but the traffic wasn't too bad as we followed a long straight road between shops. The red, white, blue and orange street lights stretching in a line of twinkling dots into the distance made me think of the flank of a newly-caught salmon, in its death throes on the banks of the Clyde long ago when this area was open country.

Olly found our destination – one of the few Clydebank tenements to survive the blitz – and after I'd carried the ridiculous mannequin upstairs all the women started a fierce jangle so I retreated back to the car and waited for her. It was getting late, and we'd have to stay the night somewhere. But I didn't want to stay with Olly's lot: I wasn't in the mood for family dissections.

For some reason – maybe it was an overflowing rubbish bin on the pavement – my mind drifted to the writings of ap Llwyd, to another of his rambles in the foothills of paradise. In a chapter entitled 'Small Gods, Big Promises' he holds forth on a household god he has fashioned for himself:

I discovered that the word *orts* can mean a morsel of food left on a plate after a meal, and I recalled an old person who always left a tiny scrap of food on the edge of his plate after every meal, presumably as an offering to a long-vanished god.

Discussing this with my friend Stefano at his Italian café that evening, he smirked and told me about one of his Corsican uncles, an old-stager who had a highly unorthodox household god: lowering his voice, Stefano whispered the Italian word *stronzo* in my ear and said it described the last little glob of shit which – eventually – follows the main business during the toilet ritual. This *stronzo*, he indicated, was regarded by his uncle as an offering to the god of the toilet; that is, to the god of the hole.

Excited by now, I told him of my own household god, a creature of my own devising.

'Imagine yourself buying a roll of binbags at your local store,' I said to him volubly, causing him to flap his hand in a sign for me to whisper.

'When you unfurl your roll of binbags, detach the first bag and place it in the bin,' I said conspiratorially, 'what's the first item you put into the bin?'

'Why, it could be anything,' he said to me, his eyes searching my face as though I were going mad.

'No!' I replied. 'The first item you put in the bin is the wrapper which held the binbags together – and *that* is an offering to the god of the bin!'

I looked at him, full of pride. His eyes sparkled with admiration at my inventiveness. I can trace our friendship back to that very moment, in his café, clutching my mug in both hands, listening to the espresso machine screeching its astral scream of appreciation as I unveiled my new creation...

Meanwhile, here I was on a mad mission with a woman I hardly knew, a mannequin and a beat-up mother with a wig. And my main motive, I suspected now as I watched the reds, whites, blues and oranges of the salmon's flank, shimmering in a dozen roadside puddles, was to pacify the god of the trousers.

We quarrelled. She wanted to stay in her Scottish baronial tenement, I wanted out. I'd had enough wigs and bruises for one day.

'Fuck it,' I said when she finally re-appeared. 'I'll go to Dumbarton. Got a mate there. Can I take the car?'

'Go on then,' she said wearily. 'Pick me up in the morning.'

Half an hour later I was outside the empty-looking home of a ginger-haired midfield terrier called Willie, with whom I'd hung around too many bars, so I had to settle for bed and break-fast on the Stirling Road. Jim, the host, was friendly and he filled me in on the local history. Run-down dockyard town, Cutty Sark built here, big whisky distilleries closing down gradually, one of them now the set for a popular TV soap, *River Side*. Small maritime museum, star attraction the Denny ship model tank, size of a soccer pitch, where they used to test hulls. Stag's Head a Rangers pub.

Jim had a football stuck in an apple tree outside his back window, in a shaded corner of the garden. I didn't know if that signified anything, though it looked totemic.

Main attraction, without any doubt, was Dumbarton Rock – a gigantic Bactrian double hump rearing straight out of the marshes by the side of the Clyde. Basalt plug, the remains of volcanic activity. Ancient capital of the kingdom of Strathclyde, one of the old Celtic mobs allied to the Welsh and speaking the same language – the fabled men of the north. According to one legend this rock was visited at one time or another by the origi-nal Merlin; the real McCoy, a man who bore very little resemblance to the Hollywood Merlin – a man who went mad during battle and spent the rest of his miserable life hiding in the Caledonian Forest. His Scots name – Lailoken.

Late in the evening I brave the steady rain, which is coldly unsympathetic, and tramp into town. I knock back a few jars in the Stag's Head. Then I decide – foolishly – on a Chinese meal, but by the time I trudge back the food is cold, my appetite has deserted me, and I don't want to pong out my room, so I put my soggy box of grub in the boot of the car, thinking it might do for tomorrow. That's what a bevvy does to you.

After a good breakfast I make my way down to the rock. There's a bowling club at its base, laid out for a wedding feast, and I chat to a couple of men standing in the doorway.

'So this used to be a Welsh stronghold,' I say to them, jerking my thumb at the rock.

'We'll teek yor worrd for it,' says one jovially, dousing his fag. After the gloom of yesterday we have a bright, light-blue day; it's a shame to waste it so I jack up on a bit of fresh-air happiness.

I survey this magnificent mini-mountain lying by the cold

waters of the Clyde; its twin mamillae bulge 240 feet straight up into the air, a big pair of tits jammed into a rock-hard bra. I enter the Governor's House and pad around for a while in the baited trap of the knick-knack shop. I walk up through a deep cleft in the rock, between the twin mini-peaks, straight to the highest point, below a flapping, wind-ravaged saltire on its flagpole. To the north, up the Vale of Leven, I look towards Loch Lomond, about five miles away; Ben Lomond lowers in the distance. If I'd stood in the same position 1,500 years ago, my eyes would have scanned each fold of the landscape for approaching bands of Picts, my sworn enemy. To the north west lay the kingdom of Dalriada, equally hostile. Dumbarton comes from Dun Breatann, or fortress of the Britons. As a fortress it has a longer recorded history than any other in Britain. The earliest mention of it is in 450 when St Patrick reprimanded Ceretic, king of the Britons, for kidnapping Christians and selling them into slavery.

This was the ancestral home of the 'great sturdy men' of Strathclyde. Welshmen.

Down below me there's a lot of history. The town is untidy, dominated by its concertina-roofed distillery buildings. The neat, newish Dumbarton football ground shelters below me in the shadow of the rock; over the road lies the Blackburn aircraft factory where 250 Sunderland flying boats were made during the last war. Although it's Sunday an orange claw-machine chunters and gnaws at the remains of one of the old distilleries. Red-brick walls topple to the ground, soundlessly, in the distance. Another fortification is being demolished...

I descend a flight of stairs to an old jailhouse known as the French Prison. Peeking through its grimy windows I see two costumed mannequins, dressed in what looks like eighteenth-century garb, conducting a desultory conversation. And then I spot the well. According to history it dried up 'miraculously' when Olaf the White, the Norse king of Dublin, laid siege to the rock in the ninth century. The Britons held out for four months, but when their well expired the Vikings overran them, plundered their treasure and took a 'great host' of slaves to Ireland, on a fleet of 200 ships. This feat earned Olaf a slot in the Icelandic sagas as the greatest warrior in the Western Sea. It didn't improve his life prospects – he was dead within a year. Incidentally, his wife was called Aud the deep-minded.

I kneel by the concrete-covered well and look at it through a side-grating. Coins glisten softly in the shaded water. I select a tenpenny piece, toss it in plopfully, and make a tenpenny wish.

As I prepare to depart I consider the importance of this rock in the Merlin tale. It was the home of Rhydderch Hael (Rhydderch the Generous), who ruled the men of Strathclyde between 580-612. And, according to legend, Rhydderch led an expedition 120 miles south, to a place near the present Scottish border, to sort out an upstart warlord named Gwenddolau. One of the victims of that encounter was a court jester or poet going by the name of Lailoken – the protean Merlin.

I felt sure now, as I left the rock and walked through a small public park to the edge of the Clyde, that I wanted to follow Rhydderch south, to the battle site, to the place where Lailoken had gone mad and walked out on everyone. But first I had to pick up Olly. I said goodbye to Dumbarton Rock and its deep history: from here William 'Braveheart' Wallace had gone to his execution in London. For some reason I feel impelled to tell you that Wallace suffered a terrible fate; after being hung, drawn and quartered he was kept alive long enough to see his own intestines thrown onto a fire: his head was impaled on a spike on London Bridge, his right arm was displayed on the bridge at Newcastle-upon-Tyne, his left arm went to Berwick, his right leg to Perth and his left leg to Aberdeen. Yes, I'm fascinated by the macabre. You too?

Soon I'd fetched Olly and told her my plan: to head for the battleground, the ancient parish of Arthuret on the Cumbrian-Scottish border. She acceded.

I was in gentler mood on the way down. Motherwell's lumbering warrior-flats were frozen in motion, as if caught in a game of grandmother's footsteps. Down we went, back through the upland hills, which had lost their menace and were now an assortment of multi-coloured Play-doh blobs on a playschool table, bathed in weak sunshine. Flocks of lapwings, balancing commas on their heads, wandered around at random to punctuate the green prose. The grasslands reminded me of Gwyn Thomas: *The colour of the snooker table fascinates me. Having an allergy to lawn mowers, I find a deep calm in the sight of anything green that doesn't grow.*

We turned off the motorway just south of Gretna, drove into

Longtown, and parked in English Street. We surveyed the broad main street of an old market town.

According to the Arthurian expert Professor Norma Goodrich, we are at the epicentre of the Arthurian kingdom. The battle of Camlan, she says, was fought just a few miles to the east. Arthur was interred in this very parish, Arthuret. That is what she says.

So we drive a short way out of town to the red sandstone church, which is close to the ground and pretty. Without entirely realising what I'm doing, I get the Chinese meal from the boot and tuck it under my arm.

'What the hell are you doing?' she asks, waving the air away from her nose. 'And what the hell is that smell?'

I explain.

'So what are you going to do with it?'

'Eat it.'

She pulls a face.

'That's disgusting. You can really go off people you know. Revolting.'

But I take no notice, and while I'm looking for a level grave-stone to sit on I spot a sign directing me to St Michael's Well, on the hem of the churchyard. We sit by the water and I polish off some cold spare ribs while she looks into the distance – we're on a bit of a stage here, raised slightly above the plain.

'I've seen everything now,' she says. 'Former Captain of Wales Eats Chinese Spare Ribs at Arthur's Burial Site.'

'What of it?' I respond. 'A man's got to eat.'

'Yuk!'

She looks kinda pretty when she's disgusted. Gorgeous. I lick my fingers and parcel the food. I've got to stop thinking about it. She's about to be married. Strictly off limits. But with a body like that... well, you know what I mean. Feral desires.

'Tell me why we're here, will you?'

I flick some stray rice grains from my lap and roll my tongue around my mouth, trying to get rid of the spare ribs.

'I'll try,' I say to her. 'But as soon as you say *Merlin* a smoke machine starts up and soon you're up to your eyes in fog. There's a different version of his story for every day of the year.'

I tell her about Lailoken.

Story of a madman: Once a certain fool, or *homo fatuus*, called Lailoken served a chieftain called Gwenddolau. In 573AD Rhydderch Hael and his men travelled to Arthuret and gave Gwenddolau a good hiding at the battle of Arfderydd, just north of Longtown, between the river Liddel and Carwinley burn. The battle became famous in Welsh legend as one of the three most futile battles ever, because it was on account of a lark's nest. Lailoken lost the plot during the battle. The heavens opened and he saw a *vision of intolerable splendour*, with a huge army of warriors brandishing their weapons at him, dazzling him hopelessly. He was seized by an evil spirit which drove him into the forest.

'So that's it – we've finished here now, have we?'

'No, not quite.'

'There's more?'

'Yes.'

'Well, come on then, let's have it.'

I fiddled about in my pocket and found some loose change. Finding two tenpenny pieces, I handed one of them to her, and then tossed mine into the well. It landed in the middle of the rising water, which bubbled delicately on the surface, as a bird's throat bubbles when it sings.

I made my wish. When I opened my eyes I saw that she was staring at me as though I were the local madman now, not Lailoken.

'You expect me to join you in your childish games?'

'Up to you.'

Pointedly refusing to shut her eyes, she chucked her coin and turned immediately towards the gate into the churchyard.

'Aren't you going to make a wish then?' I asked.

'Made it, but you're still alive.'

'Ha bloody ha.'

I followed her through the gravestones. I'd wanted to poke around, but the church was locked so we headed back into town.

'Where am I going now then?' she asked, rubbing the driving wheel, trying to warm it. She was slightly more cordial. 'Home?'

'No. Let's call at the community centre, see what we can find out.'

She didn't complain. In a few minutes we were inside the centre and getting plenty of help. On the telephone, local historian Ken Campbell directed us a few miles north, to a motte and bailey on a prominent site overlooking the plain. Soon we were standing in a damp and drizzled tangle of undergrowth, on the tumescent Liddel Strength, and there was no doubt in my mind, as we looked down on the plain, that we were close to the site of the battle. I felt sure that if we had a Geiger counter which could sniff out old blood it would be beeping away like mad. The Caledonian Forest into which Lailoken fled has been eroded but there are patches everywhere in Mohican spikes. Looking into the gloom of a copse I could imagine the sound of a moaning lament coming from a madman talking to his pig. This was where the original Merlin went loopy. Or was it? Perhaps he was already a myth by the time of the battle – a naked, hairy madman condemned to live among wild beasts as a punishment for abandoning his fellow warriors during battle. He prophesied his own triple death: he would be ambushed by shepherds who'd beat him with cudgels and throw him into the Tweed. His body would be pierced by a stake.

'Charming,' said Olly.

I was bloody glad that my own battles had rarely lasted more than ninety minutes and had always ended with a bath and a bellyful of beer. There were other rewards, too...

A farmyard dog bared its teeth as we approached the car, so I drew her towards me.

She shrugged my arm away and said:

'Hands off. I'm spoken for, remember?'

'Sorry, I wasn't thinking.'

She looked at me with a neutral look and said:

'You should know the offside rules by now.'

Later, in the car, as we entered Wales, she said: 'Are you going to kill off this character of yours?'

'Cassini? Yes. I've got to, haven't I... or he's going to get me.'

'Any ideas how? A threefold death, like Lailoken?'

I looked at her profile, framed by the bland, milky opacity of the window behind her. The curl in her hair as it folded made me think of the sensuous, undulating pleats made by newly-turned furrows on upland fields as the ploughmen dipped in and out of the contours. Her shining hair clips were gulls on the wing, above the naked earth.

'Ideally, the death should be foretold,' she said.

'U-hu,' I replied, nodding to give her encouragement.

'I think Mr Cassini needs a special sort of death, something exceptional.'

It took me a minute or so to remember his name. I had to go through the alphabet twice before I came up with it: 'Aeschylus.'

'Pardon?'

'Greek dramatist, died in a very strange way. Killed by a tortoise.'

She gave me a dry look.

'Let me guess. In the library, with a dagger?'

'No, really. An eagle grabbed hold of a tortoise, flew high in the air, then dropped it to shatter its carapace. Unfortunately for Aeschylus, the tortoise landed on his head and killed him.'

'Must have been the first person killed by fast food,' she replied.

We laughed.

She was funny, Olly. She could really make me laugh.

The clouds are boat keels throbbing overhead, preparing to drop their depth charges. And then the rain arrives, at last... by the time we get home the ground is covered in a gleaming meniscus, the sleeve of silver around a newborn puppy.

We are coursing in and out of the folded skin of old Britain, and I'm also moving through the brain's enfoldments, through the geography of the mind: through fossilised forests and moonlit mines, in the vanished realms of childhood.

'Anyway,' she says, 'it's quite obvious – you've got to kill him off. Straight away, before he gets a hold.'

'How do I do that?' I ask.

'With a funeral,' she says. 'It's time we had a funeral. If this was *Taggart* we'd have had ten funerals already. The coffins would be lined up in rows. Get rid of him!'

'I'll try,' I say. 'But it may not be quite that simple.'

4

THE TIDE COMES IN

Mr Cassini's death.
His lavish funeral

WHEN the end came it came quickly. Quite unexpectedly, with no sign of ill-health, Mr Cassini was found dead in his bed. There was an air of disbelief in the town. Cats in this country have nine lives, in Iran they have seven. Mr Cassini simply ran out of lives. A remarkable feature of the case was that the walls of his bedroom were furred over with a film of white ice when he was discovered, though the weather wasn't particularly cold. Another peculiarity was that he'd died clutching the receiver of his telephone (which he kept by the side of the bed), and stranger still, the receiver's black earpiece was cracked and brittle, as if it had been subjected to extreme cold. PC 66 noted in his report to the coroner that Mr Cassini made frequent telephone calls to an unknown person, often becoming loud and aggressive.

What killed him? No one knows to this day. But his icy bedroom was full to the brim with flowers, and only a handful of people knew that Mr Cassini suffered from an acute form of anthrophobia – a profound fear of flowers. There was another peculiarity. Among the irises and the chrysanthemums and the carnations, a pair of miniature wind-up dancers, entwined around each other in an eternal waltz, were still going round and round, mechanically, on his bedside table when he was found. The female dancer's gauze skirt had made a precise circle in the dust. No one got to the bottom of that mystery either: it was PC 66 alone, probably, who knew that Mr Cassini detested all forms of dance.

The funeral was held, according to Mr Cassini's meticulous instructions, on a day of sublime Welsh rain. The raindrops were microscopic, almost illusional, fine and warm, and the mourners might as well have been wrapped in blotting paper. The sky's weepy breakdown started at first light, and a seeping dampness invaded everyone, insidiously, hissing with pleasure as it spread in a stain all over their helpless white bodies. Children made big saucer eyes when the rain leached into their underclothes; women put their backs to the town walls and protected their street-facing parts with their hands, as if they feared a damp spider might scuttle into their gussets, or maybe a farmer might plant a great big swampy hand on their bottoms.

All the townspeople gathered like a convocation of frogs croaking on the muddy steps of an antediluvian bog-church, tilted and half-sucked into the sodden sphagnum; they felt that day as if the water had a new consistency – as if a demonic scientist had meddled with it, since they all felt as though they had too much oxygen inside them, and gulped as amphibians do when they move between one world and the next. Their faltering hymns were straggly weeds, wilting in the crazy paving of new Wales, for they had no heart for modern deities, those people: the retinue mourning him that day worshipped far older gods.

Everyone wore black.

Mr Cassini had already constructed his own grave at the end of his back garden, which runs to the edge of a small, dark, recessive stretch of water known locally as Afon Ddu, or the black river. This river spends most of its time skulking behind slippery rocks or slipping through the gloomy trees which loiter around its banks in sullen gangs, waiting to mug passers-by.

His oblong grave was made from four granite slabs laid edgeways in the earth; the capstone was circular, since Mr Cassini always added his own unique touch. Mr Cassini had ordered his body to be kept on ice until a wet and windy day came along – he thought that fair-weather funerals lacked atmosphere and gravitas – and he ordered the whole town to gather for a cremation in the manner of Dr William Price.

A note on the famous Dr William Price: He was born in 1800, the son of a clergyman, and became a doctor, caring for the old farming families and the new colliers as Glamorgan grew a great crop of iron and coal for the world. Dr Price was tall and strong with a hooked nose, glaring eyes, long hair and a long beard; he was normally dressed all in green, white or scarlet, and on his head he wore a fox-skin with its front paws on his forehead and its tail hanging down his back. He was incredibly eccentric, and violently radical. He was a vegetarian who believed that everything in nature, from a mole to a mountain, had a soul, and he was also a revolutionary republican. He condemned marriage as a form of slavery and took a common-law wife when he was 81; their two children were called Iesu Grist and Iarlles Morgannwg, or the Countess of Glamorgan. He was equally eccentric as a doctor: he concentrated on causes, not symptoms, and he charged his patients only when he failed to cure them. He wouldn't treat them at all if they smoked. He never wore socks, on hygienic grounds, and he washed every coin that came his way.

After the collapse of the Chartist rebellion in 1839 he ran away to France, where he spent seven years. Constantly in trouble with the law, he always defended himself, though in one court case he employed his infant daughter as assistant counsel.

Dr Price started to build a great Druidical temple with a tower and a *camera obscura* on top. He was to be its resident Archdruid: but it came to nothing. When Dr Price's baby Iesu died the doctor was heart-broken, because he believed the child was destined to restore the lost secrets of the Druids.

He took the little body to a field above Llantrisant and cremated it, but his neighbours thought he'd burnt the child alive and an angry crowd assembled. The doctor drove them away with a pistol in each hand; his partner held a shotgun.

Dr Price was arrested and charged with the illegal disposal of a body. He defended himself, wearing tartan and a white linen smock with scalloped cuffs, and at Glamorgan Assizes he won a momentous decision. The burning was declared lawful, and cremation became legal throughout the British Empire. When he died in 1893, a huge crowd of mourners witnessed his cremation. Each had bought a ticket with the words *Cremation of Dr Price, Admit Bearer*. His last act had been to drink a glass of champagne.

And so, in the manner of Dr William Price, Mr Cassini ordered his body – still thawing as it travelled – to be borne from the mortuary in a plain oak coffin, and burnt on a huge bonfire on the beach (the rocks nearby are still black from the flames). In emulation of the great man he had printed his own tickets with the words *Cremation of Mr Cassini, Admit Bearer,* which he had sold for many years before his death. As the coffin arrived on the outskirts of town all the townspeople assembled in groups, as he had taught them, and formed a huge human MR CASSINI on the sands.

A note on funerals: The Betsileo men of Madagascar fight with bulls and drink themselves unconscious while waiting for the burial ceremony; they cover their faces with shroud-cloths and engage in orgiastic and incestuous sex. 'I am drunk! I am animal!' they cry. Even sisters are not respected.

All the usual rituals of the high church were observed at Mr Cassini's funeral because he loved drama and respected history: a cowled cleric walked slowly before his coffin as it was carried through the town, with the church bell tolling its sad homage. All the pallbearers were right-handed, as Mr Cassini had instructed in his magnum opus, *The Dexter Propensity.* The priest was chanting, *In my Father's house are many mansions: if it were not so, I would have told you. I go to prepare a place for you.*

The priest's voice was dramatic and sonorous; it was a fine piece of theatre as the bell clanged mournfully above on its rusty spindle. PC 66 thought of Mr Cassini in God's mansions. He would have found a room for his own use by now. Would it have dummies sitting in it already, all of them sitting quietly like the dummies in Mr Cassini's front room?

His exact wishes were followed respectfully. All the children were given lachrymatories to collect their tears, and there was a large crowd of hired mourners. The ashes were put in an urn or ossuary, which Mr Cassini had thrown and fired himself, and this was placed in his riverside grave. After the capstone was hoicked into place by the strongmen of the village, sweating and crushing their fingers in a torrent of swear words, a mound of earth was raised over it so that it resembled a massive molehill. Burnt with him as requested, in the coffin, was a description of Branwen's death from a broken heart in the *Mabinogi,* plus Mr Cassini's own annotated copy of *The Dexter Propensity,* and the maps he had made of his children's bodies (front and back) on graph paper, noting all their scars, birthmarks and blemishes.

Because Mr Cassini had himself been a funeral photographer, PC 66 took a formal picture of all those present, since they wanted to follow his instructions to the letter. PC 66 used Mr Cassini's own box camera and tripod, and he asked everyone – just as Mr Cassini did – to strike a pose and look away from the camera, as if following a bird in the sky. Afterwards the crowd dispersed, some surrounding the embers of the funeral pyre, others stalking off to the Blue Angel where they became tremendously drunk. The wind howled that afternoon and the entire town closed down. The tallest oak in the long avenue of trees between the Blue Angel and the docks was ripped out of the ground, creating a strange visual effect, as though a tooth had been yanked out by a kid, leaving an unaccustomed gap in a normally fulsome smile. This breach in the line became known as Cassini's Revenge. When the woodsmen cleared the tree and sawed off its stump, to tidy it, they found an odd kink in one of the age-rings. Dendrologists later matched the kink to a year of very odd events in the locality; and strangely enough, Mr Cassini had arrived during that very same year.

PC 66's version of events, recorded in his black notebooks:
The shops had shut and drawn down their blinds; the vegetable store had covered its produce with paper and locked up, and even the newsagents had closed early. The bookshop closed altogether, for good, since Mr Cassini had sustained it for years by buying books with previous owners' addresses in them and sending them back to the same address, with a letter, even though a hundred years might have elapsed since the address had been written down; in some cases the houses had been demolished. His actions brought results occasionally: some highly unusual people walked into town looking for him. He made them stand in his darkened front room among the mannequins and he questioned them about their lives. Some of them stayed for a day or two, intrigued by his mesmerising presence; three of them stayed for good and accompanied him to the shoreline daily, waiting for him to dispense his legendary wisdom.

Rainwater poured down the hill past the Blue Angel and formed a swirling, bubbling trap by the back door. The tempest blanked us out and tried to wash us away; it rattled our doors and shook our windows; it flicked our ears and noses. It bullied us – it ripped our clothes and stung our faces with a wet-nettle wind which yowled through the eaves and screamed in the trees. Every hallway was cold and damp, miserable with muddy footprints in soggy newspapers strewn on the floor; everywhere I saw stinking, steaming dogs and runny noses, crying children and irritable old people. Mr Cassini would have been delighted. He loved regions of sorrow and doleful shades, whether human or geographical. To make matters worse, a car accident on the eastern headland blocked the road, preventing anyone from leaving the town. There was a wake at Mr Cassini's house, which is called Mortlake, and I wore my uniform still, with my helmet held under my left arm, though I was wet through like everyone else. I will describe his house to you. It is the custom in this town to paint the sea-facing houses in a host of pastel colours, alternating sky blues and daffodil yellows, or blushing pinks and mineral greens, and Mr Cassini had also given his house a hue – a strong matt red to ward off evil spirits (which is why his everyday over-alls were splashed with red paint, giving him the appearance of a murderer who had gone on the rampage). I will tell you now, to put you in the know, since I hate silly little secrets, that his nick-name was Blue Murder, partly because of the splashes of red on his navy blue overalls, and partly because of his notorious temper. But he was completely colour-blind himself. His children were obliged to sit in his darkened front room almost every day, describing colours to him, even if it was sunny outside and they wanted to play. I can hear their little voices, reciting:

Jack the Ripper's letters – written in red...

His pig was called Golly. She was a fat saddleback sow who was fed first every mealtime, even before the children, and there-fore loved her master very much and her little piggy eyes followed him everywhere. She had enormous strength and I treated her with great respect.

So the outside of his house is red, with small windows (many of them broken, with bits of cardboard covering the holes) and a slate roof with moss growing on it. The front door is of heavy oak with two solid black hinges and a big black doorknob in the shape of a pig's head with a ring through its nose. Mr Cassini hoped it would answer every question put to it, like Roger Bacon's brazen head, but it never did. However it makes a very loud clang, which is answered by a rare polysyllabic echo in the gable of the Blue Angel – a mere seven doors away. The front doorstep is very old and has a foot-worn groove in it; this was kept sparkling clean by Mrs Cassini when she was with us, but now it is dirty and scruffy, with bits of rubbish lodged in the cracks.

When you enter, there is a small, gloomy hallway with a floor of red quarry tiles, cracked and uneven; it always smells of boiled cabbage. The stairs are carpeted with a worn and frayed green runner which Mr Cassini stole from an empty house on the edge of town. On the bottom step there is a big orange stain where he left a piece of red cheese, half-chewed, while he was putting up a picture: he trod this cheese into the carpet as he walked backwards up the stairs with the picture in his hands, trying to find the right spot for it on the wall. It is a large black and white engraving – called *The Frown* – and it shows some little children sitting on a low bench facing you. It has the words

Full well the busy whisper circling round
Conveyed the dismal tidings when he frowned.

One of the boys has a dunce's cap and another has a handkerchief knotted around his head. A little girl, smaller than the rest, is obviously very tired, rubbing her eyes. Each child is trying to study a book, and the frown they're so afraid of is clearly coming from their schoolmaster. It's quite a big picture, and I like it. Mr Cassini left it to me, so it is mine now, and it will look dandy on the wall of the police station.

The rain stopped, the sky cleared at six o'clock or thereabouts. I have been looking at the waves and feeling sad, because Mr Cassini loved the shore. He said that Britain had a Count of the Shore once. Mr Cassini spent a lot of time down there. He said it was the place to wait for wisdom and knowledge. There is a ghost down there, a little girl who runs from east to west in the sea mists: people can hear her laughing at first, and then she cries in the marshes. I used to play football with Mr Cassini on the sands with me in goal, between two pullovers. He used to cheat because I never got to take any shots but I didn't mind. Then we'd go off together to beachcomb and to study all the living things, and we collected many shells which I have on my windowsill in the big room where the public come to see me at the police station. I can name them all – scallop, limpet, periwinkle, wentletrap, dog whelk, nautilus, baby ear, Venus comb, giant false triton, and so on...

Being with Mr Cassini was fun. When the birds swirled around us and the sand was soft under my feet, they were the happiest times. Out there in Little Bay, him sitting on his big rock and me sitting on my little rock next to him, singing *The Teddy Bears' Picnic*, making him laugh. I never met anyone, man dog or child, who doesn't enjoy messing around on the beach. I used to fly my kite and Mr Cassini would let me bury him in sand if he was in a good mood. Some people said, spitefully, that when I was with Mr Cassini I was like a dog's leg, shaking involuntarily when the beast's belly was being scratched. I think that was cruel, don't you?

The fountain: Late in the evening, after the funeral, a new fountain broke out near the eastern headland; its pure waters poured along the hollow of the valley, towards the sea. PC 66 went to see it; he sat down on the grass and marvelled at it. As he sat there a rainbow formed above him and a lone figure approached him, dressed in shimmering blue. PC 66 recognised him immediately as the second rainbow messenger, who sat down and also expressed admiration for the new flow of water.

'How unfortunate that Mr Cassini is dead,' said the messenger. 'Anyone who drinks freely and bathes his temples in this fountain will be made whole again, sane and intact with his reason restored.'

After a while he turned to PC 66 and offered him a gift – a smooth, round object, the pale pink obsidian stone used by Dr John Dee to summon angels, before the conman Edward Kelley ruined everything with his naked spirit Madimi.

'Everything will change soon, when the snow comes,' said the messenger.

PC 66 nodded and thanked him before he departed swiftly through the trees.

Extracts from PC 66's black notebooks: Why did Mr Cassini have mannequins sitting around the big table in his front room, with the curtains drawn and the dust gathering? Though God knows where the dust came from, because Mr Cassini kept that room locked at all times, and even I, his very best friend, got to see it only twice. There were long-dead flies caught in shoals in the cobweb-nets which hung in every window. It smelt musty and damp, a bit spooky too. Mr Cassini liked it that way. He was crazy, I guess.

No cockle-gathering today. This is the oldest trade around here, and Mr Cassini made a big study of it; he wrote a paper for the university and they made a big fuss of him, until they discovered that his essay was a straight crib from a big cockle-toff at Swansea University, who knew more about cockles than he knew about his wife's knickers. That's what Mr Cassini said.

You want to know what it's like, this town of ours – where every-one is either possessed or dispossessed? Let's go to the top of the church tower, where the jackdaws congregate under the squeaky bell. If we look straight out to sea we can see all around us – but only sometimes, because we live on the edge of light here, in a region of near-constant mists. Perhaps we will see the soldiers – a state of emergency has been in force for some time now, but we've got used to it. When night darkens the streets we all stay indoors. Offshore from the marshes lies the island, low in the water, and it makes me think of an alligator lurking there, about to snaffle a passing boat. We can have a fine time up here watch-ing the island move in and out of the winter mists, or sinking suddenly in a squall. Sometimes it lies as still as a sleeping slug on a glass table in summer. We can listen out for the great bell on the eastern tip, which frightens children in the night because it's being rung by the Bwci-bo, sent to punish all naughty kiddie-winks; and we can watch the immense beam of the lighthouse (spurned by ships, which have fallen madly in love with satellites and follow them lamb-like, everywhere) as it searches out thieves and adulterers tip-toeing around the bedrooms of the town.

'That lighthouse,' said Mr Cassini one evening in the twilight, sitting on his throne-rock in Little Bay, cleaning his nails with a razor shell, 'reminds me of a kid lying on his back, playing with a torch like I did when I was a kid. Ever do that boy?'

'Yes sir.'

'One of them torches with green and red filters, I shone it up at the stars because the teacher told us that the light would reach the end of the universe, and I did it for hours hoping little green men would come to take my ma and pa away.'

'Never did that.'
'Did you have a torch?'
'Yes sir.'
'What the hell did you do with it then?'
'Pretended I was a spy. Sent Morse Code signals to the ships.'
'No kidding…'
'No sir.'

In the bell-tower above the slate roof-pattern, a pattern which all the little green men have in their space atlases so they can identify Wales in the *how to recognise countries from above* section, I can also see a massive headland, glowering above the water, falling down steeply into the sea. The top has been sliced off by the quarrymen and I wait for a big spoon to come out of the sky and dip into its yolk.

Between the headland and the town there is a magnificent crescent beach called Big Bay. It ends at the mouth of the river, down below us at the foot of the town, where there's a small but busy port decked with brightly-painted boats, and nets hung out to dry on the quayside. A small blue fishing boat is leaving the harbour, I can see smoke coming from its exhaust. On the other side of the river, to our left, there's another bay, much smaller but also perfectly formed, covered in shells of all shapes and sizes. This is Little Bay. Then there is a hundred-yard length of rock-pools, ideal for children to play around in, and then there's a long walk along the edge of a marsh, before you come to a matching headland which is almost a replica of the one on the other side of us. Visitors – when they came, before the troubles – generally used Big Bay, whilst local children and the cockle and mussel gatherers, and waifs and strays, use Little Bay. Last summer a young porpoise was found washed up in Little Bay and the children (and me!) ran from the sea in relays with buckets of water to keep it moist, but it died before we could get it back in the water. Mr Cassini took it away with the harbourmaster's tractor and trailer and dumped it in the marshlands. Mr Cassini had great big muscles, as big as rats, moving up and down his arms. He also had a very big conk.

Seven descriptions of Mr Cassini's nose:
Bogey warehouse
Double-barrelled snotgun

Mank tank
Slime against humanity
Chute to kill
Finger buffet
Pick 'n' mix.

'Shanti Shanti, Dahat Dahat...'

Mr Cassini was walking around a lump of clay, and he was chanting.

I remember it all like it was yesterday, the two of us in a quiet nook upriver, where the Afon Ddu calms down in a black pool, a witch's cauldron topped with ghastly froth. There is a bank of bluish-white clay in that spot, cold as a corpse, and Mr Cassini had taken me there one winter's afternoon, with a bottle of whisky, some old clothes and an axe. He lopped branches from an alder and set to work.

'What are we doing sir?' I asked, looking at the water lapping around my regulation police issue boots, size 14, polished to perfection (I like to see the sky reflected in them) but smudged now with clay.

'A golem.'

'A golem?'

'Yes boy, a golem.'

I searched my mind for the meaning of that word, and it came back to me from somewhere, eventually. I had come across it in that terrifying book he'd made me read, all about Templars and Masons and Rosicrucians... the cabbala, gnostics, alchemy, underground rooms, elixirs. It nearly sent me crazy, I felt funny in the head for weeks afterwards. There was another book he'd made me read, about a Rabbi Loew who'd moulded a man of clay – a golem – and walked around it seven times chanting *Shanti Shanti Dahat Dahat...*

It came to life, and delivered the Jews of Prague from evil. But Mr Cassini wasn't Jewish. I asked him why he was making a golem. It was then that he mentioned the name of John Dee, who was a master of the dark arts. Mr Cassini was fascinated by magic but he wasn't very good at it – he spent years trying to get colourful handkerchiefs to stream out of his pockets but he never got it right and afterwards he was in a bad temper every time.

A note on Dr John Dee: His amazing career started while he was a student at Cambridge, with a fantastical stage effect: an actor was carried upwards on the back of a great beetle, up to 'heaven' during a performance of *Peace* by Aristophanes; the startled audience was convinced that Dee had magical powers. In Elizabethan times, having a reputation as a magician and a necromancer was a short cut to the gallows. Dr Dee survived, but only just. Star Chamber chewed on him and spat him out. He set Elizabeth I's coronation date, and he was called to the court to reassure her when a comet appeared, inexplicably, in the sky. He coined the word Britannia and he talked to angels. He was an alchemist, a cabalist, a crystallomancer; he was a world authority on the occult and mathematics and he put a hex on the Spanish Armada, claiming responsibility for the bad weather which blew the Spaniards off course.

When he lectured at the Sorbonne, students climbed the outside walls to hear him through the windows. He believed that numbers could lead to complete understanding; he emphasised the straight line and the circle, the sun, the planets and the zodiac. When asked to reform the calendar he suggested taking away 11 days from the year, and this was indeed adopted – nearly 200 years later. He had the largest personal library in Britain, which included Arabian books on astrology. But while he was on one of his trips abroad his library was attacked by a mob and set on fire, because they thought he was malevolent. Five hundred books were destroyed, including rare old manuscripts. But Dr Dee worked on.

He was a close friend of Walter Raleigh, Christopher Marlowe and John Donne – but having friends in high places didn't prevent him from being arraigned before Star Chamber in 1555, falsely accused of killing a child and blinding another by practising wizardry; he was also accused of using his supernatural powers to attack Mary while she was queen, though she still commissioned him to do her horoscope. He spent three months in jail. He also did Elizabeth's horoscope and once, having dined out, she called at his home and insisted that he walk alongside her horse so that they could talk; she sent him sweets from her table when he was ill. Shakespeare reputedly based King Lear and Prospero on him.

Elizabeth licensed Dee to conduct alchemic experiments. And so his great search began... later, much later, he was to sell the Voynich Manuscript, the most mysterious cipher ever known (now at Yale University and still undeciphered) to the Holy Roman Emperor, Rudolph II, for a pot of gold. Which is where the golem comes in.

John Dee went to Prague to experiment with gold. Everyone was seeking renewal, it was a golden century: some pored over magic texts, others laboured at forges, melting metals; some sought to rule the stars, and others invented secret alphabets and universal languages. In Prague, Rudolph II turned his court into an alchemic laboratory, into which he invited the most brilliant minds of the age: men like Comenius and John Dee.

Dee believed that throughout the ages a Great White Fraternity, a cohort of a few wise men, were journeying through human history in order to preserve a core of eternal knowledge. History did not happen randomly – it was the work of the Masters of the World. Dee's visit to Prague coincided almost exactly with the creation of Rabbi Loew's famous golem, that marvellous man of clay brought to life when the Rabbi fed pieces of paper bearing a cipher into its mouth.

Further extracts from PC 66's black notebooks: Night is approaching. The memorial rites have been completed. The storm has abated; the lords of misrule, wanting more fun later, have applied a tourniquet to the sky's haemorrhage and the clouds have clotted into sullen, cheerless scabs, although streamlets still course down the cobbled streets, seawards. I look out on a deep tract of hideous ruin and combustion, bathed in a mournful gloom. The townspeople, however, are in carnival spirits – they seem glad that he's gone for good.

Who went into Mr Cassini's house on the day of the funeral, after the plume of blue smoke had drifted over the sea, after the capstone's rasp on the granite slabs?

The first to walk past the pig-head knocker was his daughter, Olwen. Next to walk past the pig-head knocker was PC 66. Last to walk past the pig-head knocker was Mojo the Fair, Mr Cassini's diminutive but perfectly formed son, fair-haired and blue-eyed, hairless of face and body, who was sent to frighten the birds with his rattle in the crop-fields on his fifteenth birthday. But they flocked around him as if he were St Francis of Assisi because no living creature, great or small, was frightened of Mojo

– a tatterdemalion dot in the high acres: he sits with his rattle in his hand, at the edge of a lake in the mountains, a lake with an island which seems to float on the water. He wears gloves. He has never spoken a word to anyone.

So there we were, in the kitchen, the ghosts of Mr Cassini and Mrs Cassini, and – in the flesh – Olwen and me and Mojo the Fair. That kitchen stank. Mr Cassini's great big fry-ups revolted everyone. The first thing you saw, on a grease-splattered wall, was a strange map. Mr Cassini had become enthused one night, after his customary ten pints in the Blue Angel, and he had torn the Wales page from an old road atlas. On it he had glued a thread of red yarn which snaked along all the roads taken by a coach when the WI had gone to Cardiff. Mrs Cassini had been with them – it was the only time she'd left town. Some of the yarn had become detached and now looped through impassable mountain ranges around Pumlumon in the mid-part of the country. I realised, suddenly, that I was sitting on the reason for Mrs Cassini's trip to Cardiff – a red cushion with a patchwork map of all the counties of Wales. It had won first prize in a national WI convention. The cushion stuck to my arse when I got up to look at it better. Mr Cassini had dropped so many sausages on it that it stuck to anything near it, like Velcro. I feel sick when I remember Mr Cassini's hideous breakfasts. Mr Cassini had an ancient belly which had been prepared for excess since his childhood with vast quantities of cold lumpy porridge, fetid goat's cheese and rancid mutton.

The story of the golem fascinated Mr Cassini, and that is why he made his own man of clay, who sits silently – expectantly? – among a group of figures in Mr Cassini's living room, waiting for Mr Cassini to feed him a cipher, so that he can spring to life and startle all the sharks in the Blue Angel by walking in and demanding a pint of the landlord's best elixir. He's a little shabby now.

I feel honour bound to be straight with you from the start, since after all I am a policeman, an upholder of verity and true law. Mr Cassini was fascinated by borders. I suppose we all are, really. Boundaries between land and sea – why else would we spend so much time at the water's edge? – and boundaries between truth and fiction, good and bad, sanity and madness. Mr Cassini said the insane know far more about sanity than the sane know about insanity.

'Porky,' he would say to me down there on the strand, 'you must remember this, boy. Poets, the oracles of long ago, believed that all wisdom and knowledge was to be found at the water's edge.'

The Tiwi people, who live on a group of islands off Australia, bury their kin immediately after death but delay the funeral ritual for several months, until the family's grief has subsided. How sensible. Here am I, full of grief, trying to direct you through the last stages of my friend's life, and my eyes are full of tears. Yes, like plays and films, funerals have their directors too; the bit part actors have all learnt their lines, and I am left to ponder a few last-minute changes to the script, on the phone to my lead actors maybe, suggesting a change of pace...

Tomorrow, another court case starts.

I'm tired. Also angry, I think. Not angry because so many people were killed – just angry that I was involved at all, since I wasn't on duty that night. I was, in fact, at a party. Since no one will read this deposition except the two of us, I can tell you that the party was, how shall I put it, slightly irregular. Not quite a shebeen, but I didn't question the provenance of the hooch which flowed from an enormous pan, it looked like an old cockle cauldron, in the middle of the floor. God knows where the pan came from, though Mr Cassini said he'd bought it from an Irish tinker. Mr Cassini sourced all his 'doubtful' acquisitions to travellers and tinkers from across the water – it was a handy device, which he used often.

Anyway, we were on the island, opposite the marshlands, in a rickety old shack and we were roaring drunk. Mr Cassini, his big knobbly nose gleaming sweatily between his eyes, was arm-wrestling with one of the hairy-arsed farmers who till the meagre soil above the town. It was then, apparently, though I didn't hear it myself, that one of the revellers heard a voice screaming above the wind outside, a supernatural scream in the night. A storm had broken suddenly while we drank Mr Cassini's potion (had time stood still, or had we drunk ourselves insensible? We had been in that shack for three days without knowing it.) My notes tell me that in the midst of that barbarous dissonance a number of the men heard a fell shriek in the darkness; a hag-voice which screamed the words *vengeance is coming*. Just the once, but the incident was enough to wake us all from our drugged state. We realised, suddenly, how ill we felt from the drink, and how pitiably small we were in the teeth of that storm. A huge depression settled on all of us; through the one cobwebbed window I saw a flight of swans disappearing seawards, into a bank of rolling clouds.

Since it was a priority for me, as a policeman, to get back to civilisation, I commandeered the little blue dingy drawn up on the island's sole landing-point and cast myself into her, then Mr Cassini launched us into the boiling surf and threw himself in also. It is less than a hundred yards between island and shore, but we only just made it: the boat was swamped some twenty yards out and we were carried for the rest of the way by thunderous breakers which pummelled us and spat us out on the strand. We saw now, in a pallid dawn, that the sea was high up against the shore, higher than we had ever seen it before. In the distance, just within vision, we could see a wreck thrown up on the eastern headland. The wind howled and whistled all around us, and we could barely stay upright. Even then I wondered how we had failed to notice this gale brewing as we supped in the shack.

I dried out in the police station and as soon as I'd done so a wild-eyed man arrived at the door, pointing eastwards beyond Big Bay, and urging me to go with all haste to help the people there, for they were in dire straits. The sea had inundated the land, he said, and many had drowned. Whole villages had disappeared.

Three days later, in a mountain bothy, I apprehended the dyke-keeper who was responsible for maintaining the embankment, and charged him with neglecting his duties. It was now that things got difficult for me, since – by a horrible quirk of fate – he had been one of my fellow-revellers in the island shack on the night of the storm. It transpired that he was a friend of Mr Cassini's, involved in the smuggling trade (he supplied the Cassini empire with tobacco and spirits), and was delivering a cache to Mr Cassini on the night of the inundation. This was lucky for him, but extremely infortuitous for me. Mr Cassini had a word with him, and I don't know what he said, but this fellow has promised to say nothing of my inappropriate behaviour, though I am fair sweaty with fear.

It was a relatively small inundation, as inundations go – that's what Mr Cassini said. But I tell you, that night was to change our lives for ever. It was sometime during that terrible storm that Mr Cassini told me his plan. For the next dummy in his front room he had set his heart on a woman close to both of us. Mrs Cassini. Worse still, it was me who would betray her. My guilt weighs on me heavily. But I loved that man. I feared him too – he wielded such power over all of us.

Mr Cassini had planned it all out for me. A Stone Age death for a Stone Age woman, he said. And that meant getting rid of her. He had already chosen a day. My task was simply to put a leaf in her hair, surreptitiously, and then draw attention to it, asking Mr Cassini, in public, how a leaf had become entangled in her tresses. Mr Cassini would seize upon this opportunity to accuse her of infidelity; she had lain in the grass with another man, they had consumed their passion under a tree. He would rip out the leaf and her hair with it. He would be justified in slaying her. It would be a crime of passion.

What can I say, except that Mrs Cassini is no more... and now her husband, Mr Cassini, is dead too. We will never make a sandcastle together again. We will never play in the caves.

5

THE TIDE GOES OUT

The Irish connection.
Caves – and a disappearance

I can't remember Olly's exact response when I told her about Mr Cassini. He was a dead monster: a pile of ashes in an urn in a grave in a mound in a dream.

'Swivel on that, baby!' I wiggled my hips and waggled my middle fingers at an imaginary crowd, imitating the once-famous goal celebration I trademarked in the glory-glory days. 'Get out of that you big piece of shit!'

Olly pretended to laugh at my antics, but she didn't celebrate much.

'No more mad mannequin stories,' I said. No more astrology, no more alchemy. No more crazy talk and no more confessions from PC 66 – there's nothing worse than a bent copper.

'Justice at last, even if we are dealing with a couple of fictional characters,' I said.

'You know something,' said Olly, and I was looking at that sensuous mouth of hers, 'I've a feeling that true justice only happens to people in stories. That's what stories are for.'

I didn't know what she meant by that.

'Pardon?'

She looked tired. 'Stories... isn't that what they're for? To get some sort of justice – I don't think justice is possible in real life, do you? It's just nominal. A symbol. There's no such thing, really.'

That gave me plenty to think about as we got ready for another Mystery Quest – yes, we were off on another picnic. We'd decided to continue the Arthurian theme – our trip north had raised a hare so we gave chase.

'We've started so we'll finish,' she said to me after our trip to Arthuret. The experience had intrigued her. Something to do with madness, perhaps – there was a tenuous link in that vein between Mr Cassini and Merlin. Madness as background hiss. Olly was disappointed I hadn't given Mr Cassini a more dramatic death. She mentioned Michael the Scot.

'Who?'

She told me about him – a twelfth-century translator and philosopher at the Court of the Holy Roman Emperor, who became famous for his extraordinary metal helmet. Michael had a reputation as a wizard because he dabbled in astrology, astronomy and alchemy. He predicted that a falling stone would kill him – and he forecast its precise weight. He always wore his helmet as a precaution, except once, when he took it off before entering a church for mass. A stone fell from the ceiling and hit him, fatally, on the head.

'*That's* the sort of death he needed,' said Olly.

It's February. A jumbled-up jigsaw. Some days are blue and some days are grey, it's hard to find a pattern. A fine rain is visibly rusting the landscape. The clouds drift slowly, skybergs in a long delirium... the mountain-tops are islands in pack ice. Blackbirds are ready to pair off and sing of love. Vixens fill the night with their ghostly shrieks. The wild daffodil – with its narcotic bulb – struggles airborne: it has spent the winter in the meadows of the underworld. Many ducks are already on their way to their Arctic breeding grounds. There's a boat about to leave the harbour and I want to be on it too, I want to go somewhere that's not here.

Snowdrops, which escaped from monastery gardens long ago (and which were worn as a sign of purity by village girls) huddle in clusters, war tents in a frosty battlefield. A few squirrels dig down for nuts hidden last autumn, though it's clear from their errant scrapings that they have faulty memories, and many fail to find their hoards.

Memory. I'm still trying to find mine. The first ten years are lost. Should I continue my quest? Is it dangerous? And what exactly is memory?

Memory as a sheath – if the silkworm moth is allowed to emerge from its cocoon the silk becomes uncommercial, so the chrysalis is suffocated while it's still inside its silkspun home.

Memory as an electric cable – sometimes underground, nearly always hidden, flexed for ease and convenience, always covered up and dangerous if exposed; useful yet dangerous, like water.

We're going on a picnic, Olly and me, in the hills. Another wintry day has been delivered, wet and mucous, on the world's maternity ward. The air is sharp and scentless. But we're warm and cosy in Olly's kitchen – she's making sandwiches. The chopping board is all knives and crumbs. I know what you're thinking – Olly is always the one who makes the sandwiches, but actually I make a pretty mean sandwich myself. It just so happens that she's into making the sandwiches: I think it's a way of keeping busy, keeping her mind off things. And since I gave you the recipe last time I shall do so this time too: peppered pastrami with green olives and baby tomatoes in a home-made dill pickle bread. Really yummy. To wet our whistles I've bought a bottle of Spatone water from Trefriw Wells Spa, a spring reputedly discovered by the tenth Roman legion. Mining debris closed the site until 1833, when 'an aged inhabitant' led Victorian entrepreneurs to the source of the iron-rich water, a spring gushing from a cave hewn nearly 40 feet into the rock; patients flocked to be cured of anaemia, skin diseases, indigestion, rheumatism, palsies, stomach disorders and nervous complaints.

Butties are much more enjoyable in the outdoors, and today we're off to the wilds of Snowdonia. We're going in her motor, and my first job is to haul a big dog-stinking blanket into the car and lay it on the back seat for her hound Gelert. Yet again I have to avert my eyes and suppress some wayward thoughts as she belts herself in and her scent drifts towards me. Today she has an Elastoplast on her neck, one of those long oblong strips, waterproof. I remark on it.

'Spot gone septic,' she says, wrinkling her nose and smirking disdainfully.

She's run down, perhaps. Or the aliens have been down for another visit.

We start the journey, though Gelert has delayed us by steaming up the windows with his great lolling tongue. I smell a dog's dinner – last night's – in the air so I keep my window open. I daren't say anything because she loves that hound more than anything or anyone, even her boyfriend Fit Boy. And talking of Fit Boy, I have a rendezvous with him tomorrow, when I'm due to take him to Holyhead. He's taking a ferry over to Ireland – but more of that later.

It's suddenly warmer this morning, after a cold snap, and a minor thaw is taking place. I see snow on the tops, and snowdrops under the trees, a spillage of milk in the crisp green grass. Full-bellied rivers ache with water. Reflected in a lake's cold clarity, cotton-wool clouds, stained pink by the dawn, are surgical swabs stuck to gashes in the ravines. The air is very still; hardly a leaf moves as we coil upwards through the Llanberis Pass and then descend to the Pen-y-Gwryd Hotel, base camp for the 1953 Everest Expedition when it trained in Snowdonia. The full name of this mountain pass is Pen-y-Gwryd-Cei. Cei was Arthur's main man in North Wales; in the ancient story *Culhwch ac Olwen* he was a giant-slayer and Arthur's foremost warrior. He could be as tall as the tallest tree in the forest. He had mystical powers and could hold his breath under water for nine days and nights. No physician could heal a wound from his sword. The heat from his body kept his companions warm on the coldest of nights.

She's crying again, soundlessly, and her shoulders look as small as a child's. I feed her sweets as we snake down the pass, and she smiles little wobbly smiles sometimes when I hand her one. Her tears are torn silk, a snapped cobweb falling to earth.

This is our personal history: a private liquid which hardens as it leaves our spinnerets, then holds us in place. Tenuous yet surprisingly strong, a web from which we view the world, tremble in its winds. Waiting for something to happen, waiting for it all to fall apart.

A distant sun blowlamps the sea, and the upland fields are green phosphorescent seas crashing in giant waves onto the hillsides: their crooked walls are tidemarks flotsammed with sheep. I lie back in my seat and I dream…

Arthur is all around us: he's above us and he's below us. Last night, as I scanned the sky with my telescope, I dwelt on the brightest star in the northern hemisphere – Arcturus, to the left of the Plough in the constellation of Bootes. This star has been connected with Arthur for a very long time: its name is rooted in the Greek word for bear. The Welsh word for bear is *arth...*

Arthur's warriors sleep in a cave in Snowdonia, according to legend. There are many stories about him 'living' underground: in the fourteenth-century English poem *A Dispute between a Christian and a Jew*, he and his knights live in a magnificent dwelling reached by a path under a hill. In many of the tales Arthur and thousands of his men sleep in a circle, waiting until a bell hanging in the cave is tolled to wake them so that they can lead Wales – the Britons – to glory again. This subterranean abode or kingdom is magical and otherworldly; the Celtic Otherworld is always underground, located with great difficulty within elusive hillside caverns. These legends have beautiful touches.

In the *Chronicon de Lanercost*, Peter de Roches, Bishop of Winchester, saw a magnificent house while hunting and accepted an invitation to dine with the master, who turned out to be Arthur. The bishop wanted to convince sceptics that he had truly seen the ancient lord of Britain, so Arthur gave him the miraculous power of producing a butterfly whenever he opened his closed fist.

From Merlin's crystal cave to St Benedict's bolthole, caves are full of meaning (if nothing else). A dictionary of symbols includes these connotations:

> A symbol of the universe; the world centre; the heart; a place of union between the Self and the Ego; where the divine and the human meet; where dying gods go and where saviours are born; inner esoteric knowledge; that which is hidden; a place of initiation and second birth; the womb of Mother Earth; a place of burial and rebirth; a place of mystery; a place of sacred marriage between heaven and earth; a place of obscurity and illusion.

When Carl Jung recorded his first *active imagination experience* in 1913, he sat at his desk and decided to *let himself drop*. He felt as though the ground had given way under his feet. He plunged into dark depths. After a while he 'landed' on soft ground. When his eyes adjusted he began to see details in the gloom. Before him was an entrance to a cave, in which stood a dwarf with leathery skin. Jung squeezed past him and waded through icy, knee-deep water. At the other end of the cave a red crystal glowed on a rock. When he lifted the crystal he saw a hole which allowed him to overlook a river. Soon he saw the corpse of a boy with blond hair floating by, followed by a gigantic black beetle; then a red sun rose from the water. Blinded by its rays, Jung wanted to replace the crystal but blood poured from the hole.

In his second *active imagination experience* Jung descended into a 'cosmic abyss'. He saw something like a moon crater and felt he was in the land of the dead. Near a steep rocky slope he saw an old man and a beautiful young girl. He approached them and listened. A large black snake slithered by...

The car weaves to left and right, a shuttle in Snowdonia's moss-woven carpet, as we head down the pass towards Beddgelert. I'm voyaging towards a prism in my past: towards my own very little bang. Singularity. Will it be an event in time, or in space, or in fantasy? Why worry about it... after all, life's just a bout of insomnia before the big sleep. What did Fernando Pessoa say? *Madness isn't the failure to make sense but the attempt.*

'Enough petrol, have we?' I venture.

'Yes.' Her response comes in a hiss, and I realise immediately that I've put my foot in it again. Her whole mood changes. Suddenly her shoulders tighten, the sinews in her neck tauten. She blowpipes her mouth and fires a fruit gum at me; it hits my cheek in a warm green splat. Cheeky little madam.

'Sorry,' I say.

'Well just think before you speak again,' she says. 'I told you it'll never happen again, right? Don't treat me like a bloody kid.'

'Sorry Olly.'

I clam up, hoping I haven't ruined the morning. Olly's tense again; she's nervy and jumpy. Thin, tired, hollowed out. But why?

A few miles further on she floors me with a lightning question which has me on the canvas.

'Do you believe in God?'

I look across at her, running through all my databanks, my head's whirring as I try to establish if she's serious.

'Well, do you?' she asks again.

I'm flummoxed.

'Does he believe in me?' I counter. I don't like talking about God. Makes me nervous. There's a pause, and then (stupidly) I ask: 'Why?'

She pushes a loose strand of hair back into place and lets out a long stream of air, making a whirring noise with her lips.

'Don't really know. I've been thinking about it recently, that's all. A lot of people say they're not religious, then they turn round and say *all this can't be here by chance,*' and she waves her hand at the scene around us.

I keep mum. I don't want to get involved. I've lived long enough for everyone around me to say the same thing twice – in completely contradictory ways.

Instead, I admire the russet bracken breaking in waves on the slopes around us. The fields have been ironed by an amateur or a drunk, because all the folds are in the wrong places. A huddle of hills looks like a tug o'war team, braced, straining at the rope of the horizon. The road is a glistening snail-trail of silver after a shower. Fortunately for me, the crisis passes. No more talk of God because soon we're there; Gelert the hound is leashed, and we're booted and coated ready for our excursion.

We face a rotunda hill, tortoise-napping by the side of the road near Llyn Dinas – the lake in which Vortigern hid the throne of Britain, allegedly (the case hasn't come to court yet). There's a girl canoeing with her hair in bunches and she looks like a grebe. Skirting a row of caravans, we climb along the vertebrae of a wooded ridge which takes us towards the top of Dinas Emrys. We're in a kingdom of luxuriant mosses which cushion and constrain a soft green half-light. The path is surrounded by sessile oaks and their rheumatoid branches are festooned with water droplets which light our path – candelabra in the hallway of the mountain king; we walk through a tree-lined vestibule decorated tastefully in the muted colours of bark and lichen. It's the sort of place you'd expect to meet a *woodwose,* a wild man of the woods. Long ago they were thought to live in the forests which covered Britain, and they make frequent appearances in medieval art. Naked, clothed only in their hair, they appeared in masques to portray rustic or primitive folk. The *Speculum Regale* (the King's Mirror) written in Norway around 1250 says:

> It once happened in that country (and this seems indeed strange) that a living creature was caught in the forest as to which no one could say definitely whether it was a man or some other animal; for no one could get a word from it or be sure that it understood human

speech. It had the human shape, however, in every detail, both as to hands and face and feet; but the entire body was covered with hair as the beasts are, and down the back it had a long coarse mane like that of a horse, which fell to both sides and trailed along the ground when the creature stooped in walking.

Above us, on the slopes of Craig Wen – the White Rock – I hear dogs barking and the faint sound of a bugle: the Eryri Hunt is out. The whipper-in is trying to recall three muddy hounds which have become detached from the hunt and lope along the valley floor. Meanwhile, we examine the remains of the fortress on Dinas Emrys. Archaeologists have found evidence of human activity during the Roman occupation and in the ensuing Dark Ages. They also discovered the site of a pool, a small waterhole which lies at the centre of the most important Welsh myth.

History of a hole: Once there was a king called Vortigern who fled from his enemies, to the remotest part of his kingdom. He decided to build a fortress at Dinas Emrys, but as soon as any building took shape it sank without trace into the ground at night. Wise men told Vortigern that this could be prevented by pouring the blood of a fatherless boy into the foundations. Such a boy, Ambrosius, was found in Glamorgan. Transported north to Dinas Emrys, this wonder-child declared that two dragons, fighting in a pool below, were the cause of the problem. Digging down, masons discovered a red dragon fighting fiercely with a white dragon. The red dragon won. Impressed by the boy, Vortigern named the fort after him (*Ambrosius* equals *Emrys*). Some use this episode to explain the red dragon on the Welsh flag; others compare the dragons' fight to the conflict between the Britons and the Saxons. Mediterranean pottery found at the site points to a rich Christian household from the fifth or sixth century: the shards may have been mistaken for broken dragon's eggs, or the container in which they fought. The fabled pool, now little more than a reedy hollow near the summit, was a water cistern, probably. It was Geoffrey of Monmouth who muddied the waters. In his epic work, *The History of the Kings of Britain*, the most influential book ever to emerge from Wales, he welded the story of Emrys to the British myth about a madman in the woods. Geoffrey of Monmouth was a literary alchemist who turned a collection of folk tales into a major book which kick-started the golden age of the Arthurian cycle. He was to have a profound effect on the whole of Europe, and still exerts a magical influence via Hollywood.

I stood on Dinas Emrys, enjoying the view. For although it appears to be little more than a hillock from the road, it commands a glorious view of the pass. As I looked down on Llyn Dinas, which shone like a burnished shield, Gelert lunged forward and very nearly disappeared over the ramparts. He squealed to a halt on the edge of a 200-foot drop, and his target – a black and white billygoat – romped away from us towards a flock on the other side of the river. I screamed at Gelert but he took no notice of me. Then a single whistle rang out and he froze to the spot. Olly took control and he was on his leash almost immediately. Long dribbles of saliva drifted from his mouth as he looked longingly at the goats. In the silence we could hear the hunters' bugle drifting away from us, up the mountain. And I was reminded, suddenly, of the Demon Hunter and his seven magic bullets.

Turning to view the valley floor again, I saw a huge spotlight of sunshine beaming down from a chink in the clouds, capturing a green field by the river and turning it instantly into a brilliantly-lit stage. The river, the roadways, and all reflective surfaces glittered in this dazzling light. Then a pair of choughs passed by, the light waned and the slopes of Cnicht blued over in a wintry haze; in the darkening woods a purple hue of regret and melan-choly fell in folds over the ribs of the silver birches. A great tit sawed in the branches below me. Fallen trees all around me testi-fied to the many storms which had buffeted this eyrie, but it was preternaturally still that day. I ate my sandwiches, leaving a crumb or two for the sparrows, and Gelert left a pint of dog-drool for the ghosts of Dinas Emrys. As I ate my dill pickle bread on that blue-forgotten hill I thought I heard children at play, their fluid shapes moving along the bole of a wind-snapped tree. You may think I'm being fanciful, but that was the mood of the moment. The loss of my children hit me with a deep pang; they should have been there with me – playing in my present, not in my past. I had taught them to love the light, and birdsong, and darkness and silence too... today they would be encased in breeze blocks, listening to hoodlums from the Bronx.

I am a ghost to them now as they play in this country inside me, this lost terrain.

Olly pointed over the valley, to the Sygun Copper Mine, now a tourist attraction.

'That's where they filmed *The Inn of the Sixth Happiness*, isn't it?'

I'd never heard of it – apparently it's a film starring Ingrid Bergman, set in China, about a real-life missionary called Gladys Aylward. When the Japanese invaded she led about a hundred Chinese kids to safety over the mountains.

'I had her hat once,' said Olly.

'No kidding. What hat?'

She ignored my superciliousness.

'The coolie hat which Ingrid Bergman wore in the film.'

'What's the sixth happiness, anyway?' I asked. 'And what were the other five?'

Olly seemed to know all about it. This Gladys Aylward was a missionary who opened an inn out there for muleteers, and when it was time to put a name on the sign above the door she chose *The Inn of the Sixth Happiness* because Chinese people traditionally wish each other five forms of happiness – health, wealth, virtue, longevity and a peaceful death in old age. The sixth happiness, presumably, was the Christian message.

The sixth happiness. I wondered if it was possible for mankind to discover previously unknown forms of happiness; after all, a tenth planet had just been discovered revolving around the sun. It might be a simple form of happiness, spinning around inside us; we could announce it proudly to the world at a crowded press conference.

Ladies and gentlemen: today we bring you the seventh form of happiness – discovered yesterday by Duxie the well-known but generally disparaged former football player. The World Happiness Forum has verified the name of this new happiness as Duxieness. Please feel free to laugh or express joy and contentment.

'Tell you what,' I said, 'I've got an idea.'

This time it was her turn to be supercilious, pulling a silly face. I ignored her.

'Remember those seven rainbow messengers in my crazy dreams?'

She nodded. 'How could I forget?'

'Right,' I said. 'We'll aim for the seventh happiness. That's what we'll look for at the end of this rainbow of ours – the seventh happiness. Deal?'

She dropped her head and looked at her sandwich, then tossed it into the reedy water below us.

'Yeah, if that's what you want.'

'Hey,' I complained, 'I could have used that sandwich myself.'

'Tough shit.'

We got up, and she stuffed the remains of our picnic into her rucksack. I started to move away, but she stopped me.

'Haven't you forgotten something?' The hand which had halted my progress remained on my chest, and I pushed against it gently… provocatively?

'What?'

She jerked her head towards the reeds, and the murky water beneath them.

'Go on.'

I didn't get it. 'What?' I said again, pushing against her hand.

'It's time to put your penny in the pond, dummy.'

Of course. I laughed quietly and moved away from her, then ferreted about in my pockets. No cash, not a single bloody penny. She put her rucksack down and scrabbled around in a side-pocket, then handed me a twopenny piece.

'That's all I've got, I'm afraid. It'll have to be a very small wish.'

She was already on her way when she heard the plop.

'If it's about the seventh happiness you can forget it,' she said. 'I need some of the others first.'

Our mini-quest over, we turned the car eastwards, drove through the piled-up mountains and dropped to sea level again. On the way, Olly told me she was going to delay the wedding. Big fuss, lots of pissed off people. Her father had been playing up again; he'd made a number of impossible demands. He was being a pig, as usual. There was a medical problem, too. The blood tests had revealed an unspecified illness. She was having sensory tests… the doctors were concerned about her eyesight. Her peripheral vision was impaired; the world in front of her was clouding over. But there was no easy diagnosis. They thought the problem was psychological.

I'd heard of artists going mad or losing their eyesight because of the pigments in their paints; Olly was losing her vision because of a pigment in her history. Her brain, apparently, might be trying to block out the present, as mine was blocking out the past. I tried to understand what was going on, but it was difficult. I don't have much experience of this sort of thing. Away from the bar and the bedroom, sportsmen have pretty one-dimensional lives. As I've told you already, I'm a professional footballer, retired. The end-game was a bad experience. Ageing player-managers don't get much sympathy:

> Duxie laboured towards goal like a pit pony released from the shafts after a lifetime lugging coal: half-man, half-carthorse, he looked more like a centaur-forward than a centre-forward – *Cambrian News*.

> Duxie's boys eat, drink and sleep football – what a shame they can't play it. In the end they lost five nil, and they were lucky to get nil – *Rhyl Journal*.

My wife ran off with a younger model three years ago. Barry Town goalkeeper. Safest pair of hands in Wales. Too damn right. He'd had plenty of practice juggling with my wife's tits. The papers had a field day. I was standing in the front room when I found out, looking at a trail of wet footprints on the carpet, and I was shocked to the core. The handset was brittle and chilly against my ear, and my legs – up to my knees – were cold and wet because the phone had rung as I was stepping into the bath. This time it was *The People*. Long-distance camera shots of her in a hotel room, fuzzy, but I could see it was her behind the net curtains. The way she was holding him told me everything I didn't want to know. I had a bad time with it all. Perhaps I took her for granted, I can't tell you for sure. Other beds, yes, but they meant nothing and she knew it. I never fell in love, that must count for something, mustn't it? But she had to go the whole hog, didn't she? She remarried as soon as the decree absolute arrived. I'd been forced to move into a particularly gruesome flat and I remember vividly the morning I went down to check the mail and found the envelope lying on the cracked hallway lino. It was one of those cold, dirty hallways shared by half a dozen people who hardly ever spoke yet knew more about each other than they did about their own brothers and sisters. You learn a lot from the mail: Save the Sardine, Royal Society for the Protection of Bison. Penis enlargements, hospital appointments, dole cheques, summonses, debt claims, double-glazing, the endless folderol.

Banks, charities, governments, aliens, the multiple horrors of bedsit-land. Moans, groans, rows, silences, all of them as revealing as my own centre spreads in the Sunday papers. We hit a disastrous losing streak and things were never the same again on the pitch. Confidence, I suppose. I felt as if the whole damn crowd, every single one of them, were grinning and thinking of her at it in that hotel room. I had the kids most weekends, though it was hard moving all five from her place to mine. The smallest lay in the well in the back of the car in case the coppers saw I was overloaded. They don't come now. They're doing their own thing. Their interest ended, pretty well, when I fell to earth.

I moved out of that flat eventually, before the dry rot sucked out all my juices. Got myself a nice gaff now, up at the top end of town, looking down on the football pitch as it happens. Sometimes, on Saturdays, I watch them playing from my bedroom window. I'm trying to get some qualifications, though I don't know what for. Don't know what I want to do, never did really. I just did what people wanted me to do, all my life, and you know what happens if you try to please – they soon have you running round like Maradonna on speed. Willing horse and all that.

I keep the place clean, I have a telly and all that sort of stuff. I listen to music a lot. I like to have books around. And of course I've got a lot of pictures. The most important – taking the Cup at Wembley – I keep tucked away in my computer room. People get the wrong idea if you stick something like that by the front door. I keep the medals locked away. I've got some nice memories on the walls: team pics, presentations, meeting some of my heroes – Pele, Cruyff, Rushie, Giggsy, even Maradonna – the man himself – at a nightclub in Rome.

Those pictures mean a lot to me, so I'm going to tell you about ap Llwyd again. Remember him? The loner who wrote *Water-Divining in the Foothills of Paradise*. His book seems to be regular bedtime reading for me these days.

Here's a passage I read last night – in the middle of the night to be honest, because my sleep patterns are all over the place. As usual, ap Llwyd is in the café with his Italian buddy Stefano, and they're having one of their animated conversations (I wonder, sometimes, just how much time ap Llwyd spent in those foothills of his).

Stefano was keyed up that night – more excited than I'd ever seen him before, swiping at the condensation on the window so that we could see the landmarks below. He pointed out the individual colours: red for the glow above the pithead wheel; orange for the long line of dwindling haloes around the lamp standards edging away from us along the main road, towards civilisation; green for the boat-lights, dim and diffused, in the harbour. He was going through one of his anarchist phases and he wore a black tee-shirt bearing a stark white message:

> DON'T VOTE
> SHOW THEM
> YOU CARE

'You seem excited tonight, Stefano,' I remarked.

'Do you think so?' he replied. '*È vero*, I suppose I am a little on edge.' As the condensation returned to the windowpane he traced a pattern among all the lights, which somehow resembled the outline of a bird in flight.

'What a strange coincidence,' he said, loudly enough to gain everyone's attention in the café. They turned round and stared at him in unison, reminding me of startled cows in their stalls, white-eyed and steaming, waiting for the farmer to give them some winter feed.

'Today this is not the only bird to be there – yet *not* there – *caro amico*.'

Stefano's English was weak at times, so I asked him for a clarification.

'The bird on the window – it is there, yet it is not there, *sì*?'

'Yes, what of it?'

'Today I was looking at a famous painting which should have had a bird in it – but the bird wasn't there.'

'Yes? Go on,' I said encouragingly.

'This painting is by Gainsborough, and it is called *Mr and Mrs Andrews*.'

I knew the one; it shows a gentleman and his wife in the Suffolk countryside in about 1750 – he with a gun slung nonchalantly under his arm, she sitting on a rococo bench, in an azure blue dress, her hands held meekly in her lap.

'Did you ever look at that picture?' asked Stefano.

'I've seen copies, yes.'

'Did you ever look closely at her hands?'

'No, I never did.'

'You look next time. There's nothing there, because this Gainsborough never finished the picture.'

'And what's that got to do with a bird?'

He chuckled and took a draught of coffee. He seemed calmer.

'Well, there are two theories. Some say that Gainsborough meant to paint Mrs Andrews holding a child. Others say that Gainsborough meant to paint her holding a pheasant – but she wouldn't hold it because it was dead. The bird was meant to be a symbol of her husband's prowess with the gun. But she didn't want any blood or guts anywhere near her, no thank you very much.'

'And so there's nothing there,' I remarked. Warming to the subject, I told him a story about Cézanne: after 115 sittings for his portrait in 1899, the art dealer Ambroise Vollard noticed that two tiny patches on his right hand remained unpainted in the picture. Cézanne warned him that putting the wrong colour on either patch would ruin the painting, forcing him to start again from scratch. The two spots of bare canvas – hardly visible – were never covered.

'Aha,' my friend interjected, 'so it was more important for Cézanne to be satisfied artistically than for him to finish his pictures completely.'

'Seems so,' I replied.

After a full minute's silence he raised his eyes from his coffee mug and stared at me intently.

'You may remember that some time last year, when you came to my home, you noticed something unusual.'

'Yes, I have a clear memory of that day,' I replied. 'I had just returned from the foothills, and we were due to celebrate my discovery.'

What I had found was unique in the history of water-divining: seven interconnected wells, all yielding water of the very highest quality. I'd discovered they were connected by dropping a red dye into the first – only for it to colour the second, and the third to a lesser degree, and so on. In a similar fashion, the Greeks had used pine cones to track sinkholes from the mountains, through limestone channels, to coastland springs down below in the Gulf of Argos.

'What did you remark on that day, when you visited my house?'

'I commented on the fact that a very large picture in your vestibule had been turned to face the wall.'

'Indeed. What you couldn't know, since you did not visit every room, was that every single picture and photograph in my house had been turned to face the wall.'

'And why did you do that?'

'I *thought* you'd be interested,' he said, clicking his fingers and ordering two more coffees with a simple rotation of his right fore-finger over our empty mugs.

'For one month of the year, every February, I turn all my pictures to the wall. You find that a strange thing to do?'

'You can't deny that it's unusual…'

'Yes, I admit it. But for that month, as I pass each picture, I try to remember the scene it portrays, the people it depicts. I try to remember all the details, and why I like each picture – why I have it on my wall. And do you know why?'

'No idea, my friend.'

'Because I realised something one day. I realised that if I was forced to look at any of my pictures every single day, for hour after hour, I would soon be sick to death of them. In fact, a major part of my enjoyment was *not* being in the room for long periods, and *not* being able to see the picture for days on end.'

My dear friend Stefano gave a soft, musical laugh. His eyes gleamed. How I admired him that day. What wonderful thoughts he had!

But he hadn't quite finished. As the fresh coffees arrived at our table in a small cloud of steam he bathed me in one of his most intense gazes and added:

'And so it is with our own lives, my friend. If we spend too much time in the company of our own histories they soon tire us. We must turn them to the wall at regular intervals, hide them in case we become sickened by our own pasts.'

I clapped him on the back and congratulated him. And then I astounded him with a quotation I had learnt off by heart one night as I sat by my campfire in a cave-mouth just a few yards from the seventh well; a marvellous quotation from a man called Julian Barnes:

The past is a distant, receding coastline, and we are all in the same boat. Along the stern rail there is a line of telescopes; each brings the shore into focus at a given distance. If the boat is becalmed, one of the telescopes will be in continual use; it will seem to tell the whole, the unchanging truth. But this is an illusion; and as the boat sets off again, we return to our normal activity: scurrying from one telescope to another, seeing the sharpness fade in one, waiting for the blear to clear in another. And when the blear does clear, we imagine that we have made it do so all by ourselves.

Now it was Stefano's turn to clap *me* on the back. Our friendship was set in stone from that day onwards.

Olly took me home and I put my feet up. I didn't even try the coffee routine. After a quick bath I sat on the couch in a damp towel and turned on the telly to get the footie scores. Onto the screen came a rugby match and I groaned because I'd forgotten, God knows how, that an international was being played that day.

In fact it was *the* international, against the old enemy, and a spiky-haired kid with silver boots was about to take a penalty. You could tell it was a mighty important kick. Four minutes to go and Wales were 9-8 down. As he placed the ball and prepared himself, my thoughts raced back to Dinas Emrys: to a long-ago battle between a red dragon and a white dragon, watched by anxious eyes. Things didn't change much, I thought, except that millions of eyes were watching this particular tussle. He got the kick – it was Gavin Henson I think – and he was a hero that night. No nerves at all – he just did the job. That's what makes heroes: they can kill the nerves and deliver the goods.

My next task was to run an errand for Olly on Sunday. I didn't feel like doing it, but promises are promises. I'd agreed to run Fit Boy to Holyhead. He was taking a ferry over to Ireland. Something to do with pigshit – apparently the Irish have dreamt up a new way of dealing with farmyard sewage; instead of saving it up in sewage pits they channel it into wetland lagoons and let reeds filter out the poo. Fit Boy was going out there to find out more – something to do with his course at the college. Smelly business, but Fit Boy always came up smelling of roses. Not much love lost between us – I think he's a poser – but Olly loves him (there's no accounting for taste) so I try to be nice to him.

I picked him up in my own jalopy, a decaying yellow Toyota pick-up, and we headed over the Suspension Bridge and across Anglesey. I wasn't in the mood for chit-chat so I let him do the talking. When he ran out of topics I switched on the radio and we picked up the news. That little girl in the well was still down inside it, and they were having big problems. One of the big engineering companies was drilling a shaft alongside the well in an attempt to get to her. She was still alive, but they couldn't get any water to her (deeply ironic, I thought). By now it was a race against time.

'You two going to have any kids?' I asked him in an attempt to make conversation.

'Loads,' he said. 'Though the way things are going I'm not sure there's going to be a wedding, never mind kids.'

'How come?'

'Oh, problems. Loads of stuff. And Olly seems to be going through a bad time, no one knows why. She won't talk to anyone about it,' he said.

'Not even you?'

'No.'

'I'm really surprised.'

I could see him looking at me through the corner of his eye.

'To tell you the truth, I thought she was talking to you about it. She seems to be cavorting with you most of the time.'

I told him the truth about her and me – though I would have told him exactly the same story if we'd been at it like rabbits, which unfortunately we hadn't. We were helping each other with course work at the college, I said. Besides, I was old enough to be her father, etc. etc. I didn't tell him about the crying though. He had to learn about the tears himself. Perhaps he was too vain or too arrogant to register other people's emotions. Of course, there was a possibility he knew everything. We didn't talk about it.

I drove steadily through the centre of the island, on the old road. We were overhung by a large black saucepan-lid cloud, in the centre of the sky above us, leaving an encircling ring of blue all around us, along the horizon; helicopters swayed drunkenly through this slit of blueness as if they were bees arriving at a hive. The hedgerow-tops on either side of the road had been given a crew-cut recently and tail-up blackbirds strutted their stuff along the flat parade-ground surfaces, hurling shrill commands at the surrounding countryside. And then, on the grey verges, we saw flowers for the dead everywhere. We came across bouquets at many lonely spots: against walls, tied to fences. They had been left in memory of people killed in road accidents, and clearly there had been a spate of fatal accidents. Colourful blooms wilted in their cellophane wrappers. There were skid marks, churned-up verges and broken walls. I survived a bad crash once and as I looked at the flowers I relived those last few seconds before impact. After a while my mind returned to the world around me, and I felt glad I was still there to appreciate it. Death is so absolute, isn't it?

I took him to Terminal One and accompanied him to the departure lounge. There's a circular glass reception area beyond the ticket desks, so I sat on a bright blue chair, looking over my shoulder at a forest of masts in the harbour, whilst he sorted his ticket. A skein of wild geese struggled across one of the panes, in the far distance.

'Bloody hell,' he said when he returned. 'Bit steep.'

I wasn't particularly bothered, since I wasn't paying, so I had a gander at the people around me, trying to spot the Irishmen going home to guzzle some Guinness.

I hadn't been scanning the crowd for long when my eye landed on a head of curls and a rugged profile which I recognised straight away, or thought I recognised anyway. Was it him? Surely to God it was – the man himself again. Adam Phillips, the Cardiff brainbox who said such memorable lines as *'you can change childhood by deciding what not to say about it'*. Yes, I felt sure it was him. Yet again I found myself listening in on his conversation, and I nearly moved to the seat next to him, but I thought he might think I was a crank and stop talking.

I listened intently. By the Christ! He was telling that marvellous story about Procrustes. Never heard of Procrustes? You've never lived. Procrustes lived in Greece a long time ago. Adam Phillips was telling his mate all about this man, and I felt like shouting over: 'Hey Mr Phillips, I know all about this geezer,' but I didn't say a word of course. Procrustes liked to entertain. He made a point of inviting lots of guests to his house. Procrustes believed that size matters.

Adam Phillips (if it was indeed him) was telling the story real good.

Procrustes lived in a house by the side of the road and he offered hospitality to passing strangers. They were invited in for a pleasant meal and a night's rest in a very special bed. Procrustes told his guests that the bed was unique because it was always the same length as the person lying in it, no matter how big or small the guest was. Naturally, the guests were intrigued by this one-size-fits-all sort of bed and they all gave it a try. And that was a very big – or possibly very small – mistake. Because Procrustes had his own way of making them fit the bill. As soon as the guests lay down, Procrustes went to work on them, stretching them on the rack if they were too short for the bed or chopping off their legs if they was too long. Theseus turned the tables on Procrustes by making him fit his own bed.

I like that story. I can't remember why Adam Phillips was telling it – I think it was something to do with the need to tailor the way we listen to the people around us.

I spent about five minutes plucking up courage, but as I stood up to go to him Adam Phillips got up too, put on his coat, shook hands with his mate and bounded towards the departure gates. I'd missed my chance again. I was pretty pissed off with myself, I can tell you, but I comforted myself with the thought that, such was the frequency of my accidental meetings with Phillips, I was bound to have a chat with him sooner or later. Hoping that some of that brilliance might rub off on me I sat down in the very chair he'd used, settling my arse into the blue fabric, which was still warm. If I expected any exchange of genius-atoms I was sadly disappointed. Things like that may happen in Cardiff but they don't happen in Holyhead.

Anyway, as I was sitting there, wondering what to do next (Fit Boy had gone to the gents, and I felt obliged to wait until he re-emerged), I picked up a magazine which had been left on the seat beside me. I opened the mag at random, and my eyes nearly popped out of my head. Ever since I'd started all this phooey, coincidences had come along in droves. But the coincidence which greeted me now was beyond the pale. I had said farewell to my last mannequin in Glasgow, or so I'd thought. I would never have to deal with another mannequin ever again, or so I'd thought. But as I leafed through that glossy magazine, full as it was with the twaddle of Britain's salon society, I noticed that all the girlie models looked like mannequins: lifeless, representational, consumed. When I looked at that magazine I felt that the whole of the twentieth century had been a missed period in the history of western civilisation. And then, to top it all, I came across an article on Lester Gaba and his beloved Cynthia. Lester Gaba was a soap sculptor who became a mannequin artist. During the thirties he created Cynthia from plaster of Paris. Cynthia became a famous 'socialite' who sat languorously, cigarette in hand, at the Stork Club. She became Lester's constant companion – at the opera, riding through the city. She needed at least three strong men to carry her, but she looked exquisite. She became a celebrity: couturiers sent her clothes, Cartier and Tiffany lent her jewellery. Sadly, Cynthia slipped from a chair in a beauty salon and shattered into a thousand pieces.

Fit Boy went his way and I went mine. I headed towards the eastern tip of the island – to Llaneilian, where I had some business in hand. I drove past some of the milestones on my countrymen's long road to the Promised Land – Abarim, Soar, Bazrah, Carmel: the wayside chapels where my ancestors fell in love with the original – and best – pyramid salesman. There are over 6,000 chapels in Wales, most of them named after places in the Holy Land. I don't suppose that many people in Palestine walk around looking at shrines called Llanfrothen, Nefyn, Narberth, Dwygyfylchi...

Their hymns had a sexual rhythm; their prayers ended in climactic exultation. The old people would be troubled by that comparison, yes, shocked. But love dies, sooner or later. And it died in the chapels. Something to do with unrequited love, I fear. They lie there sleeping, those chapels, post-coital, still in the missionary position.

At Amlwch the sea was a topaz aquarium, so I parked up to admire the view. I looked towards the horizon and imagined out-of-sight Ireland stuck to a glassy sea-panel on the world's rotating mirrorball, in the eternal disco of the cosmos – her people waiting for the music to start, waiting for the music to stop. Waiting for the darkness, waiting for the light. Waiting for a kiss, conception, compassion, death. In that silent, magical realm over the horizon birds wove their paths through the air and animals cropped the rich pastures – but I heard them neither bleat nor caw. I could hear the people, however. Some of them were laughing as they played on the flutes of love, some were lamenting as they beat on the drums of hatred. Some were sane, some were mad. For just like the Scottish and the Welsh, the Irish also have a wild man in the woods. His story is told in *Buile Shuibne* – the frenzy of *Shuibne* (pronounced Sweeney). The wild man was known as a gelt, and this is how a thirteenth-century Norse text described him:

There is also one thing which will seem very wonderful about men who are called *gelt*. It happens that when two hosts meet and are arrayed in battle-array, and when the battle-cry is raised loudly on both sides, that cowardly men run wild and lose their wits from the dread and fear which seize them. And then they run into a wood away from the other men, and live there like wild beasts, and shun the meeting of men like wild beasts. And it is said of these men that when they have lived in the woods in that condition for twenty years then feathers grow on their bodies as on birds, whereby their bodies are protected against frost and cold, but the feathers are not so large that they may fly like birds. Yet their swiftness is said to be so great that other men cannot approach them... for these people run along the trees almost as swiftly as monkeys or squirrels.

Sweeney, the son of a king, is supposed to have lost his reason at the Battle of Moira. But his madness also gave him strange powers: he could levitate, and he could utter beautiful, magical poetry.

As I meditated on his story I tried to compare Sweeney to Mr Cassini. But it was a different type of madness, I could see that clearly now. Sweeney and Lailoken had both gone mad in almost identical circumstances, during battle. Their minds had snapped, suddenly, while under severe strain. But Mr Cassini's madness was quite different: he was able to live in society, and affect (infect?) other people around him. He showed no outward manifestation of unreason; in fact, his madness could be passed off as harmless eccentricity. My dreams were trying to say something. I had to get to the bottom of this.

I enjoyed my journey along the coast. Olly had been in my pick-up and I thought I could smell traces of her perfume. I felt as if I was travelling with her in spirit – as if the scent, or shampoo smell, was her soul hovering around me. I opened a packet of Everton Mints and chewed contentedly. Although she wasn't there I felt closer to her than in real life. I daydreamed about her – in an honourable way. Yes, certainly, I liked her physically. But there again, just about every man on the planet might desire her carnally. She was extremely beautiful.

There was not among the Welsh a woman more beautiful than she. She surpassed the fairness of the goddesses, and the petals of the privet, and the blooming roses and the fragrant lilies of the fields. The glory of spring shone in her alone, and she had the splendour of the stars in her two eyes, and splendid hair shining with the gleam of gold.

She turned heads wherever she went. Men stood in lines, frozen into statues, just gawping at her when she got off a bus or a train. Whole streets ground to a halt when she walked through town. Even women stopped what they were doing and watched her pass. But that was only part of her. I have already mentioned her intelligence and humour. She was also an ecstatic dancer – it's true, she partied like there was no tomorrow. Men fawned, pleaded, begged, threatened, but they got nowhere. Until Fit Boy won her heart. Even he didn't make it all the way to her bed. She was a classical, traditional girl. No ring, no fling.

And yet there was something wrong with it all. Something not quite right. At times I gained the impression that she was going through with the Grand Plan merely as a matter of form. As if the whole thing was the re-enactment of a story written long ago. She had the bearing of an Electra or an Antigone. Has it ever struck you that some people are different – elevated, removed, segregated by a glass wall of other-ness? You know, those occasional kids at school who are treated in a different way to the rest; everyone feels, secretly, that they'll achieve something big or die tragically young. Is the mark upon them from the start? I don't know. Some people, just a few, are cast in ancient moulds; they move and act as if they're reincarnations of the mythological heroes and heroines of the antique world. They rise to dizzying heights or they fall into the bottomless pit. They disappear from view, then suddenly they're in magazines, newspapers; they're on telly, in films.

I'm standing by Ffynnon Eilian, the well in Llaneilian, and I've got something in my hand. It's not a handkerchief. In one Welsh parish long ago, girls who wanted to discover their lovers' intentions would go the well and spread a hanky on the water: if it drifted to the south their lovers would be honest and honourable; but if it went northwards they were in for a hard time.

What I have in my hand is a small piece of slate, and there's a name on it. I drop it into the water and I make a wish. Why? Am I finally losing it? All that pressure over the years – to win at all costs, to bring glory to my country, has it all been too much for me, finally?

No. I'm playing games again. Not with a football, this time. I'm playing the game of life. That's what it is, after all. Just a game. Don't you agree? Take it seriously for just one second and it'll have you by the neck.

Let's go back to 1925, when a strange discovery was made at Ffynnon Eilian. Out of the depths of the well came a small piece of slate, about three inches by two inches, with a pattern etched around its border. Someone had carved the letters RF in the centre of the slate and pinned a wax figure to it. This effigy had a head, body, legs, and one arm – the left arm had been broken off. It seems likely that this voodoo token was put in the well by someone who bore ill-will towards RF. Ffynnon Eilian was a cursing well. It fell into disrepair over the years and nearly disappeared altogether, but the council has made some repairs recently. Local farmer Tom Owen put his hand in there one day and pulled out a couple of corks with pins sticking in them. Someone, in the past, had been cursed...

Healing wells, wishing wells, cursing wells – they're all variants on a theme: people went to them hoping to cure a disease, ignite a romance, or skewer an enemy. The Romans had well spirits or gods such as Sulis or Mercury. They threw inscribed lead tablets into the water – many have been found in the area around the Severn estuary. Roman curse tablets had four major themes:

Pleas for the return of stolen goods
Pleas for success in a lawsuit
Pleas for success in love
Curses on charioteers and their horses.

When the wells became Christianised they were given saints' names. At Ffynnon Gybi near Holyhead the names of the people to be cursed were written on paper which was put in a hidey-hole near the well. People often dropped pins into cursing wells: bent pins for curses, straight pins for good wishes. At one well a live frog was skewered and a cork placed at each end of the skewer. The frog was then floated on the well, and the person being cursed would suffer ill-fortune for as long as the frog remained alive. Some well-owners made good money: one man earned nearly £300 a year from curses. In 1820 the standard charge was five shillings for a curse, fifteen shillings for lifting it.

So I drop my bit of slate in the water. And the name I curse? You know very well.

I entertain myself on the homeward journey with an imaginary film clip. It's the second part of my *picnic in the snow* idea. Remember Captain Oates, stumbling out into the snow? My next clip is from *Three Colours: White*. The Polish hairdresser Karol Karol, divorced by his Parisian wife because he can't consummate their marriage, and left penniless, is smuggled back into Poland inside a trunk. But misfortune strikes yet again and the trunk is stolen by baggage thieves. The action moves to a rubbish dump outside Warsaw where the thieves leave him lying in the snow, after beating him up. Karol wakes up in the snowswept dump and cries out: *Home at last!* He forges a new life for himself: he makes a fortune and he fakes his own death… in fact, he's ideal. Karol Karol can join Captain Oates on the tartan rug in my film. Perhaps I should have a polar bear too. I share something with polar bears – a blockage. Mine's in my memory. But bears have a more unusual variety – a plug of faeces, dead cells and hair which forms in their bumholes when they're hibernating. It's called a *tappen*. No kidding.

As soon as I drove into town I knew something had happened. There were a couple of cop cars outside Fit Boy's house. So I stopped.

The coppers were sitting in their cars, waiting. Since I knew that Fit Boy was on Irish soil by now, I thought I'd better help out. I walked up to one of the cars and knocked on the driver's window. It slid down slowly and the copper looked at me unemotionally, wafting copperish smells towards me: shower gel and chewing gum. I looked at their numbers, but there wasn't a PC 66 among them.

'Yes?'

'He's not there,' I said. 'He's in Ireland.'

The cop looked at me all over, up and down.

'You're Duxie, aren't you?'

He'd recognised me.

'Yes.'

He grinned. 'I was there when you scored that second goal against England. Bloody great. What a day that was.'

I dropped my eyes to the ground, briefly.

'What's going on?' I asked.

He let a few seconds go by, then he turned to his mate, who eventually nodded.

'You know a girl called Olwen?'

'Yes, I'm at college with her.'

'Friend of hers?'

'Yes, we do a lot together.'

He smiled, cunningly.

'Oh yes? Haven't changed much then, Duxie?'

'Nothing like that.'

'Sure.'

Again, some time went by, so I straightened up. In the distance, over the sea, I could see a dense cloud coming in, and it had the yellowness of snow about it.

'Something happened to her?' I asked.

'Perhaps.'

I was getting a bit edgy.

'Are you going to tell me?'

Again, he played a waiting game.

'We're trying to get hold of her next of kin.'

I told him that her mother was in Scotland and her boyfriend was in Ireland.

'Don't know much about the father,' I said, 'but I think he lives in Holywell.'

'OK,' he said, and the window started rolling upwards.

I put my hand on the rim, to indicate I hadn't finished. He stopped.

'Well, are you going to give me a clue then?'

He pondered for a moment or two.

'I suppose you'll find out something sooner or later,' he said, 'but don't go spreading this around yet.'

He told me what had happened.

Olly's car had been found. At least they thought it was hers. It had crashed into a wall on one of the passes high above the sea, east of the town.

'No one in it,' he said. 'Smashed windscreen but no sign of the driver. Would you recognise her car if you saw it?'

'Yes, it's a little blue Polo.'

He conferred with his mate.

'Do you mind coming with us to see it?'

'Nope.'

'Jump in then.'

When I saw the car, which had been towed to a lay-by, I recognised it immediately. I told the copper it was hers, and we circled it slowly, looking at the damage.

They were searching for her body on the rocks below.

'No blood?' I asked.

'No.'

I looked inside, and on the back seat I could see a big buff envelope, recycled by the looks of it, and it had my name on it. I pointed it out to the copper, and he fetched it for me. After pulling out the contents – a wad of paper – and giving it all a brief once-over he handed it over to me. The long and the short of it was that Olly had disappeared – and Mr Cassini was back, making a nuisance of himself again. She'd written me a letter, and it went like this:

> It's no good, Duxie. Playing games won't make it better. Perhaps you think you've got rid of him, but he's back. Remember, this is *our* story. He's got hold of me now too. I dream about him every night. I wrote it all down.
>
> I think you're using me. You're not interested in me as a person. You've projected your own neuroses onto me, like a novelist – you've never allowed me to be myself. I might as well be a character in a fairy story, or a mannequin in Cassini's front room. And all that stuff you have in your head about magical islands – what about Diego Garcia? What about those people robbed of their homes by the British and Americans? What about Guantanamo Bay? What about those poor men in orange suits? Islands can be bad places too, you know, places of tyranny. Face up to reality, Duxie. When you're ready, come to me.
>
> I'm going to eat sweets and cry!
>
> Love, Olly.

And she left me seven kisses, but I think that was her idea of a joke.

6
THE TIDE COMES IN

Mr Cassini's dramatic return: Olly takes up the story

BEFORE his sudden death, Mr Cassini had painted a marvellous door on the western wall of the public bar at the Blue Angel. It was a fake door – a *trompe l'oeil* – and although it was in black and white, it was very realistic; many customers had tried to open it. In their hurry to get to the toilets some men had gone crashing into it, because Mr Cassini had painted *gentlemen* on the mock timber. It was his little joke. Newcomers were made to look stupid as they fumbled for the non-existent door-handle.

'You shouldn't be trying it anyway,' Mr Cassini told a juvenile shark as the boy turned away from the door one evening, his face red with beer and embarrassment. 'It's clearly marked *gentlemen*, and you're certainly no gentleman.'

One morning, when the one-eyed landlord went downstairs to open up, he found the fake door open – or it appeared to be open, since a totally new door had been painted on the wall. The paint was still wet. He'd smelt it as he walked downstairs.

And there was a shock in store. There, sitting at the bar, as large as life – and with fresh paint on his overalls – was Mr Cassini. He was back in the land of the living. There was one striking difference, however: his hair had turned completely white.

He demanded a pint, and was given one, free.

After downing three pints in quick succession, Mr Cassini waved an arm in the general direction of the new door and said: 'Well, what do you think? Is it as good as the first door?'

Never one for saying much, the landlord nodded. From where he stood it seemed real enough. It appeared to open onto a dark hallway paved with cracked quarry tiles. A flight of stairs disappeared upwards.

Nothing about Mr Cassini surprised him. This was the man who observed his own nine-day week, with a normal weekend and seven shorter days sandwiched in between so that days went faster in winter or merged into each other in summer, if he so wished. Mr Cassini had offered to cremate the landlord when he died and put his ashes in an egg-timer which could be used on the bar of the Blue Angel when subsequent landlords called time. He was probably mad. What did they say about men like him? *The looser the connection the brighter the spark...*

Mr Cassini explained sooner rather than later.

Finding a mangled fiver in the top pocket of his blue-and-red overalls, the man they called Blue Murder ordered yet another pint and said: 'I take it you know your quantum physics?'

The landlord nodded, since he did try to keep up with all the latest developments. He was a five-dimensional, bouncing universe man himself.

'We live in a cosmos which has many dimensions, isn't that so?'

Again, the landlord nodded.

'Eleven dimensions at the last count, all swirling around us now, as I speak,' said Mr Cassini, wiping a snowfall of froth off his top lip with his sleeve. 'Let me explain where I've just come from,' he continued. 'Scientists don't know this yet, but the eleven dimensions are all participles of the verb *to be*. They are:

I might be, I might not be, I might have been, I might not have been, I can be, I cannot be, I will be, I will not be, I am, I am not, I have been and I am again.

So, at this precise moment, eleven versions of me are swirling around you in the public bar of the Blue Angel. I have chosen, however, to appear to you as the eleventh and final dimension, *I have been and I am again.* Thus I make myself immortal. Got that?'

Again, the landlord nodded. He had no idea what Mr Cassini was talking about; he was completely lost. Why were the dead so demanding?

'Another pint?' he asked Mr Cassini. 'This one's on me.'

Meanwhile, PC 66 was feeling pretty despondent, sitting on his rock in Little Bay, looking at the turnstones as they weaved and sifted along the water's edge. He was trying to digest all the official orders which had landed on his desk that morning: identity cards were being introduced, followed by restrictions on movement. He was depressed. In front of him was a slopping chamber pot full to the brim with frothy yellow sea-piss; behind him somewhere he could hear a cockle woman singing an aria to a group of men huddled around one of the steaming cockle cauldrons. And sure enough, as she sang her violet notes, a rainbow shimmered into life; seven unbraided plaits bridged the river; seven dreambands rippled in the water's subdued reflection. Then zap – the third rainbow messenger arrived, moving faster than light itself as she materialised on Mr Cassini's throne-rock, next to PC 66. Yes, it was a *she*. Initially PC 66 thought he'd been joined by a boy, but the unmistakeable swell of her bodice and the curve of her hips betrayed her sex. They enjoyed the rainbow, mutually, in silence.

'You know the Muslim view on rainbows, don't you?' said the rainbow messenger eventually.

'No, I'm afraid I don't.'

'The colours represent the seven different types of clay used to create mankind.'

'That's rather nice, isn't it,' he answered.

A car, glinting in the brilliant light, appeared to balance on the apex of the rainbow as it crawled along the mountain pass to the east. It came to a sudden stop, and PC 66 wondered if he should investigate.

'Personally, I'm with Keats on the subject of rainbows,' said his visitor.

PC 66 raised an eyebrow.

'He believed that all the poetry of the rainbow was destroyed by science – that something was lost for ever when Newton unwove its magic, reduced it to prismatic colours.'

PC 66 mused on this.

'By the way,' she added with studied insouciance, 'indigo was probably added merely to create a seventh colour because the God Squad weren't happy with the number six. Something to do with 666.'

She looked closely at his police number and grinned. 'Seems you're pretty close to evil yourself.'

'I'm a good copper,' he replied firmly, 'and I'm certainly not into cheap symbolism. Now can you tell me why you're here?'

'I have a present for you,' said his visitor as she prepared to leave. She withdrew a book from the folds of her vests and handed it to him. It was a copy of Mr Cassini's great work, *The Dexter Propensity*, which PC 66 had heard so much about but had never seen. The *only* copy, apparently. After wiping his hands on his regulation police trousers he took it reverentially, and flipped it open at random pages.

'It's all yours now,' she said. 'Do with it what you will, but be careful whom you show it to; only sturdy minds can withstand its malignance.'

As she prepared to leave, the messenger added: 'Before I forget, the seventh rainbow messenger sends his best wishes. He's rather fond of you, it seems. He sends a warning – beware the nation's collective and elective amnesia. Remember Erich Fromm's words about the retreat from liberty – towards author-itarianism, destructiveness and robotic conformity. Get out before you succumb too, he says.'

And as soon as she came, she went. PC 66 touched the boulder on which she'd sat – Mr Cassini's throne-rock – but it was stone cold.

In the gloom of Mr Cassini's front room there are many effigies. The first has been described in detail: a crumbling *eminence grise* – the golem. The left arm was never completed, since Mr Cassini was an unashamed despiser of all things sinistral, anti-clockwise or laevogyrous. Strips of plaster have been taped to the golem's neck to prevent its head from falling off, and it looks as though it's been in an accident.

The second effigy, sitting next to the golem, is that of Mrs Cassini. Its *principium* is a red mannequin, stolen deftly by Mr Cassini from the window of the ladies' haberdashery shop one lunchtime when the proprietress, Mrs Evans, was in the back room eating her light lunch (always two ryebread biscuits, a slice of cheese and an apple, since she was forever on a diet). He had waited for the right moment, pounced, and stuffed the inanimate into the back of his battered ex-delivery van which had been painted roughly, by hand, in the same colour as Mr Cassini's house: a matt red with big droopy paint-runs. A very sloppy job indeed, but Mr Cassini simply didn't care.

'I am a moralist, not a mechanic,' he would say whenever

anything went wrong with his chariot. It was PC 66 who sorted out the problem, always.

This red mannequin has a nice feel to it, a soft bristly texture, close-cropped and comforting, like an old bus-seat, or the worn but comfortable sofa in your grandmother's front room. Mr Cassini undressed the mannequin (mannequins were never left undressed in Mrs Evans' window) and then he dressed it again, in Mrs Cassini's Sunday best (all charity shop stuff) – a flimsy dress with a marigold pattern and a revolting purple tapestry coat made from Welsh wool, heavy as a wet tarpaulin; it made PC 66 feel nauseous. Mr Cassini added a pair of opaque fifty-denier stockings used by women to hide varicose veins, and a pair of blue lattice-effect shoes. All these items she had worn on her WI trip to Cardiff, to collect her award for embroidery. Mr Cassini added her ash-blonde wig, and this lay on the mannequin's crown like a tuft of coarse dead marram grass, sun-bleached; finally, he added her spectacles on their silvery chain. Mrs Cassini's effigy appeared to be writing a letter: a pen had been stuffed into her left hand. Below this was a sheaf of papers, with her actual writing on them (Mr Cassini had rummaged in the box he kept below his bed and had found some of the love letters she'd sent him during their courtship). Why did she have a wig? Mr Cassini said she'd had treatment for cancer. Some of the townspeople whispered that he'd pulled out her real hair during regular beatings. Mr Cassini laughed at this and said: 'Let them say what they like, the woman loves me. I know that for sure because she proves it to me every night.' And here he always gave his great roar-laugh.

Scattered among the slippery seaweed strands, among the rock-pools, Mr Cassini and his steadfast companion PC 66 found many shoes and gloves. They found large quantities of black and green Wellingtons, also boots, espadrilles, pumps, plimsolls, sandals, brogues, moccasins, sneakers, loafers, slippers, in fact just about every sort of footwear you could imagine, in every conceivable size and colour. They also found gloves, rubber or otherwise, mittens and gauntlets, again in all shapes and sizes. Mr Cassini collected all these and created a piece of installation art not unlike the Terracotta Army, with all the shoes assembled in lines, all pointing in the same direction. This he exhibited in a shed at the docks, in a show called The Mermaid Murders. The highlight of the show was a large outline of a mermaid figure, rather like one of those white lines drawn around murder victims in cartoons, except that Mr Cassini's victim was huge and delineated in tiny white sea shells sprinkled together. It looked rather striking, though the local paper gave it a slating under the heading *One foot in the wave*. Mr Cassini never forgave the editor and slandered him whenever he could. Mr Cassini conducted a lengthy survey of the castaway shoes and found, to his joy, a preponderance of right-footed shoes. This data he converted into the principal chapter of his great thesis, *The Dexter Propensity*. Mr Cassini loathed left-handed people. PC 66 thought there was definitely something behind this hatred; he simply refused to believe that it was a completely irrational, unreasonable prejudice. But he never got to the bottom of Mr Cassini's sinistrophobic tendencies.

'Porky,' said Mr Cassini indulgently as they strolled along Little Bay, looking for new shells. 'I don't suppose you know where the word sinister comes from, d'ya?'

He had a close-to-your-heart way of speaking, as if you were the best friend he'd ever had. He talked to you like a brother or a father, all warm and easy, and funny with it, quite different to his appearance, because he was a fearsome physical being, cratered and pocked, with hair springing out of him like thick undergrowth.

'Nope,' said PC 66 amiably, 'no idea where sinister comes from.'

'Well,' said Mr Cassini, spitting a gob as big as a jellyfish onto a rock, where it quivered with oystery slitheriness, '*sinister* is the Latin word for left. Are you with me so far, boy?'

Mr Cassini talked like this all the time, like he was a big kid really.

'Truth is boy, the old people believed that the left half of your body was bad. Honest injun. Them medievals thought yer left half belonged to the Devil. So that's why sinister means harmful or menacin' and all that boy.'

Here he popped another shell into his jacket pocket, so that he looked increasingly like a donkey with bulging panniers on each flank.

'And the right part of yer body is yer *dexter* half, and that comes from the Latin word for *right*. Them oldies thought the right hand side of the body was better and stronger. Right is might and might is right.'

'Jeez,' said PC 66, 'I didn't know that Mr Cassini.'

He had a great store of one-liners, Mr Cassini, as limitless as the shells on the shore.

'I'd give my right arm to be ambidextrous,' he'd say, and then he'd laugh his stupendous, roaring laugh.

Mr Cassini told PC 66 all about being right-handed. He said the right hand path was straight and true. The left hand path was bent and skewed; it led to the dark woods, evil and misfortune. Left-handed people were a freaky minority. The Muslims' left-handed toilet ritual was deplorable, and he commended a North American Indian tribe who restrained their children's left arm to ensure right-handedness... didn't Christ sit on the right hand of God?

Mr Cassini, he was a helluva fellah, everybody said that. What a brain, they'd say.

What a brain, and funny with it too.

Mr Cassini was a hell of a man.

When *The Dexter Propensity* fell open in PC 66's hands, it was at the letter H.

His attention was caught, in the first instance, by an entry entitled **Household Winds**.

Mr Cassini wrote in large block capitals, and this is what his entry said:

After exhaustive studies, I have discovered that each house has its own household wind. No two sound alike. The household wind at my own home is tethered to the guttering outside the front bedroom and has a range of five descending half-tones followed by five ascending half-tones in the key of E Minor. They are close to a sequence in the lento of Elgar's E Minor cello concerto (composed immediately after the First World War as a lament for an irrecoverably lost world). My own household wind has three identifiable mood ranges, namely

a) Mistral, Rhone Valley, strong and freezing
b) Tramontana, Italy, brisk and cool
c) Baguio, Philippines, cold with driving snow.

I have named the household wind at my own abode – Caliban (A).

I would describe it as a windling with a flugelhorn parent, a fluted and mournful night-stalker, a tune whistled by the Fifth Horseman through his teeth on the Day of Judgement. It is exceedingly sad and I enjoy it most of a night immediately after a funeral, when I lie on my bed listening to it before and after * with Mrs Cassini.

As PC 66 read this entry a wind-riffle caught the page and turned it over (rather spookily, he thought), revealing another heading: HARRIES (see Wizards of Cwrt-y-Cadno).

PC 66 turned to the back of the book and found WERE-WOLVES. Under this there were many entries, ending with:

In Galician folklore, the seventh son will be a werewolf. In other folklores, after six daughters, the seventh child is to be a son and a werewolf. In other European folklores, the seventh son of a seventh son will be a vampire.

Next to this entry he found WIZARDS:

Just a short walk from the Dolaucothi gold mines at Pumsaint, up the richly-wooded Cothi Valley, in a quiet corner of Carmarthenshire, there once lived two wise and cunning men, and they practised magic: a mixture of folk remedies, conventional medicine, and the dark arts. They were not unique in Britain; it was an age when superstition crackled and surged along the country's goblin-crowded lanes (very few people ventured out at night).

John Harries and his son Henry – the Wizards of Cwrt-y-Cadno – were among a cadre of charmers, fortune-tellers and diviners who were given the titles white witch, wise man (or woman), wizard or conjuror. In Wales the charmer was known as a *dyn hysbys*. Charmers didn't set bones or treat the major organs. They dealt with skin diseases, bleeding, and mental well-being. And what magic they held at their fingertips.

Abracadabra: A local girl had disappeared – she'd been murdered by her boyfriend. John Harries was asked to locate her body. He told the authorities where they could find the corpse – but when it was found he was charged as an accessory to the crime. Summoned to Llandovery Court, Harries challenged the magistrates to test his powers, saying: *You tell me which hour you came into the world and I will tell you the hour you will depart from it.*

They dropped the case.

The Wizards of Cwrt-y-Cadno were chosen to sit in Mr Cassini's dingy front room, facing the venerable John Dee: since the Harries boys were wiz-kids with astrology they would have much to talk about. Mr Cassini faced a problem obtaining two new mannequins: they had to be taller than usual, since John Harries was reputed to be six feet two inches tall, with short dark hair and mutton-chop sideboards. He was always cheerful, bright of eye and pleasant of speech.

So Mr Cassini went to work with his usual industry and ingeniousness.

The do-it-yourself shop had two large windows on either side of the main entrance. In the left hand window there was a model kitchen, and in the right hand window a model bathroom. In the kitchen stood a tall, silvery mannequin – alien-looking, faceless and sexless – with a saucepan in its hand, standing by the stove. In the model bathroom there stood another silvery mannequin, taking a dusty shower. Mr Cassini waited until the New Year revels had died down, heaved a brick through the main entrance, and snatched the dummies. He then spread a rumour around town that Mrs Evans' son had been seen in an upstairs window at the haberdashery shop wearing women's clothing, and it was he who had broken into the do-it-yourself shop to steal the dummies in a drunken fit of perverted lust. Everyone believed the rumour, naturally. Secreted in Mr Cassini's front room, the dummies were dressed in a countrified manner, in knee breeches.

The people of Carmarthen believed the Harries family derived their powers from a large book of spells which was kept padlocked, because even the Harries family were terrified of it. Some believed it was the Book of the Seven Seals. Once a year the wizards took it to a secret place in the woods, unchained it, and if Abaddon, the angel of the bottomless pit, allowed them entry they would delve into the book's vertiginous secrets. Thunder would reverberate in the Cothi Valley and people would mutter to each other: *O! Mae'r meddygon wedi agor y llyfr du… the doctors have opened the black book.*

The sick and the sorrowful came from all parts of Wales. John Harries was so good at charming away pain that people believed he was in league with the Devil. Lunatics were taken to him from as far afield as Pembrokeshire and Radnorshire, and he had a wonderful power over them with his water treatments, herb treatments and bleeding treatments. Sometimes he took patients to the banks of a river and fired an old revolver; this frightened them so much that they fell in the water and often recovered their sanity.

Mr Cassini, too, kept an old Luger in the box under his bed...

Charms, herbal treatments and shock therapy were the Harries' main tools. Their ancient knowledge was fused with modern learning, making them marvellous and magical in the eyes of their uneducated and illiterate patients. Both had the power to stop bleeding instantly through laying on of hands and prayer (a gift they shared with the notorious holy man Rasputin, and a craft still practised in parts of Russia). At Cwrt-y-Cadno they believed that pure spring water was a cure in its own right.

Hey presto: A deranged man believed he was bewitched. Various doctors had failed to cure him. The Harries diagnosis: the patient had swallowed an evil spirit (a tadpole which had grown into a frog). After consulting texts and invoking spirits the patient was forced to be sick. His vomit contained a frog, and the man was cured.

Mr Cassini goes to the Blue Angel every day without fail. He sups at least ten pints, quarrels with the one-eyed landlord and sells contraband to the juvenile sharks. They're scared to death of him. But like PC 66, they're in awe of him too. After a game of snooker and a display of his famous trick shots (none of which he ever gets right) Mr Cassini and PC 66 are in the toilets, which stink. Shit on the pan. Graffiti. Phone numbers, lewd suggestions, the usual stuff. Mr Cassini's coming to the end of a good night. He's about twelve pints good. He's almost ready to go home for his midnight fry-up and * with Mrs Cassini. Right now, he's talking about death. Mr Cassini always wears his vampire teeth in the toilets, to frighten strangers – he stares at them in the next cubicle, with his huge bloodshot eyes, and then he opens his mouth slowly to reveal his luminous plastic fangs.

'You think people will miss you when you're gone Porky?' asked Mr Cassini.

'Not much,' replied PC 66. But he knew that in thirty years' time the sharks would come over all nostalgic and say *do you remember 66*, and then someone would say *surely you mean 99*, and there'd be a rare old flare-up, and they'd have to call the police.

Mr Cassini nearly deafened PC 66 with his boom-laugh, then he went twelve-pints misty-eyed and said:

'Reckon there'll be a right old to-do when I finally go.'

'Reckon you're right there Mr Cassini.'

'I can't decide, y'know.'

'Can't decide what, Mr Cassini?' asked PC 66 as he washed his hands.

Mr Cassini never bothered with that sort of thing; he just made a great big show of killing the biggest snake in the jungle (as he described the act of shaking his whatsit before he put it back in its cage). No wonder Mrs Cassini always looked startled. She always looked as if she'd just seen the biggest snake in the jungle.

'I can't decide what sort of funeral I'd like,' said Mr Cassini. Being a funeral photographer and all that, Mr Cassini was always going on about death.

'Ya gotta say goodbye to the dead, Porky, you gotta do it proper or they comes back to haunt yer boy.'

Swaying in his cubicle, killing the biggest snake in the jungle, he told PC 66 about the scattered tribes who live in a vast area stretching from mid-Russia to Siberia.

They believe that death is foretold by the unusual behaviour of birds. When people are dying the birds become agitated: some want different foods, others want to drink water from a different well. After a death all mirrors and reflecting surfaces are covered. Anyone who dies with his head on a feather pillow will have to count all the feathers in the otherworld and will never be absolved. Witches must confess their misdemeanours and pray. A witch can die only after someone has agreed to take over her skills. Then the witch spits three times into the apprentice's mouth. For forty days after the death, while the soul is still around, fresh water and bread are put out every day. Some believe that during this period the dead revisit all the places they've been to during their lifetime.

'Me too,' said Mr Cassini. 'I'm going to visit everywhere, I'm going to visit you all, you jus' remember that boy.' And surely to God, PC 66 saw a tear roll down his friend's cheek. Mr Cassini wiped it away mighty quick, mind you. Mr Cassini wasn't a man to be seen crying. Mr Cassini was a real man.

The Estonians have an unusual custom. The hands and feet of the dead are tied until the burial, when the limbs are freed again, so the deceased can move around in the otherworld. Afterwards the bonds are either placed in the coffin or used for magic: they can cure diseases, or sometimes the bonds are secretly sewn inside a drunkard's pockets to put him off alcohol, or sewn into a wife-beater's clothes to prevent him from harming his wife ever again.

The Harries family had an astrological almanac and a book of incantations which told them how to make spirits appear. Years later a powerful invocation was found in the Harries library; apparitions could be made to appear in a crystal ball – *the wizards could expect to see travellers on a beaten road: men and women marching silently along… there would be rivers, wells, mountains and seas, after that a shepherd on a pleasant hill with a goodly flock of sheep, and the sun shining brightly; and lastly, innumerable flows of birds and beasts, monsters and strange apparitions, which would all vanish with the appearance of the genie of the crystal ball…*

A discourse on vampires: The sharks at the Blue Angel believed Mr Cassini was a vampire. One of them claimed that Mr Cassini had cried in the toilets and his tears had been red. No one believed this story, because Mr Cassini never cried.

You don't believe in vampires? Before you dismiss the notion completely, listen to the story of Nicolas Strathloch. With a Welsh father and a Russian-Romanian mother, Nicolas lives in Los Angeles today, but he was raised by his grandparents in Wales. Three of his 14 brothers are also 'vampires'. Every lunchtime Nicolas, a print shop foreman, goes to a nearby park where he 'feeds off' human energy. Strathloch is one of 300,000 or so people worldwide who follow a vampire religion. They come from all walks of life; some are scholars, artists and teachers, some are members of the clergy (allegedly). They 'feed off' other people's emotional energies, though many will only feed off willing donors. Killing is strictly forbidden, as is taking energy from the sick.

Los Angeles has a large concentration of vampires, but there are many living in Japan, Rome, Vienna and London. India has a large following of vampires devoted to Kali, the Hindu goddess of creation and destruction. Modern vampires are drawn to the darker forces and enjoy a nocturnal lifestyle. Many claim psychic powers, saying they can leave their own bodies and occupy others. Some say they can actually fly and enter people's dreams. Some vampires say they suffer from porphyria, a rare metabolic disorder which causes reddening, pain and blistering of the skin in direct sunlight.

Vampires believe they're immortal. When their spirit leaves the body it seeks out a new host. 'The greatest punishment there can be is to lose immortality,' says Strathloch, who is a high-flyer in the Temple of the Vampire, a Washington-based international organisation. Other organisations, such as the Order of the Dragon, the Vampire Church and the Vampire Grove, also follow the vampire religion.

The Wizards of Cwrt-y-Cadno also had the ability to know the movements of their enemies, and inflict harm on them. They could 'freeze' people with a look, make them see items appear or dance before their eyes, and force them to act irrationally.

Abracadabra: Having been overcharged for meat at Swansea, one of the wizards cast a spell on the butcher, who was forced to dance and sing

> Eight and six for meat!
> What a wicked cheat!

His wife, servants and children also succumbed. After removing the spell the wizard said: *That'll teach you to overcharge people!*

The wizards could also 'mark' thieves and malicious people. And they could retrieve stolen goods. Suspecting a servant, a woman who had 'lost' several spoons announced she would consult Dr Harries. Scared of being marked, the servant returned the spoons. Mirrors were sometimes used in magical ways to 'reveal' the culprit.

But neither wizard was able to forestall death. One died young, the other died strangely.

Do you ever die? Is it possible for your memory to live on for ever? Mr Cassini thought so. Mr Cassini had a system all of his own.

One afternoon he whistled at PC 66 and lassoed his attention as the policeman cycled home. It had been a tiresome shift and he'd been busier than usual. The heat had brought out all the juvenile sharks, who'd shoaled in the Blue Angel beer garden. As usual, things got out of hand; one of them was sleeping it off in the cells. PC 66 had handled it pretty well, but his uniform had taken the full force of a trayful of full beer glasses, and he smelt like a brewery.

'Psst!'

PC 66 hadn't seen his friend. The brakes squealed horribly as he wrestled his bike to a stop. Eventually his eyes found Mr Cassini, sitting with his back against an oak tree by the side of the road, on the banks of the Afon Ddu. He was shrouded in the deep shadow of the tree's summer canopy. His cobra-rising hand waved PC 66 towards him.

'You need some oil on that wheel, boy.'

'U-hu.'

'By the way, you smell like a brewery.'

That was bloody rich, coming from him. Mr Cassini stood against the bole of the tree, a Cerne Abbas giant outlined in black. PC 66 could even see the silhouettes of his jutting lugholes.

Mr Cassini lumbered out of the shadows.

'Come on, I've got some oil in my workshop. Then we're going on a mission.'

He laughed, and lifted his eyes to the high meadows way above them.

PC 66 followed his gaze. Shading his eyes, he searched for a small black dot. He knew Mojo the Fair, smooth-skinned and blond, was up there somewhere, a microdot among the molehills. Mr Cassini pointed, and PC 66 tried to follow the stubby brown finger, but he couldn't see anyone. Mr Cassini laughed and said something. Then they made their way to Mr Cassini's workshop, which was also his photographic developing room. PC 66 was seldom allowed in there. Mr Cassini found the oil and lubricated the bike-wheels. As he spun a wheel, testing it for squeaks, PC 66 pondered his companion's manifold eccentricities.

Was it possible to be remembered for ever?

Mr Cassini certainly believed so. In his search for everlasting life, Mr Cassini engaged in some cunning stratagems – and they were curious to say the least.

Some days he would catch a bus to the castle and he would loiter in the crowd. Then, when a photo was about to be taken, he would press forward so that he was standing immediately behind the tourists being photographed. In this way he inveigled himself into countless holiday snaps. During one of their drinking bouts he informed PC 66 that many thousands of Japanese and American photograph albums contained at least one picture of him. Mr Cassini the hairy hominid grinned at grandparents, cousins, lovers, even total strangers in Tokyo and Nagasaki, Washington and Denver.

'Think about that boy,' he said to PC 66. 'I'm all over the world.'

And there was another ploy, even more bizarre. Knowing that call centres recorded voices for training purposes, whatever that meant, Mr Cassini frequently spent hours with the Yellow Pages on his lap, calling corporations at random. Some days he'd be Mr Angry, other days Mr Confused; he cultivated a whole repertoire of telephone archetypes.

'That way I'll live on,' he said. 'My voice'll be played over and over again in rooms all over the world. Isn't that marvellous boy?'

And you had to concede, it *was* marvellous.

'Mystery,' he said. 'Mystery is the key to it all. Make yourself into a mystery, an enigma, Porky. You'll be remembered for ever if you're a riddle.'

Or a serial killer, or a complete bastard, thought PC 66.

For a while Mr Cassini contemplated a scheme so ambitious it was breathtaking. But in the final analysis he couldn't afford it. Well, let's put it like this, he couldn't afford it and drink alcohol in the quantities he did.

'I've struck on a brilliant plan,' he said to PC 66 in the bogs at the Blue Angel, his plastic vampire teeth gleaming like jaundiced glow-worms. His overalls had acquired some extra splashes, and PC 66 was trying to pluck up enough courage to broach the subject.

Mr Cassini's brilliant plan? It was brilliant all right. He would 'disappear' like Lord Lucan – and then post 'sightings' of himself all over the world; he'd send letters, postcards, cryptic notes to newspapers. He'd create the biggest mystery story ever. He was going to sneak into the Millennium Stadium (*nothing* was beyond Mr Cassini) and he was going to plaster his own home-made banners over the advertising hoardings: WHERE IS MR CASSINI?

'What d'ya think Porky? That'll keep them guessing, won't it?'

'No doubt about it, Mr Cassini,' he answered.

But drinking twelve pints a day rules out world travel, even trips to Cardiff. Twelve pints a day discounts pretty well everything except dreams and cirrhosis of the liver (Mr Cassini had a small rowing boat which he'd named *Cirrhosis of the River*).

Even Golly the pig had to go without occasionally. And he *loved* Golly the pig.

Despite all his magical abilities, Dr John Harries failed to forestall his own tragic death – he'd had a premonition that he would die in an accident on May 11, 1839.

In an attempt to cheat death he stayed in bed throughout the day. But during the night he was awoken by cries that the house was on fire and in his haste to extinguish the flames he slipped from a ladder and was killed. He was 54. Even in death he was unable to avoid controversy: it was said that his coffin suddenly and inexplicably became lighter while it was being carried to the churchyard. It was widely believed that the evil spirits which had taken his soul when he died had returned to take his body too; as the coffin 'lost' its contents, a herd of cows in a nearby field became frightened and stampeded: they didn't stop running until they reached the waterfall at Pwll Uffern (Hell's Pool) four miles away. John Harries is buried with his son Henry, who died of consumption at the age of 28, at Caeo churchyard.

Mr Cassini, funeral photographer *sans pareil*, knew all about photographs – developing, printing *and* doctoring. He knew all about the power of photographs.

He could have been Stalin's right hand man (or left hand man, come to that, since he moved people around or rubbed them out altogether with breathtaking dexterity).

In his workshop, hanging above the developing trays, he had a copy of the most famous ghost photograph ever taken – *The Brown Lady* who haunted the oak staircase at Raynham Hall in Norfolk. The ghost belonged to a wife who'd been locked away in a remote corner of the house after a sham funeral. Mr Cassini showed his collection of 'doctored' photographs to PC 66. They were quite frightening.

'This is a secret, mind,' he said. 'Our little secret – you mustn't tell anyone. Promise?'

'I promise Mr Cassini sir.'

And he revealed more of his wonderful theories to PC 66.

'Some primitive people think their souls will be stolen if they're photographed,' he said. 'They also believe their shadows and reflections are sacred, magical. They think they'll die or get hurt if someone takes their shadow from them, or trample on it. Your shadow's part of your soul, Porky. Your reflection in water, or in a mirror, is also part of your soul – that's why breaking a mirror brings you seven years bad luck.'

Some ancient cultures fear that water spirits can use the reflection to drag the soul underwater. Many people still fear the camera lens – the *evil eye*.

'How many people do you know who won't be photographed?' he asked PC 66. 'You think it's vanity? Insecurity? You're wrong, boy. We're talking about ancient forces.'

A photo captures and freezes you in a single moment in time, cutting you off from the past and the future too, he said. A photo can evoke strong emotions: tears, laughter. It can reveal a lot about your nature and your personality. It can paint a truer portrait of you than a psychologist can.

Naked Lunch author William S Burroughs used a Polaroid camera to cast a 'spell' on a coffee shop he'd fallen out with. And since the photo 'removed' the shop from normal time and space, the shop became vulnerable to sorcery or enchantment. The Polaroid technique opened magical doors because the image could be seen developing slowly, and the image could be influenced as it formed on the paper, Burroughs believed. A sigil (magical sign) could be drawn onto the photo as it developed. Elements of the snap could be eliminated with a match, or with Mr Cassini's skull and crossbones lighter, the one with red luminous eyes.

Is it possible to love the dead – whilst also fearing them?

Does love end when the coffin lid rattles; does something else take its place: a ghostly love, a spirit-love which floats up and down the stairs on windy nights?

Mr Cassini loved the dead – and he feared the dead. He feared, more than anything else, retribution. Reprisals from beyond the grave.

Mr Cassini was in the bogs. He was twelve pints maudlin.

'I loved her you know,' he said, killing the biggest snake in the jungle. 'And I still talk to her every night, boy. She still loves me she says.'

Mr Cassini believed that he could only talk to people properly when they were dead – when they'd reached the afterlife. He also believed he'd be able to communicate with the living when he was gone. He even toyed with the idea of having a microphone buried with him, connected to a loudspeaker on top of his gravestone.

'That'd look rather dinky, don't you thing so, Porky?'

He told PC 66 how to treat the dead.

'Close their eyes so their spirit can't re-enter the living world. Burn their homes to prevent their souls from returning. Carry them out of the house feet first to prevent them from looking back, to stop them from beckoning to the living, saying *follow me*. Cut off their feet so they can't walk. Cut off their heads too like the Aborigines do – the spirit will be too busy searching for it to haunt the living. Hew monumental tombstones to encumber ghosts and weigh them down. Make a maze around the tomb to frustrate the departed, since ghosts travel only in straight lines.' Mr Cassini finished killing the biggest snake in the jungle. His vampire teeth glowed in the feeble light.

A storm was blowing in from the north, driving a high tide onto the crumbling cliffs beyond Little Bay, onto the marshes. No one seemed to care. Everyone was drunk or drugged to the eyeballs; all the townspeople in their tawdry hovels had blanked out danger, turned a blind eye to the mounting fury of nature. Mr Cassini had sent his children to patrol the margins of the marshlands; PC 66 feared for their safety, but Mr Cassini expected booty that night, another boat driven up on the shore, another hold full of contraband. PC 66 felt helpless: he should go to the marshlands, he knew it in his heart of hearts, but he had urgent business elsewhere. He had to appear in court again; a *subpoena ad testificum* had ordered him to the Coroner's Court to give evidence in a strange and troubling case.

The bells of the church rang wildly in the wind. There was an air of foreboding; all the dogs howled, the cats caterwauled and Golly the pig screeched and yelped in her sty. The tempest bullied and blustered. Children mewled and whimpered.

Through the police station window PC 66 looked out on the wild sea, the fountains of the great deep, and he heard a faraway cry on the shore, eastwards, near the marshes.

There were two new mannequins in Mr Cassini's van, rolled up in a stolen carpet. The omens massed around him... PC 66 had to do something. They would expect him to do something.

Tomorrow... when the storm subsided. When it was all over. When the looting was finished – he could hear the soldiers down by the museum, firing into the air. The sirens went off again, and he could hear feet scurrying past the police station as people headed for the shelters.

He looked at himself in the mirror and pressed down his newly-ironed uniform with his hands. He combed his hair and adjusted his helmet. He found himself humming; it was a habit he'd caught from Mr Cassini. It was the same song too – *If you go down to the woods today you're sure of a big surprise* – every time Mr Cassini hummed it PC 66 would sing out the last line: *Today's the day the Teddy Bears have their picnic...* and they would have a laugh together.

'Life certainly ain't no picnic at the moment,' he said to himself.

The impending inquest troubled him. A young farmer tending his flock by the shores of a lake in the high pastures – where Mojo the Fair ran among the birds – had met a beautiful girl at the water's edge. She was dazed, and streaks of blood ran in the water draining from her flimsy clothes. A herd of splendid and unusual cattle surrounded her. She had been in an accident, it seemed. He comforted her and took her home; everyone marvelled at her beauty. She was under the impression that she had come from the water, together with the cattle. She was distressed; she talked constantly about her father, a dark and brooding presence *beneath the water*. They thought she was concussed; a bruise around her left eye seemed to show that she'd been struck. She recovered slowly but exhibited odd behaviour: she wept at weddings, laughed at funerals. Over the next year she received counselling, but she continued to experience night terrors; the rings under her eyes refused to fade, and she remained watchful, tense, insecure.

They married, eventually. She was gifted and funny, poetic and sad. They were happy for quite some time and made children together. But there was an underlying tension. The farmer knew, as he looked into the lake's blackness, that his wife had some unfinished business. She was exceptionally firm on domestic violence.

'You can hit me once by accident and once in the heat of the moment, but hit me three times and I'll be gone for ever,' she told him. He believed her.

Once he struck her by accident, when he flung a spoon towards the kitchen sink and it rebounded, glancing against her face. Once he struck her in anger, when he slammed a car door on her and trapped her fingers. And once too many, he struck her again: he kicked the ironing board in a rage because she wouldn't iron a shirt for him to go out; the smoothing iron, still hot, toppled onto her foot and hurt her badly.

The next day she was gone. The cattle had gone too.

He went looking for her. He was found drowned in the lake.

PC 66 dusted and rearranged some of the shells he'd collected with Mr Cassini, now on show in the police station; then, stretching himself to his full height, he put on his regulation gabardine coat and strode out of the police station, into the teeth of the gale.

And so ended Olly's story. At the foot of the last page she left a simple message:

Duxie – I give up. He's hanging on in there. Even his ghost won't go away. So it's me that's going. I'm getting out of the story. I can't take it any more. I can make a fresh start somewhere else, in another bloody story. Please try to understand. It's the only way I can cope. Can you tell everyone else? Can you look after Gelert? I'll get in touch when I've sorted it all out. Also, there's another problem. I couldn't tell you earlier for obvious reasons – but I'm not sure about the marriage, and I've got too close to you recently – seems like that anyway. Don't flatter yourself, I'm not in love with you. But I need time to sort things out. I think you've put two and two together about my father. There's a lot else I can't tell you about. I need to sort it out in my head. See you on the ice… or by a well somewhere (any of your wishes come true yet? I don't think so, and they never will. Mine never did.) Do you like my dream story? It's better than yours!

Love, Olly.

Part 2

Daydreams

7
THE TIDE GOES OUT

The search for Olly:
I turn detective

WHAT do you do when a friend goes missing? When the police have gone, when kith and kin have been comforted? When countless mugs of coffee have been drunk, shoulders shrugged, eyes wiped, hands held, blanks drawn?

Wait? Hope? Despair? All three of those emotions, in varying degrees?

Yes, we did all of those things, and more. But as I've told you already, Olly left a note for me at the end of her dream story (which I told no one about). She also left letters for her mother and Fit Boy.

I decided to do some detective work of my own. It was just something to do; I couldn't sit around waiting for something to happen. I read psychology books, tried to find the cause of Olly's marasmus. I remember that time very well: it was a cold period; we felt as though a huge finger had pulled down the Arctic Circle like a rubber band and snapped it over us, trapping us in an igloo of ice. The wind combed the trees too hard, and snowy furrows in the fields spilled onto the hedgerows as if they were slices of frozen bread. The trees were stark and bare, coathangers waiting for damp leaf-green pullovers to be draped over them in the spring.

Time collected in puddles.

Lost in a colourless, painting-by-numbers landscape, waiting for paint, I stood at my sea-facing window and kept watch for rainbows. I was waiting for a moment like Paul Klee's moment in Tunisia, when he said, exultantly: *Colour has taken hold of me; no longer do I have to chase after it. I know that it has hold of me for ever. That is the significance of the blessed moment...*

And there's a blue boat down there in the harbour, bobbing slowly on the ripples as its crewmen uncoil their ropes. I am ready to go with them under the wheeling gulls, under a parting plume of smoke. This leaving is inside me, perfectly formed, waiting for me to take it to the water's edge.

I had no experience of detection work. Sure, we watched videos of the opposition before most of the big games, and I got pretty good at working out their patterns of play, set pieces, offside tactics and penalty preferences (left or right of the keeper). Call me naïve if you like, but at least I tried. What was I meant to do? Go to a psychiatrist and say: *One of my friends has lost the plot and she's done a runner. What do you think has happened to her? Where is she likely to be now?* Yeah, sure.

Something had burst inside her. Those pipes linking us to the past can never be disconnected; washers can be changed and taps tightened, but when the burst comes it brings water from deep underground, from a long time ago.

I nearly wrote to Dear Deirdre in *The Sun*, honest to God. While I puzzled out what to do I worked on my fitness because I was getting plump. I also took a look at some famous detectives, to pick up some ideas. The Sherlock Holmes style was a possibility, I thought, until a few problems cropped up: I didn't like the deerstalker image, I sure as hell couldn't play the violin, and although I wasn't averse to taking cocaine in a seven and a half per cent solution, like the great man, I eventually chickened out because I'm terrified of needles. There was another thing: Holmes was famous for his razor-sharp intelligence and his super-analytical brain. Regrettably, I am not. So I took a look at Raymond Chandler, and I liked him a lot, right away. When I was writing up my notes about Olly I could come up with some classic lines: *The girl gave him a look which ought to have stuck at least four inches out of his back...*

Doing it the Chandler way would give me an opportunity to come up with stuff like this bit in *The Long Good-Bye*:

A girl in a white sharkskin suit and a luscious figure was climbing the ladder to the high board. I watched the band of white that showed between the tan of her thighs and the suit. I watched it carnally. Then she was out of sight, cut off by the deep overhang of the roof. A moment later I saw her flash down in a one and a half.

Spray came high enough to catch the sun and make rainbows that were almost as pretty as the girl.

But there was one big problem – Chandler's hero. Initially, I could compare myself favourably with Philip Marlowe; just like him I was about forty and tall with grey eyes and a hard jaw. I too was a man of honour, a modern day knight in shining armour with a college education (almost). At this point, however, Marlowe and I diverged. He listened to classical music and played solo, imaginary chess games against the grand masters of history. Me, I hate classical music, and although I could give you a good game of draughts, I wouldn't last long in a game of chess. I simply don't have the concentration. Besides, Marlowe seemed to take regular physical beatings (from the good guys as well as the bad guys) and his hair was parted by a bullet nearly every day. I wasn't into that at all. No, I wasn't up to that Marlowe malarkey. So I cast my net into the waters again and this time I came up with an ideal role model. If I was going to be a detective, I was going to be just like Precious Ramotswe. We had many things in common. Both of us were sensible and down-to-earth but very cunning underneath our veneer of normality. Both of us lived in former British colonies – she in Botswana, me in Wales. I read all about her *No 1 Ladies Detective Agency*. She was dignified. She was humorous. And she got results every time. So I followed her example whenever I could and stuck to the tenets of her professional bible, *The Principles of Private Detection*. I thanked God that my enquiry was fresh, because this is what it has to say about stale enquiries:

A stale enquiry is unrewarding to all concerned. The client is given false hopes because a detective is working on the case, and the agent himself feels committed to coming up with something because of the client's expectations. This means that the agent will probably spend more time on the case than the circumstances should warrant. At the end of the day, nothing is likely to be achieved and one is left wondering whether there is not a case for allowing the past to be buried with decency. Let the past alone is sometimes the best advice that can be given.

Precious Ramotswe concluded that there was far too much interest in the past, and people were forever digging up events which had happened long ago. *What was the point in doing this if the effect was merely to poison the present?* she asked.

But the past is inextricably connected to the present, as surely as ap Llwyd's wells are linked in *Water-Divining in the Foothills of Paradise*. Everything that has gone before is fibre-optically linked with events happening around us now. Look at Olly. There were elements of her story which were eternal. Pretty girl meets pretty boy but her father puts all sorts of obstacles in the way; the boy must prove himself before the two can wed... they call on a hero to help them. Every story ever told seems to stretch way back into the past: nothing much changes, except that every age adds its own impressions and changes the fable slightly. So how do we construct a new story for ourselves from those seven basic strands mentioned at the start of our story? You tell me. Another thing: did Olly run away – or did she *escape* from something? Here's Adam Phillips:

> If you want to escape from someone, they have become very important to you... we map our lives – our gestures, our ambitions, our loves, the minutest movements of our bodies – according to our aversions... as though our lives depend, above all, on accurate knowledge of what we are endangered by...

Yesterday I was on a train. The girl opposite me – early twenties, mixed race – bought a bottle of water from the trolleyman for close on £1.50. The water was in a well-presented bottle and she sipped on it during our short journey. You'll have to pardon me; I'm old-fashioned and I was born in the country, so I'm slightly perplexed when people buy water at exorbitant prices, especially when there's good clean water on tap, free; after all, a huge chunk of the world has almost no water at all. But there's something else, more important. I'm pretty sure that the girl on the train, typically urban, had never seen a well or a spring, never seen water bubbling to the surface; never witnessed its *magic*. To her it was a commodity, not a life-giving force; for a child born in the Kingdom of Advertising it was a liquid in a bottle, not a thing of beauty. To her, the bottle was more important that the contents. The age we live in is about euphemisms and avoidances, because few want to face reality – as if we were all living in a fairy tale without fairies.

I know, I'm going on a bit. But this *fin-de-siecle* feel to Britain at the moment – am I imagining it? A country in which 99 per cent of the population watches the least talented one per cent in a bread-and-circuses parable called *Big Brother*, or some such dull opiate? Over the pond many Americans, in a deliberate annulment of the brain, have abrogated any sense of intellect and returned to a dark age of religion and war.

Nothing changes. I was reading a book called *The Age of Arthur* last night and I came across these statements:

...for nations, like people, tend to form habits in infancy that their adult years harden and modify...

...as men began to lose respect for the state, they transferred their hopes to religion; and for the rest of the century, religious conflict mattered more and more in the political life of the Roman world...

...the core of the story has always been melancholy regret for a strong and just ruler who protects his people against barbarism...

No, nothing much changes. But man is never in stasis; he mutates constantly to fill the vacuums he creates in his never-ceasing motion. Like a plane's aerofoil in flight, the force of his existence keeps him in perpetual motion – feeding, fighting, fleeing and fucking. I know, it's time I had a lie-down. Binge thinking is bad for you.

I searched for Olly. The next thing I did was to comb our dreams for clues. I noticed that the rainbow messengers came from some of the old Welsh romances, such as *The Dream of Macsen Wledig*. Macsen was a Roman Emperor, handsome and wise, who dreamt he went on a great journey through many regions and across many seas, to a wonderful castle where a beautiful maiden lived. But as he was about to embrace her he awoke. Having fallen in love with his dream woman, Macsen sent messengers far and wide to find her, and they located her, eventually, in Wales.

I though about this story, long and hard. I wondered if Rome might have a part to play in my search for Olly: if I reversed the story, starting with a beautiful young woman living in Wales, I would end up in Rome. With this in mind I telephoned an old friend of mine, Dafydd Apolloni. Dafydd is a Llanrwst boy with an Italian father and, as a fanatical Roma fan, he certainly knows his football. When I phoned him he was cooling off on the balcony of his flat in the Testaccio district of Rome. Fresh in from teaching English to a businessman, and with a cool bottle of Peroni in his hand, Dafydd was in good form: Roma were on line to win the *scudetto*. After the initial greetings, our conversation went something like this (in Welsh, of course):

'Dafydd, I need your help.'

'OK – fire away.'

'One of my friends has gone missing, and I'm trying to find her. We're fairly sure she's alive but she's been very down recently – something bothering her – and she's done a runner. Her passport's gone too so I'm exploring every possibility. Something she said made me think of Rome.'

'And you want me to find her? Do the words needle and haystack mean anything to you?'

'No, I've got something in mind. We've been visiting some wells recently and I've been tossing a coin into each of them, making a wish and all that.'

'That sounds like you, Duxie. Still playing games, eh?'

'Don't be cheeky Dafydd, or I'll put a bottle of *spumante* in the fridge and support Lazio next time you play them...'

'You wouldn't do that to me Duxie, never!'

'Are you listening to me, Dafydd?'

'OK – carry on.'

'This girl is very beautiful. She's even more beautiful than your Italian girls (sound of raucous laughter on the other end of the phone). Anyway, if I wanted to toss a coin into a well in Rome where would I go?'

'Duxie, there are dozens of wells in Rome. But you're being a bit slow, aren't you?'

'How do you mean?'

'Just think about it, you plonker. Where do people go in Rome to make a wish? It's probably the most famous place in Rome.'

[he sings a snatch of song – *Three coins in a fountain...*]

'Shit! Of course Dafydd – the Trevi Fountain!'

'Bloody right. Took you long enough.'

[sound of swigging from a bottle]

'How often do you go anywhere near it?' I asked.

'The Trevi? Now and then, not very often. It's snowed under with tourists all the time.'

'Snowed under?'

'OK, bad choice of words.'

'If I send you a photo of the girl, will you go and check out the place now and again?'

'Sure Duxie, I'll keep an eye open. Just how beautiful is this girl? I think you've fallen for her yourself, Duxie. Am I right?'

'No way.'

'And she's run away from you, like they all… [pause]'

'Thanks for reminding me, Dafydd.'

'Sorry, Duxie. Wasn't thinking. Anyway, you send the photo, I'll do the business this end, though I can't promise anything. I'll try to go there as often as possible, and I'll tell my mates… on second thoughts, you'll never get her back if they get to her first.'

'Thanks Dafydd.'

We made smalltalk about *Serie A* soccer, then he hung up on me. He'd probably seen a bit of skirt going into the bar below him. I blame the hot Latino blood in him, only partially diluted by Llanrwst water (and there's plenty of that, as we all know).

Let's have a look at the scenario again.

As I've already told you, I'm trying to discover what happened to the first ten years of my life. My past is intangible. Somehow I must rig up an internal modem to Google my childhood – but it's ciphered in a lost language. At the moment my past is a black hole. Deep Space, Deep Time, Deep Nothingness. Astronomers in Cardiff have discovered an invisible galaxy which is almost completely made of dark matter. With no stars to illuminate it, the galaxy was found using radio waves. Meanwhile, in Geneva, a 17-mile underground tunnel, nearing completion, will recreate the moment when the universe was about the size of Dr John Dee's obsidian stone. In effect, scientists have built the world's biggest microscope to find the most elusive fragment in the universe. And there's a new breed of detectives called forensic astronomers who have identified the time and place in which van Gogh painted two of his most famous paintings, by analysing his notes and details in the pictures. Can you believe that? It's so advanced – and there are people in this town who are still complaining about the Window Tax.

For a long time now I've been walking along an endless circular corridor, looking for my past. This corridor is made of glass: it's like a neon halo, but on a much bigger scale – it could stretch all the way around the world, perhaps. It's clear, but tinted a very light green. As I walk in my glass corridor I am surrounded on three sides – above me, below me and to my right – by deep space: planets and moons and stars twinkling in a vast bluey-black void. But I'm not scared. To my left is a black hole, and my circular glass corridor is bent around it. I'm walking along my own event horizon. Somewhere to my left, in the void, is my own singularity. If I move out of the corridor, to my right, I will be sucked into deep space. If I move to my left I will be sucked into my own singularity, triggering another big bang in my own history. But I'm safe as long as I keep on walking in the glass corridor. So I walk all day in the green-tinted corridor, and along the lefthand side, from beginning to end (I have never completed a circuit) there are millions of orange Post-it notes stuck to the glass. Sometimes I stop and read these notes. Some of them are from my past and some are from my future. None of them make any sense on their own, but I've a sneaky feeling that if I managed to get them in the right sequence they would tell me all about those lost years. Pulling them off the wall and trying to rearrange them, however, smacks of madness so I'll carry on walking for now at least, until I'm impelled to tear down some notes and stick them in random order on the floor. People reading orange Post-it notes on the floor tend to attract attention.

Self-absorbed? Yes, but we all are, aren't we. Some want to hide it, some don't.

Through the glass, in deep space, I can see a transporter ship carrying another little batch of genes to their destination. My own. Genes are never happy. After their raid on your body they always make a quick getaway. They always want to go somewhere else – *inside* someone else as quickly as possible.

A little question for you: from the amount of darkness surrounding us can we always assume that there will be a certain amount of light also; or is it the other way round? If we look at those little pinpricks of light within and without us, should we always infer a terrible and sucking darkness?

> My dark past is behind me now... I made sure I let go of my past, accepting the fact that that part of my life was only a small fraction of my life. I knew the black hole was out there, waiting to suck me in and forever control my destiny – but only if I let it
>
> – Dave Pelzer, *A Child Called 'It'*.

OK, I've gone on a bit. I'll stop now. A bit worked up, that's all. So here's something to soothe you – something about a hole: but it's definitely not black. It's very beautiful. I want to take you back to the annual fiesta – called Sa Cova (the cave) – which took place every year until recently at a small fishing village called Farol, on what is now the Costa Brava. Every year one of the village girls was chosen to be the central figure in a very old mystery; indeed, its meaning has long been forgotten. On the day of the fiesta the child and her mother were taken in a boat to a secret cave. Followed by several other boats, all of them full of women in fine clothes, the chosen one would be rowed several miles to Sa Cova, a sea cave containing beautiful water suffused with a strange blue light. There, the mother would strike her daughter lightly, the child would pretend to cry, and they would all return home. Make what you will of that tale. But it's marvellous, isn't it?

In early February I had gone for a picnic with Olly to the Glynllifon Country Park near Caernarfon. It's set in the grounds of a mansion built by one of the old magnates who stole large chunks of land from the Welsh peasantry; I wanted to roam around it to see what we'd all missed out on. Before we went I cooked a special cake for our picnic. I don't know if you like a dollop of dope in your chocolate cake, but my own belief is that the secret lies in the quality of the bud butter. I melt about a pound of butter in a pan and mix in the hash, then I leave the mix to mature. Don't let it boil or you'll ruin the taste. Then I make a chocolate cake the normal way. I've had very few complaints. My own cakes are guaranteed to get twelve people floating, eight people flying, or four people into outer space. I had a magic chocolate cake right there in my rucksack when I went with Olly to Glynllifon. We took a bus; it's better that way sometimes. You get to feel the mood of the country.

We set off in a bitterly cold easterly wind and, judging by the number of seared plants and bushes on the wayside, it must have been a pretty smug little wind. The sky was split neatly into two, as if we were inside one of those plastic sweety eggs you get in 20p machines: grey to the west, blue to the east. The sea was on the way out, and it looked sharp and cold; if you stepped in that water you'd feel like a slipper in a basket full of puppies. As we waited for a bus we changed colour slowly, chameleon-wise, becoming purple and blotched to match the others in the queue. In their multi-coloured coats they were songbirds garbed too soon in mating plumage, dying now in starved flocks on the frozen ground.

A few blossoms had popped out in the hedgerows but the blackthorn bushes were making a real effort to keep their buds inside them, as if they were children desperate to go to the toilet but forced to stand around awkwardly, trying to keep it all in. February enfolded us; the defeated land was besieged in a garrison of greys. When the bus came we found a seat near the back, behind a group of youngsters who were chatting about *stuff 'n' fings*. One of them had glitter on her face, the remains of last night's fun scattered on her crusty make-up and around her spots. I felt a pang of envy. The old people vanguarded the front, front line fodder ready for slaughter. Rolling past the crematorium I wondered who'd be buried first: Mr Cassini or me?

A girl was trying to read a book but her mind was elsewhere. Another girl scrutinised a hospital letter; by the way she pored over the doctor's scrawl I wondered if she was going in for tests. It could be the most significant day of her life. A horde got off at the hospital, hurriedly, as if they hoped to leave their diseases on the empty seats. *No, it's not mine, honestly.*

Outside the window the estuary was a mud-wound; the leafless trees were stark and brachiated, upturned lungs in a medical textbook. Happy in a shit-spattered field I saw an orange pony, fat as a toffee apple and snug in a canvas coat pithed with dry white mud. I thought there was a mood of expectancy in the bus, as if we were all sitting in a cuckoo clock about to chime. I enjoyed the countryside flashing by. None of the kids looked out. Flicking from TV screen to computer screen to mobile screen, they live in a virtual world now. I felt sad... about my constant search for stories, symbols and similes hidden among the clouds, the seared plants, the emaciated branches. The Green Man on a dirty bus. A cherry tree snowed gently onto a hedge. Big deal. Perhaps the kids are right. What is blossom to them – bush-bling? Why bother with the real world. Perhaps their mobiles change tone subtly with the seasons, when it's time to mate: *Behold, O Fortuna, our Nokias sing of nookie and nippers.*

We approached Caernarfon, and in that light the concrete came into its own; it bloomed in grey outbursts of melancholy. People thorned the streets, and in a pause between buses we had breakfast in Caffi Gronant. I listened to a conversation in Chinese on a nearby table. Cosmopolitan Caernarfon. Sometime between the sausages and the beans I talked to Olly about wells, for the last time. They had served no purpose in my quest to recover the past. Why should they?

> You tease your personal history until you tire of it; and then it
> becomes an old toy in a cupboard, waiting for the final throw-out
> — ap Llwyd.

I thought about the little girl in the news, trapped in a well far away. A shaft had been sunk; a local potholer had descended and was boring through the clay to connect the two holes; he was a yard or so away from her. No signs of life were being detected. Time was running out. The media swarmed all over the area; the nation paused and millions turned to face the well.

There are many ghostly stories about maidens falling down wells, or throwing themselves into the water below. These legends may echo human sacrifices long ago.

Some wells were oracular – people prayed by them and waited for guidance. A person who'd been robbed might throw bits of bread on the water and name a suspect; the bread sank if the thief was named. Prehistoric wells were sacred and may have been guarded by divine maidens or priestesses. In some legends, the well-maiden was a dark nemesis: if a warrior encountered her washing bloody linen he knew he was doomed. Some wells were guarded by sacred fish, dragons, serpents or eels. Killing or removing them brought dire consequences. Well-dressing is probably a residue of well-worship. According to one tradition a Waste Land was created when brutal men violated the well-maidens and stole their golden cups. The land became barren; trees withered and the waters dried up. The Waste Land was also a landscape of spiritual death. The chief Celtic well divinity was the three-in-one goddess Coventina, closely identified with the Greek goddess Mnemosyne, mother of the nine Muses, who personified memory. Mortals were given a choice after they'd consulted the Oracle: they could either keep their memories and drink from the Spring of Mnemosyne, or they could forget the past and drink from the Spring of Lethe. The Delphic Oracle could supposedly tell the future because of a sacred spring which emitted vapours. Science has an explanation: the fumes contain ethylene, a sweet-smelling gas with an intoxicating effect.

Olly and I enjoyed our breakfast at Caffi Gronant. Afterwards I popped into a store over the road to stock up on some grub for our picnic at Glynllifon. There was a special offer on the chicken salad sandwiches: chicken breast with mayonnaise and salad on malted wheatgrain bread. Sounded great. And there was a *two packs for the price of one* offer on the marshmallows, so that was that. To make sure that Olly was happy I grabbed a bottle of Ty Nant in its cobalt blue bottle – water drawn from a vast underground aquifer near Llanon, south of Aberystwyth. The aquifer was discovered below farmland by a noted water diviner in 1976; after a borehole was sunk through 100 feet of rock he declared it to be the purest water he had ever tasted.

Soon we were on another bus, heading out of town. An old headmaster of mine got on and slumped into the seat in front of me; he looked like a ghost among all the other pensioners, and my journey began to feel like a spectral ride into the past – to a museum, where we'd all be stuffed and propped up in cobwebbed corners, ready to whisper our polite conversations, like the dummies I'd seen on Dumbarton Rock. Mannequins again. During a lonely childhood Carl Jung – who felt compelled to live near water throughout his life – carved a comforting *friend*, a little wooden mannequin which he hid in the attic.

These passengers were different: as we changed longitude – travelled westwards, into old Wales – they became more direct, less formal with those around them; they bantered and pointed. The cadence changed; voices were higher.

Most of them looked ravaged – straggly survivors of a generation which had subsisted on black humour, booze and fags, but the good times still struggled inside them. At one bus stop an old man struggled for breath, his goldfish mouth filtering the thin air around his haunted face; he had two bundles of kindling wood in orange nets, and he looked as though he'd carried them all the way from Neverland.

It was a nice ride. I felt comfortable and happy. There was snow on the mountains – exposed bone in a tureen of hills – and I could see a little figure on each of the peaks, waving at me. I'd been to the top of each and every one of them. I loved it all that day. A few flakes of snow gyrated in the air. Some people say it's harder to love your country when it's cold. Do the Italians love Rome more than

Inuits love the tundra? I'll have to ask Dafydd Apolloni.

We arrived at Glynllifon in wan sunshine. If you like trees, this is a good place to go. There are trees from all over the world. Towering redwoods, tactile cypresses. There's even a tree from China called the Seven Son Flower of Zhejiang. I probably climbed trees a lot during those lost ten years. Like that little boy with a bad haircut in *The Singing Detective*, whose parents quarrelled all the time. He escaped up trees, seeing things he shouldn't see. Even now I like to sit in the branches of a tree, swaying gently in a breeze, looking at the world go by.

There are lots of sculptures in the park at Glynllifon, and an art installation in the shape of a ruined house with two trees growing inside it, and Welsh poetry on the wall, plus a picture of seven quarrymen from long ago. This is what the poetry says:

> Voices come in waves *daw lleisiau yn donnau*
> Along the white road, *ar hyd y lon wen,*
> I have remembered *yr wyf wedi cofio*
> And I have forgotten, *ac rwyf wedi anghofio,*
> The fire is fading in the grate: *mae'r tan yn mynd i lawr yn y grat:*
> I will go to bed, *af i'm gwely,*
> Tomorrow will come *fe ddaw yfory*
> And I will still be able to ask questions *a chaf ddal i ofyn cwestiynau.*

I am standing by the seven quarrymen: I say men, but two of them are just boys (one of them looks beaten, he's so tired he can hardly hold himself up – his arms loll in front of him, exhausted). The men have big moustaches and Klondike hats or bowlers. There's still a lot of humour in those faces, and some anger, also some bitterness, wariness, tiredness. They'll never go home to study the fire and mull over hard times because they're painted on a wall by the side of a large field. Close by them there's a lake (a real lake). OK – it's a pond, and its surface is green, clogged with watercress and weeds. Jutting out of this pond is a female arm, straight in the air, with outstretched fingers, as if a mermaid has stretched out, from under the slime, to catch a ball. There are two little holes in the wrist; I point to them and I say to Olly: 'Look, those holes look like the needle marks on your arm after they took blood samples.'

She doesn't say anything back.

In the palm of this metal, chocolate-coloured hand there's a bolt. It's obvious that the hand held a sword once, but the sword is no longer there. Stolen, probably. That would make sense.

Olly and me, we had our dinner among the trees. There's a little picnic site at Glynllifon, and as the sun crept up the slats on our table I bathed in the shade of a magnificent evergreen oak. A farmer whistled to his sheep and they responded emotionally, bleating with pleasure as they ran towards him. The power of food. *Murder me, steal my lambs, but first give me a handful of Ewe Nuts.*

I don't suppose you want to know this, but sheep can remember the faces of ten people and fifty other sheep for at least two years. That sort of information comes in handy when you're standing next to a stranger at a bus stop and need to break the ice.

The snow on the mountains reminded me of marbled bathrooms, the sort you want to get in and out of quickly because they're so inhospitable. The colours had been sucked from the fields, as if they were polar bear hides which had been gnawed by used-up Inuit women before they stumbled out into the snow to be eaten by bears. Or is that a pathetic fallacy, too? Recycled ancestors, their spirits passing through the bear and re-entering their children via succulent bear steaks. Alimentary, my dear Watson.

So many words for ice. But no words at all for modern, urban yearnings – for snow, for purity, for white bears and simple myths.

Olly and me, we ate two large slices of chocolate cake. After that we were extra happy. Olly became a bit strange. Sort of dreamy, and a bit giggly of course.

Duxie makes exceedingly nice cakes.

I remember the time I stood looking at the Lady of the Lake's damaged hand. Olly was standing very close to me; I could smell her intricate femininity. I reached out and took her hand in mine, and she let me, but I sensed immediately, as you do, that it was an appeasement. She didn't respond in the way I wanted, with one of those incredibly sophisticated messages which flit through you; the sort of message Schumacher gets when the lights turn green. We were standing by the water, and I thought of Jack and Jill, and the smell of vinegar and brown paper. According to a Scandinavian myth the moon god Mani captured two children while they were drawing water from a well and their shadows can still be seen, carrying a bucket on a pole between them, when the moon is full. My own children... they might as well be on the moon. Are they missing me? Do they ever cry in the night, as I do?

I relinquished Olly's hand. That was probably the last time I tried it on with her.

She smiled her tired little smile, and the shadows under her eyes dragged me towards her, filling me with moonlight and desire. Perhaps it was the cake. I wondered if she was going to cry; I imagined the elemental, underground taste of her tears, the metallic tang of the water, its geyser warmth. A miniature Excalibur in every drop.

To bridge the silence between us, I made smalltalk about my picnic in the snow project. I'd already found two film characters to join me on the tartan rug – Captain Oates and Karol Karol, the Polish hairdresser; now I was searching for a third.

Olly suggested the little boy in *The Road to Perdition*, riding his bicycle through the snow. Within a few days his whole family would be wiped out by mobsters. I wasn't sure about that one so we compromised with a good old-fashioned bit of schmaltz. *Dr Zhivago*. Yes, that snowed-up cottage on the steppes and two mournful eyes in the frosted window; the crazy dash by Yuri – Omar Sharif – as he escapes from the claustrophobic confines of his home, flees from his pregnant wife, and heads for the arms (and bed) of his lover Lara. Julie Christie. Yes, *Dr Zhivago* would do fine; I could have a clip from the film, and then a Sharif look-alike arriving at my picnic. And so we dreamed on...

Standing by our lake-pond, I made a sudden connection. A tremor ran through me.

'Bloody hell,' I said slowly, 'I've just seen something.'

She peered into the pond, trying to see what I saw.

'No, not in there,' I said. 'In *here*,' and I tapped my temple.

She made a face. Olly could be quite hurtful, actually.

'Go on then,' she said.

I checked my pockets, found a tenpenny piece, and flicked it into the pond. She rolled her eyes. My offering disappeared in a silver flash and sank near the well-rounded shoulder below the swordless hand. I almost expected a swish, for the arm to salvage my coin and hold it aloft.

I'd made an intriguing connection. Slow, yes, I've always been a yard behind the rest, mentally. But I've been granted a few special favours on life's great soccer pitch; that's the way it seems to work.

I went through it all again.

Wells were probably seen as leading to the womb of an earth mother. The Celts probably believed in a well of knowledge. Nine hazel trees grew over Connla's Well in Ireland and their nuts contained knowledge, wisdom and inspiration. When the nuts fell in the well they were swallowed by a salmon, and the spots on its flank revealed how many nuts it had eaten. In turn, anyone who drank the water of the well or ate the salmon attained knowledge, wisdom and inspiration.

The Celtic Well of Wisdom was a place of healing. Well-pilgrims drank the water in a special cup made from a skull, creating a direct link with the dead in the Otherworld.

Some wells had special powers on May Day or Midsummer's Day when the gates of the Otherworld were open. Fairies or pixies were frequently sighted on these days.

Some wells overflowed when negligent maidens forgot to cover them, creating lakes such as Llyn Glasfryn on the Lleyn Peninsula. As a punishment, the maidens were changed into fish or swans.

Some wells held a malignant spirit which stole naughty children if they wandered away from their homes in a mist; this evil sprite was sometimes called Morgan.

The name Morgan is linked to Morgan le Fay, one of the three queens who escorted Arthur to Afallon. The three queens were another version of the triple-goddess Coventina.

Olly prompted me, again.

'Well Duxie, come on, spill the beans.' She smirked a bit and hurt me some more.

'Who was the Lady of the Lake?' I asked her. 'Who exactly was she?'

'You're trying too hard,' she said. 'You need to take a rest. Why not go away for a while? Somewhere sunny, where you can relax. This business with the wells has messed up your brain.'

'No, listen,' I said. 'I've cracked it.'

Olly waited, her arms folded (rather defiantly) across her chest.

'The Lady of the Lake presented Arthur with his magical sword Excalibur and reclaimed it when Bedwyr hurled it into the lake after Arthur's defeat at Camlan. Right?'

'Yup. Get a move on, it's getting cold.'

'Arthur was escorted to Afallon by three queens, right?'

'Trust you to mention an escort agency.'

'You really are trying to hurt my feelings this afternoon, aren't you?'

'No, of course I'm not. Just joking, right?'

I continued. 'The Lady of the Lake was a three-in-one figure just like Coventina. When we throw coins into a wishing well, what are we doing?'

She makes an idiot-face. 'Doh! We're making a wish, right?'

'To whom, exactly?'

'I dunno. Does it matter?'

'Yes it bloody well does. We're making a wish to Lady Luck. And who do you think Lady Luck is?'

'Frankly my dear, I don't give a fuck.'

'The Lady of the Lake, dumbo! The Lady of the Lake has become Lady Luck. Get it?'

'Sounds feasible to me. Yeah, OK, I'll go along with that one. Can we go now?'

But I hadn't finished.

'So when I throw a coin into a well or a fountain and make a wish I'm going back a long, long way – into the distant past, when primitive people threw swords and other bits of metal into lakes, and to King Arthur himself and Excalibur. Clever, eh?'

'OK smart arse, I'll take your word for it. Now let's go.'

We were both subdued on the return journey. Coming down a bit from the cake. We sat on the back seat, me in the middle and Olly sitting with her back to a window, with her feet on my lap. As usual, I ended up massaging her tootsies. Pretty feet, clean feet, so no problem. I sometimes think it was the sole (ha!) basis of our friendship. We were as close as moan is to groan when I stroked her feet.

'You're the best,' she'd say coquettishly. And I ended up stroking her feet, for hours, all over the place, not just on buses – in pubs, on cliffs, even at lectures. It was the most pleasure I ever gave a woman, I'm pretty sure of that.

The old people were creaking to a halt; each movement was getting slower, jerkier, as they boarded or left the bus. Outside they froze into menhirs, propping up the bus shelters as if the tin roofs were cromlechs. Odd sights came our way: a huddle of garden gnomes, in committee, on the roof of a porch above a crooked pathway; a charnel of council houses, burnt onto the landscape with a poker; a man sitting in front of me wearing a cap inscribed *Information Security Forum*. That sounded spooky – perhaps he was Brains from *Thunderbirds*, fresh from dealing with another international incident in Nefyn.

Only one person got on the bus when we reached the hospital – the girl who'd scrutinised her doctor's note earlier (all the rest had died, presumably). She looked a lot happier; I had a feeling that this particular day would be framed on the wall of her life for some time to come, possibly for ever.

Anyway, on with the story – and the search. I was about to quit the wells meditation; I'd hoped that a handful of recollections would come rattling into the sunlight, floating about in a rusty bucket, and if I was quick enough I could grab some of them before they escaped through the holes, back into the well. I read so much about wells my friends became worried about me. I even read some stories by HG Wells. Does that sound a bit nutty? Yes, I became a bit concerned myself at that point.

I was using wells as a symbol of the forgotten past, the unseen, the hidden, the unconscious, and the subterranean vaults in my mind, whatever. I was trying to use wells as a mnemonic, as a bradawl to bore into the past. But nothing was happening. I decided to have one last go, by reading one of the most powerful books ever written about wells – *The Wind-Up Bird Chronicle* by the Japanese author Haruki Murakami. The main character in the book is Toru, a young man living in a Tokyo suburb. Toru's cat disappears and then his wife fails to return from work. His search for them involves a bizarre collection of characters, including two psychic sisters and an old soldier who saw many horrors during the Second World War. The book is all about trying to get answers – through wells, mainly – and it's about responsibility, both personal and national. Atrocities committed by the Japanese army in China keep rising to the surface of the book, as if they were repressed memories bobbing about in a well-bucket. Toru enters a netherworld beneath the placid surface of Tokyo, and below the history of Japan itself. Wells play an important part in his search for his own true self, and for the truth behind his country's past. Here are a few passages from the book:

'I don't mind fighting,' he said. 'I'm a soldier. And I don't mind dying in battle for my country because that's my job. But this war we're fighting now, Lieutenant – well it's just not right. It's not a real war, with a battle line where you face the enemy and fight to the end. We advance, and the enemy runs away without fighting. Then the Chinese soldiers take their uniforms off and mix with the civilian population, and we don't even know who the enemy is. So then we kill a lot of innocent people in the name of flushing out 'renegades' or 'remnant troops', and we commandeer provisions. We have to steal their food, because the line moves forward so fast our food supplies can't catch up with us. And we have to kill our prisoners because we don't have anywhere to keep them or any food to feed them. It's wrong, Lieutenant. We did some terrible things in Nanking. My own unit did. We threw dozens of people into a well and dropped hand grenades in after them. Some of the things we did I can't bring myself to talk about. I'm telling you, Lieutenant, this is one war that doesn't have any Righteous Cause. It's just two sides killing each other. And the ones who get stepped on are the poor farmers, the ones without politics or ideology…'

We travelled north for two hours or more, coming to a stop near a Lamaist devotional mound. These stone markers, called oboo, serve both as the guardian deity for travellers and as valuable signposts in the desert. Here the men dismounted and untied my ropes. Supporting my weight on either side, two of them led me a short distance. I figured that this was where I would be killed. A well had been dug into the earth here. The mouth of the well was surrounded by a three-foot-high stone curb. They made me kneel down beside it, grabbed my neck from behind, and forced me to look inside. I couldn't see a thing in the impenetrable darkness. The noncom with the boots found a fist-sized rock and dropped it into the well. Some time later came the dry sound of stone hitting sand. So the well was a dry one, apparently. It had once served as a well in the desert, but it must have dried up long before, owing to a movement of the subterranean vein of water. Judging from the time it took the stone to hit the bottom, it seemed to be quite deep.

The noncom looked at me with a big grin. Then he took a large automatic pistol from the leather holster on his belt. He released the safety and fed a bullet into the chamber with a loud click. Then he put the muzzle of the gun against my head.

He held it there for a long time but did not pull the trigger. Then he slowly lowered the gun and raised his left hand, pointing towards the well. Licking my dry lips, I stared at the gun in his fist. What he was trying to tell me was this: I had a choice between two fates. I could have him shoot me now – just die and get it over with. Or I could jump into the well. Because it was so deep, if I landed badly I might be killed. If not, I would die slowly at the bottom of a dark hole. At last it dawned on me that this was the chance that the Russian officer had spoken of. The Mongolian noncom pointed at the watch that he had taken from Yamamoto and held up five fingers. He was giving me five seconds to decide. When he got to three I stepped onto the well curb and leaped inside...

How much time went by after that I do not know. But at one point something happened that I would never have imagined. The light of the sun shot down from the opening of the well like some kind of revelation. In that instant, I could see everything around me. The well was filled with brilliant light. A flood of light. The brightness was almost stifling: I could hardly breathe. The darkness and cold were swept away in a moment, and warm, gentle sunlight enveloped my naked body. Even the pain I was feeling seemed to be blessed by the light of the sun, which now warmly illuminated the white bones of the small animal besides me. These bones, which could have been an omen of my own impending fate, seemed in the sunlight more like a comforting companion. I could see the stone wall that encircled me. As long as I remained in the light, I was able to forget about my fear and pain and despair. I sat in the dazzling light in blank amazement. Then the light disappeared as suddenly as it had come. Deep darkness enveloped everything once again. The whole interval had been extremely short...

What happened down there? What did it mean? Even now, more than forty years later, I cannot answer all those questions with any certainty. Which is why what I am about to say is strictly a hypothesis, a tentative explanation that I have fashioned for myself without the benefit of any logical basis...

Outer Mongolian troops had thrown me into a deep, dark well in the middle of the steppe, my leg and shoulder were broken, I had neither food nor water: I was simply waiting to die. Before that, I had seen a man skinned alive. Under these special circumstances, I believe, my consciousness had attained such a viscid state of concentration that when the intense beam of light shone down for those few seconds, I was able to descend into a place that might be called the very core of my own consciousness. In any case, I saw the shape of something there. Just imagine. Everything around me is bathed in light. I am in the very centre of a flood of light. My eyes can see nothing. I am simply enveloped in light. But something begins to appear there. In the midst of my momentary blindness, something is trying to take shape. Some thing. Some thing that possessed life. Like the shadow in a solar eclipse, it begins to emerge, black, in the light. But I can never quite make out its form. It is trying to come to me, trying to confer upon me something very much like heavenly grace...

I would not have minded dying right then and there. I truly felt that way. I would have sacrificed anything for a full view of its form.

Finally, though, the form was snatched away from me for ever...

The light shines into the act of life for only the briefest moment – perhaps only a matter of seconds. Once it is gone and one has failed to grasp its offered revelation, there is no second chance. One may have to live the rest of one's life in hopeless depths of loneliness and remorse. In that twilight world, one can no longer look forward to anything. All that such a person holds in his hands is the withered corpse of what should have been.

After reading *The Wind-Up Bird Chronicle* I decided to end my study of wells.

I had bored into the crust of my past, drilled with all the energy I had, but I had failed to tap any hidden memory – that's assuming, of course, that I had any memories to uncover. For many months I had behaved like the solitary spiny mason wasp, which bores into sandbanks or into the mortar of old walls, stocking its nest with small caterpillars; or another digger wasp, *ectemnius cephalotes*, which drills into rotten tree stumps and then stocks its nest with paralysed flies. I had dug down too, but to no avail; I had failed to line my nest with a single grubby memory. There was either nothing there to discover or I had failed, miserably, to reach the subterranean river I had hoped to find. It seemed possible that I had put my past into a paper boat, while I was still small, crouching on a riverbank, and sent all my memories spinning into the darkness beyond. Or maybe all my memories had been taken – like nectar – to a glass beehive inside my brain, and the glass now prevented me from touching the honey.

There is a marked change of mood in chapter seven of *Water-Divining in the Foothills of Paradise*. The jaunty, optimistic air of the previous chapters is swept aside as ap Llwyd deliberates the pros and cons of embarking on a bold and dangerous descent into the heart of the mountain beneath him. Although he has discovered seven interconnected wells containing water of the highest purity, he feels impelled to go a stage further: as he sits in sombre mood by his campfire, at the mouth of a cave, he muses thus in his unfinished diary:

LLOYD JONES

It is now, more than ever, that I need Stefano's advice. The seven wells are fed by a deep and untraceable source which seemingly emanates from the centre of the Earth itself. Should I attempt to trace it? What would Stefano say? The cave behind me, sunk as it is in limestone, bears plentiful evidence of having been a water conduit in times past. It seems logical, therefore, to assume that it would take me to the source of the well water. But I am daunted by the many dangers I face. The cave is likely to go down a very long way, and I have only two spare batteries for my torch. I am alone, and there is no one to summon help if I become trapped or lost. I feel sure that Stefano would say: This is a foolish mission my friend, it is too dangerous for one man to face alone. Go in haste to the town, fetch your friends, they will wait at the mouth of the cave, and they will follow the rope down if you do not come back. But a voice inside me says: Now is the time. Seize the moment.

There is another issue, and I must face up to it now. If I am to discover the truth about what is inside me, True Self or False Self, this is the time to find out. In the dark bowels of the mountain I will discover which part of me will survive in a crisis; whether my True Self will emerge victorious through the mouth of the cave, or my False Self. That is the issue I must face alone, in the darkness beneath me. Perhaps I have been seized by a temporary madness, but of one thing I am utterly sure: tonight is the night when I will find out.

As I sat on the bus, studying the stark contours of Carnedd Llewelyn and the rest of the range around it, and massaging Olly's feet (she was almost asleep now), I considered that last sentence again. It seemed as though a magnetic force was pulling him towards the cave, an irresistible power dragging him downwards. And it became clear, also, that a battle was raging inside him: a battle between two forces – one called True Self, the other called False Self. I had never heard those terms before. What, exactly, was ap Llwyd doing?

He was a diviner, a water witch whose preferred instrument was the hazel rod, rather than metal, or whalebone, or the pendulum, or even a twisted coat hanger.

Since that journey with Olly I have studied ap Llwyd's *Well Diary*, which is kept in a vault at Aberystwyth. He was aware of the tendentious nature of his work, but he was a firm believer in its virtues. His own studies had been exhaustive. Ancient wall paintings in the Caves of Tassili in the foothills of the Atlas Mountains of North Africa depicted a tribesman dowsing for water. The Ohio Supreme Court ruled as late as 1861 that ground water was too

164

secret and occult to be adjudicated by law. In the 1920s a Major CA Pogson, the Government of India's Official Water Diviner, had ranged for thousands of miles finding wells and bores.

There was another branch of the science: *radiesthesia*, which attempted to locate missing people and detect illnesses. Medical diagnosis through dowsing was permitted in Britain and Europe but not in the United States. Some dowsers operated telepathically, using maps and pendulums. Some modern theorists believed that diviners became attuned to the object they sought; others believed the dowser's nervous system was stimulated by electro-magnetism. Einstein was fascinated by dowsing.

It seems that ap Llwyd was an experimentalist, regarded as a maverick by his contemporaries. But he had some rare results. We can only speculate on what he discovered before he had that terrible accident deep inside the mountain. The misfortune put paid to all his adventuring; he worked for Stefano thereafter, in the Italian café at the top end of town, near the notorious 43 Club. He was noted for his limp, his acute sense of humour, and the inner radiance which shone from him throughout the rest of his life, after his recovery. For although he lost a leg he gained something else down there at three thousand feet below the foothills of paradise: he gained an inner awareness, a self-knowledge which brought him great happiness... a hidden lake of contentment.

I had such a lovely time that day at Glynllifon. But now I must put aside my memories of ap Llwyd and Olly, our trip on the bus, my wave of farewell to Olly as she slipped off homewards, still a bit zonked by the chocolate cake. It happened some time ago, and all that remains is a soft and muted remembrance of things past. When Olly disappeared I was forced to formulate a new plan. It was my turn, not Olly's, to go to the dark side – to a sinister substratum in our tale. It was time for me to act on her behalf, before my tiredness overwhelmed me. Olly and I had failed to eliminate Mr Cassini, to eradicate him from our dreams and our daily thoughts. He had attached himself to us parasitically – and don't forget, almost half of all living things are parasites. I had a cunning plan: in Olly's absence I would continue the task on her behalf. I would purge the monster known to all of us as Mr Cassini. And I would do that by invoking a character in her dreams – PC 66. Who better? He was an accessory to the fact. At best he was guilty of inertia, at worst collusion. Maybe he and Cassini were crude symbols of the state and the church, I don't know. The ambivalence of his number – 66 or 99 – seemed to point towards a central ambiguity. But he seemingly wanted to redeem himself. So I would give him an opportunity to do so now. I would send for him, metaphorically, and outline a possible plan of action. I would show him how he could get rid of Mr Cassini – a man who stole childhoods. But PC 66 needed some allies, since he couldn't do it all alone.

I will weave a web to catch me some luck. Like the moon-struck Russian scientist Kozyrev I will train my telescopic mirrors to catch starlight in chorus from the past, the present and the future. I will fight back with words – for words are a form of witchcraft too, my friends. PC 66 – you are summoned to the police station, at once.

8
THE TIDE COMES IN

I interview PC 66 and we assemble
a goodly band of men

Mr Cassini must die. But he won't – he's a grotesque vampire-man who refuses to lie down. He has survived his own funeral, and now he's prowling around downstairs, in the cellar of our story. Clatter, bang, shatter – can you hear him down there, shouting at someone? Having crept into the story he has spread his dark stain over the narrative: he has infected nearly every page and forcibly added his name to a bestiary of hobthrusts and monsters, a band of baddies ranging from the Minotaur to Faust and Frankenstein's Monster, Prospero, Dracula, Caligula, the Demon Huntsman, Freud's Wolf Man, Pedro the Cruel...

You've never heard of Pedro the Cruel? A fearsome king was Pedro – recognisable only by the clicking of his arthritic knees, he stole out from his Spanish fortress at night, in disguise, to pick a quarrel with – and murder – any luckless subject who happened by. We have to reverse this process and pick a quarrel with Mr Cassini; we have to rebirth the monster and then destroy him if Olly is going to survive. Mr Cassini has stalked along the ley lines of her mind every night, looking for trouble; he's asleep now, so let's make the most of his quiet period – let's nab him.

If we go back to the first story ever recorded, the 4,000-year-old Epic of Gilgamesh, we find the sky-god Anu responding to the pleas of the human race, which is being oppressed, by creating someone who will deliver it – the wild man Enkidu, who lives in the untamed forest and has the strength of a horde of wild animals.

Ring any bells? Yes, remarkable isn't it – Merlin, our very own wild man of the woods, has been around for a long time in one form or another. But how could a wild man save the oppressed majority? Because he speaks the truth? Because he has experienced ultimate degradation and knows, exactly, the depth of Abaddon's pit – and how to climb out of it? Or is it because he knows that our fears are often more troublesome than reality itself? And is there a wild man in all of us, a Janus who swivels the mirror playfully now and then to show us sanity then insanity, order then disorder, yin then yang? Who knows... maybe Enkidu was just another drugged-up tree hugger.

First, we have to set the scene. Conditions must be just right.

Let us go down to the shore again, to that liminal strand between land and sea. Why? Maybe because nobody owns it, not really. The National Trust and the MoD lay claim to some of it, and the Queen says she owns more than half of it. But the truth is that no human can own this realm. It's the dominion of children, a land of dreams. The first and last place of safety. A separate world exists here, but don't imagine for a moment that nothing much happens between a rock and a hard place, because every beach is divided into zones and territories which have their own citizens and their own unwritten laws. Some of the citizens have been around a long time, others are new kids on the block. Take that smallish barnacle which clings tenaciously to its rock: it came from Tasmania, on the keel of a flying boat which landed in Milford Haven, and now its offspring are spreading at a fantastic rate along the Welsh shoreline. No matter how small or insignificant we are, there's always someone or something ready to feed on us. So it is with the humble barnacle, too. The common dog whelk drills holes in its shell and sucks it up for dinner. Then there's the Chinese mitten crab: having conquered swathes of Europe and North America it landed at Chelsea in 1935, and now threatens a number of native species as it burrows into river banks and crosses dry land in a steady march northwards, obliterating the natives as it goes. Likewise the American red crayfish – a vicious invader which is on a murder spree in Britain's waters; it can climb up nearly anything and live out of water for months. Little fleas have smaller fleas... there's a bird in the Galapagos Islands – the sharp-beaked finch, also called the Vampire Finch – which lives by drinking the blood of other birds, and there are plants in Wales

which live on flesh – sundew, butterwort, and the rootless blad-
derwort. Which brings me back to another blood-sucker – Mr
Cassini, and the cunning plan I have in mind. I've been extremely
resourceful. I think you'll be impressed with my stratagem.

As the sea gathered its forces before the equinox, and the tides
waxed big, Mr Cassini set about his next gargantuan task. He
decided to build a massive stone man on the shoreline, to paral-
yse sailors with fear so that they would be driven onto the rocks
below. He laboured every day under his rusting scaffolds, carrying stones to a promontory in the paludal wastelands beyond
Little Bay, using the harbourmaster's tractor and trailer. This area
of bogland was far bigger than any of the great bogs of Wales:
Fochno, Caron, Crymlyn. Gradually, the sea-facing colossus
(which he eventually painted matt red, the same colour as his
house) took shape: it was fifty feet high by the time he finished.
As he fashioned his creation, rumours spread around the town. A
ghost ship had been sighted repeatedly in Big Bay. A polar bear
had passed by on an ice floe. Three Inuit kayaks, empty save for
whalebone fishing tackle, but steered in a perfectly straight line
by phantom paddles, had been seen by local fishermen. Finally,
Mr Cassini unleashed a wave of panic with Little Michael. He
told the juvenile sharks drinking in the Blue Angel that he had
found a small but superbly-crafted coffin on the shore near his
colossal Red Man, a coffin which was precisely fourteen inches
long. Inside it lay a perfectly formed human called Little Michael.
This tiny man, dressed in a black suit, was dead… but Mr Cassini
knew how to bring him back to life. A wave of agitation and
unrest swept through the town.

While Mr Cassini basked in a new wave of notoriety I
prepared the way for his final demise. I knew a way to eliminate
him, once and for all. One day I went down to the shore, looking
for PC 66. Sure enough, I found him moping around on his
throne-rock in Little Bay. There, amid the scuttling crabs and
many single Wellingtons, pumps, moccasins and boots, I inter-
viewed him. I told him about myself, and about Olly's
predicament. He was anxious to help us, to tell the whole truth
and nothing but the truth.

'It's time to get it all off my chest,' he told me. 'I'd like that.
Maybe I could relax a bit afterwards. That calm, drugged feeling

you get when an ordeal is over. Actually, I was thinking about it yesterday, on the beach, walking along aimlessly. Daydreaming, really. I imagined the seawater all gone, just for a day, so that I could walk along the bottom of the sea looking at what's there. Maybe I would meet other people wandering along the bottom of the sea bed and we'd laugh and say *did you see this* and *did you see that*. I want to start with a clean slate. I'll tell you all about it. Don't rush me though – I want to figure it all out first.'

We decided to form a team. A classic *nice cop – nasty cop* routine. He could be the nice cop for a change.

'Do your duty before it's too late,' I urged him. 'Iron your uniform, polish your truncheon, do whatever you have to do. We must get rid of this monstrous man!'

Our first step was to recruit some aides to help us dispose of Mr Cassini. We needed men with special powers, and our first choice was a man much famed for his exploits: the soldier, magician and poet Huw Llwyd. We travelled westwards to find him at Maentwrog, and luckily for us he was available. We found him at a loose end, and he was quickly persuaded to join our hit squad.

His first question was: *would there be any fighting?* I assured him not. I was well aware that he had fought bravely for a Welsh regiment raised to fight the armies of Spain in the Low Countries, but I needed only his fabled mental powers. 'Good,' he replied, 'since I have been dead for over 400 years now.'

Let me introduce Huw – or to give him his full name, Huw Llwyd of Cynfael.

He was the seventh son of a Maentwrog family and he was a wizard, according to the old people. If you walk through Ceunant Cynfal nature reserve near Llan Ffestiniog you'll come across a pillar of rock known as Huw Llwyd's Pulpit: according to local tradition he came to this spot regularly to meditate. He was a renowned huntsman who wrote odes to both the fox and the hound. He had a thorough grounding in medicine, and he was skilled in wizardry. It's said that he studied books on magic and ate the eagle's flesh so that his descendants could charm away diseases for generations to come. To ease him into his new role, as one of my interrogators, I asked Huw to tell me about the famous occasion when he'd outwitted the cat burglars of Betws.

'With pleasure,' he said expansively when we met him at the

Grapes Hotel. I had difficulty keeping his attention, since he could hardly keep his eyes off the barmaid, who was extremely pretty and engagingly industrious.

'I hear it's a great story,' I said, to egg him on.

He called for our glasses to be replenished, though it was clear he'd already had a few snifters. He grabbed the barmaid as she served us and began singing a ballad to her, gazing forlornly into her eyes, his cheek pressed against her bosom.

'Huw,' hissed PC 66, 'people don't do that sort of thing any more! Let her go!'

He looked dumbfounded, but slowly unclasped her.

'The cat burglars of Betws,' I prompted.

'Ah yes! This story is quite famous you know,' he said with a hint of mock-modesty. 'One day I called at an inn kept by two sisters near Betws-y-Coed. I pretended to be an official on my way to Ireland, and asked for a night's lodging. But I had a reason for calling – travellers who stayed the night there were consistently robbed, and I'd promised to unravel the mystery. But I was puzzled – the bedrooms were kept locked throughout the night, and it was impossible for anyone to enter them.'

He took a slurp from his beer, to wet his whistle.

'Anyway, at supper there was a bit of a duel of wits between the sisters and I: they tried to entice me with their beauty and their racy talk, while I entertained them with fantastical tales about faraway countries. When bedtime came I asked for a plentiful supply of candles, to keep my room lit all night. I locked the door, got into bed, and pretended to sleep. But I kept watch all night long, with my sword unsheathed beside me on the bed. Before long two cats came down the chimney and romped around the room. As I watched them through half-closed eyes I saw them play among my clothes. They were cunning – but not quite cunning enough! They thought I was asleep, so one of them put her paw into my purse-pocket. I sprang out of bed and lashed at the paw with my sword. There was a hideous yowl and both cats disappeared up the chimney. I saw no more of them that night!'

Huw sank the remainder of his porter – he was a thirsty man that night – and burped loudly before continuing with his tale. He was beginning to slur a little now.

'Next morning only one of the sisters came down to breakfast. So I asked her where the other was. I was told she was ill, and wished to be excused, so I ate my food in silence. When I'd finished I prepared to leave, but before going I insisted on saying farewell to the absent sister. I listened to many lame excuses but I refused to be fobbed off, and finally she came down to say goodbye.'

There was a pause, and Huw's eyes misted over as he contemplated his story.

'When I held out my hand to bid her farewell she held out her left hand, instead of her right, but I refused it, saying in a light-hearted way *I'm not going to take your left hand: I've never taken a left hand in my life, and I'm not going to begin with yours, white and shapely though it is.* Very unwillingly, she extended her right hand. It was swathed in bandages!'

Huw winked at me, and scratched a livid sore on his right cheek. I noticed that his teeth were yellow and rotten, and his breath smelt indescribably foul. Still, if I was going to summon aid from other dimensions I would have to put up with some unpleasant side-effects. He finished his story.

'I had solved the mystery. Those two sisters were witches who took on the form of cats to rob travellers lodging under their roof. Drawing myself up to my full height I told the injured sister: *I have drawn blood from you and henceforth you will be unable to do any mischief.* Turning to the other sister, I said: *I will make you equally harmless,* and with that I seized her hand and cut it slightly with a knife, just deep enough to produce some blood. Do you know what? There were no more robberies at that inn, and for the rest of their lives the sisters behaved like model citizens. What do you say to that?'

I laughed uproariously and clapped him on the back, though I'd heard the story at least a dozen times before.

The time had come for me to lay my cards on the table.

'I have a mission for you Huw,' I said conspiratorially. 'You are just the man I need – brave and clever – to rid the world of a fiend called Mr Cassini.'

For a moment I thought I'd overdone the flattery, since he frowned and cupped his chin in his hand thoughtfully.

'That's a very strange sort of name,' he said. I explained the scenario.

'Fine,' he said boisterously. 'I'll do it. When do we start?'

I told him to be on the summit of Pumlumon Arwystli at

such-and-such a time, where he would meet three other adven-
turers plus PC 66 and myself. Together, we would wait for Mr
Cassini and question him about his misdeeds, then send him
towards his nemesis.

As I started to rise, he tugged at my sleeve, playfully, as children or friends do if they want to prolong a conversation. 'A word
to the wise,' he said. Did he snigger, ever so slightly?

'This tomfoolery about wells. Forget about them. Wells are a
dead end, you'll get nowhere with them.'

I looked at him steadily, refusing to look surprised.

'Explain that to me,' I replied after a suitable pause.

'You've experimented with water, and it's got you nowhere.
Look at those divers who drown in the Dorothea Quarry pool all
the time. What are they after? Some inner truth? Why do they test
themselves to the limit like that? Do they expect to see some
strange white light of revelation when they reach the bottom, or
to arrive at the centre of their being? Give it up, my friend.
There's nothing at the bottom of the well – only death.'

He looked me in the eye.

'You're filling your mind with water. You're filling it up with
nonsense so that you *won't* remember anything. Do you understand what I'm saying? Thinking about wells is having a contrary
effect. You'll never remember anything while you're slopping
around in water – and you know it!'

Perhaps he was right. But why would I do that?

'Because you don't want to remember,' said Huw, reading my
thoughts. 'The mind is very powerful. It chooses what to remember and what to forget. Perhaps it's trying to protect you, yes?
What did Michael Hamburger say… *memory is a darkroom for the
development of fiction*. Heed his words, my friend.'

I liked this man. He seemed to have my interests at heart. I
smiled at him, and laid my left hand on his right shoulder, as a
friendly gesture. He smiled also.

'You've tried Water,' he said. 'That leaves Earth, Wind and Fire.'

I rolled my eyes. 'And chocolate,' I said.

He looked at me quizzically, so I elaborated. 'Food… the taste
of things. Good for bringing back memories, yes?'

He shrugged his shoulders and turned to admire the
barmaid's rump.

When we left Huw he was enthusiastic about the quest; I

wondered how eager he would be the next day when he woke up with a demonic hangover. He looked like a man who'd woken with plenty of hangovers, so we went on our way.

Next on my list was a minister of religion known simply as the Reverend Griffiths, so we travelled eastwards to find him: I'd been told he lived somewhere on the edge of the Llandegla Moors between Wrexham and Ruthin. One of his most celebrated devices was to chalk two circles on the floor of a haunted room; he would stand in one of them and command the ghost or evil spirit to appear in the other. I managed, eventually, to arrange a tryst with him in the churchyard at Llandegla, a pretty little village on the Offa's Dyke Trail. I broke the ice by expressing an interest in the local wells. He knew much about the subject.

'Did you know that children were dipped up to their necks three times in one of the local wells to prevent them from crying at night?' he asked me. 'And talking of water, did you know that the dolphin family spent a period on land, long ago, before returning to the sea? Might that nugget of knowledge help you with your quest?'

PC 66 entertained us with snippets about the Reverend's exploits as an exorcist, and his specialist knowledge of poltergeists; he mentioned the ghost of Ffrith Farm and the Llandegla Rectory poltergeist. The Reverend was surprised by his acquaintance with the facts.

As PC 66 inspected a circle of bright yellow celandines around our feet I sat on a gravestone and spread the contents of my rucksack – a picnic – on the lid of the grave.

'I've been told you have a unique way of conjuring up evil spirits before you destroy them,' I said to the cleric casually. I sampled one of the sandwiches – egg and cress in a plain white bread – and yawned comfortably in a brief ray of sunshine.

He turned to me and, after giving me a look of horror, he tore up and swiped my picnic off the gravestone.

'You mustn't do that!' he said angrily. 'What in heaven's name has got into you? Have you no respect for the dead?'

I'd forgotten that his mores were from a different age, and I apologised profusely.

I told him that I'd been distracted by a mission which I had undertaken, to rid the world of a monster who preyed on women and children. He was mollified by my admission, and stood quietly while I rescued the sandwiches and repacked them. We adjourned to a more suitable spot, a low wall nearby. I offered him a sandwich, and after nibbling on it suspiciously he took a good bite and munched on it ruminatively. 'Wonderful bread,' he said. 'How do you get it so white? And the egg and cress is such a fine marriage, I'm sure it'll be all the rage soon.'

Having repaired the damage, I continued.

'I believe you have a unique way of dealing with evil spirits,' I repeated.

'Indeed,' he replied, polishing off his fourth sandwich and eyeing a trio of jam doughnuts.

'Help yourself,' I said, and he did – to all of them.

'It's quite simple,' he said, ploughing into the third doughnut, which left a large wodge of cream on his nose. 'I transform the spirits into beetles or small black flies and then I conjure them into a small bottle.'

He rifled one of his inside pockets. 'Look – I always have a bottle with me.'

'And then what happens?' I asked.

'Getting rid of demons is quite easy once I've captured them,' he said. 'I simply tie a piece of lead to the bottle and toss it into the River Alun. Once they're submerged under water they can harm no one ever again.'

I expressed admiration for his ruse, and waited until he'd relaxed after his repast. Then I delivered the *coup de grace*: with a flourish, I uncovered a bottle of the finest port and two crystal glasses in a brown leather case (PC 66 never drank on duty). The Rev Griffiths was enthralled, and as he savoured his drink I asked him if he would help us to rid the world of one last fiend. It would be his masterstroke, I said.

He acceded.

'Can you be on the summit of Pumlumon Arwystli when I need you?' I enquired.

Moving his glass from his right hand to his left, he presented me with his hand and said:

'Friend, I wouldn't miss this opportunity for anything in the whole wide world. I shall be there.'

He wiped his mouth with his sleeve, and closed his eyes briefly, as a sign of utter contentment.

'I feel obliged to ask you something, however,' he said dreamily. 'Are you sure that water will constrain this monster of yours, Mr Cassini?'

'You have doubts, yourself?' I asked.

'Water's all right for sorting out the small fry, but you need a good deep cave to trap a really big monster like Mr Cassini. You need a big hole where you can bury him for ever. You do realise, don't you, that the Cassinis of this world never die? All you can do is trap them and seal them in. An *oubliette*, or something like that. Understand?'

I didn't. I didn't understand at all, so I thought about his advice as I nibbled on an orange-flavoured Kit-Kat.

'What's an *oubliette* when it's at home?' I asked him.

'It's a dungeon below the floor, and the only way in is through a trapdoor. French speciality – they threw people in and forgot about them. *Oublier* is the French word for *to forget*. Don't they teach you *anything* these days?'

'OK mister,' I said. 'What's your plan to get rid of him then?'

'The only way you can sort him out is with words,' he said. 'What are you reading at the moment?'

I started listing the books on the little table by the side of my bed, where I seem to do most of my reading these days. *Water-Divining in the Foothills of Paradise, The Wind-up Bird Chronicle, Rings of Saturn...*

He interrupted me. 'Any caves in them?'

I didn't have to think for long because I'd come across a strange story about a cave in *Rings of Saturn* the previous evening. I told him.

'Excellent,' he said. 'That's the way to get rid of him. How many rings around Saturn?'

'Seven main rings, if I'm not mistaken,' I replied.

'Even better,' he said with unfettered pleasure. 'When we've got him cornered on Pumlumon Arwystli we'll ensnare him with words – is that clear?'

'Yes, sure,' I replied, though I had little faith in what he proposed. Still, if I was going to employ eccentrics I must expect some pretty eccentric behaviour.

We shook hands, and after finishing the whole bottle of port with him I bade him farewell and headed off with PC 66 to our next destination – Carmarthen town.

The next person I seek, to help me with our quest, is Merlin – or Myrddin as he's known in Wales (he has many personae, wherever he goes).

Although I can choose from dozens – or possibly hundreds – of different Merlins I decide to eschew the faker, impostor and itinerant trickster depicted in many of the tales. Instead, I select the kind and rather absent-minded Merlin who appears in TH White's *The Once and Future King* – a magician who has already lived in the future and therefore knows what's what. Those of you who've read *The Once and Future King* know that King Arthur – or The Wart as he's known in the book – falls asleep in a dark forest, and when he wakes up in the morning he discovers an old man with a long white beard drawing water from a well near a cottage. Naturally, the old man is dressed in a pointed cap and a gown with embroidered stars and runic symbols. Who else could he but our old friend Merlin, in one of his many guises (remember, we have already met him as a raving lunatic living with a pig in a dripping wood on the Scottish border, so let's wink at him, hoping he'll wink back, and so compound our confederacy. He does!)

'I know exactly why you're here,' he says calmly as we approach him. He's sitting by a picnic table at Alltyfyrddin Farm, also known as the Merlin's Hill Centre near Carmarthen.

I've chosen this spot for many reasons.

First, I've chosen a modern Merlin so I want a modern setting – a tourist attraction. Here's part of the brochure blurb:

Walk the nature trails to the Iron Age Hillfort Site and experience breathtaking views enjoyed by Merlin the wizard. According to legend, Merlin is still imprisoned there.

Wander around the farmyard heritage centre and watch the cows being milked. Picnic area. Open daily.

A magical day for all the family

Diwrnod i gofio i'r holl deulu.

In 1188, Gerald of Wales wrote that Merlin was born in Carmarthen.

Merlin – King Arthur's guardian with magical powers – is believed to have lived in a cave on Merlin's Hill. This cave was to serve as his home and tomb as, according to legend, he was locked there in bonds of enchantment by his lover. Alas, the cave has become lost with the passage of time but many still hear Merlin clanking his chains on Merlin's Hill.

'I'm sure as hell glad you chose this place,' said Merlin when we sat opposite him. It was one of those picnic benches with low seats on either side, and the whole contraption see-sawed slightly as the weight of our bodies counterbalanced his.

'I'm sick and tired of that wild man of the woods lark, so I'm looking forward to a stroll around the farm and a bite to eat,' he said.

'By the way,' he added thoughtfully, stroking his right eyebrow, 'what do you get if you cross a wizard with a dinosaur?'

My brain fogged with puzzlement. 'No idea,' I answered.

'Tyrannosaurus hex!'

I could hardly believe it. A Merlin who told cheesy jokes? I was incredulous. But he was full of childish humour, as I was about to find out.

Merlin studied me with his penetrating eyes and said:

'I hear you're a bit of a wizard yourself, with the sandwiches. And the cakes too!'

I blushed modestly. 'I'm sure you could do a whole lot better.'

'I'm sure I could,' he said comfortably, 'but when you've made sandwiches for the entire court of Camelot for well over a thousand years you tend to run out of inspiration.'

There was something about the timbre of his voice which reminded me of someone else, but I couldn't figure it out.

'Adam Phillips,' he said nonchalantly. 'I've been masquerading as the well-known Cardiff writer and psychoanalyst at a motorway service station in Scotland and at the ferry terminal in Holyhead.'

I laughed heartily. 'That must be very enjoyable,' I said. 'Being able to pop up wherever and whenever you want.'

'It has distinct disadvantages too,' he said morosely.

'Such as?'

'Such as this foolish errand you're about to send me on.'

'You know about it? Of course you do... you've already been to the future, haven't you?'

'Yes – but don't ask me what's going to happen. I can't tell you that, any more than I could tell Arthur himself. And look what happened to him, poor sod – sent off to an island. I think it's called *extraordinary rendition* nowadays. He's waiting to liberate you all, if he's ever called upon. Modern society has got it all wrong. Arthur is just a *symbol* of fair play and justice – concepts which are as alive as ever, but people couldn't be bothered, could they? It's you lot who've gone to sleep, not him. Nobody seems to care a toss.'

He sounded quite angry.

'Olly...' I urged him to say something about my friend.

'No news. I'm allowed to tell you, however, that she's well and trying to be happy. She'll pop up in your life again very soon. Lovely girl. Great taste in music, though I'm more of a Dolly Parton man myself.'

'Where is she?' I asked anxiously.

He pressed a finger to his lips and merely whispered 'Shhh...'

He allowed a few seconds to pass, and then added: 'Incidentally, if you want some advice, give up the wells thing and have a go at caves. You might get somewhere, though memories aren't all they're cracked up to be you know. They can do you more harm than good, just remember that!'

He sat quietly, looking at a group of visitors.

'Another thing,' he said, picking his nose in an absent-minded way, 'you're dealing with some very old symbols here. Don't you think you should update your references?'

'But I think wells are quite relevant,' I said. 'They reflect changing times. They started off as pagan symbols, then they became Christian symbols, and when science came along they became spas – scientific symbols. Now they're forgotten places. I ask you, Merlin, is it better to have ignorance and a sense of wonder, or knowledge and cold cynicism as we have today?'

He guffawed at me.

'Myths, wells, rainbows, caves... old hat, my friend. You need something contemporary. You know what you remind me of?'

I looked at him expectantly.

'You remind me of a child playing with one of those match-the-shape toys – you know, those boxes with holes in them and kids have to push square bits of wood, or round bits, whatever, into the holes. The problem is that your shapes are all wrong – you're standing there, trying to push your old bits of wood into the holes but they won't go in because they're the wrong size and the wrong shape. You've got to move on, use different shapes and symbols. It's the same with your sanity, mate. It's a lesson I learnt a long time ago, a bloody long time ago. Sanity is all about using the right symbols. If your head is full of field symbols, or flower symbols, or peace symbols, then you've got no hope at all if you're suddenly pushed into a battlefield – and that's what urban society is, after all – you've got no chance of matching the symbols because there are no flowers or fields left, no peace either. Get my drift?'

I nodded, but his line of thought was too difficult to follow. Why were my symbols all wrong? Was I supposed to use television symbols, or mobile phone symbols – modern plastic symbols?

'That time you went mad,' I said, 'what happened?'

He took quite some time to answer my question.

I pressed him further. 'You saw something awful? Something really terrible?'

He nodded, slowly.

'*Monstrum horribile nimis.* A sight horrible beyond measure.'

'What was it?'

Again, he looked at me for a lingering moment, as if he was weighing me up – trying to get the measure of me.

'Something from the past, Duxie, something from the past. That's why you should be careful. You're playing with fire. The past is a minefield. Just be careful, OK?'

I needed to think about this, so to buy time I unzipped my rucksack and spread a picnic on the table between us. I'd even packed a small white linen cloth, and Merlin gave a bit of a girlish giggle and said in a camp sort of voice: 'I haven't been treated this well for *ages* duckie.'

I put his packed lunch in front of him and he unwrapped it slowly, melodramatically, putting his finger into his mouth and rolling his eyes with mock-childishness. He really was a complete idiot, an absolute buffoon.

He picked up a roll, gingerly, and held it within an inch of his eyes, pretending to examine it in microscopic detail.

'My, my, my. A home-baked poppy seed roll,' he said in a shock-and-awe sort of voice, adding sarcastically: 'Delia Smith recipe – if I'm not mistaken, Norwich City use these as practice balls. Only joking!'

He took a bite and munched away. 'Lovely cheese – cambazola, right?'

As usual, he was dead right. 'And hey, there's some mango chutney in there too! You little tinker! A real surprise – that's what you are! I'm well impressed!'

He demolished the roll and reached for another.

'Just as well you didn't put any ham in them – I can't touch the stuff, can't even think about pigs without feeling suicidal. I'm sure you understand why. Years living alone with a pigling ain't no good for nobody. Christ, how I miss bacon butties. My dear little pig died years ago but I still carry his grunt around with me (he points to his breast pocket), as a reminder of our times together. Rude bedfellow or not, he gave me all the love he could...'

Merlin dropped his head and covered his eyes with his right hand.

I commiserated with him by patting his shoulder and saying 'There, there...'

'Only joking!' he said, whipping his hand away and grinning manically. He really was potty.

'What do you get if you cross a snowman with a vampire?' he asked.

'No idea,' I said wearily.

'Frostbite!'

I buried my head in my hands. I'd expected something better than this.

As a diversion I asked him to do a trick.

'With water?' he asked, teasingly.

'Yes, fine,' I replied, expecting something marvellous. A wave of the wand, a flash of beautiful light, a tiny fairy ice-skating in the tumbler of water in front of me, perhaps. Instead, he ambled over to a nearby horse-chestnut tree. After sitting down again he opened his right hand and revealed a few strips of bark taken from the twigs of the tree. He gave them to me and nodded to the glass of water in front of me.

'Go on, put them in,' he said.

I eased the twig-bark into the water, and let it soak for a while. It was magic: very simple magic, but undoubtedly impressive; after a while the water took on a fantastically pretty sky-blue fluorescence. I was amazed.

'This is the only sort of magic I do, actually,' he said. 'Natural magic. It's your age which has added the flash bang wallop stuff. You're all children now, not just the young.'

I questioned him further.

'Is it true that you became invisible when you climbed into your apple tree?' I asked, perhaps a little naively, trying to maintain the conversation.

'Maybe, maybe not,' he said. 'That story goes back a long way you know – to an ancient hope that fleeing warriors could climb to the tops of trees and vanish, or turn into eagles and soar to safety. We've wanted to escape from something or other ever since we came down from the trees, Duxie. And the apple tree is the Celtic fruit of immortality... the island where Arthur was taken – Afallon – means the island of apples. There are apple stories from all over the world.'

'Adam and Eve... ' I said.

'Yes, and elsewhere too. In Norse mythology there's a story about Odin, king of Heaven, and his little brother Loki, god of fire, sliding down a rainbow from Heaven to a green hill on Earth to go camping. There's an eagle and some apples in that too... these stories are very primitive memories. Have you ever dreamt about falling?

'Yes, of course I have.'

'It's one of the commonest types of dream Duxie – and it goes back millions of years, to the time when we were clambering about in the trees.'

'You mean this dream goes back to when we were monkeys?'

'Too right mate.'

Merlin scoffed the last of the cambazola and mango chutney rolls, then looked expectantly in my direction.

'Yes?' I said, innocently.

'Would I be right in thinking that you have a freshly-baked cake in that bag of yours, a nice, squidgy, dark brown chocolaty sort of cake, or has my sixth sense let me down? – and if it *has* I'll be bitterly disappointed, because:

a) it has never let me down once, in thirteen hundred years, and

b) I hear that Duxie makes exceedingly good cakes.'

He drummed his fingers on the table lightly as I pulled out my cake tin, levered off the lid, and fetched a miniature candle from my bag. I stabbed it into the centre of the cake and lit it. He looked at me quizzically.

'That's for the 1,432 birthdays you've had since you lost the plot at the Battle of Arfderydd,' I said.

His eyes went all misty and emotional.

'Why, that's beautiful,' he said. 'You old romantic, you. For that, I'll try extra hard to shift this Svengali of yours. What's his name again?

'Cassini.'

'Mr Cassini will be mostly motionless by the time I've finished with him,' said Merlin.

'Another slice of cake?' I asked.

'Too bloody right. *[He mumbles through a mouthful of crumbs – something about the male brown argus butterfly smelling of chocolate when courting.]* What's the plan then?'

I tell him about the others, and about our rendezvous point.

'Can you be on top of Pumlumon Arwystli at such-and-such a time?' I asked him, finally.

'Can I? Wouldn't miss it for all the hemp in China. Feels like I've spent 1,432 years waiting for this tosser to come along. I've got some bad anger in here *[he thumps his chest]*. Need to get rid. Revenge! *[He stands up, brandishing a slice of chocolate cake in the air. Small children run to their parents.]*

'An actor,' I tell the startled picnickers. 'He's an actor, we're making a promotional video...'

They don't look convinced. They eye my cake suspiciously.

We depart, quickly, in the direction of Merlin's Hill so that Merlin can clank his chains, as per brochure. When we get there he waves his limbs around and I hear chains jangling, though there are none in sight. He looks pleased with himself. An almighty squeal comes from his top pocket.

'Just testing the sound effects for your video,' he says.

We part on very good terms. 'By the way – I forgot to ask you something,' he says. 'Will you bring a cake to Pumlumon Arwystli?'

He grins, and thrusts his hands out in front of him in a Tommy Cooper pose.

He does a fantastic Tommy Cooper impression.

'What do you call a wizard from outer space?' he asks.

Before I can open my mouth he delivers the punch line:

'A flying sorcerer! *[Stupid Tommy Cooper laugh.]* Just like that!'

Then he giggles, turns away from us, and slopes off into the trees.

The fourth and last person we turned to for help was the redoubtable Arthur Machen, who'd secured a special place in my heart. He had many claims to fame, and I still chortle, guffaw, and generally make bubbles in the bath when I think of his best scam ever. Working for a national newspaper, he wrote a spoof obituary, which was published. The obituary lamented the death of his employer – who was still very much alive. Arthur was promptly sacked.

Born at Caerleon, Gwent, in the 1860s, Arthur Machen – real name Arthur Llewellyn Jones – wrote gothic horror stories set in the Welsh countryside. It was he who 'discovered' the White People – and I wanted his strange, frightening imagination to be my secret weapon in the disposal of Mr Cassini.

Arthur let me know, from the start, that he didn't mess with the ganja.

'I'm a man of God and I believe in sanctity,' he said in a serious, slightly quavering voice when we met on one of his rare visits to Wales. He was a Christian: his father had been an Anglican priest. I was a pagan who had devised my own elaborate pantheon of lesser gods and demons, as pagans do. I tried my best to skirt around the issue. My first impression of Arthur was of a man possessed. Not by anything evil, you understand. I'd say he was possessed by a raw energy, a driving force which had pressed him into a rigorous life: he'd written hundreds of thousands of words and traded many thousands of thoughts. I was rather surprised to see that he'd shaved off his trademark beard, black and bushy, a growth which had given him the demonic appearance of a Rasputin in early manhood. Clean-shaven now, his strong nose and forceful mouth betrayed his strong personality. His thinning hair was straight, lank, and combed forwards, giving him the damp-palmed look of a public school organist – but I do him a disservice.

Arthur spent a solitary childhood playing in the countryside around his home. According to one source he took an unfamiliar path through the hills one afternoon and encountered something that touched his soul – something he struggled to put into words for the rest of his life. He found terrors and wonders in that early landscape – and his fertile mind embellished the wonders he saw and heard: weird pagan sculptures dug up by archaeologists, shady dells, fairy rings, music carried on the wind. His world was haunted and mysterious. A temple dedicated to the Romano-British god of healing, Nodens, was excavated at nearby Lydney Park during his boyhood, and his lush imagination fed on this and other episodes, picking out threads of foreboding and terror. If you ask me, Arthur was more in need of my special chocolate cake than all the rest put together, but he was adamant.

'My dear friend,' he addressed me as we sat on a grassy bank in the splendid Roman amphitheatre at Caerleon, 'there is naught you can say to persuade me. Marijuana, dope, grass, weed, hash, pot, puff, blow, call it what you will, I have no intention of touching it. I may, however, suffer one of your highly regarded sandwiches to pass my lips in due course. First, we have a matter in hand.'

He lay back on the grass, studying a flock of puffy white meringue-clouds far above us in the sky.

'We are beset by huge changes,' he said. 'All is not well with the world. Mr Darwin preaches strange heresies, yet his arguments are powerful and seductive. Like me he is plagued by digestive disorders. But instead of praying to the great God above for good health, he worships the humble earthworm. Did you know that?'

'No,' I replied truthfully.

He pulled out a well-thumbed book and opened it at a marked page. It was by Charles Darwin, and its title was *Formation of Vegetable Mould through the Action of Worms*.

When we behold a wide, turf-covered expanse we should remember that its smoothness, on which so much of its beauty depends, is mainly due to all the inequalities having been slowly levelled by worms. It is a marvellous reflection that the whole of the superficial mould over any such expanse has passed, and will again pass, every few years through the bodies of worms...

'Well! What do you think of that,' said Arthur in an extra-quivery voice.

I rolled over onto my stomach, and traced my right forefinger around a worm cast in the soil.

'So the little fellow at the end of this hole, living and dying in absolute obscurity, has had a big say in the story of humanity,' I ventured. 'Incidentally, did you know that earthworms cap their burrows to prevent water seeping in?'

He looked astonished. 'These little animals have won my respect and admiration today,' he said with great feeling.

It was Arthur who told me the story of Bladud. He thought it might be relevant.

Bladud was a Celtic prince – legendary founder of Bath – who was disowned and banished by his father when he contracted leprosy. His mother gave him a gold ring before he left, as a means of identification. Shunned and despised, Bladud became a pig-keeper but some of his pigs caught leprosy too and one of them, crazed by the disease, rushed into a bog. In his struggle to free the animal, Bladud was covered in mud – which cured him, and the pig too. Returning to court, he was recognised by his ring and ruled wisely for twenty years, creating the temple of Aqua Sullis. But he died tragically when a magical experiment went wrong. In the manner of Icarus he made a fantastical pair of wings, but they gave way and he crashed to his death.

Arthur warned me about my quest.

'Duxie, we're all bubbles in the breaking wave of time – no more than that. Be careful at the end of your story. Please don't try to fly.'

Arthur, the London journalist, had tasted poverty at first hand. He got to know the city intimately and fell in love with her nooks and crannies. His first book, *The Anatomy of Tobacco*, was followed by three French translations. And then, married to Amy Hogg, he turned to 'decadent' fantasy fiction laced with sexuality and horror. *The Great God Pan* – which features a pagan demoness – caused a scandal.

Arthur propped himself up on his right elbow and regarded me in the brittle light of a February afternoon in Caerleon.

'Let me tell you something,' he said, flopping onto his back again. 'A man like you, searching for something in his past, is in mourning. Did you realise that?'

I murmured something to bide time.

'Mourning your childhood probably,' he said. 'Or mourning a suitable explanation for your existence... or mourning your own impending death, perhaps.'

I countered him swiftly. 'How about you then. You're in perpetual mourning for a man who died two thousand years ago, and in perpetual mourning for an unknown date in the future when you'll get to see him again. That's a whole lifetime in mourning. Am I right, or am I right?'

He seemed rather shocked.

'How can you talk about God like that,' he said in a hushed tone. 'These modern notions of yours...'

I placated him.

'Yes, you're quite right.'

I explained, in a soothing voice, that there had been a great crisis in faith – of any kind – since his death. People were looking for other ways to feel happy and optimistic. Like shopping and eating chocolate.

'I'll give you a quote from a book I'm reading at the moment,' I said. 'It's by a man called Adam Phillips. He's Welsh, actually, like us.'

I rummaged in my rucksack and brought out a paperback with a dark blue cover.

'This line comes from *Darwin's Worms*,' I told him.

> It is the consequence, if not always the intention, of both Darwin's and Freud's writing to make our lives hospitable to the passing of time and the inevitability of death, and yet to sustain an image of the world as a place of interest, a place to love.

'So you don't believe in *anything* any more,' he said.

'Belief is a commodity sold by people who want you to buy their story and nobody else's,' I replied. 'And it's a very dangerous commodity. If you don't keep it in a safe place it's likely to blow up in your face any moment.'

Arthur chuckled over my homespun philosophy. As I repacked my bag he questioned me about modern science. Had Richard Dawkins really described our DNA codes as islands of sense separated by seas of nonsense, and what did he mean by that?

I lay back on the grass, trying to summon up some courage. Would he join my gang on Pumlumon Arwystli? Would he reactivate the White People? I went over the reasons in my head, my plan of action.

When war broke out in 1914, Arthur had gained a new and freakish notoriety. Soon after the Battle of Mons he wrote a story called *The Bowmen*, describing how celestial archers from the age of Agincourt appeared in the sky above the battle and fired arrows at the Germans, saving the British from defeat. The story took on a life of its own and soon the public believed in *The Angels of Mons* – a real life version of Arthur's story. He became famous despite his repeated avowals that *The Bowmen* was a work of fiction.

I wanted to use his novella *The White People*, in my bid to exorcise Mr Cassini. The story features one of Arthur's favourite themes – the 'little people' of folklore: the children of Danu, who 'disappeared' into the Welsh hills many years ago but who live on in another dimension or otherworld; he believed they still exert an obscure and menacing force on humanity. In *The White People*, a girl on the cusp of puberty is fatally sucked into this fairytale world.

'I have an idea,' I said to Arthur. 'Does the name Ti Bossa mean anything to you?'

A faint negation reached my ears.

'A voodoo priest who lived in Haiti... he had forty wives,' I said. 'Did a trick with white powder.'

His response was immediate, as I'd anticipated. He jerked to life, rolling onto his side and putting his face close to mine; so close that I could smell peppermint, which explained the regular, furtive movements of his hand between a pocket and his mouth.

'White powder?' he rasped excitedly.

'Yes – apparently he could make people invisible merely by sprinkling a small pinch of this powder over them.'

His eyes burned into me, two black coals set in the embers of his bloodshot eyes.

'My God! You do realise, of course, that I myself have used a white powder in one of my own stories?'

'*The Novel of the White Powder*,' I replied cunningly. My ruse had worked perfectly.

'You've read it?' he asked, with that strange mixture of disbelief and pride which rises like a dove from the author's fragile breast.

'Of course,' I answered.

A brief silence fell over us as we contemplated the conversation which had passed between us. There was no doubt in my mind that we had formed a friendship, based largely on white powder. I was glad I hadn't brought any cocaine (not that I had any, you understand). Arthur was an aesthete in such matters, and I might have scuppered my project in its infancy.

'Let me get this right,' he said. 'You want me to meet you on the top of Pumlumon Arwystli, together with Merlin, Huw Llwyd of Cynfael, the Rev Griffiths and the singing policeman. There, we will encounter a teardrop vampire or animagus called Mr Cassini, a man who siphons life from other people, and together we will banish him from this earth by utilising a number of tricks and wiles, my white powder being among them. Is that right?'

'Perfectly correct, though I also want you to bring the White People along, since I have a part for them to play also.'

'I hope you don't mind my saying this,' he said in carefully considered tones, 'but the whole thing sounds rather childish.'

Now it was my turn to roll over onto my side and regard *him*.

'That's the whole point,' I said. 'I am seeking to return to my childhood – to be specific, to the first ten years, in the hope that I will be able to recall some of my earliest memories. As Dylan Thomas once said, *I hold a beast, an angel and a madman in me, and my enquiry is to their working.* Surely you can appreciate what I'm trying to do, since you yourself have based most of your fiction on the fragments you've retained from your youth. Childhood, after all, is the supreme fiction. Am I speaking truthfully?'

Again, he waved his hand languorously and murmured assent.

And so our pact was made; my plan of action was completely in place and, as I bade him farewell and watched his black shadow receding into a Caerleon dusk, I put together the last few pieces of my jigsaw – the gambit with which I would entice Mr Cassini to the summit of Pumlumon Arwystli on an insipid day in mid-February.

That night I dreamt the next development in my story, or should I say *our* story, since Olly had helped me gestate the malevolent incubus whom I now sought (as a ghostwriter) to extinguish in my own private *auto-da-fe*. In my dream, PC 66 felt a frisson of magnetism one morning, and it drew him towards the shore; he walked to the edge of the pounding surf and trembled with cold and shame by the side of the turbulent sea. He took off his huge police issue boots, and then his socks, which he crammed into the still-warm leather interiors. He stepped into the sea and walked steadily into the briny, until the super-cooled waves encased his legs and shackled him, numb, to the rocky seabed. He wanted to swim out to the island. He wanted to escape from the pointing fingers, the knowing looks, the shaking heads. The people were demanding action. For years they had turned a blind eye to Mr Cassini's familial cruelties, but now, with the arrival of Little Michael, they'd been pricked into action. Tales of the supernatural sped from shop to shop; the aldermen held agitated meetings behind closed doors; superstitious townspeople talked of vengeance and supernal intervention. PC 66 turned back. He went for his boots, but one of them had already been carried away by the tide; he put the other on his left foot and limped away from the scene. A magnetic force dragged him back to the police station, wet-legged and miserable, to face his destiny. When the sun sank below the liverish waves a large crowd, silent except for the crackle of their torches, laid violent hands on Mr Cassini and interned him in the police station. As he sat in his cell, unmoved, an inquisitorial court was convened to try him, and while it deliberated, the crowd enacted a macabre and sinister practice which takes place during the carnival at Villanueva de la Vera, in the high and lonely sierra south of Madrid, every year. At the height of the jollifications a man-sized doll – *Pero Palo* – dressed in seventeenth-century clothing, is delivered to the crowd to be torn to pieces. At one period this act of light-hearted destruction was preceded by a semblance of castration, now omitted from the festivities, but there is still fierce competition for the possession of the carved, wooden head. Differences of opinion exist in Villanueva as to who the effigy represents, a common view being that in real life *Pero Palo* was an inquisitor, finally lynched by the populace in retribution for intolerable abuses...

But even then Mr Cassini displayed no fear. A traditional sin-eater was summoned and the mob witnessed his vicarious act of contrition; presented with a small loaf of salted bread, a mazer full of beer, and a small denomination coin, he symbolically consumed the sins of the man inside the police station. Mr Cassini laughed.

Now, as the seven rainbow messengers arrived simultaneously at the door of the cell, PC 66 executed his *coup de main*: he arranged for the seventh rainbow messenger to enter the cell and foretell Mr Cassini's death. The omens had to be right.

The seventh rainbow messenger said to Mr Cassini in his cell: 'Beware the snow: when the windows of heaven are opened a white host will come – the snowflakes will arrive as a swarm of remembrance. The taste of snow is the taste of violence. Do you understand me?'

'Yes.'

'The mannequins in your room will come to life, they will hunt you down. I can see that room very clearly. There are many people sitting in that room and they are thawing.'

Mr Cassini hung his head, he made no response.

Moving towards the door, the seventh rainbow messenger said: 'Go to Pumlumon Arwystli without delay, take yourself to the centre cairn, the middle of the three, and look to all points of the compass, as the sun rises. Your future will become known to you. Do you understand me?'

Mr Cassini lumbered to his feet and nodded.

'Come then, leave this place. Your fate awaits you.'

PC 66 turned to the rainbow messengers and said, simply:

'Go with him, guide him to the top of the mountain. I shall see you there.'

And that was the last time that Mr Cassini saw Big Bay or Little Bay, or the island, or the marshes beyond, or his colossus – the Red Man – looking out to sea.

PC 66 took Mr Cassini's matt red van (with his bicycle inside it) to the top of the eastern pass above the town and he drove it as fast as he could without injuring himself into a gap in the wall, simulating an accident. Then he cycled back and prepared himself for the day ahead.

9

THE TIDE GOES OUT

Sherlock Holmes
and the seven rings of Saturn

TOO many things are happening at the moment. Hoping to hear news of Olly, I've started listening to the radio again and looking at the telly, and that's always a bad sign. It's February and it's cold. I feel as if I'm sitting in a dark kitchen with the fridge door ajar – there's a nicotine glow, the hum of snow to come. Outside, the earth is flat and colourless – clingfilmed ready for reheating; the barcode trees are stark and black, waiting for spring's leafy new price tags. I wait for each dawn as a sick man waits for medical results.

I'm standing by the sea-facing window, next to my telescope, looking down at the harbour. If I concentrate all the lenses of my mind I can focus on a tiny upstairs window in Bangor in the nineteenth century. A man called John Jones is training a large telescope on the snowy cap of Mars. He calls his telescope Jumbo. He made it himself. By day he counts slates in the local docks; he has already been a farmer's boy and a servant. But after reading *The Solar System* by Dr Dick he has become enamoured of stars.

There's a blue boat in the harbour and its chains are rattling, its capstan spinning. Soon it will glide seawards and I need to be on it – I want to be a dot on someone's horizon. And strangely, portentously, there's a ghost moth in the hallway, clinging to the glass pane above my front door. It hasn't moved for days. I stand there, sometimes, willing it to life. There's sadness in moths. In times of drought, without dew, they may travel in clouds for many miles, looking for water. When they find it they drown in large numbers as they try to settle on its surface.

I have some final business to attend to. I am in need of friends. I have called upon them all to help me – and here's one of them now, scurrying up the path.

He was with us a short while ago: magnifying glass in hand, one eye larger than the other in the best cartoon fashion. The man who used his brilliant deductive skills to free two innocent men from prison – in real life. He introduced skis to Switzerland. He voyaged to the Arctic as surgeon on a whaling ship. He enthralled the public with his creation, Sherlock Holmes. Yes, Arthur Conan Doyle is with us again, though in a different guise – as a spiritualist. For him it was a great crusade, and if you don't believe me, read his two-volume *The History of Spiritualism*. To tell you the truth, Sherlock Holmes meant very little to him. Ready cash. He thought his historical novel *The White Company* was his best work. Like most of us, Conan Doyle had a skeleton in the cupboard – his father drank enough of the hard stuff to sink Baker Street under a sea of bottles. One of seven children, given to fits of violence, Doyle senior spent much of his life in mental asylums or nursing homes for alcoholics.

Already fascinated by psychic research – séances, telepathy and thought transference, Conan Doyle was devastated by the death from pneumonia of his son Kingsley, and the tragedy refracted his mind; at a sitting held by a Welsh medium his son 'spoke' to him. Conan Doyle was hooked.

Sherlock's sleuthing tips were of no help in the search for Olly. And there's even worse news. The police have given up. Even Dafydd Apolloni in Rome has thrown in the towel, and we all know what he and his hot-blooded compatriots will do to find a pretty girl. So I'm going on a different tack. I'm going to get in touch with her through spiritualism.

'Oh well,' I hear you say as you lay down my book. 'Pity – he'd kept it together pretty well until now, for a lunatic that is. But communing with the lost and the dead? Forget it.'

The truth is, I have a confession to make. During the last few months a creeping sensation has spread over me. Not a realisation, exactly – more a suspicion. A hunch? A little orange Post-it note from Sherlock, or my Sixth Sense, saying: *Everything is happening now. The past and the future, too. All that has happened and all that will happen is happening now. Without beginning, middle or end, the performance is continuous and ever-happening. Whatever has been in the past and whatever will be in the future is happening now, all at the same time.*

I know, sounds barmy to me too. I don't believe in all that tosh either. But hang on for a sec. Don't go yet. I wouldn't bother you with this if I didn't have something to go on. A solitary clue.

Lately I've been having a recurring *déjà-vu*, but it's a *déjà-vu* with a difference. It's not a sharp, tangy repeat from the past. It's from the future. It happened yesterday, when I was travelling up-country, from the sea towards the foothills of Snowdonia. Meandering up the valley, following the curves of the river – I was somewhere near the old Roman ford.

There I was, travelling along in my pick-up, when I had a typical *déjà-vu* experience but it was from the future: I was transported by my senses to exactly the same place *after* my death. It was the same old world, pretty much, and it felt familiar in a *déjà-vu* sort of way. But time had moved on a bit, and I wasn't there. I was acutely – and not unpleasantly – aware that I'd left the stage; I was simply not there any longer. Don't get me wrong. I don't believe in an afterlife. No – my senses (or my mind) were merely playing tricks with me. Happens to loads of people, apparently. Nothing new under the moon. But how about the millions who *do* believe in all that, all those who *have* believed in spiritualism? A surprising number of Welsh people, actually. Superstitious lot. I should know. Few people have spent more time than me avoiding ladders and tossing salt around by the sackful. Research has shown that the average Welshman spends a total of thirteen weeks of his life touching wood and saying *Touch Wood*.

I'm joking! *Never* take me seriously.

Let's examine the Welsh and their penchant for the super-natural.

Take Jack Webber, born in one of the South Wales valleys in 1907: he spoke through trumpets and his presence affected electrical equipment.

Or how about Treherbert-born Alexander Frederick Harris. At one Christmas séance featuring a luminous ball he caused the decorations and balloons to be pulled down by spirit children who played on tambourines, mouth organs and drums. During the war he 'reunited' a woman with her dead son. At a séance the young man appeared dramatically, held out his arms to the woman, and said: *Mum, it's Derry.* With a cry of anguish she jumped from her seat and wept tears of joy in the arms of her 'dead' son.

I, too, decided to try a spot of spiritualism in my search for Olly. I got in touch, via the internet, with a spiritualist medium who *makes your angels accessible to you*.

'I am bestowed with the gifts of clairvoyance, clairaudience, clairaroma and clairsentience and I have been psychic all of my life,' she says on her website. 'As a child I experienced the joy of playing with Spirit children and enjoyed their unconditional love. These same Spirit children are still with me, they are my guides who have grown up along side of me; and with their love and light they help me to link with the Spirit world.'

She continues: 'By connecting with the Angels I will help you to be more able to understand the *synchronicities – the planned coincidences* which happen to all of us at some time in our lives.'

I emailed her, and while I waited for guidance I did a bit of detective work, since I am a Welsh Sherlock *manqué* (manky Welshman, more like it).

I sensed that the medium would never reply. She didn't...

I had a bit of luck though. I met that man again, the Cardiff psychoanalyst and writer, or maybe it was Merlin, messing around again. He was sitting in a little café on the hill, and when I saw him I went straight up to him. No messing around this time.

'You must be Mr Adam Phillips,' I said as I sat down opposite him (if it was him). He looked a bit startled but he held his own counsel and nodded amenably as he ate his breakfast and listened to me.

'I loved *Houdini's Box*,' I said enthusiastically.

Houdini's Box, one of his books, examines four different escape artists. One of them is a little girl who has been abused. She plays her own version of hide-and-seek. You may not have realised it, but hide and seek is a subtle game. If you put yourself out of reach, or refuse to hide, you're not playing the game.

I grabbed some paper napkins and scribbled down a few of the sentences which passed between us, over the tomato ketchup bottle, that morning:

        ✲   We can't describe ourselves without also describing what we need to escape *from* and what we want to escape *to*.

* People often feel most alive when they're escaping, most paralysed before and after.

* What we want is born of what we want to get away from.

* Sandor Ferenczi: do people colonise the world with fear to distract themselves?

* Hungarian proverb: It is better to fear than to be frightened.

* When it doesn't starkly and literally save our lives (when we shoot our approaching lion) fear sustains our ignorance... what is being escaped from is often shrouded in mystery.

* The opposite of fear is choice. Indeed, the whole notion of choice may have been invented as a counter, an alternative, to fear.

* We transgress to find out if we can escape, create havoc to see what will survive.

* All symptoms are a kind of geography; they take a person in certain directions, to certain places and not to others. They are a schedule of avoidances, a set of warning signals.

* It is fortunate that pain has made us so inventive.

Adam Phillips (if it was he, I'll never know now) finished his breakfast and thanked me for my company. It had been an exhilarating conversation. I had learnt much, and I thanked him effusively. 'Absolute pleasure,' he said as he enveloped himself in a large and warm-looking coat. Perhaps it was my imagination, but his step seemed to quicken into a near-run as he disappeared into the crowd. He liked to keep fit, obviously. But my thoughts were already elsewhere, since a faint but perceptible rainbow was forming over the town, as if to salute this transference of ideas from one mind to another.

The Yanomami people who have survived marauding gold diggers, loggers and Christians in the rainforests of South America like to hunt, fish, and cultivate gardens – when left alone. To communicate with the spirit world, their shamans snort a hallucinogenic snuff made from the bark of the virola tree. Their spirits appear to them as miniature humans, magnificently decorated with ceremonial ornaments. They are the spirits of the forest – mammals, birds, fish, amphibians, reptiles, insects. There are spirits which represent trees, leaves, vines, water, also stones and waterfalls; spirits representing the sun and the moon, storms, thunder and lightning, and mythological beings. There are also humble household spirits such as the dog spirit, the fire spirit and the clay pot spirit. Finally, there are spirits representing the white man and his domesticated animals. These white spirits are conjured as an antidote – to ward off epidemics.

Shamans control the fury of the storms, the tic-toc of day and night, the seasons, and the abundance and fertility of game. They prevent the arch of the sky from falling down (the present earth is an ancient fallen sky); they also control the forest's aggressive spirits and cure Yanomamis made sick by sorcery.

Shamans 'die' when they take their snuff and they enter a visionary trance. White men who have joined them in this rite have seen brilliant sights: rainbows trapped inside the shamans' feathered headdresses, flowers weeping in their hair, trees trying to soar into the sky, leaves falling to the ground with great howling noises. They report that the stars throb; the sky opens and a great wind destroys everything in its path; the ground opens and snakes slip away into the earth. Then they are engulfed by terror and death hovers all around. They lie under a canopy of immense sorrows.

I am not the brightest of men, but I'm making a connection here. Forests, men behaving as if they were possessed, generally off their heads, but treated by everyone else as if they were wise beyond measure, awesome, visionary...

Yes, we're back with our old friend Merlin again. The madman in the woods. Perhaps he wasn't that mad after all. Just off his head. Shitfaced. And where did all the Druids and the *vates* hang out? In the groves. Sounds like a good excuse to me. Merlin the local dealer.

The time has come for me to describe my own descent into the underworld. You know already that my experiment with wells failed: that I was unable to journey into the past as I had hoped. The first ten years of my life were still a mystery to me.

So I turned to the ground itself, because over the years a few tiny shards had risen, slowly, as if they'd been transported – like miniature surfboards – to the surface of my memory on incredibly slow-moving waves created by the activities of a trillion mind-worms. Those shards reminded me of the poems which once formed part of an epic Welsh saga known as *Canu Heledd*. The poems are all that remain of a great myth; the basic story, told in prose (long ago) has been lost.

Looking back now, I can see that my descent below ground had started (unconsciously) a few weeks previously. Olly had been with me then too.

We'd been sitting in Merlin's café bar in Ystradgynlais, I remember it as if it were yesterday. You know the place – red and green façade, big leather Chesterfield in the window to let you sit and watch the world go by. Me and Olly, just the two of us, loafing about and enjoying it. Good energy in Ystradgynlais, too. Steady community or, as they say down the valleys, *tidy*.

'Let's go down a pit,' I said to Olly, but no, she wanted to go to the Dan-yr-Ogof caves up the road. I stood my ground and prevailed (for a change).

The Lewis Merthyr Colliery in the Rhondda seemed the obvious place to go. I asked a friendly man standing in the doorway of a shop on the crossroads: *Brian Davies menswear, footwear & protective clothing etc:* 'How do we get to the Rhondda?'

There was a sharp intake of breath and he shook his head, as if to say that a blood-soaked man had crawled into town less than an hour ago... last stagecoach through the pass ambushed by Arapahos, all dead and scalped, mainly women and children. I felt excited by this, as if we were at the far end of the Silk Road, in Mongolia perhaps, not just round the corner from Lower Cwmtwrch.

We got there eventually, via Neath and Blaengwynfi. First a Sherpa bus full to the brim with people who bubbled with language: Welsh, and English, and even sign language too. Raindrops chandeliered the dirty windows in liquid constellations (I saw Hydra, Draco); my star-streaks glimmered against a dark backdrop of forests and ravines climbing up on either side – for most of the journey we were in a deep cleft matlocked in the moorland. Giant wheels appeared, as if newly invented, rearing above their dereliction; skeletal pithead wheels, abandoned like so many upturned supermarket trolleys, rusting above the coal shafts: spinsterish, spindled, bespoke. There be dragons.

A lonesome whistler on the back seat harrowed my brain. The wipers, I thought, were trying to reach out beyond their ambit, trying to suck in the unobtainable raindrops just beyond their sweep; and I saw parallels with my own search for meaning, beyond the constraints of my own blades, sweeping the glassy plains of my past.

The villages we passed had an Austrian feel to them, perched on ledges, but there were windows patched up with cardboard and flowerless gardens. King Coal took the money with him. Onwards we lurched in our bus, crammed into our seats as if we were spiders pushed into a matchbox by a bored child, and spinning from our backs – from all of us – came the silken thread of our lives, swirling though the rear window, entwining to form a history, a gossamer cord dragging the parachute of *what has happened between us today, and may never happen again.*

We hitched a lift over the mountain and descended into Treorchy. If Honolulu is the rainbow capital of the world, overarched by a vibrant bow almost every day of the year, then Treorchy was the capital of the clouds that day. Capital of the clouds... the appellation would look nice on a nameplate somewhere in Wales:

CERRIGYDRUDION
Capital of the Clouds

You could have a competition based on rainfall, cloudfall, and the number of angels seen walking the streets.

Through the rain-mottled window of the rain-mottled car I looked down on the Rhondda, half in awe. The place is legendary. This is where the Great Jehovah lives, the Great Redeemer – this is the barren land. This is where they bake the Bread of Heaven. Terraces of miners' houses stretched away in long miles, some of them dead straight and some of them following the bendy contours of the valley.

A brief history of Hwntws: South Wales is riven by deep valleys, each with its own coal-mining history. South Walians are knows as Hwntws (North Walians are Gogs).

Hwntws are divided into Straight Hwntws (born in straight terraces) and Bendy Hwntws (born in bendy terraces). Telling one from the other is quite easy. Straight Hwntws prefer rugby, which has lots of straight lines in it: they sit in straight rows in the stands watching straight lineouts and straight three-quarters. The rugby ball, which is fighting the circle and gradually straightening out, is kicked between two very straight posts. Also, Straight Hwntws will frequently converge in long straight lines, standing in comfortable silence (often in pubs, as it happens). There is no point in walking to either end of this line, looking for the object of the queue, since there isn't one – they're merely drawing strength and comfort from each other in emulation of their houses. If you want to identify the Bendy Hwntws, simply throw a party and wait until everyone's drunk, then start a conga. The Bendy Hwntws will adapt happily to the conga's snake-like path, but the Straight Hwntws will eventually revert to the norm, stiffen into a straight line, and punch a hole in the side of your house before disappearing into the distance; thus the phrase *to bring the house down.*

The Rhondda is a place where pretty words bow their heads and stay silent, out of respect and politeness. All these valleys have been drilled out by a bad dentist and the gaping holes overlaid with poorly-fitted dentures – rows of houses, pitted with caries, which sit uneasily on the blackened gums of yesteryear. Never has so little beauty been compressed into so large a space, as Gwyn Thomas put it.

We arrived in a squall; the tired rivers and industrial-sized puddles were pocked by the rain in acne-rings, and a weaselly mandrel-wind slipped in and out of every hole in our clothing. Needless to say, the people were magnificent. Somewhere above us in the mist (we were lost in the spout of a kettle all day) was the ancient well and shrine at Penrhys, almost as important for pilgrims as Holywell.

When we arrived at the Rhondda Heritage Park in Trehafod we passed under a six-foot high model of a miner's lamp (a memorial to the many thousands of Welsh miners killed over the years) and walked into the restored colliery buildings. Over half the visitors come from outside Wales. I wondered what they make of the Black Gold experience, with its reconstruction of a village street in mining days, art gallery, restaurant and gift shop. The surrounding village dropped 14 feet when the mine was working and it's a wonder it's still standing.

After sniffing around for a while we were taken on a guided tour by an ex-miner who'd spent a long time below, in the heart of darkness, at the cutting edge.

His voice slipped like a chisel occasionally and sent sparks into the gloom; he'd either smelt firedamp or had spent too many hours trapped in the sclerotic arteries of the past because there was a distinct whiff of mania in the air around him. He had a black, trammelled sense of humour and he scared the children once or twice. The canaries seemed fond of him though. Yellow and black go together quite nicely, I noticed. Compatible colours. We sat down in a metal cavern and struggled to understand an audio-visual show. Exciting and emotional, said the publicity. These people ought to get out more. Girders loomed in the vaulted darkness, and their dimlit cavities reminded me of those lovely little hollows behind girls' knees. I half expected it to start snowing coal dust from the shadows overhead; soft black coal-flakes which glinted in the murk and turned us all, slowly, into minstrels with itchy collars and very white teeth, gleaming in luminescent rows. Dirty blackleg miners.

Coal seams, as you well know, are buried ancient forests. Which brings me back (neatly) to the Yanomami wise men, who snort hallucinogen snuff in faraway rainforests. Next time you look into a coal fire, when the tic-toc of time has brought you to the end of your working day, I invite you to look into the eye of the firestorm. You will see brilliant sights: rainbows trapped inside the shamans' feathered headdresses, flowers weeping in their hair.

Lewis Carroll always maintained that *Alice's Adventures in Wonderland*, a story told during a series of picnics, was just a book of nonsense. But he was certainly influenced by *The Seven Sisters of Sleep*, published in 1860 by the naturalist and mycologist Mordecai Cooke; very popular in its day, it was an entertaining survey of the best known psychotropic drugs of the Victorian age: betel, cannabis, opium, coca, datura, and fly agaric mushrooms.

> The Caterpillar and Alice looked at each other for some time in silence: at last the Caterpillar took the hookah out of its mouth, and addressed her in a languid, sleepy voice.

Alice goes on 'a trip'. She experiences a slowing down sensation. She sees hallucinogenic animals. A baby turns into a pig in the story, reminding some of the curse of opium, which affected about five out of six Victorian families and killed many children – the infants *shrunk up into little old men* under the influence of the drug.

Drink Me! says the bottle and Alice shrinks until she's 10 inches high. *What a curious feeling!* says Alice. *I must be shutting up like a telescope…*

Inside a glass box there's a very small cake. *Eat Me!* So Alice grows enormous.

Don't tell me that this nonsense has nothing to do with drugs. Or eating disorders.

It all ends in tears:

> Poor Alice! It was as much as she could do, lying down on one side, to look through into the garden with one eye; but to get through was more hopeless than ever: she sat down and began to cry again…
>
> 'I wish I hadn't cried so much!' said Alice, as she swam about, trying to find her way out. 'I shall be punished for it now, I suppose, by being drowned in my own tears!'

And there's implicit danger, a lurking threat in the background:

> How doth the little crocodile
> Improve his shining tail,
> And pour the waters of the Nile
> On every golden scale!
>
> How cheerfully he seems to grin,
> How neatly spread his claws,
> And welcome little fishes in
> With gentle smiling jaws!

Crying is good for you. Butterflies gather salty tears from the eyes of otters and turtles along the Peruvian Amazon. But no one knows the exact nature of tears. Are tears – high in protein – the residue of an ancient emergency feeding system for babies? Another crackpot theory…

Going underground: Plutarch (45-125AD) reported that vestal virgins who broke their vows were sealed alive in underground chambers and left to die. Medieval monks and nuns who broke their vows were often walled into niches with just a small amount of food and water for company. When graveyards became full in the mid-18th century, following a particularly busy era for the grim reaper, many graves were 'recycled' to accommodate new residents. When the old coffins were dug up something horrifying came to light: scratches, kick-marks, and even teeth-marks seemed to indicate that about one in every 25 of the 'dead' had been buried alive. So being buried alive became a huge fear factor for the Victorians, many of whom arranged for one of their fingers to be connected – via a small borehole and a piece of string – to a bell on the surface so that they could ring for attention. Doom service. Graveyards had someone on standby around the clock – the graveyard shift. In his book *Buried Alive*, in 1895, Franz Harman recorded over 700 incidents of people who were literally saved by the bell.

I've a little joke up my sleeve, for my fellow Taffies. There's a word for the fear of being buried alive... taphophobia! No kidding.

So we went on a ride in a cage, that day, to the bottom of the mine. Could have been seventeen hundred feet down, could have been seventeen. Didn't matter. It felt mighty authentic. There were great big iron hoops to keep the roof up, and nogs and sprags festooned all over the place like beads in a Rastafarian hairdo. We were inside a whale's ribcage, a great big mechanical whale creaking and clanking through a coal tar sea. Swallowed by the darkness, we were all little Jonahs inside the whale's belly.

So we were there at last, in the small intestines of the Rhondda Valley, and it was treacle black in there. Sloe black. A landscape of smells. I've always liked the smell of coal and pencils. Carbon. Compacted a bit more it turns into jet, then diamonds. It's the same with people. The richer they are the harder they get.

But it's no good. Down here in the dark, the past won't come back to me. Pity. It smells just right. Musty and old. I'd hoped that the darkness, the drop in temperature, would help. But there are others humans snuffling around me, and I can't concentrate. I would have to be alone.

We prepare to leave. Darkness has failed me; my obdurate memory has sealed itself in and refused to cooperate. I'm not even allowed to have Korsakov's Syndrome, a drunkard's complaint in which lost memories are replaced with fantastical inventions. Or euphoric recall, the romantic false memory system used by cocaine addicts to exaggerate the pleasures and diminish the pain of their trips.

Back on the surface I mentioned food.

'Fancy a nibble?' I asked as we sauntered around the knick knack area. 'Because I've made some rather special sandwiches for us today.'

I looked smug, and she made *I'm like soo impressed* eyes.

We walked out underneath the oversized miner's lamp and found a rough-hewn bench near a children's maze. As I unpacked my mini-feast I regaled her with some facts about Britain's commercial sandwich industry, which now employs more people than the farming industry – over 300,000 according to some estimates.

Top varieties:

1 cheese
2 unflavoured chicken
3 ham
4 tuna
5 bacon
6 flavoured chicken
7 cheese salad.

Each year more than 5.5 billion lunchboxes are packed for children in the UK.

'Wow,' said Olly through a mouthful of food. 'That's a hell of a lot.'

That morning, as the dawn chorus twanged my ears, I had stood in the garden for a while, drawing in some fresh air. I've told you much about telescopes; but I also like looking at the small things around us, the little things in life. I watched leaves take shape in the gathering light. On one leaf I noticed a squadron of flies in military formations, parked neatly in rows on the blade, between the veins, all of them painted gunmetal grey. They stood completely still. I admired their microcosmic tidiness. I like standing in the garden while most people are asleep, looking at very small things. Detail therapy. Tiny animals and thumbnail Monets in the lichen patches. Droplets lodged in the petals, tumescent water-boulders.

Anyway, as I studied the flies I thought of the day ahead and made plans. Having formed a mental itinerary I dwelt briefly on food. In particular, I considered what sort of sandwiches I'd provide for our trip, since it really was my turn. I'd insisted.

I settled on something special: a mango and mint salsa sandwich with diced mango, red onion and vine tomatoes plus fresh lime juice, rice vinegar, sunblushed tomato chutney and fresh mint leaves, sliced. All this went on a tomato and chilli bread smeared liberally with crème fraiche and low fat cheese. The best yet. Out of this world. To accompany it I chose individual bottles of Brecon Carreg water, high in calcium and magnesium, and an ideal compliment to the mango. You may be surprised to know that some of the world's top restaurants now employ a water *sommelier*. Absolutely no bloody kidding.

Olly was knocked out by the picnic. We rounded it off with two tubs of sherry trifle. Brilliant. We chatted comfortably about various things, including my *picnic in the snow* film project at college. I'd already chosen Captain Oates, Karol Karol the Polish hairdresser, and Dr Zhivago to join me on the tartan rug – but which film character should I choose next? Actually, I'd already decided. I wanted a wise fool, an eccentric, a madman who'd keep us all entertained with his tall stories – who better than Baron Munchausen, the daddy of all bullshitters? I couldn't remember if Terry Gilliam's 1988 version, *The Adventures of Baron Munchausen*, contained the famous snow story but I found a version of it in Rudolph Erich Raspe's original book and it goes like this:

I set off from Rome on a journey to Russia, in the midst of winter...

The country was covered with snow, and I was unacquainted with the road. Tired, I alighted, and fastened my horse to something like a pointed stump of a tree, which appeared above the snow; for the sake of safety I placed my pistols under my arm, and laid down on the snow, where I slept so soundly that I did not open my eyes till full daylight. It is not easy to conceive my astonishment to find myself in the midst of a village, lying in a churchyard; nor was my horse to be seen, but I heard him soon after neigh somewhere above me. On looking upwards I beheld him hanging by his bridle to the weather-cock of the steeple. Matters were now very plain to me: the village had been covered with snow overnight; a sudden change of weather had taken place; I had sunk down to the churchyard whilst asleep, gently, and in the same proportion as the snow had melted away; and what in the dark I had taken to be a stump of a little tree appearing above the snow, to which I had tied my horse, proved to have been the cross or weather-cock of the steeple!

Without long consideration I took one of my pistols, shot the bridle in two, brought the horse down, and proceeded on my journey.

The Baron was just perfect, and Olly agreed with my choice as we sat together in the Rhondda that afternoon. My project was coming together. Soon I would have a fine group of people stumbling out of their films and joining me for a picnic. All I had to do now was to write a dialogue for all of us as we sat and munched our way through the chocolate cake.

Before the aptly-named Walter Coffin sank the first pits in the 1850s a squirrel could cross the whole of this area by leaping from one branch to another. But huge deposits of high quality coal made the Rhondda one of the biggest coal-producing areas in the world by the end of the nineteenth century, with 53 collieries in a strip of land only sixteen miles long. The population soared from about 3,000 in 1860 to over 160,000 in 1910. At one stage a miner was being killed every six hours.

On an April morning in 1877 a huge inundation of water, which had built up in an abandoned seam nearby, burst into the mine at Tynewydd. Two of the fourteen men underground were drowned immediately, as were a number of horses. The flood waters chased five of the miners onto higher ground, where they were trapped – and with the waters rising it was only a short matter of time, seemingly, before they were drowned too. But a bubble of air held the floodwater at bay.

The men started digging themselves out and by the following morning they had burrowed eight yards through coal and rock. Their picks were heard by rescuers, who started digging towards them. With only a thin wall of coal left between them one of the trapped miners – a young man named William Morgan – broke through, but the sudden outflow of compressed air flung his body into the narrow opening, killing him instantly. His four workmates, including his father, who witnessed his terrible death, were rescued.

Spotting air bubbles coming through the water from the workstation of a miner called Edward Williams and his fetch-and-carry boy, Robert Rogers, rescuers sank a shaft towards their faint voices and taps, which suddenly fell silent. When they finally broke through it was too late – both had drowned in the rising water.

Rescuers concentrated their efforts on another part of the mine, thought to be the likeliest place to find survivors. Four deep-sea divers searched the flooded galleries, venturing over 600 feet into the black waters, but strong currents forced them to abandon their mission. Massive pumps were put to work and after two days the water had lowered enough to allow a tunnel to be cut downwards. Four teams of four men worked around the clock in three-hour shifts, and eventually faint tapping sounds indicated that men were still alive below. The news spread like wildfire throughout the country and newspaper reporters flocked to the Rhondda. Before long the rescuers were close to the imprisoned men, who were huddled together on a ledge in a tiny cavity. Hunger had forced them to eat the wax from their candles, and they were completely exhausted. They sang hymns to raise their spirits, although one of them, a young boy, became distraught and frequently cried out for his mother. The rescue, which was complex and incredibly dangerous, ended when the leader of the four men on shift, Isaac Pride, aged 24, broke through to the trapped men, alone and in complete darkness. Isaac was thrown down by escaping air but recovered quickly and enlarged the hole. Trapped for over nine days by now, the men were too weak to stand and Isaac used his body as a human bridge so that they could be pulled to safety. Many of the rescuers were given medals and jubilant newspapers ran headlines like *Life from the dead.*

We left the Rhondda to its own devices in the rain. The greys were frolicking like lambs by now. We were on a bus again and we were all thrown into the air when we hit a bump in the road, or an iceberg, or maybe it was a coalberg. Farewell to thee fair Rhondda. As we zoomed up the dual carriageway to Merthyr I thought I saw an endless conga, black-clad but happy, snaking its way along the banks of the Taf. The experience had been too much for me, obviously.

Inscribed on the tomb of that famous iron man of Merthyr, Robert Crawshay, is the epitaph: *God Forgive Me.*

It was the task of the twentieth century to forgive Robert Crawshay.

But many people in Merthyr are still trying to forgive God.

I am a footballer. I have told you this, many times. I was in the business of making connections. Pass-pass-pass-pass-goal. A movement on the soccer field is a sentence with clauses and punctuation marks. There are some who argue that words are the curse of mankind, that they constrain the mind rather than free it. Like many, I am fascinated by the word on the page, by the fact that the sea of white around each letter is sometimes more meaningful – more emancipating? – than the words themselves. Books as liquid charts, slopping from one hand to the next. Sentences as sea-bound glaciers with their stony meanings trapped inside them, debris. Memories as terminal moraines. Each page a white mist, a spell upon the land, crowded with words which have forgotten their childhoods. *Oblivion*: etymology unknown.

And so I navigate this last dangerous sound using the words of others; listening to the sonic of their experiences and trying to find my own position on the map.

In 1992 the German academic and writer WG Sebald, who spent many years working in England, set off to explore Suffolk. His tour was a carefree one, initially. But as he walked through the countryside he experienced a series of intense encounters and witnessed *traces of destruction reaching far back into the past*. His health collapsed during that year and he was admitted to hospital.

He recorded his travels in *Rings of Saturn*, a phantasmagoria of fragments and memories in which the past and the present intermingle; the living seem like supernatural apparitions, while the dead are vividly present. Exemplary sufferers such as Joseph Conrad and Roger Casement people the author's solitude, along with various eccentrics such as Major George Wyndham Le Strange, who lived in a Suffolk manor house, and who became incredibly eccentric as he grew old. Since he had worn out his wardrobe and saw no point in buying new clothes,

> Le Strange would wear garments dating from bygone days which he fetched out of chests in the attic as he needed them. There were people who claimed to have seen him on occasion dressed in a canary-yellow frock coat or a kind of mourning robe of faded violet taffeta with numerous buttons and eyes. Le Strange, who had always kept a tame cockerel in his room, was reputed to have been surrounded, in later years, by all manner of feathered creatures: by guinea fowl, pheasants, pigeons and quail, and various kinds of garden and song birds, strutting about him on the floor or flying

around in the air. Some said that one summer Le Strange dug a cave in his garden and sat in it day and night like St Jerome in the desert. Most curious of all was a legend that... the Major's pale skin was olive-green when he passed away, his goose-grey eye was pitch-dark, and his snow-white hair had turned to raven-black.

This cave I will mark on my map; I may need to find it later. A rainbow above the town is strengthening. Wouldn't it be strange if the colours were reversed, with the red on the inside... would our aesthetics be altered completely? By the way, if you look closely you'll notice that the inside of the rainbow is always lighter than the outside.

The Lakota Indians of North America have a story about colours. Two men out hunting meet a beautiful young woman dressed in white buckskin, carrying a bundle on her back. Overcome by bad thoughts, one of them approaches her – but a white mist surrounds him and he disappears. Nothing remains but a skeleton when the mist rises. The second man is told by the woman to return home and prepare a lodge for her, and when she walks into his village he has completed his task. *I have come from heaven,* she tells the people of the village, *and I am here to tell you how to live, and to teach you about your future on earth.* She gives them maize, introduces them to the pipe, and teaches them the seven sacred ceremonies. She gives them colours for the four winds or directions. When she has finished teaching them she turns into a buffalo calf which changes colour – from white to black, to red, and finally to yellow, representing the colours of the four directions. Then she disappears.

Which brings me to a fitting coda – another passage from ap Llwyd's masterpiece, *Water-Divining in the Foothills of Paradise.* I must ask you to return with me to that little Italian café some-where on a hill in Wales, in a busy town, looking down on a harbour. Ap Llwyd gives no clues, and we cannot even guess where it might be. You may remember that, when we left him, ap Llwyd had found seven interconnected wells which had a common source, deep inside the mountain below him.

Torch in hand, he had stood at the mouth of the cave, wondering whether or not he should go down in search of the source of the water. To do so alone would be very dangerous. But he believed that deep within the earth he would resolve some-thing important about himself: he would put himself to the ultimate test, and he would emerge either whole or damaged beyond measure. I quote ap Llwyd:

As I stood at the entrance to that cave, my mind flitted back to the café, and to my great friend Stefano. He had been in high spirits when I left; if I remember correctly he was going through an intensely religious phase at that time and invariably wore a T-shirt bearing the slogan:

A CHRIST IS FOR LIFE
NOT JUST FOR DOGMAS

of which he was immensely proud. 'I pray for you every hour,' Stefano had shouted through a cloud of steam as he dispensed one of his wonderful cappuccinos. I paused in the doorway to look back at him. What a crazy man he was, with his heavy Hoxton Handle moustache and his hairy, ape-like arms. His teeth gleamed through the festoonery on his face, and his Groucho eyebrows arched up and down in caterpillar waves as he greeted his customers.

'I will see you in a week or so,' I said across the room.

'Maybe, maybe not so quick,' he shouted back, and he suddenly looked serious. 'Something big is happening, yes? You go careful. You mind out. I have a feeling about this one. Think before you jump. Remember the Well of Souls. I don't want to pay for your requiem.'

I laughed. 'Don't worry Stefano! I know what I'm doing.'

He cocked his head in that appealing way of his and his lustrous eyes questioned me in the shadows of his caterpillars. I became aware of a body close to me, trying to enter the café, so I stepped aside and extended an arm towards Stefano, who froze and stopped what he was doing; indeed, a lull fell over all his patrons. I turned, and realised why they were all mesmerised, for the girl who walked in was so beautiful I was stunned into silence too. I glimpsed her face as she gave an almost imperceptible nod of thanks. I waved goodbye but no one noticed. And there was no one to notice me now, either, as I walked the first hundred yards into the cave. I noticed some marks made by a mammoth sharpening its tusks, so I knew immediately that this portal was very old. Dimly, in the far distance, I thought I could hear a whisper of water. Bats chittering above me in the darkness made the last noise I heard as I started the long, slow descent into the interior. You may wonder what went through my mind at that point. It was this, for I am in no position to withhold information from you now: a vague plan, a strange formulation had been occupying my mind ever since I had discovered the link between the wells, and a common source of water for them. I knew that in finding that source, and in staying by it for seven nights in total darkness without food or human company, I could put myself to the ultimate test. It would be like dropping a huge weight on myself and seeing if I would survive. I increasingly saw myself as two people: one was a building and the other a scaffold, and either the scaffold had to be dismantled or the building had to be thrown to the ground and then rebuilt. But I had no idea where to start. So my sojourn underground was the equivalent of testing both structures by dropping the whole weight of my life onto them. I hoped that one of them would survive, making it possible for me to start a new life with a True Self. The *real* me.

There was another possible outcome, of course, and it sent a frisson of fear through me as I plunged deeper and deeper below ground. The chill of that possibility seeped into my body as I heard the murmur strengthen, as my ears began to respond to the torrent of liquid life below me. And that possibility, of course, was that the house and the scaffold would both be destroyed, and that there would be nothing left. Nothing at all – and that I would be no more…

As we all know, ap Llwyd did survive. One can only wonder what happened to him during those seven nights. How, for instance, did he keep track of time? Did his mind play tricks with him? Was he frightened? Did he reach a state of enlightenment? Was it his True Self which survived or his False Self – and how could anyone tell them apart? I am told that he felt unable to tell the whole story in *Water-Divining in the Foothills of Paradise*, but that he intended to reveal all in a sequel. Unfortunately, that sequel has not yet been written. Many years have drifted by. I am told he is *too happy* now to commit his memories to public record. I'm not sure what he means by that. Can anyone be *too happy* to remember, or to want to remember?

But we have to leave him now. He has already taken up valuable time. We have our own little quest to complete, as we wait for the fair Olly to surface again.

I went in search of an explanation of *True Self and False Self*. The trail led me to a man called Donald Winnicott, regarded by some as the British Freud.

'We have yet to tackle the question of what life itself is about,' he wrote late in his career, in 1967.

He proposed a theory of True Self.

The experience of aliveness can't be taken for granted, he said. People need to *feel* real. People who experience a severe failure in their early environment often feel as if they never started to exist. And although they have complied with their surroundings their lives feel futile.

'Feeling real is more than existing, it is finding a way to exist as oneself... and to have a self into which to retreat for relaxation,' said Donald.

The child who cannot develop a True Self retreats into a false existence, a False Self. The False Self hides and protects the True Self as a nurse looks after a child. It replaces the True Self and acts out the role of the real person.

The True Self lives a secret subterranean life, waiting for the day when it can thrive again. Only the True Self can be creative and only the True Self can feel real.

I have a childish analogy for you. Imagine a new house – it hasn't been built properly. There's something wrong with the foundations: plenty of sand but no cement. So scaffolding has been erected around the house, and hoardings put up to disguise the problem. To complete the cover-up, a perfect copy of the ailing house has been painted onto the hoardings, so that no one can see the difference at a distance.

Are you still with me? Because I'm off now. Do you remember our quest? I have summoned four eccentric Welshmen to meet me – and PC 66 – on the summit of Pumlumon Arwystli, smack bang in the centre of Wales. And why?

To complete some unfinished business. To kill off, once and for all, the monstrous man known to us all by now as Mr Cassini. There will be seven of us in all, waiting for him, if you include Gelert the dog. Our mountain has three sumptuous cairns on its summit. In short, my friends, I have summoned every source of magic at my disposal to rid us of this tinpot tyrant, so that Olly can sleep safely in her bed again.

10
THE TIDE COMES IN

The trial on the mountain:
Mr Cassini's nemesis

I WANT to tell you why I'm on Pumlumon Arwystli, a mountain in the middle of Wales. The day is dawning and I'm in a little world of my own again: I'm indulging in a spot of detail therapy – I'm lying with my chin on the soggy ground, looking into a miniature world of heather stalks lit by fairy lights (shiny little dewdrops) and pretending to be Lemuel Gulliver – tiny, afeared, and lost in a forest in Brobdingnag. I'm a small boy again and I'm taking part in a children's play: a fairy tale without fairies. Don't ask me why. Who shouts *look behind you* loudest at the panto: the child or the parent? It's something to do with that. We're at a panto, and the grown-ups can be as childish as they like. Go on, pretend. Boo and hiss when you see Mr Cassini. Shout *look behind you* when he enters stage left, pursued by bears.

Gelert the dog is lying by my side, panting his revolting doggy breath into my left ear. It's cold and it's dismal – yes, conditions are perfect. We wouldn't want Mr Cassini to face his nemesis on a nice sunny morning, would we?

To set the scene: we're in a region of bogland. *Uncertain sponge with black pitchy water*, as WF Peacock described it two centuries ago. It hasn't changed much. *Dark herbage thrives and its complexion is just about as ghostly and healthless as you can imagine,* he added rather uncharitably. Somewhere on the slopes below me, at Hyddgen, the fabulous Welsh hero Owain Glyndwr rekindled his great rebellion in the summer of 1401 by routing a force of English soldiers and Flemish mercenaries – a great victory and a highpoint in Welsh warfare. Owain is regarded with mixed feelings: to many he is still the ultimate icon of Welsh independence; others see him as an ancient Arthur Scargill who led his men to a final, doom-laden battle against the forces of evil. Like all mythical heroes, from Christ to King Arthur, Owain Glyndwr has never been allowed to die. His death was never recorded: he simply vanished into the mist. Like Arthur, he is expected to return one day to save his country.

But I have chosen Pumlumon Arwystli for other reasons. It *feels* right. Two great rivers begin their journey on either side of it: the Severn and the Wye. Perhaps this mountain is given its tinge of gravitas by the massive cairns on its summit; or perhaps the regret I detect in the air around me comes from another sad story from Wales' past: the story of Hafren. According to legend, Hafren (the Welsh name for the Severn) was a little girl – and a king's love child – who was bound and thrown into a river, together with her mother, by a vindictive queen.

'The land between the two rivers is known as Fferllys, and is the home of the Tylwyth Teg, the fairyfolk,' says Richard Sale in *Best Walks in Southern Wales*. 'On this land the ferns (of which there are not many) bear a small blue flower on St John's Eve. If the seeds of the flowers are gathered in white cloth – no hand must touch them – the gatherer will become invisible so that he/she may enter a lover's room undetected. Alternatively, if you stay at Fferllys, an elf will exchange your seeds for a purse of gold.'

Please, I beg you – no jokes about the national elf service.

There's another reason for choosing this tump. We're at the centre of my homeland. As in Ireland, France, England, Egypt and India, the traditional division of Wales is into North-South rather than East-West. So I stand on a fulcrum. And there is yet another reason, a third motive for being here. As in Ireland, there is evidence that Wales was divided into five realms long ago, and that the realm between the Wye and the Severn was the fifth dominion (the *pum* in Pumlumon means five). This fifth dominion symbolised the whole. There's a five-peaked world mountain in Chinese tradition too. So, as I await the arrival of Mr Cassini, I will have invoked all the major magical numbers of the Celtic world:

Three (cairns)

Four (eccentrics)

Five (dominions – North, South, East, West, and *Here*, or where we're standing, the navel or *omphalos* of the world: similarly, the Islamic Kaaba inside the great mosque in Mecca, containing the sacred Black Stone, is the point of communication between God and man, the heart of existence; the seven anticlockwise circuits made by pilgrims symbolise the seven attributes of God)

Seven (four eccentrics, PC 66, me, and a dog in attendance)

Nine (following a Welsh tradition, I have lit a small symbolic fire made from nine sticks collected by nine men from nine different types of trees)

Twenty-seven (the number of seeds from the aforementioned fern with a small blue flower which I've eaten to render myself invisible – thus making me feel quite woozy, incidentally).

PC 66 has implemented a cunning ploy of his own; he has instructed one of the rainbow messengers to lodge a couple of possibilities in Mr Cassini's wicked mind: that *The Dexter Propensity* will be an international best-seller, and that the men he's about to meet on the mountain will make excellent mannequins in his front room. PC 66 has been ingenious. I too, have been resourceful: I have found a relevant passage in the *Vita Merlini* to amuse me while I digest my magical seeds:

> In happened one time while we were hunting in the lofty mountains of Arwystli that we came to an oak which rose in the air with its broad branches. A fountain flowed there, surrounded on all sides by green grass, whose waters were suitable for human consumption; we were all thirsty and we sat down by it and drank greedily of its pure waters. Then we saw some fragrant apples lying on the tender grass. The man who saw them first quickly gathered them up and gave them to me, laughing at the unexpected gift. I distributed the apples to my companions, and I went without any because the pile was not big enough. The others laughed and called me generous, and eagerly attacked and devoured them and complained because there were so few of them. Without any delay a miserable sadness seized them; they quickly lost their reason and like dogs bit and tore each other, and foamed at the mouth and rolled on the ground in a demented state. Finally, they went away like wolves filling the vacant air with howlings.

All I need, to complete the picture, is a Yanomami shaman by my side to instruct me in the journey of the soul: a journey to a sacred place to discover cosmic intent – an act of mental dissociation, brought on with sacred plants, or fasting, or sensory deprivation accompanied by chanting and beating of drums. We have only to wait now. Everything will fall into place. *I'm in control* I say to myself over and over again. *I'm in control.*

I'm sitting in a little niche within the tumbled rocks of the central cairn on Pumlumon Arwystli. It's a dank and dismal morning in February. Gelert the dog is sniffing the air and whining. Is there someone approaching? Yes indeed! We have our first visitor of the day. I scramble to the top of the cairn, and the bleached stones make an odd clonking noise as they bang against each other. Down below me I see a head bobbing in the heather, and it belongs to Huw Llwyd of Cynfael. He has kept his tryst.

He scrambles to the top of the mountain, and he's talking to himself. He sees Gelert. He approaches him warily, making those appeasing *there's a good boy* noises we make when we're trying to make friends with a donkey-sized wolfhound. Gelert licks his hand, and I say *Hullo Huw Llwyd of Cynfael*. He nearly jumps out of his skin. He fetches a knife from his belt and crouches aggressively, looking around him warily.

Silly me. I've forgotten I'm invisible on account of the 27 seeds I've swallowed. I'm feeling pretty mellow, actually. I have a fit of the giggles.

'Don't worry Huw,' I say. 'It's me, Duxie. I'm over here, on top of the central cairn, but I'm invisible on account of the 27 seeds I've swallowed.'

Huw growls, puts his knife in its scabbard, and sits down. He holds his head between his hands. Another hangover, I assume. 'You'll find a bottle of grog in the picnic basket,' I say.

'The what?' he replies tetchily.

'In that basket over there,' and I point (uselessly) to the foot of a neighbouring cairn.

He finds the bottle and jokes with Gelert about *the hair of the dog*. That's an old joke, then. Next to arrive – I can see him walking along the path from Glaslyn – is the Reverend Griffiths, and he's singing *Psalm 23* in an unshakeable, unshaking voice:

The Lord is my shepherd; I shall not want.
    He maketh me to lie down in green pastures: he leadeth me beside the still waters...
    Yea, though I walk through the valley of the shadow of death, I will fear no evil: for thou art with me; thy rod and thy staff they comfort me.

Thou preparest a table before me in the presence of mine enemies: thou anointest my head with oil; my cup runneth over...

I wasn't sure whether to *lie down in green pastures* and *preparest a table* constituted the first reference, ever, to a picnic, but I had a present ready for the Rev Griffiths – another bottle of the excellent port we'd enjoyed a few days previously in Llandegla. He sat down next to Huw and swigged it contentedly. 'This is the life,' he said.

'Too right,' said Huw. I was glad they were getting on.

Soon we had two more guests. Merlin appeared out of nowhere, made a beeline for the picnic basket, and opened the wicker lid. 'Aha!' he said triumphantly. 'I see you've bought the cake tin, Duxie!'

I had to restrain him. 'Later,' I said, tugging it from his grasp. He wasn't pleased. I noticed that he wore an amulet and held a *grimoire*, or book of spells, containing words of power. And then came Arthur Machen, rather morosely I thought, panting along the saddle from the direction of Pumlumon Fawr, with a small brass telescope tucked underneath his left arm. 'Didn't know it was going to be this far,' he complained grumpily. 'Might not have come if...'

I appeased him with a king-size bar of Twix and a bottle of Montgomery Water. Sitting next to Merlin, munching away quietly, he seemed mollified. Merlin eyed the Twix enviously so I gave him one too. Everyone seemed happy. I hadn't intended to start the picnic until afterwards, but what the hell. They deserved it. They were my friends now. We were a company of men, capable of anything. Great deeds. The expulsion of Mr Cassini was a minor matter. Arthur Machen told me, in a splutter of crumbs, to view the mountain peaks of Wales, in every direction.

'Behold,' he said. 'Look what I've arranged for you. Neat, eh?'

I looked all around me, to the North and the East, to the South and the West. On every peak, near and far, I could see little figures, standing expectantly.

'They're all looking towards us, waiting,' he said, cramming the stub of a finger of Twix into his mouth.

'Who are they?' I asked.

'The White People of course,' he said. Merlin clapped him on the back and laughed.

'Wonderful,' he said. 'We shall have such fun.'

Mr Cassini was late arriving. He was in a *very* bad mood. I could tell at a distance; at a very great distance, in fact – as he emerged from the Hafren Forest way below me, because I'm good at that sort of thing. It's a gift I have. I can tell from a long way off what sort of mood someone's in, and how drunk or how high he is – to the nearest glass or toke. Mr Cassini strode towards us at twice the speed of darkness, his face knotted into a gargoyle mask.

He was being trailed by the rainbow messengers, spread around him in a fan, as if they were holding the train of an invisible mantle. One of them held a writ of *habeas corpus* – a brilliant touch, which hadn't even occurred to me. I was stirred, suddenly and strongly, by waves of emotion. A hot spurt of feeling welled up inside my chest. That old clenched feeling inside me. And then the warm tears. The well inside me bubbled and flowed – it's an ancient, primitive force within us all. By now the effects of the 27 seeds had worn off, I had re-materialised, and I was feeling awful. Arthur Machen put his arm around my shoulders.

'Been there mate,' he said consolingly. 'Don't worry – we'll sort this one out for you. Just you sit and watch.'

I was grateful to him. I sat down on top of the central cairn and watched Mr Cassini as he arrived at the summit. I was seized, suddenly, by a fit of dread. I quaked. Every particle of self-control seemed to drain away from me. My face went numb, I was struck dumb. Mr Cassini stood with his legs apart and his hands on his hips, in High Noon style. He stared hard at me.

I dropped my gaze and wiped my nose with my right sleeve. What next? Should I say something? Fortunately for me, Merlin came to the rescue. With an almost imperceptible flicker of his right forefinger he indicated to Mr Cassini that he should sit on a large boulder, and our guest slumped on it as if his legs were about to buckle. Thank God for good friends, I thought. The rest of the company formed a circle around him and studied him in silence for a while. No one seemed to expect me to do anything, and I was glad. I could watch and listen, let everyone else get on with it. I felt an enormous sense of relief. I stopped trembling. Merlin had taken over the reins. He was in charge, comfortably and competently. I began to wonder what he might do. How would he conduct the trial? Would it be a trial by compurgation – would jurors swear sacred oaths regarding Mr Cassini's guilt or innocence? Would it be a trial by ordeal, or a trial by battle, or a trial by torture?

In the event, Merlin adopted his own irregular course of action. The trial would be conducted through the medium of books. Merlin indicated that he would choose at random from the many books I had read recently: *Water-Divining in the Foothills of Paradise, Rings of Saturn, The Wind-Up Bird Chronicle*...

'Mr Cassini,' he said. 'You have been summoned here today to face grave charges of cruelty towards your wife and children. How plead you?'

Mr Cassini said nothing, but he looked at me in a very frightening way.

Merlin fished a book out of his pocket. I recognised it immediately – it was *The Wind-Up Bird Chronicle* by Haruki Murakami. He flipped through the pages until he came to a certain point, then he addressed Mr Cassini in a steady and authoritative voice:

'Since you are apparently unwilling – or too cowardly – to make a statement on your own behalf, I will read out a passage from *The Wind-Up Bird Chronicle*,' (and here he gave me a kindly glance). I smiled back at him feebly, though I had no inkling as to why he was reading from a book I had read myself only recently. This is the passage which Merlin read out on the summit of Pumlumon Arwystli:

I must say, Mr Okada, for a man without a wife, you do keep the house clean. I'm very impressed. I myself am completely hopeless, I'm embarrassed to say. My place is a mess, a garbage heap, a pigsty. I haven't washed the bathtub for a year or more. Perhaps I neglected to tell you that I was also deserted by my wife. Five years ago. So I can feel a certain sympathy for you, Mr Okada, or to avoid the risk of misinterpretation, let me say that I can understand how you feel. Of course, my situation was different from yours. It was only natural for my wife to leave me. I was the worst husband in the world. Far from complaining, I have to admire her for having put up with me as long as she did. I used to beat her. No one else: she was the only one I could beat up. You can tell what a weakling I am. Got the heart of a flea. I would do nothing but grovel outside the house; people would call me Ushi and order me around, and I would just suck up to them all the more. So when I got home I would take it out on my wife. Heh heh heh – pretty bad, eh? And I knew just how bad I was, but I couldn't stop. It was like a sickness. I'd beat her face out of shape until you couldn't recognise her. And not just beat her: I'd slam her against the wall and kick her, pour hot tea on her, throw things at her, you name it. The kids would try to stop me, and I'd end up hitting them. Little kids: seven, eight years old. And not just push them around. I'd wallop them with everything I had. I was an absolute devil. I'd try to stop myself, but I couldn't. I couldn't control myself. After a certain point, I would tell myself that I had done enough damage, that I had to stop, but I didn't know how to stop. Do you see what a horror I was? So then, five years ago, when my daughter was five, I broke her arm – just snapped it. That's when my wife finally got fed up with me and left with both kids. I haven't seen any of them since. Haven't even heard from them. But what can I do? It's my own fault.

There was a brief silence after Merlin had ended his reading. Our wizard closed *The Wind-Up Bird Chronicle* and folded the book into his robe. He looked Mr Cassini straight in the eye and said:

'Mr Cassini, you now have an opportunity to defend yourself. We will ask you a number of questions, and you may redeem yourself or incriminate yourself, the choice is yours. Are you ready?'

Mr Cassini sat there, stooped, his arms resting on his knees, his head bent low, studying his hands which were clasped together. He rubbed him thumbs together, idly. He didn't seem unduly concerned. I almost admired his composure.

'Mr Cassini,' said Merlin again, 'could you please tell us, in your own time, if your cruel behaviour can be ascribed to any form of brain damage – some sort of injury which you sustained in the past?'

Mr Cassini: I take it that you're alluding to frontal lobe damage (at this point he stood up, brushed away a small amount of debris from the surface of his rock-throne, and then made himself comfortable again). Now let me see. Very important part of the brain: an emotional control centre, the seat of my personality. It's involved in planning, problem-solving, spontaneity, judgement, impulse control, and social and sexual behaviour. And it's the most commonly injured area. Even a relatively minor car accident can damage the frontal lobes. Many partners report that people who suffer frontal lobe damage can be different people afterwards: emotionless, detached, unloving. Their attention span and memory can also suffer. There can be a dramatic change in sexual and social behaviour. A damaged person may exhibit abnormal sexual behaviour or lose their sex drive altogether.

But in answer to your question, I have never, to my knowledge, suffered frontal lobe damage (Mr Cassini rolled himself a thick cigarette and lit it with his skull and crossbones lighter).

At this point, Merlin bowed to the company and sat down.

The next interrogator was Huw Llwyd of Cynfael, who unsheathed his knife and tapped it on a nearby rock as he formed his question: the blade gleamed in the wan sunshine, sending rays directly into Mr Cassini's eyes. I think Huw did this purposefully. Having planted himself squarely in front of Mr Cassini, so that his shadow fell on the tyrant, he asked him this question: 'I have been told that violence in the home may be rooted in alcohol abuse, mental illness, brain damage and social deprivation. But people who are repeatedly violent may be psychologically *different*. The word psychopath is used sometimes. Would you define yourself as a psychopath?

Mr Cassini cleared his throat and drew unsuccessfully on his roll-up, then threw it in the heather.

Mr Cassini: There are problems with discussing the term psychopath, since there are differences between American and European definitions. A psychopath is often an intelligent person who displays a poverty of emotions, no sense of shame, and exceptional – but superficial – charm. He is manipulative, prone to irresponsible behaviour, shrewd, and mentally agile. He can talk very entertainingly but is incapable of understanding personal values. He shows no interest in human tragedy or joy as presented in literature or art. He is indifferent (except in a superficial sense) to issues of beauty and ugliness, goodness, evil, love, horror, and humour. Importantly, he cannot detect other people being moved either. He has no empathy with the emotions of other people.

At this point Mr Cassini requested something to drink and one of the rainbow messengers handed him a bottle of water from the picnic basket. It was the Decantae, I noticed, taken from a spring in the old county of Denbighshire. Mr Cassini put the bottle to his lips and glugged greedily. 'Anything stronger?' he asked Merlin, but the wizard sniggered and shook his head slowly and tellingly.

'I would like you to continue your discussion on psychopathy,' said Huw Llwyd of Cynfael.

Mr Cassini: Robert Hare's *Psychopathy Checklist*, created in the 1960s to separate psychopaths from the rest of the prison population, is still used throughout the world. The *Checklist* identifies psychopaths as impulsive, glib and superficial; egocentric and grandiose; deceitful and manipulative. They also demonstrate shallow emotions, a lack of remorse or guilt, a lack of empathy and poor behavioural controls. The typical psychopath needs excitement. He displays a lack of responsibility, extreme behavioural problems early on, and antisocial behaviour as an adult.

Huw Llwyd: You seem to know a lot about the subject, Mr Cassini.

Mr Cassini: Indeed, I have made a special study of it.

Huw Llwyd: Why would you do that?

Mr Cassini: We all want to know about things which are close to our hearts.

Huw Llwyd: Perhaps you could cite some famous cases.

Mr Cassini: Of course. You may like to know about Jack Abbott. He killed a waiter who asked him to leave a restaurant. Denying he'd done anything wrong, he said *there was no pain, it was a clean wound, and the victim wasn't worth a dime.*

Another good example is the serial killer John Wayne Gacy who murdered 33 young men and boys but claimed that he was the victim because he'd been robbed of his childhood.

Huw Llwyd: Psychopaths appear quite at ease with themselves. They can be articulate, highly intelligent, charming and convincing. True?

Mr Cassini: Yes. And to muddy the waters, we don't know if psychopathic behaviour is influenced by such factors as low birth weight, obstetric complications, poor parenting, poverty, early psychological trauma or adverse experiences. The jury is still out.

Huw Llwyd: One striking feature of psychopathy is that extremely violent and antisocial behaviour can appear at a very early age. Other telltale signs include casual and thoughtless lying, petty theft, a pattern of killing animals, early experimentation with sex, and stealing.

Mr Cassini: Correct.

Huw Llwyd: Do you consider yourself to be a psychopath, Mr Cassini?

Mr Cassini: Certainly not.

Huw Llwyd: A narcissist then? Self-obsessed, constantly in need of a woman who'll tell you how wonderful you are?

Mr Cassini: No.

Huw Llwyd: A sadist?

Mr Cassini: You imply that my wife was a masochist, and she wouldn't thank you for that.

Huw Llwyd: Perhaps you need cruelty to feel alive?

Mr Cassini: No.

Huw Llwyd: Mr Cassini, during military service I witnessed a strange affinity between the torturer and the tortured. Was yours such a relationship?

Mr Cassini: Quite definitely not. You're barking up the wrong tree, mate.

At this juncture Mr Cassini rolled a super-thin cigarette and tried to light it with his skull and crossbones lighter, which seemed to have run out of fuel; he cursed it; Merlin flicked his thumb and offered him a blue flame, much to Mr Cassini's astonishment.

The next interrogator was the Rev Griffiths, who adjusted his cassock after balancing his (nearly empty) port bottle against a rock. Was it my imagination, or had his voice thickened; did he slur his words occasionally? The Rev Griffiths adopted an air of flamboyance, with his left hand planted dramatically on his hip and his right forefinger prodding the air in front of him.

'British psychologists and criminologists tend to use the phrase Antisocial Personality Disorder,' he said to Mr Cassini. 'Do you have this disorder?'

Mr Cassini paused awhile, puffing meditatively on his ciggie. Then, using his right hand as a thought-wand, wafting cigarette smoke around him in the air, as if he were wielding a miniature incense burner, he said:

'A typical person with Antisocial Personality Disorder resorts quickly to aggression, including violence. He displays a callous unconcern for the feelings of others, a gross and persistent attitude of irresponsibility, a disregard for social norms, rules and obligations, an inability to maintain enduring relationships (though having no difficulty in establishing them) and a very low tolerance to frustration.'

Rev Griffiths: And you have displayed all of these symptoms at one time or another?

Mr Cassini: Yes.

Rev Griffiths: Pray continue.

Mr Cassini: A person with this sort of disorder won't experience guilt and won't profit from experience. Punishment means little to him. He often blames others, or gives odd reasons for his actions.

Rev Griffiths: Let me continue. Personality disorders tend to appear in late childhood, do they not? Experts look for wayward attitudes and enduring and pervasive behaviour. Later on, significant problems emerge in the workplace and in society. Am I right, Mr Cassini?

Mr Cassini: Quite correct.

Rev Griffiths: People with this sort of disorder often start off as school bullies.

Mr Cassini: Yes, about two million British people can be classified as suffering from Antisocial Personality Disorder and many of them started off as junior bullies.

Rev Griffiths: Mr Cassini, I challenge you to answer my question: do *you* suffer from an Antisocial Personality Disorder.

Mr Cassini: Categorically, no.

Rev Griffiths: How can you be so sure?

Mr Cassini: May I remind you that when Sherlock Holmes – or any detective for that matter – arrives at the scene of the crime he considers all the obvious possibilities first, and all the outlandish possibilities second. About three quarters of all murders are committed by members of the same family. The statistics are surprisingly consistent. And about three quarters of all sexual crimes are committed by members of the same family. Statistically, the family is more corrupting than the Mafia and the home is more dangerous that the fast lane of the M6 on a wet Bank Holiday Monday. Look to the family if you want reasons for my behaviour.

Mr Cassini puffed at his cigarette and appeared calm, but I couldn't help noticing that he cast furtive glances, occasionally, at the Rev Griffiths' bottle of port. Merlin noticed it too. As soon as the Rev Griffiths had finished his cross-examination I grabbed the bottle and stood provocatively in front of Mr Cassini. I swung the bottle slowly, as if it were a pendulum, in front of his eyes. Perhaps I could mesmerise him; perhaps I should click my fingers and say *look into my eyes, when I count to ten...* but Mr Cassini merely sat there, silently. He sneered at me, and said *sit down boy, this is men's work*. I didn't know how to respond to that, so I did as he said.

In the meantime the Rev Griffiths sauntered over to me and wrested the bottle from my hand. I was surrounded by a bunch of dipsomaniacs, evidently.

Merlin clapped his hands and said, 'I call Mr Arthur Machen to the stand'.

By *stand* I presumed he meant a little knoll to the right of Mr Cassini. Arthur Machen presumed so too and he walked over to it now, looking grave. Mr Cassini sniggered and said 'Bowmen of Mons? The nearest you ever got to any bowmen was a bottle of cider, mate.'

'Be quiet, Cassini,' was Arthur Machen's tart reply. Arthur raised his right hand to his mouth and a piercing whistle rang out across the land; looking around me, looking all around Wales, I saw small white figures dropping down from the summits around us and scurrying towards us along the valleys and ravines. Arthur had summoned the White People, and soon they were clustered around us, whispering incomprehensibly in their own tongue, the Xu language. And it seemed to me then that I could hear every blade of grass in Wales sibilating in the breeze.

I cannot describe these people to you because their company merged into a whole which was a feeling, an emotion rather than a physical presence. We all became aware that they could make us either supremely happy or utterly miserable. There is a brief description of them in *The Green Book*, found in a drawer by the little girl who narrates the story of *The White People*:

But a wonderful thing happened when I was about five. My nurse was carrying me on her shoulder; there was a field of yellow corn, and we went through it, it was very hot. Then we came to a path through a wood, and a tall man came after us, and went with us till we came to a place where there was a deep pool, and it was very dark and shady. Nurse put me down on the soft moss under a tree, and she said: "She can't get to the pond now." So they left me there, and I sat quite still and watched, and out of the water and out of the wood came two wonderful white people, and they began to play and dance and sing. They were a kind of creamy white like the old ivory figure in the drawing-room; one was a beautiful lady with kind dark eyes, and a grave face, and long black hair, and she smiled such a strange sad smile at the other, who laughed and came to her. They played together, and danced round and round the pool, and they sang a song till I fell asleep. Nurse woke me up when she came back, and she was looking something like the lady had looked, so I told her all about it, and asked her why she had looked like that. At first she cried, and then she looked very frightened, and turned quite pale. She put me down on the grass and stared at me, and I could see that she was shaking all over. Then she said I had been dreaming, but I knew I hadn't. Then she made me promise not to say a word about it to anybody, and if I did I should be thrown into the black pit.

I looked at the White People around us, and they fitted this description perfectly. After calling for silence, Arthur Machen addressed Mr Cassini with the following words: 'Mr Cassini, do you know that the British Government defines domestic violence as any incident of threatening behaviour, violence or abuse – psychological, physical, sexual, financial or emotional – between adults who are, or have been, intimate partners or family members, regardless of gender or sexuality?'

Mr Cassini: Yes, that sounds about right.

Arthur Machen: I'm sure that you are fully aware, also, that domestic violence is rarely a one-off incident. Almost always it's part of a pattern of abusive and controlling behaviour. The abuser seeks power over the victim. In some cases he has been heavily dependent on his mother and he transfers this dependency to his wife; there is a conflict, often, between hostility towards his wife and dependency on her. The hostility is kept in check while the wife satisfies him; but when he no longer receives her full attention – when a child is born, for instance, or when his wife looks at another man – he can become violent.

Mr Cassini: Yes, you're quite right. And domestic violence occurs across the whole of society – regardless of age, gender, race, sexuality, wealth or geography. Mostly the violence is by men against women. As long ago as 1427 Bernard of Sienna was suggesting to his male parishioners that they should exercise restraint and treat their wives with as much mercy as they would their hens and their pigs.

Arthur Machen: Children are also affected. Many are traumatised by what they witness, and there is also a strong connection between domestic violence and child abuse. One in three girls hit by her parents goes on to be abused by her boyfriends. In a way, poor behaviour by parents is adopted as a model by their children in much the same way as good parenting is adopted by children in safe homes. True?

Mr Cassini: Yes, that's correct. I believe a recent NSPCC survey revealed that one in four teenage girls believe it's acceptable for a boyfriend to hit them under certain circumstances. A third of the girls had witnessed violence in the home. A woman dies every three days at the hands of her current or former partner. One in ten mothers is sexually abused in front of her children; 33 per cent of children try to intervene during attacks on their mother.

90 per cent of children are in the same room or the next room during attacks on their mother; nearly 27,000 incidents are reported to the police in Wales every year – that's a quarter of all recorded violent crimes; there are more than 500,000 assaults on women in the home every year in Britain.'

Arthur Machen: And predatory men target vulnerable girls, don't they?

Mr Cassini: Yes, I can spot one a mile away. Insecure, quiet, damaged. They come from families of secrets and lies. They're often desperate to leave home and they're attracted to men who have a protective image. My motto is, *keep them pregnant.*

Arthur Machen: I want to concentrate on emotional and psychological abuse. Have you ever told someone they're worthless, that no one else wants them?

Mr Cassini: Frequently. My late wife was trapped by fear, paralysed by it. She'd been abused herself and she was a compulsive carer – she'd forgive me anything because she couldn't imagine herself surviving alone.

Arthur Machen: Did you force her to do things at exactly the same time or in exactly the same way?

Mr Cassini: Yes, and I kept her financially dependent – she had to come to me for every penny.

Arthur Machen: Did you try to make her believe she was mad?

Mr Cassini: Yes. Mrs Cassini actually went mad because of it. Now that's what I call a result.

Arthur Machen: No doubt you told her that the violence and abuse were her fault?

Mr Cassini: How *did* you guess. *You've made your own bed, now lie in it,* I'd say. *Don't go bleating to your family – they warned you against me right from the start.*

Arthur Machen: You turned away her visitors, controlled her friendships?

Mr Cassini: Too right I did.

Arthur Machen: You didn't allow her to go out, or to see her family and friends... you didn't allow her to be alone with other people, or to use the phone, or to send letters?

Mr Cassini: Worse than that mate. I sometimes locked her in a room. I told her she was a bad mother, I encouraged the children to upset her. I kicked her cat, I broke her belongings, I accused her of lying...

Arthur Machen: Every trick in the book. You disgust me. And you continued to belittle her?

Mr Cassini: I told her she was fat, I told her she was ugly and useless, I made her believe that no one else liked her.

Arthur Machen: Did you threaten to abuse her in front of the children if she didn't obey your every whim?

Mr Cassini: I took it all to the absolute limits, Arthur. I even told her I'd find her and kill her if she left me. I'm a tyrant, after all. Tyranny begins in the home. I have to act the part of a domestic despot, isn't that right?

Arthur Machen: Is that how you see yourself?

Mr Cassini: Too right. Once you've taken that first step – slapped your first slap, threatened your first threat, a force greater than gravity itself takes hold of you, pulls you, drags you into the role. You become an actor. And some people actually encourage it. Let me give you an example. When Eisaku Sato, a former prime minister of Japan and a Nobel Peace Prize winner, was revealed as a wife-beater, his popularity rocketed. His wife commented 'Yes, he's a good husband, he only beats me once a week'.

Arthur Machen: But you could have changed. You could have rewritten the script.

Mr Cassini: It's not as easy as that. There are forces beyond our control. Many husbands who batter their wives are extremely weak men who have suffered great insecurity as young children – they are emotional people, who tend to act first and think later. The more powerless a person is, the more likely he is to compensate for his weakness by sadism. He may even risk his life for a moment of absolute power. In the final analysis, domestic violence is an advanced form of attention-seeking. Traditionally, society has colluded with men by giving them the right to do as they wish in their own home.

Arthur Machen: Excuses, excuses.

Mr Cassini: No, I'll give you an example. Take the A55, running along the North Wales coast. It's merely a strip of tarmac, yet it has a profound influence on the region, and that's because it brings things in and takes things out. New things travel inwards from the New World, old things travel out from the Old World. The road is a rent in the fabric of time, so to speak. Likewise with domestic abuse: once you've torn the fabric of reason and compassion you can move in and out of it. A prolapse has been created, a hernia... a weakness.

Arthur Machen: But you could have taken physic, you could have cured the sickness.

Mr Cassini: It's not as simple as that. Once you're cast in a new role it isn't easy to dive in and out of the two parts you're playing, the old and the new. It becomes easier to stay in the same costume. You don't find Cassius changing his part in mid-play, do you? That's because it's easier to keep the frown than to change your expression all the time. And the gravity pulls and pulls... it talks to you, it says *just how far can you go with this?* It says to you *now they all fear you anyway, you might as well do the job properly.* And they all look at you so accusingly, so bloody hurt, and you feel like doing it all over again just to fulfil their expectations. I raged against the world. I hated seeing *others* happy when *I* couldn't be happy.'

There was a sticky pause while Arthur Machen mopped his brow with an old red silk handkerchief which had large yellow spots all over it. He looked pale: this had become an ordeal for him, and Merlin spotted that too – he ambled over to him and put his arm gently around his shoulder.

'That's fine Arthur,' he said. 'Take a rest now – you deserve it.' And Arthur was only too glad to rest his body on a cairn. He kept his eyes on Mr Cassini throughout; I could see the revulsion growing in him, that a man could carry on hurting people whilst recognising so well the forces which impelled him.

Now Merlin himself took a stance in front of Mr Cassini, closer than anyone else had stood. He studied the seated man. Under normal circumstances a man such as he might be stewing in his own guilt, but Mr Cassini showed no signs of remorse. He relit his crumpled rollie, pinching the stub between thumb and index finger.

Merlin addressed him thus:

'Mr Cassini, are you aware of the Welsh term *angel penffordd, cythraul pentan?*'

Mr Cassini: Indeed I am.

Merlin: Could you give me a rough translation?

Mr Cassini: Something like *an angel on the highway, a devil in the home?*

Merlin: Yes, it's used quite often to describe men who act impeccably in public yet behave appallingly in their own homes. And there are many such men, are there not?

Mr Cassini: Millions, I should think.

Merlin: Are you such a man?

Mr Cassini: Yes.

Merlin: And do you believe that alcohol played a part in your behaviour – did it act as an agent when you abused your wife and children?

Mr Cassini: Indubitably. I think it played a major part. As you well know Merlin, alcohol suppresses your inhibitions, encouraging you to take the brakes off and career in any direction you wish. Basically, it comes down to this: alcohol makes nice people nicer, nasty people nastier. You can split heavy drinkers quite neatly down the middle, into benign alcoholics and malign alcoholics. Unfortunately for my family, I turned nasty with it.

Merlin: Do you regret that now?

Mr Cassini: It's a bit late for regret, isn't it? There was a time, right at the beginning, certainly, when I had regrets. But a vicious circle kicks in pretty soon. You beat your wife, you loathe yourself, you get drunk, you beat your wife. The vicious circle becomes self-fulfilling; in the end it's a comfort blanket for the abuser. We all like routine.

Merlin: And would you have acted differently, do you think, if she'd done something as soon as you started abusing her?

Mr Cassini: Yes, that's a possibility. But the daft cow loved me. She just took it.

The clouds drooped onto the hilltops around us. Soon they would lactate a soft fall of snow onto this region around us. I looked to the North and to the South; I tried to eradicate from my mind all the hurt which had been wrought by men like Mr Cassini.

And then I saw a corpse candle hovering in the air above us, and said to everyone that death was near. We all looked up at the mysterious red flame of the Jack O'Lantern and studied it for size, for we all knew that its dimensions would indicate the age and size of the victim. It was a tall rush light, foretelling the death of a man. We looked towards Mr Cassini, but he merely laughed.

'You can never kill me off,' he said dismissively. 'None of you can do that. Imprison me perhaps, but kill me? No, you can't do that. You haven't got the power.'

'We'll see, Cassini,' said Arthur Machen, who evidently hated the man by now.

The time had come for us to wind up the interrogation. We were all tired. A flock of huge impasto clouds had spread themselves over the western horizon, and we knew that snow was near. It was Merlin, running out of patience by now, who brought the proceedings to an end. He questioned Mr Cassini one last time:

Merlin: Did Mrs Cassini do anything in response to your actions?

Mr Cassini: She left a couple of times, but I wheedled, I begged... she always came back. And then I used the children. She was truly frightened then.

Merlin: You were beyond help by now?

Mr Cassini: On a weird, out-of-control carousel. It was burlesque... I was a painted villain with a blacked-up face. Life became fundamentally unintelligible; I was an excess to others and myself. If there are such things as yin and yang, black and white, good and evil, then I was being polarised... my whole being was being reconfigured along the magnetic lines of yin, and black, and evil. I was being sucked into a black hole. The prophesy of the past became self-fulfilling.

Merlin: How do you mean?

Mr Cassini: Evil, sin, call it what you will, uses a system of echoes and photocopies.

Merlin: You're about to blame your past, I can see that. You're going to bleat about your own childhood, aren't you?

Mr Cassini shrugged his shoulders and looked at the ground wearily. I almost felt sorry for him.

Mr Cassini: The slaps of history echo down the years, that's all I'm saying.

Merlin: And each generation memorises the sound, repeats it as faithfully as it can like a nursery rhyme – a clapping song in the playground. Is that the angle you're going to take?

Mr Cassini: Possibly. I'm looking for causes. There do have to be causes, don't there? I wasn't created in a vacuum, was I?

Merlin: No, you've got a point there, but I don't want any feeble excuses.

Mr Cassini: I'm past looking for excuses. I wouldn't mind knowing the causes myself. We're just photocopiers, I know that. We photocopy the past, we photocopy our parents.

And we photocopy all the mistakes too. History keeps the misspellings. It's something to do with colour, also. You can photocopy for so long with a black and white cartridge, but there comes a time when you've got to work in colour.

Merlin: Go on...

Mr Cassini: You've got to have a colour cartridge in there too. My own childhood wasn't particularly happy either, you know. It was all black and white, no colour.

Merlin: OK. We're getting somewhere now.

Mr Cassini: There were five of us. My father was drunk a lot of the time. But he wasn't that bad, looking back. Not as bad as me, certainly. But he beat me. None of the others – just me, if I was naughty.

Merlin: And you felt a sense of injustice?

Mr Cassini: Yes, very much so. I had a deep resentment burning inside me for most of my childhood.

Merlin: And you carried it with you into adulthood?

Mr Cassini: Yes, there's little doubt of that. It smouldered inside me. Pain is a form of energy – you can't dispel it, only displace it... pass it on to someone else perhaps.

Merlin: If you were asked to use one word to describe the cause of your behaviour, what would it be?

Mr Cassini had a long hard think at this point. He flicked his cigarette end into the heather and began rolling another. He also looked longingly at the picnic basket.

Mr Cassini: Any grog in there?

Merlin: Quite possibly, but you'll have to wait.

Mr Cassini: (angrily) Listen, pal, don't come the high and mighty with me. You were a bloody lunatic yourself once, remember?

Merlin: Calm yourself, man.

Mr Cassini: Fuck you, pal. Just because you've reinvented yourself as Captain Bloody Marvellous, don't think you can lord it over *me* OK? Don't think for one bloody second that I've been taken in by all that tosh about you, the Mark Twain and Hollywood bullshit... I know all about your own past mate. Mad as a bloody hatter. *I talk to the trees*... and the social services wouldn't swallow that shite about your friendship with the pig either. Got one of my own. You can have a lot of fun with a pig, can't you Merlin...

Merlin: How *dare* you.

Mr Cassini: Well shut the fuck up then.

(Merlin makes an almost imperceptible movement, and Mr Cassini's newly rolled fag is dashed out of his hands in a yellow, sulphurous flash.)

Mr Cassini: Ow! What did you do that for? Bastard!

Merlin: I asked you a question. I'm still waiting for an answer.

(Mr Cassini looks confused.)

Merlin: I asked you for one word to describe the cause of your behaviour.

Mr Cassini: OK, OK. Just wait a moment – you've burnt my fingers (he rubs some of his digits in the cooling dew of the heather). Right. (slowly) I think that word would be *frustration*. Yes, the word that comes to mind is *frustration*.

Merlin: Yes, go on...

Mr Cassini: I was never what I wanted to be. I could see it all out there – money, fame, people doing what they wanted to do. I read about it, I watched it happening in films. But it never arrived. It was always a fingertip away, just beyond reach. Do you understand?

Merlin: But you've got to *make* things happen.

Mr Cassini: I never knew how. That was the problem. I could see what I wanted. I wanted to be successful, I wanted to be loved. I wanted magic but I didn't know how to use the wand, which words to use. *Abracadabra* didn't work. When I tried to get the things I wanted I always messed it up somehow. And the further it all went away from me the angrier I got. I lashed out at everything, everyone. It was just bad luck for my family that they were the closest to hand. Also, I was appearing in two plays at the same time: I was Mr Good and Mr Bad in two separate productions and I didn't want to leave either stage; I wanted to see how both plays ended.

Merlin: Fine, that's enough. You've told us enough now. We know the scenario. Nothing special after all. A nasty little control freak like the rest. Just the same old story. Ah well...

Mr Cassini (rising to his feet, infuriated) It might be the same old story to you pal, but it's my story all the same, so don't take the piss. Fuck off the lot of you. Think you're all perfect? Don't make me laugh.

Mr Cassini reserved a special look of anger for me, as good as to say that he would get me later. His eyes snarled at me, and I started shivering.

'That's enough,' said Merlin. 'He's guilty, and he hasn't even tried to hide it.'

'What shall we do with him now?' asked Huw Llwyd of Cynfael.

'Send him to the Towers of Silence!' cried the Rev Griffiths.

'Make him lie for ever among the Parsee dead and let the vultures eat him alive!'

I was warming to this idea when Huw Llwyd of Cynfael suggested: 'Send him into space like Clough Williams Ellis!'

'Pardon?' we all said, simultaneously.

'Clough Williams Ellis – the man who built Portmeirion. They sent his ashes into space in a rocket, a special firework... something like that.'

But Williams Ellis was a *nice* bloke, I complained. 'We could always give him to Cloacina, goddess of the sewers,' I added lamely.

'Listen, listen to me,' said Arthur Machen, who was almost at the end of his tether.

'Why do you think I invited the White People? Who could deal with him better than they?'

''Tis true,' added Merlin, 'they're the best in the business.'

Arthur Machen cleared his throat and addressed the encircling throng of White People, asking them how they might deal with the tyrant Mr Cassini.

There was a brief hush, and then the Queen of the White People stepped forward.

She was as beautiful as *The Green Book* portrayed her. She was whiter than any of them and taller; her eyes shone like burning rubies, and she spoke movingly about the secrets of the secrets, and about the ceremonies of the White People: the White Ceremonies, the Green Ceremonies and the Scarlet Ceremonies. Read Arthur Machen, he's the one who invented them.

The Queen of the White People produced an *aumbry* – a great golden bowl – and a green jar containing wine. She poured some of the wine into the bowl and then she laid a mannikin – a little man made of clay – very gently in the wine and washed it in the wine all over. We were frightened. A great ring of snow-topped hills appeared, encircling the hills of Wales, the little hills I loved so much. I had never seen these outer hills before. The entire world became very still and silent. The sky was heavy and grey and sad.

'What will you do now?' I asked the Queen of the White People.

With a look of utter contempt she tossed the *mannikin* on the symbolic fire I had made from nine sticks collected by nine men from nine different types of trees. Mr Cassini gave a cry of pain, and as he did so the fire went out with a startling hiss.

'Fools,' he cried, clutching the left side of his body. 'You can hurt me but you can never, ever kill me. Be aware of that fact – I am eternal. I will live in your heads for ever...

'And *you*,' he said, turning to me. His eyes screamed at me in a very angry way.

'Don't ever relax, not once. One day I'll come to get you. You'll hear a knock on the door and it'll be me, coming for you. Remember that, always.'

I shuddered. He sounded as if he meant it.

Stepping quickly onto the knoll, which had been used as a witness stand during the trial, Merlin cried: 'But we have other ways of getting rid of you, Cassini!'

From then on everything happened very quickly.

The Rev Griffiths sprang forward, grabbed Arthur Machen's brass telescope, and unscrewed the eyepiece as quickly as he could. He ran forward and took a stand immediately in front of Mr Cassini, who was still groaning with pain.

Merlin produced a vial, poured some white powder into his right palm, and threw it over Mr Cassini. There was an enormous flash, and Mr Cassini disappeared in an explosive burst; the sight and smell was very much like a reeking, noisy firework being set off. Briefly, a small black dot floated in the air, and upon seeing this the Rev Griffiths – who had very keen eyesight, evidently – swung unto action. Darting forwards with the telescope in one hand and the eyepiece in the other, he entrapped the black dot and held the telescope aloft, triumphantly.

'Behold!' he cried exultantly. 'The monster is ensnared!'

We all rushed forward to examine his catch. There was a bit of pushing and shoving as we all tried to catch a glimpse of the fly-sized Mr Cassini inside the telescope. Only the White People, full of decorum as usual, maintained their dignity by stepping back and standing in a placid, patient ring around us.

A faint buzz came from within the telescope. For a few seconds I was allowed to view its contents. As the black dot came into view I could see, clearly, that it was a tiny version of Mr Cassini, hovering waspishly inside his new prison. I could hear his tinny, hornet voice buzzing shrilly.

Then the Queen of the White People stepped forward and held out her hands, as if she were a priest taking the communion bowl. I gave her the telescope reverentially.

'What will you do with it?' I asked.

The Queen studied it for a few seconds.

'This is what we will do,' she said in Xu. How softly and delicately she lisped the words. 'We will take this telescope to a little stream of water running down the valley below us and we will drink the water with our hands, and it will taste like bright, yellow wine, and it will sparkle and bubble as it runs over beautiful red and yellow and green stones, and it will seem alive, and then we will take this thing through dark woods full of creeping thorns and whispers, and it will be a long, long way, and we will creep by a place that is bitter and dreary, through many bushes, under the low branches of trees, and through thorny thickets on the hills, full of black twisted boughs, and we will pass through a big bare place, and we will come to the kingdom of Voor where the light goes when it is put out, and inside a cave will be the great well, deep and shining and beautiful, and all around it the ground will be covered with bright, green, dripping moss, every kind of moss will be there, moss like beautiful little ferns, moss like palms and fir trees, all green as jewellery, and drops of water will hang on it like diamonds, and the water in the well will be so clear, we will try to touch the red sand at the bottom but it will be far below, and the water will bubble up but the surface will be quite smooth and full and brimming, a great white jewel, and we will leave him there. And all kinds of people will come to watch, there will be gentle folk and village folk, and some old people and some boys and girls, and quite small children, who will sit and watch, and it will be dark as they come in, except in one corner where someone will burn something that smells strong and sweet, and makes us all laugh, and the smoke will mount up red. Then there will be a singing and shouting and crying like nothing you have heard before.'

That was good enough for us.

'Brilliant,' said Merlin. 'Just the job. Do you need any sort of payment?'

'We wouldn't consider it,' said the Queen of the White People. 'This is what we do. This is what we're good at.'

'Great,' said Merlin, and then the White People left us, a long stream of excited little people, babbling in their Xu language, their Queen holding the telescope aloft in front of her. In no time at all they had disappeared in the direction of the Nant-y-Moch Reservoir. They blurred into a white, ghostly, shape-shifting mass and then disappeared over a ridge.

'Good riddance to bad rubbish,' said Merlin, wiping his hands symbolically.

'You all right?' he asked, looking at me keenly. 'You look as if you've seen a ghost.'

'Yes, I'm all right,' I said, but I wasn't. I felt quite ill. I was still coming down from the 27 seeds, and I wasn't convinced that Mr Cassini's reign of terror was over. He could come back at any time, I thought. Merlin read my thoughts.

'He's as secure as he ever will be,' he said reassuringly. 'Come on, let's have a picnic. Perhaps a slice of chocolate cake would do us all good.' And he gave me one of his special winks.

We had our picnic, and it was good – though I couldn't eat anything myself. We chatted amiable about the banalities of life, under a noonday muster of clouds, as if nothing of import had happened, as if we were a ramblers' club enjoying a day out. The chocolate cake went down very well. Combined with a few bottles of port and plenty of Montgomery Water it cast its own magic spell, and they all slumbered for a while afterwards, propped up against the cairn-stones as if they were dolls and teddy bears in a little girl's make-believe world.

At one time or another during that little feast, before we parted company, before all of us went our individual ways, I took the opportunity to ask Merlin a few questions.

His eyes looked at me fondly from underneath his yucca eyebrows, and he took a few long puffs on his clay pipe.

'I will have to return to the woods again soon,' he said. 'Every century or so I get the call again, and I have to return to my madness. It is never fully purged. No one is ever fully cleared of it. There is no such thing as catharsis, I think you know that already yourself. There are cycles, patterns, mandalas, culminations and expiations. Yes?'

I nodded. As a mere mortal, my own cycles were shorter.

'And where will I find her?'

He knew who I meant.

'Duxie, she's beautiful and intelligent, and she's in a strange town. She's sad, and she's trying to work things out. She smokes too much and she drinks too much coffee. Sometimes she cries at night in bed. You'll find her very soon, OK?'

'Promise?'

'Cross my heart and hope to die.'

'You don't really mean that, because you can't die.'

'Duxie, you can be quite pedantic at times, can't you? Relax. Take it easy for a while.'

I cleared up the picnic things and packed them into the basket.

'There's one last slice of cake,' I said to the company. But they were all asleep, all except Merlin and me.

'Share it?' he said. But I was full, and I waved my hand at the slice between us, indicating that he should have it. The hunger was leaving me; I had no need for food now.

As he munched his way through the final slice I looked at Merlin and felt as if I'd found a father. A really nice warm feeling spread through me. I felt good.

'Friends for ever?' I said to him.

'For ever and a day,' he said, adding: 'Can't get over those White People – I wonder if they really do have red and yellow and green stones in their rivers.' He contemplated this odd colour scheme.

'Talking of colours,' he said in his jokey Tommy Cooper voice, 'how do you make a snooker table laugh?'

'No idea,' I said.

'You put your hand in its pockets and tickle its balls. Boom boom!'

Afterwards, as my composure returned, I walked down the flank of Pumlumon Arwystli towards home, with Gelert the dog by my side. It was snowing, and the land around me was losing its shape; the air was blurred and the pathways scrunched below me; little pyramids of snow formed on my boots. I looked round at one point and he was standing on the summit of Pumlumon Fawr, looking down at me. I waved to him. As he waved back I dwelt briefly on the three lines of poetry he'd left me with:

> Papery moths drift to the light,
> Churr in a hand's cave,
> Then out, out.

And so we went our separate ways.

Part 3

Reality

Basho, coming
To the city of Nagoya,
Is asked to a snow party.

There is a tinkling of china
And tea into china;
There are introductions.

Then everyone
Crowds to the window
To watch the falling snow.

Snow is falling on Nagoya
And farther south
On the tiles of Kyoto.

Eastward, beyond Irago,
It is falling
Like leaves on the cold sea.

Elsewhere they are burning
Witches and heretics
In the boiling squares,

Thousands have died since dawn
In the service
Of barbarous kings;

But there is silence
In the houses of Nagoya
And the hills of Ise.

The Snow Party – Derek Mahon

11

THE TIDE GOES OUT

The interview tapes (1)

Let's go back to the beginning, to the day you met. Where were you?
In the café at the top end of town – it's run by an Italian.
Stefano's?
Yes, that's the one.
When was this?
February.
This year?
Yes, I can't remember the date exactly. Wales beat England on the Saturday.
Rugby?
Yes – Henson got a penalty in the last few minutes.
Ah yes, I remember. But you're not from the town, are you? What were you doing here?
I was taking a break. It was here or Ibiza but I couldn't afford the air fare. I've a relative living down by the harbour so I stayed with her. I needed to get away. I'd been studying too hard, and I had a few personal problems.
You're a student?
Yes, I'm trying to get some A levels.
So how did you get to know him?
He was staring at me when I walked into the caff, so I noticed him straight away. The place was pretty full, so I had to sit at a table near him. He couldn't keep his eyes off me.
Dirty old man?
No, not quite. He looked at me like he was seeing things. It turned out he thought I was one of his daughters – that's what he told me later. Hadn't seen his kids for years, apparently. He said I was the spitting image of his eldest. He was acting a bit weird.

Still staring at you?
No, he stopped after a while. He was staring at the window, with his hand in the air, like he was waiting for someone to pass so he could wave to them. But he was trying to kill a fly. After a while I saw it myself, the fly, standing very still on the window by his left hand. He tried to swat it but the fly was too quick for him. He made quite a loud bang on the glass, but he was wearing gloves so he didn't hurt himself. Then he turned to me and smiled. He said: 'I wonder if there's a big hand in the sky, waiting to get me too.' So I smiled back. Then he offered me a sweet... he was always offering me sweets. I realised fairly soon that he wasn't as crazy as he looked, once he'd stopped staring.

[That fly was a survivor, for sure. Everyone was in on the joke, now. For the first day or two it had irritated the hell out of everyone. It had escaped death repeatedly, as if by magic. Stefano the proprietor had tried every trick in the book, since the blue fly-killer on the wall had failed to attract the insect. Stefano had tried stealth, and failed. He'd tried sudden rushes from behind his counter, and failed again. He quit when he crashed into a table, sending a shower of crockery and hot coffee onto the floor. The patrons started a furtive, unofficial competition to see who could kill it. Mrs Griffiths, who was into the occult, tried to trap the fly in an empty bottle; the retired copper sprinkled a small pyramid of white sugar on his table and kept watch in a silent, malevolent stake-out – but the fly lived on. Eventually the fly was given a name – Mr Cassini.]

Go on – what happened next?
The man rested his head in his hand and closed his eyes. He was very tired, he said. His work had been very demanding. That's what he told me, anyway. He said his name was Duxie and he lived in a flat somewhere in that big council complex at the tatty end of town, somewhere on the hill above the football ground. He'd sit at home, by his window, looking down at the footie games. He said it was like playing Subbuteo. He liked watching the little men run about in waves of action. It reminded him of the sea, he said. Small tides of men swarming towards each goal and then falling back again. He described it to me in his own peculiar way.

[On the wind, sometimes, Duxie heard whistle-blasts, child-screams, manly voices shouting manly things. The only thing that Duxie had ever wanted to be – really, *really* wanted to be – was a footballer. That was a long way back, when he was in his teens: before booze and fags, before wimmin. And now he was offside by about forty years, closing in on retirement. He wheezed when he climbed the stairs. Duxie was in a stale routine. He polished his shoes and kept his gaff tidy. Everything was in its proper place, and the kitchenette was woman-clean. He hoovered every evening at a quarter to seven, before going to the snooker club.]

What did you talk about?
Colours, at first. He couldn't decide between magnolia and white. That was the main topic when we met. He asked me for advice. What colour should he paint his flat? He'd thought about it for quite some time, even consulted his mates at the snooker club. We finally agreed on white. Magnolia walls seem so corporate. White's classier. Then we talked about colours. There was a big rainbow over the town. He was quite interesting, knew a lot about them. He said Honolulu was the rainbow capital of the world. He'd never been there, said he'd love to go there. I told him I'd stayed there once. He was fascinated by that. Hadn't travelled much, by the sound of things.
He was easy to talk to?
Must have been, because I told him about the raves.
How do you mean?
We must have been talking about the colour orange, because I told him about the way I used to go to raves.
What's orange got to do with it?
When we'd finished clubbing we'd gather in the car park, some-times hundreds of us, waiting, and then someone would put one of those orange flashing lights in the rear window of a car and we'd follow, for hours sometimes, until we were in the middle of nowhere, in a wood maybe, and the rave would start.
Bit risky, talking about that to a stranger?
He liked it, he was really interested.
What did he tell you about himself?
 He told me a few things. He was quite chatty.
Try it on, did he?
Not as much as you have.

Pardon?
You heard what I said.
You don't like it when people comment on your looks?
Just drop it, OK?
OK, fine. Sorry. [pause] So what did he have to say about himself?
Oh, the usual things.

[He said his flat on the hill was comfy and tidy. He said he'd tried, for a very long time, to cook something wholesome every night but the pull of the microwave had grown stronger by the day and almost every evening, nowadays, his machine went *ping*. The way he described it, his neighbour Harriet would've called the police if she hadn't heard that *ping*. He lived a simple life, which was how he liked it.]

Did you feel OK with him? Did he seem fairly normal?
Yes, he was OK. Getting on a bit – a lot of baggage I'd say. He wasn't put together quite right – as if he had the arms of a child. He wasn't in proportion, somehow. Not completely normal. Still, he didn't lay it on too much. He seemed like he was from another age. Could have been born hundreds of years ago, the way his mind worked. Always looking into the past. Trying to work out what happened when he was a kid, and thinking in such an old-fashioned way. I felt so different. My generation doesn't seem to have all that shit going on. It made me think about my history course at college... everything's happening so fast now, the whole world is speeding up. Every generation seems to be fundamentally different nowadays, don't you think?
Don't know, never thought about it. What do you mean about old-fashioned – in the way he thought?
It's hard to define. Nothing was straightforward. Everything seemed to be encrypted, or an allegory, or a puzzle. He didn't seem able to keep things simple, like we do.
He had trouble remembering, too?
Yes. He said he remembered very little from his past. Nothing felt real. He said his whole life felt as if it had been re-enacted by the Sealed Knot Society.
Did he tell you about his work?
Not that first day, no. But I got to know more about him. He always seemed to be there when I went in, and it would've been

rude to sit at another table. He didn't mind me smoking, either. 'Fraid I smoke too much. Life's a bit of a bummer at the moment. *What sort of work did he do?*
He worked for a delivery company and he took parcels and things all over the place. He drove a white van with a rainbow pattern on both sides. That rainbow thing became a bit of a joke between us. He was good at his job – he knew Britain's roads inside out. If you wanted directions to anywhere you'd ask Duxie and he'd say something like *take the A55 to junction thingymee and then the M56 to junction whatsit and then the M6 to junction thingamajig...*

[Because life was a web of junctions for Duxie. He said there was a golden mean somewhere in Britain, probably – if he visited a certain number of junctions in exactly the right order he might arrive at Shangri-la or Camelot. Duxie's mind worked like that. There had to be more to life than motorways and concrete, he said. There had to be some meaning to it all, somewhere.

Duxie's van was scrutinised everywhere he went, followed throughout the day, every day, by an eye in the sky – he was tracked by satellite. It was the way of the world. At first he hadn't minded, thought little of it. But he became more and more conscious of the satellite – unseen, undetectable – as it rotated above him in space. He began to resent it, and then he grew to hate it. He understood, now, why people went underground, politically and emotionally. He was uneasy even in his own bedroom: now and then he found himself scanning the sky through the window, wondering if he was being watched as he prepared himself for a furtive act. In his teens, as his sexuality got the better of him, when he'd sought relief, he'd imagined a row of relatives up in heaven, looking down at him over the edge of a heavenly parapet and shaking their heads, tut-tutting – and he imagined meeting them again, for the first time, up there in God's presence, and he was sure to blush and stammer, look down at the floor, because they'd all seen him at it. Maybe it wasn't like that. Maybe there was a heavenly fraternity in such matters. Perhaps all his dead relatives would do something quite disgusting, there and then, together, just to put him at ease. Maybe he ought to discuss it with his psychiatrist...

The constant scrutiny he endured, human and mechanical, had driven Duxie into his shell; his life was spent increasingly within his own imagination. His everyday work took on a robotic air as he constructed a rich and meaningful inner life based on dreams and daydreams. In short, Duxie lived in a fantasy world.

At a quarter to seven every evening, half an hour after the nightly *ping*! had been transmitted through the thin wall to Harriet next door, he vacuumed swiftly, had a wash, put on his old leather jacket and walked downtown to the snooker club.

Duxie was nothing much to look at. He was smallish – about five foot six – and he was losing his fur; a few stray wisps of light brown hair – silvered with a sprinkling of grey – fluttered around his bald patch as he plodded downhill. His face, which still bore traces of the acne which had ravaged his teens, was thin and unremarkable, though he had keen and intelligent eyes. He had a paunch and yellow fingers from smoking too much. Duxie was well past his sell-by date. He'd even started rehearsing his own deathbed scene. But a man could dream, and Duxie dreamt a lot. He dreamt he'd inherited a hole, and he either had to complete it – dig it out completely, tidily – or fill it in. In his dream he didn't know which action to take. He had another dream, about a room. It was dark in there, he couldn't see anything much. But he could feel a lot. Was the room getting lighter? Was he on the edge of remembering something? Inside the quilt of his dreamworld slept a mystery; things were being kept from him... nothing would come back to him from his early years. They were just a blank.]

Tell me something about the café.
Yes, fine. It was run by a nice Italian man called Stefano, really charming and talkative. He was helped by a small, red-haired man who was very lame. People said he'd had a nasty accident while exploring some caves. Duxie disliked him. He called him the Gimp with the limp. I liked it there, in the café. Some strange people went in there, like a big woman selling seafood – yucky things like that. It was quiet, with an old world charm of its own. It was a place for the wrinklies, people of my age kept away – but that suited me fine because I wanted some peace and quiet, and something a bit different. My boyfriend's into clubbing, big time, so I was glad for a rest. There was an ancient jukebox in there and the music was from long ago, by people I'd never heard of – a lot of jazz and soul. Some Miles Davis, a bit of fusion jazz from Jan

Garbarek, some old ballads from the 50s and 60s. The Gimp with the limp often played *Big John* to encourage the myth about his underground accident. The lighting was subdued. The whole room was painted in pastel greens, and there were lots of plants. It was a place from the past, with sad-eyed people, poets and burnt-out addicts. Duxie felt at home there.

Did he do drugs himself?

Perhaps. Hard to say. He knew a lot about them, but I couldn't see any signs. Either he liked to give the impression he'd messed about with them, or he'd stopped taking them somewhere along the line.

Go on...

He had a regular seat in the corner where he could look down on the town below. He liked the harbour lights twinkling in the far distance. We had a good view from up there, with a big bay on one side of the harbour and a smaller bay on the other – they sort of matched each other nicely. Stefano made a big fuss of him when he went in. They were old friends, by the look of it. Stefano and the Gimp always wore identical tee shirts – they'd go through a crazy phase and they'd have words like

> DON'T VOTE
> IT'LL ONLY
> ENCOURAGE
> THEM

printed on the front. Almost as soon as you'd sat down there would be a steaming cup of cappuccino in front of you. The tables were odd, made of wicker with glass tops. They served excellent Danish pastries in there.

[Happiness: this was indeed happiness for Duxie, as he bathed briefly in a pool of contentment. The satellite above him was patrolling elsewhere, in the lighter realms of the world. He could rest in tranquil peace. He breathed on his coffee to cool it, but remembered that he was in no hurry and put it down. He ambled over to the music machine to select a Garbarek number: *Mnemosyne* perhaps, or *Iceburn*, or maybe he'd choose *It's OK to Listen to the Gray Voice* because he felt a touch of empathy with the title. Driving a van with rainbows on each side tended to make one bloody-minded at times.]

Who else did he talk to?
Sometimes he'd chat with the ex-copper, a grizzly man with grey hair, cut short in a Number 2. He was a big, brooding bloke who seemed to be morose all the time. I bumped into him, often, on the seashore, early in the morning. He went down there early every day and walked about beachcombing, or sat on a rock, looking out to sea. He was always whistling a tune, the one that starts with (she sings) *If you go down to the woods today...*
Teddy Bears' Picnic?
Yeah, that's the one. The whisper was that he'd been drummed out of the force, but no one knew why. Duxie was wary of him and talked to him mainly out of politeness.
Anyone else?
Yes, there was another oddball, a really tiny fellah called Little Michael who joined us occasionally. He was a bit spooky, not because of his size. He was immaculately dressed in a dark suit and tie with a really white shirt, he looked like a miniature undertaker. Gave me the creeps. He came in with the *Daily Mail* under his arm but you knew he wanted to read Stefano's copy of the *Sun*, really.
Any pastimes – did Duxie mention any hobbies?
Yes, he played snooker every day, upstairs.
Upstairs?
Yes, there's a snooker hall above the café.

[The snooker hall was big and old and cold. Duxie climbed the stairs wearily and paused, every day, on the landing half way up. He stood on the cracked plastic floor tiles and viewed the world outside. He liked standing at this long gallery window with its expansive sheet of glass. The window took on a light green tinge from the neon sign advertising the café below. Sometimes he imagined he was in deep space, in a glass corridor, looking into the centre of a black hole. One day he stuck an orange Post-it note to the window with something he'd seen in a book written on it:

Human kind
Cannot bear very much reality

No one had said a word about it and it stayed there for weeks, until it fell to the floor. It lay in a corner for quite some time, curling up at the edges and gathering dust. Duxie's first and only attempt at public existentialism had come a cropper, and he didn't try anything like that again.]

You've mentioned children. Had he remarried?
No, he was still single. Not many takers, I'd guess. He wasn't much to look at. He said his wife had started an affair, he hadn't been able to cope, so he'd slept in his cab. That's how he described it to me, and there was still a bit of sadness in his voice, like he'd never got over it.

[One week became two, three months became six. He'd watched them all, at a distance, and marvelled at how well they coped, how little his absence seemed to affect them. He'd been the one to clean their shoes, make their sandwiches, but the eldest child had taken over as naturally as if it had always been so. Although he got a welcome from them, Duxie had sensed a glass wall between them – he was no longer part of the family machinery. He imagined a corporate rejection. By the very fact that he was *over here* and they were *over there*, grouped together, he felt himself being pushed away. He became a ghost. There had come a time when he was faced with a simple choice: he had to fight his way back in or shrug his shoulders and retreat. He backed off. His visits faltered, weakened, died. And then they all moved away, swiftly, to Birmingham, without leaving so much as a note. Duxie despaired. Despite his keen sense of guilt, he felt bereft without them physically near him. And so he played out an elaborate game on the snooker table. It was his way of coping with it all. Sad, yes, he knew it was sad. The biggest sadness of his life.]

So he played snooker every night. Did you ever go with him?
No, I never did. He liked his routine, he didn't want any disruptions. I sneaked up there once and looked at them all through a window.

[The usual scene greeted Duxie every time he entered the snooker hall, that was the main reason he went there. On the lower deck there were two rows of snooker tables – six on either side – nestling under their comforting pools of light. Then, up some steps, was the big boys' table, where the best players in town played each other for a tower block of crumpled fivers. There was a small bar up there, and you got your pint in silence. Duxie usually played in a round robin with two mates. They were all drivers and they made small talk about the weather, soccer, road conditions, and the desperate girls who knocked on their cab doors every night, in the lorry parks, willing to do anything for a fiver.

Duxie's highest break ever was 49. He was very average. So he spiced things up by playing a complicated game of his own. His friends had no inkling.

This was the game that Duxie played. The white ball represented the forces of Good and the black ball represented the forces of Evil.

The other colours: yellow, brown, green, blue and pink represented each of his five children, though he hadn't seen them for years. Every time he potted one of the coloured balls he won a life for one of his children. He imagined a lorry bearing down on one of them at a pedestrian crossing, the child on the brink of running out into the road – but saved from certain death when Duxie potted the relevant ball.

The fifteen reds represented his *aides-de-camp*, his helpers in a nightly quest to ward off the forces of Evil. The highest break possible was 147, which had mathematical significance: 147 divided by seven made 21, and 21 divided by seven made three. All the cardinal numbers of magic were there.]

Any other hobbies?
Yes, he had a telescope and he looked at the stars when it was clear enough. He mentioned Saturn a lot because there's a mission going on at the moment.
The Cassini-Huygens probe.
Yes, that's the one – you know about it then.
It's been in the papers a lot, and there was a question in the quiz last week.
That's what he called the fly – Cassini. The fly that wouldn't die. He didn't explain it properly, but it was something to do with his past. He said the fly was bloody irritating and it refused to die, so he called it Mr Cassini. The name stuck, so every time I saw him I asked him how Mr Cassini was. I picked up on his Saturn mania. He said the Cassini probe was named after an astronomer who also gave his name to a dark ring which separates the other rings of Saturn – it's called Cassini's Ring, or the Cassini Division. The number seven cropped up time and again when we

talked about the probe. Seven years of preparation, a seven-year journey through space... Duxie made a joke of it. He'd looked it up on the web, this seven-year thing. He said the body undergoes a complete change of cells every seven years. He'd made a mental list of things, like the seven-year itch, seven ages of man, seven deadly sins, seven virtues, seven works of mercy, seven years of plenty and seven years of lean, the seven sacraments. I suppose he had a thing about death. He said that burying the dead was the seventh and last sacrament.

Wasn't this an odd sort of thing to be talking about, to a stranger in a café?

Yes, I suppose it was. He certainly wasn't normal. But there's a history of clued-up drivers, isn't there? Remember that taxi driver who won Mastermind?

Yes, I suppose you're right. What else did he talk about?

There was something which was bothering him a lot, a hell of a lot. He was getting nuisance calls, and he had an idea who it was.

Something to do with his ex, perhaps?

No, it was someone from his past, he said. Someone who wouldn't leave him alone. A man in a fez, he said, but I thought he was joking. I got the impression he'd tell me sooner or later, in his own time. He said he could talk to me about things like that. And I could see no harm in it – after all, I'd be gone in a week.

Did you tell him anything about yourself?

Not much, no. I told him why I was there. I've been having a really bad time at home, it's affected my studies. My father can't cope because my mother walked out on him after thirty-odd years of marriage.

Abusive?

No, not particularly. Just a pain in the arse sometimes. They used to row a lot.

Do you want to talk about it?

No, not now. Anyway, it's not particularly relevant. But Duxie made a big thing of it. He was always asking me about it, always wanting to talk about it.

It was a big issue for him?

Yes, I think it was more of an issue for him than for me. He was preoccupied by it, he brought the conversation round to it whenever he could. He seemed really protective towards me. He told me he'd seen a little girl crying, on his way down to the café – she was kneeling by the front door in a hallway, with her face up against the glass... it looked like a druggies' house, he said. I think it had triggered something inside him.

[That first night she walked into the café his heart went all over the place. She was very pretty, but it wasn't that. He thought he recognised her, and his head went hot. He started trembling. *Everyone* looked at her. Who wouldn't? She was beautiful. Straight blonde hair, creamy complexion, cornflower blue eyes. Full red lips. Lovely in every way. He watched her as Garbarek suffused the room. Above the café window there was a two-tone neon light in a strong italic script which said *Stefano's*. It was about six feet long and *Stefano's* was split into two so that the top half was green and the bottom half pink. She sat close to him, by the window, directly below the neon sign, and the pink of the light – softened by the glass – played lightly on her hair, giving her a supernatural, angelic look. She sat quietly on her own, reading and drinking coffee, smoking one cigarette after another. She seemed preoccupied, in a world of her own. He felt sure he knew that face. But there again, she could have looked out at him from a thousand roadside hoardings or from the pages of a hundred magazines. Was she in one of the porno mags he kept under his bed in the cab? No, she was too classy. No way. He studied her. She had dark rings under her eyes... very tired perhaps, or was she on drugs? Two small Elastoplasts floated on her arm, tiny hovercrafts at rest. He watched her and he watched her. He stayed far longer that usual. He watched the gimp with the limp circling her, emptying her ashtray too often, giving her free top-ups. He was after something... not her body, he'd never get that, not even as a supreme act of sympathy, the sort of gesture women were capable of making sometimes. He wanted to bend her ear probably. To tell her about his great adventure, the cave in the mountain. Duxie had heard it all too bloody often.]

You make it sound as if he was feeding off your unhappiness.
No, it was something else. He was bothered by something, and it was to do with the nuisance calls. He was trying to come to terms with something, I guess. He described it as *decommissioning*, as if he was a used-up power station. He said to me: *If you had seven days to live, Olly, what would you do?*

I asked him straight if he only had seven days to live. He said no, he was good for another thirty years. But he still wanted to know what I'd do if I only had a week to live. Go back home, get married quick to my bloke, spend a week in bed with a crate of champagne I said. *That sounds good enough for me,* he said. But how about you, I asked. What would you do? And he said the strangest thing. He said he'd go for a picnic in the snow.

Picnic in the snow?

Yes, he was excited by the idea. It was an ambition he had. He was going to invite some people. He wanted to film it all. He was waiting for some snow.

Sounds crackers.

Well, at least it was different. It meant something to him, so I went along with it. He mentioned the weather forecast, said there was snow on the way. He was like a big kid. He was all excited, as if he had a birthday coming up.

Anything else odd about him?

He mentioned islands a lot. He laughed at the island cartoons in the newspapers, they all seem to have a palm tree in the middle and a man with a long beard trying to send a message in a bottle... and he mention a Glubbdubb-something or other, an island of magicians in Gulliver's Travels, a place where Gulliver could talk with people from the past.

What happened next?

I left the café, but I promised to meet him again. Why not? He wanted to tell me about his snow plan. He said to me as I put my scarf on: 'Olly, did you know that icebergs are blue inside? And there's an iceberg – the B15 – which is almost the size of Wales?'

'No, that one passed me by,' I said. 'Must have blinked.'

'Yes,' he said. 'Almost everything in the world is measured in Wales-units now. Part of the icecap melted away last year and they said it was three times the size of Wales. If some of the rainforest is chopped down it's five times the size of Wales. It's an international unit of measurement. A measure of disaster, usually.'

I thought that was funny. I laughed at that. Then I left him to it, and I walked down to my aunty's house by the harbour.

[She left, suddenly. They all watched her go. She wore a creamy-yellow corduroy jacket with the collar up, bunching her hair in attractive loops around her face. One particular curl swept loose over her right eye, swirling in sidewinder motions along her cheek. Light green trousers. Duxie couldn't identify the material – something like moleskin, soft and supple. Light brown boots, leather. Stylish in an understated way.

When she stretched to put her jacket on he noticed a tiny butterfly tattoo on her right shoulder. The door closed behind her and she was gone, suddenly. They didn't see her pass the window, it was as if she'd disappeared into thin air. There was a brief, animated hubbub as Stefano, the Gimp and a couple of the older males made comments about her. Weary by now, Duxie decided to get a taxi home. He couldn't be bothered walking up the hill. He saw her as they passed, and the taxi wobbled slightly as the driver – also staring – corrected a drift towards the pavement. *Never seen her before,* said the driver. *Nor me either,* said Duxie.

Later, sitting by his window overlooking the football field, Duxie rolled a joint. He liked a blow before bed, it helped him to relax. Once he'd had a run-in with the heavy drugs: acid, speed, charlie. After the break-up he'd done a lot. He'd needed something to take the pain away. It had been like falling into a hole full of cotton wool. Thankfully, he'd weaned himself away from the heavies, calmed himself down with cannabis. It was pretty harmless stuff, he reckoned. So he skinned up on his little side-table and waited for the stuff to take effect. It did, pretty soon. Duxie sat and smoked, wondered about the girl in *Stefano's*. Something stirred in him. He sensed that the girl was vulnerable; that she had been hurt badly, and her eyes spoke of a troubled past.

Duxie would return to the café every day to talk with her; perhaps he would be able to gain her confidence (if the Gimp allowed him to) and maybe he could help her. He felt protective towards her, and he reasoned – probably correctly – that he was using up some of the fatherly feeling he'd stored up inside him, unable to use it on his own kids.

Duxie rolled another joint, just to be sure of getting some shut-eye. Sleep was virtually impossible these days without a good blow first. His body gradually unfurled. He listened intently, trying to hear any noises coming from the flat below. All quiet. They were out, thank God. The rows had got worse recently, and Duxie had found himself very tense, extremely wound up as he waited every night for the raised voices, the breaking crockery.

He thought about tomorrow. It would be a better day than the day he'd just had, hopefully. There had been a long delay on a mountain pass, caused by a pile-up involving three vehicles. One of them was vintage – a Minerva Landaulette; also a blue Polo, and behind that a rust bucket, an old van painted clumsily in matt red. He'd been one of the first on the scene, but there had been no sign of any passengers: the vehicles looked as though they'd been put there for a film or an advert. Strange. He needed to start early in the morning – he had a drop in Scotland, it was going to be a long day. He was taking some bottled water on the up journey and bringing some jeans back down. He could have a good think in the van. Finally, Duxie fetched out an old tin box from a drawer in the table by his side. It was an ancient Christmas selection box, with a snow scene and people ice-skating; a scene of merriment and laughter, with lots of children running around looking happy and excited. He prised open the lid – it was very stiff, slightly rusty – and started flipping randomly through a higgledy-piggledy stack of old photographs, most of them faded. They smelt musty. They were mostly creased, many were partly perished. Family heirlooms. Some of them were so old he had no idea who was looking back at him. There were soldiers and farmers. God knows who they were: it was strange to think that most of them had shared the same genes as him, the same acid clusters, the same lettering in a very old line of seaside rock.

Duxie found what he was looking for – a picture of a man in a fez. He had a sloppy grin on his face and his hands were held out in front of him, in a Tommy Cooper pose. Duxie knew he was drunk. He was afraid of this man in the picture...

The dreams were returning – the dreams of magic and fear. Dreams from his childhood, presumably. Duxie returned the picture to the box and closed it. Methodically, as usual, he cleared away his smoking debris and washed the ashtray and his cup under the cold tap. He returned with a cloth to wipe the table.

Tomorrow he was going north on an errand. He would weave a good fantasy to cheat the satellite watching him in the sky. Then, in the evening, he would hurry from the snooker hall to watch the beautiful girl as she smoked and drank coffee under the pink neon sign. He would ask her to go on a picnic with him.

Duxie read for a while, as usual. He'd finished *Rings of Saturn* and now he was on Knud Holmboe's *Desert Encounter*, a book about a dangerous adventure in North Africa. The Italians had

blocked up some of the Bedouin wells with concrete in retribution for a rebellion. Duxie felt a deep sympathy for the Bedouins.

That night he dreamt of wells, and in his dream he went on a
long journey with Olly. The seven rainbow bands on the side of
his van had turned into seven human messengers from the past.
In his dream, Olly was in terrible trouble and only he could help
her. Outside his window the night air smelt of snow, as sharp and
medical as the smell of a swab on his arm before the anaesthetic
sent him to another land – a land from which he was exiled, a
land in a perpetual state of emergency...]

12

THE TIDE COMES IN

The interview tapes (2)

Would you like to describe the second meeting? Do you remember what you talked about?

Yes, I remember that evening very well because Mr Cassini was finally nailed. Or so we thought. There was a shout from the ex-copper's table, and Stefano came rushing out of the kitchen all excited, as if the Red Baron had been shot down. He fetched a drinking straw and played with the fly's body, leaning over the table – his nose almost touched it. Mrs Griffiths shuffled over too and studied the upturned insect. The table was covered in sugar grains – they were scattered all over the place after the copper brought his hand down on the pyramid he'd made as a lure.

'*Non corretto,*' said Stefano. 'This one isn't Mr Cassini. This one he is grey all over, Mr Cassini is blue and sort of greeny too, no?'

We all agreed. The policeman admitted his mistake, and we all sat down again. The policeman tidied his table with a serviette and started another vigil. Soon, an angry outburst from the kitchen confirmed that Mr Cassini was back. There was an explosion of noise caused by saucepans falling onto the floor: Stefano had missed again, and he was getting cross. We could hear him banging his knives on the preparation boards and barking at the Gimp.

[Duxie listened to the commotion and planned his picnic. He knew the ideal place. He would borrow a tartan rug from Harriet next door, and he had a picnic basket in one of the storage cupboards – he knew exactly where. It might need a good clean. February was an odd time for a picnic, but if they were lucky with the weather it could be very enjoyable. Snow – he wanted snow.

He'd watch cloud-shadows on the sea and look for dolphins cleaving the waves. All that water. Fountains of the great deep. The river down below would be doing a silvery conga through the trees. He would nudge her arm and point to a gleaming speck on the far horizon: the ghost ship, which had been sighted many times before. Or maybe it was an iceberg, she might say. Twice the size of Wales. He'd pull a face and make a weak joke about manic, sexually ambivalent bears in the Arctic being bi-polar and she'd bring her mug down hard on his gloved hand.

He would consult his *Bumper Book of British Picnics* and he'd choose a pleasing medley of sandwiches and titbits. No alcohol – he would select the finest water, collected and bottled at one of Wales' ancient springs. Perhaps he should take a couple of folding chairs. The mirror-calm lakes would dazzle her. Once settled, she could nibble at a sandwich and contemplate the consumptive hills, as grey and placid as sleeping hippos.

'Did you know that hippos like bananas?' he would ask across the table, and she would shake her head, her big luminous eyes brimming with wonder and doubt. He would take a couple of bananas, and apples of course. Plus one of his special cakes. He would tell her about his secret life. He would tell her about his amnesia… so many years lost, a hole in every day which needed to be darned. He would tell her about the man who forgot the word for anchor and never came to land. He would tell her about the seven swans and their flight through the rainbow. Yes, he would conjecture on man's need for the far horizon as a perpetual mystery – a paradigm for the line between the temporal and the spiritual. A grand illusion, but also a clear demarcation between feeble man and the infinite, unknowable universe beyond.

She would respond warmly, he thought. Perhaps she would smoke and study the teeming waters of the lake for a while, the lake they'd chosen as their final destination. Perhaps she would compare the mountain ravines to duelling scars. Perhaps she would comment on the sheet of water in front of them. Water was magical, she would say. It gave life to all – yet it killed and destroyed just as easily. Humans, who started off in the sea long ago, had not fully left it: they still needed water, carrying it around with them in the same way as spacemen carried oxygen in their tanks on the moon. The amniotic fluid, which surrounded each unborn child, was a perfect re-creation of the ocean, with exactly the same salinity. Tears were miniature droplets of history – liquid stigmatas: symbols of regret, signifying the last few drops to fall from our bodies when we first left the seas all those millions of years ago.

He would marvel at her beauty, even more pronounced in the limpid air. Everything in the story was true:

> Yellower was her head than the flower of the broom, whiter was her flesh than the foam of the wave; whiter were her palms and her fingers than the shoots of the marsh trefoil from amidst the fine gravel of a welling spring. Neither the eye of the mewed hawk, nor the eye of the thrice-mewed falcon, not an eye was there fairer than hers. Whiter were her breasts than the breast of the white swan, redder were her cheeks than the reddest foxgloves. Whoso beheld her would be filled with love for her. Four white trefoils sprang up behind her wherever she went; and for that reason was she called Olwen.

He would add to the conversation. Water had been an important escape route for many peoples fleeing persecution and poverty, he would say. The human race was divided into the people of the sea and the people of the land. But there came a time, eventually, when it was necessary for all of us to leave the shore. One couldn't put one's back to the land for ever and ignore it. At a critical point in one's evolution it was necessary to turn away from the sea, to head towards the hinterland. There were certain understandings which could only be arrived at on a peak in the centre of one's country. It was a different dimension. Land without sea. In the act of travelling from the sea to the centre a traveller might construe a different frame of mind which was based on the whole rather than the peripheral.

Their picnic would get off to a sound start, and if it *was* a little old fashioned in tone, then so what? She might enjoy a bit of decorum and restraint. So would he. The world had gone mad, everyone agreed on that. Souls bought with trinkets, indescribable nonsense in the papers and on television. Britain had a rancid end-of-empire gloom about it with all the decent, thoughtful people watching askance from the margins as a children's party degenerated into a disgusting and violent bun fight. Duxie was sick of it all; a society in which Prozac was being consumed in such huge quantities that it was being found in the drinking water, building up in river systems and groundwater. A society grounded on fear, permeated by nervousness, unable to sleep properly: twelve million people slept badly for three nights out of seven. We were people who raged, he'd say. We were people who couldn't cope with silence; our children lost in a virtual limbo, drifting from one screen to another, unable to comprehend the natural world – the real world – and therefore glad to expunge it, to enclose it in a hard, cold, concrete casing of forgetfulness.

He would give her a choice of sandwiches. Cheese with a subtle salad, in case she was a vegetarian. As an option he would make a ham and pickle combination with tomatoes drizzled in a boisterous vinaigrette. He would go mad and buy a selection of biscuits from the best shop in town. And he would make a chocolate cake too, just in case. He would tell her about its contents, of course. He wasn't into sneaky little tricks like that...

He would tell her about Shackleton's men, starving on Elephant Island as they waited for deliverance, dreaming of food, craving for sweets: Clark wanted Devonshire dumpling with cream, James wanted syrup pudding, McIlroy wanted marmalade pudding and cream, Rickinson wanted blackberry and apple tart with cream; but Perce Blackboro, the Welsh stowaway who had part of his frost-bitten foot, gangrenous and black, amputated under an upturned boat amid the icy rocks, had merely wanted bread and butter. Duxie felt guilty. He'd got so fat he was telling people he was going to be a Munchkin in the Christmas panto... he felt like a grub which had munched its way though leaf after leaf, waiting for respite from gluttony, waiting to be an imago at last.]

So the fly was still alive. Could you tell me, again, why it was called Mr Cassini?
He seemed to call anything or anybody who bothered him Mr Cassini. I don't know why. It was like a code. Something to do with those nuisance phone calls he received, too. He had a call on his mobile that evening and when it ended he made a funny face, shrugged, and said: *Mr Cassini again.* The colour went from his face and he was quiet for a while.
Did you ask him about this Mr Cassini who phoned him?
Yes. I said to him, 'Tell me what's going on, you might as well Duxie... in a few days I'll have gone and we'll never see each other again. Talking to strangers is good for you, sometimes.' But he turned the conversation round to me again. He wanted to

know more about my father. He wanted to know if he'd hurt me, or done other things...

I'm beginning to think...

You're beginning to think that his preoccupation with my father had more to do with his father than mine?

Yes, that's what I think.

I got that impression too. What do they call it, when you project yourself onto other people?

Transference.

Yes, that's the one. I realised that he was using me to re-enact his own past, somehow.

I take it that your own father has caused you problems?

Yes. He made things absolutely impossible for my boyfriend – that's why I came here, to get away from it all for a while. Sanctuary, I suppose. I told them to sort it all out by the time I got back. You know what men are like. One minute they're snarling and threatening to kill each other, the next minute they're in a bar with their arms round each other, friends for ever.

So you wanted to marry this man?

Mad about him.

What went wrong?

My bloody father, that's what went wrong. He was being a sod again. I'm just a normal girl, I just want a normal life. But he always makes it difficult. He made life hell for my mother. When I was small I couldn't believe he was my real father, I thought it was impossible, a big mistake. Every day I wanted him to die. Never happened, did it.

Did he abuse you?

No, not really. Now I know more about that sort of thing I realise he wasn't that bad. Duxie talked about cold cruelty and hot cruelty. If kids were mistreated but there was a lot of love around they usually got over it. But if they got cold cruelty, without any love, that was the thing that really messed them up for ever. It was cold abuse that did the real damage, he said. Those were the people who felt empty inside.

I don't think he's necessarily right about that, but did he say any more on the subject?

He asked me if I ever felt as if I had holes all the way through me, like Swiss cheese.

Have you?

No, I've never felt like that. But he said he had something wrong inside him. Bored out by little miners when he was a child, he said. There were lots of people like that. They tried filling the holes with alcohol, or drugs, or food, but they never filled them up. He said there were silos or hoppers inside him but all the switches were bust, the machinery didn't work properly, so some hoppers were perpetually empty while others were overflowing hopelessly. And there was water coming up inside him again, filling him up from below, travelling up his legs. He couldn't find the plug. That's the way he described it.

Had he tried getting help?

He mentioned a psychiatrist. He'd read some stuff too, but as he said himself, a little knowledge is a dangerous thing. He was searching for something – an explanation, I think. He wasn't that keen on psychiatry. A form of alchemy, he said. Doomed to failure, a search for fool's gold. He mentioned a doctor... Dee? He said this doctor and others like him had made millions of useless experiments, spent billions of hours chasing a dream. He thought the whole psychoanalysis thing was a bit sad, another tale of alembics and elixirs. He thought the pressure to make sense of it all was another tyranny – a useless experiment. There was no such thing as a lasting solution, and if there was, humans would destroy it immediately to create a new set of problems. But maybe he could reach a personal solution, he said... a small solution. He called it the eighth story.

Eighth story?

Yes, he said something about there being seven classical plots in the human story. The eighth, he said, involved a white room.

Was this a real room, or a room in his mind?

No idea. He said he'd sat in a perfectly white room once and it was a room of complete simplicity. He had spent all his life making thousands of small decisions every day, but when he sat in that room there was only one decision left for him to make, only one in the whole wide world.

Did he tell you what it was?

Yes.

[Little Michael moved seats to be closer to her in the cafe: he actually jostled the copper into sitting by the window, and then he moved into the warm indent left by his bum. There was something of the White Rabbit about Little Michael; he seemed to arrive out of nowhere, and he had a surreal edge.

'I'm starting a protest movement,' he said to Olly. As usual he was immaculate, in his neatly pressed black suit. He couldn't contain himself; like everyone else he had to be in on the action.

'And what exactly are you protesting about?' she asked.

Little Michael leaned across the policeman and wrote with his finger in the condensation on the window, in big capital letters:

SAVE THE FLY!

'There,' he said, 'poor little sod, he's got as much right to live as you lot. Why persecute him? He's the best entertainment we've had in here for years.'

Olly laughed. She wrote under it:

LONG LIVE MR CASSINI!

The policeman added:

EAT SHIT! 12 MILLION FLIES CAN'T BE WRONG

but Olly rubbed it out.

There was a slightly embarrassed pause, then Little Michael reignited the conversation.

'You having trouble with your pop?' he asked Olly.

'Yes,' she said wearily, 'but I think we've discussed it enough now.'

'Never mind,' he said, covering her hand with his, 'he'll get his come-uppance one day. You always pay in the end. He'll die a lonely old man. He won't sleep proper. People with a bad conscience always fear the judgement of children,' he added. 'But I can't remember who said that.'

Olly regarded him with a bemused look. 'Who rattled *your* cage tonight?'

Little Michael looked sheepish. 'Sorry,' he said. 'Do you mind if I join you for a while? Only I couldn't help overhearing.'

Olly waved her hand to show it was OK.

'I was involved with a complete bastard once, so I know what you're on about,' said Little Michael.

Duxie daydreamed for a while. They were by the lake again, having their picnic, with cloud-shoals silvering the reefs of Snowdonia. The frosty hills would loom like enormous maggots in a mist. He would offer a sandwich and tell her about the fantasy world he'd woven around himself as he drove his van around Britain. He could see no reason for *not* telling her. What could he lose? He would describe his journeys along the road-veins creasing Britain's ancient skin. He would tell her all. Well, all that he remembered. Maybe he'd tell her about the photograph of the man in a fez, looking drunkenly into the camera, imitating Tommy Cooper. He would tell her about his dreams and fantasies. He'd dreamed about her repeatedly, ever since he first saw her in *Stefano's*. In his fantasy world they were at college together. She was a girl in trouble. He wouldn't mention the sexual tension he'd concocted. What were dreams anyway? A vision of the future perhaps – a forewarning or a presentiment. That was the ancient view, wasn't it? Or perhaps there was a cinema in the mind, entertaining the brain as we slept. Or an old part of the brain was sifting through the day's events and stripping out any information which reinforced survival techniques, then threw the rest away in a dreamy jumble. No one knew, really...]

Had he been a driver all his life?
I think so. He seemed envious of me, going to college. He'd never had an education, never had a chance to go to college or a university. Perhaps his dreams reflected a hidden wish – that he wanted to be cleverer, more qualified than he was. He said he'd studied at the Mesolimbic Reward Centre, wherever that is.
It's in the brain.
So he was having me on?
Looks like it. Did he mention dopamine?
Something like that, yes.
He was talking about drugs, probably – the way you get pleasure when you take them.
The little sod. I thought he was being serious.
Did he tell you about his dreams?
Some of them. There were lots of dummies. What do you call them – those dummies in shop windows...
Mannequins?
Yes, that's the word. He talked a lot about mannequins and

murders. He mentioned holes a lot. Wells and floods. Stuff from long ago. I couldn't make much sense of it all.

The mannequins were symbols, perhaps?

What do you mean?

Perhaps they symbolised something?

Such as?

Well, they could have symbolised people who'd been dehumanised in some way. You've mentioned domestic abuse – they could be the sort of people who live with a typical domestic tyrant. All their wiring ripped out. Shells. Get my drift?

Yes, I suppose so. Sounds a bit simplistic to me.

Anything else? Did he mention anything else?

Plenty. He had so much hocus-pocus inside his head – it was like a teen flick in there. There was a room in his dreams, a dark room with a big table in the middle all set out for a meal, something like Sunday lunch. No one ever spoke a word, they all sat there like dummies.

The mannequins?

'Yes, lifeless, as if they were in a museum. No one ever said a word in his dreams.

And...?

They could hear someone coming... they could hear a key in the lock.

Go on.

But there was nothing else. Just one scene from the past, that's all he was allowed. He would feel a bit choked inside. A hot tight feeling in his chest. He felt as if his blood was bubbling slightly and his ears zinged – that's how he described it. And then a sudden plunge into depression. It felt like a freefall into a black void, he said.

[Duxie went into a daydream again, looking down at the town, his chin resting in the cup of his gloved hand. He was back at the lake again, with Olly. He would offer her some chocolate cake and watch the lake darken under a cloud grazing the air for dampness. He would press her to eat another slice. And she'd nibble gracefully without getting chocolate sauce all over her nose, like he did. Oaf that he was.

How would he explain the demonic figure in his dreams, and in his daydreams too?

He was worried. Would she get the wrong idea? Maybe her

eyes would sharpen and she'd size him up anew, see him in a different light.

'Are *you* Mr Cassini?' she might ask.

'Bloody hell *no*,' he'd reply tersely. 'Absolutely not. I *promise* you. I *swear* it!'

She might consider his answer, weigh up his response. Give him an unwavering look. He would be forced into a corner; he would have to convince her of his innocence.

'It's true, I do have a family,' he would say. 'But they live in Birmingham. I haven't seen them, any of them, for years.'

And she would respond, quite naturally, with: 'And why did they move to Birmingham? Why did they go away from you, why didn't you follow them?'

He'd reply: 'I felt rejected. I thought they would be better off without me.'

'What a cop-out. If you'd loved them properly you'd have followed them anywhere, to the ends of the earth.'

'Yes, well, I didn't.' He'd have to be truthful.

He'd notice, suddenly, that the air was thickening, that the cloud cover was not much higher than a dome tent around them. Tunnels of light and dark. He would start packing up the picnic. A grey cloud-pillow would descend slowly from above, as if intending to smother them. A few snowflakes would be puffed into the air around them, frozen eider down blown through a rent in the stitching.

'So if Mr Cassini isn't you, who is he?'

She would want to know the truth. There would be no getting out of it now. He would be cornered, with his back to the wall. He would have to be evasive.

'He's got to be someone – someone *real* for you to construct such a story in your head. He has nothing at all to do with *my* father and you know it. He's either you, or he's…'

Hopefully, she would peter off there.

But no, she was much too sharp.

'… *your* father. Tell me about your own father. Where is he now?'

The truth was stranger than fiction, so he'd tell her the truth.]

He told you about his father?
Yes, in a way. I asked him where his parents lived. He said his

mother was dead; his father was at the football ground, he said. 'Watching a game?' I asked. 'No,' he replied. 'He's a groundsman then,' I said. 'No,' he replied. 'He's with the worms, where he belongs.'

I said 'Duxie, you need to explain this to me.' And he told me. I was the first person he ever told – how he'd buried his father under the football pitch.

He'd killed him?

No, nothing like that. They'd brought his ashes back from the crematorium in a jar, but he didn't know what to do with them.

Why didn't he scatter them somewhere, like any normal person would?

He was very confused. For some reason he wanted to keep an eye on his father's remains. I asked him why. He wasn't quite sure. But there was some unfinished business. That's the way he put it, *unfinished business.*

'You see, he'd disappeared for years, gone out of our lives in a second,' he said to me. 'Then he came back, as a corpse. They'd found him dead. He'd been living in the next town. There's only one photo of him, he's wearing a fez. I think he was some sort of amateur magician. No one would tell me anything about him. He was a forbidden subject. But I knew, somehow, that he had something to do with my hands.'

His hands?

Duxie always wore gloves. There was something wrong with his hands.

What?

I'll get to that in a minute.

[Duxie had buried his father right below the centre spot. He sneaked down to the pitch one night and dug a good hole, about three feet down. Duxie put him in there, in his grey plastic jar. Then he put the turf back, carefully. Nobody noticed because they were always repairing the centre spot anyway. He was still there. Duxie watched him from his window. He was safe down there.]

Sounds as if that jar was a bit of a holy grail to him.

Yes, it was of immense significance.

But why there?

He didn't want his father sneaking up on him, that's what he said. He wanted to know where he was.

Doesn't make sense – the man was dead. And why was he so important to Duxie? He'd been missing for most of his life.

Duxie said to me once: I think it's possible, don't you, that fathers who aren't there for your childhood can often play a bigger part in your life than fathers who are.'

I think that was one reason. But the gloves... they were the main reason.

[Sitting in the café, Duxie was gripped by another panic attack. What if they ran out of petrol on their way to the lake? He'd ran out of petrol last week. He'd had a verbal warning. He imagined the scene, with Olly. The pick-up would start spluttering. It would grind to a halt, as if a huge finger was pushing against the front bumper.

'Bugger,' Duxie would say. He would grasp the driving wheel and bang his head on it. 'Bugger, bugger, bugger.'

They would sit quietly, neither saying a word as the pick-up tick-ticked and faded, a colossal grasshopper without energy, unable to make the final leap to safety. Olly would look straight ahead, with the curl waving softly in the cab's unseen wafts.

'Got a can in the back?'

'No,' he would reply softly.

'You bloody pillock. What are we going to do now?'

Duxie would consider the possibilities and then they would sit there, listening to the silence of the approaching snow.]

Where were we... ah yes, his father. Correct me if I'm wrong, but his father seemed to hold an exaggerated importance in his life, considering he hadn't been there for most of it.

That's true. He had his own theory, as usual. He said that fathers seemed to play three important roles for their children. Part of them had to be heroic, another part was anti-heroic, and the third part had to be absent.

You've lost me completely.

This is what he told me. For a small child, say up to twelve, the father is usually a superhero. He can do no wrong. Then, for adolescence, he becomes an anti-hero. It's necessary, apparently, for normal development. Kids are testing the water, seeing how far they can go before they enter society. And then there's the absent bit. It's like a painting on your wall. No matter how much you like it, if you have to look at it all the time you get sick of it.

So it has to be absent from your life, strategically, to be fully appreciated.

Like a father going to work, say, or for a night out with his mates?

Yes, that's about right. But if a father's absent all the time his absence takes on a whole new meaning, disproportionate to his importance.

[She would sit in the cab of the pick-up, and he would enjoy their steamed-up isolation in this little igloo of time. He would tell her more about his dreams, about Mr Cassini's vampirism. Drinking the tears of women and children to stay alive. That would be easy to explain, she would know all about that. Her own father had fastened alligator clips onto the nipples of all the women around him and drained their batteries.

'Oh yes, that's pretty straightforward symbolism,' she would tell Duxie. 'Your father must have been a pretty nasty piece of work. This is the biggest clue we've got. An abusive father feeds on his family's emotions, sucks up their life forces. You have to pity him just a little bit because he's cursed, like Dracula, to live in a twilight world. Abusive parents colonise the mind, in the same way as bats colonise a cave; their droppings cover the surface of the memory.'

He would look at her and marvel at her insight.

'Is that why my memory is so faulty?'

'I think so, don't you? The human memory is a wonderful thing. It can shield us from the past.'

'And why would it do that?'

'To help us survive. That's all, really. We're just survival machines, aren't we? It's like putting a blanket over a dead person – merely covering up the past.'

'OK, I understand,' he would say, getting ready to go out in the cold, to flag down the first car, to get some petrol, but in no hurry because he'd be feeling snug as a bug with Olly. Maybe he'd roll a quick joint. He'd go over everything again. His father had been an amateur magician who'd either disappeared into the darkness or who'd been flushed out of the family nest. He'd fed off other people until they were lifeless – mannequins, sitting around a table, waiting for their lord and master to come home from the pub, waiting for him to start his shouting, his throwing, his slapping, his smashing, his homeland terror... they were all dummies, pushed and pulled into odd and unnatural shapes by a one-man Khmer Rouge. The effect of his reign of terror would be felt for generations to come, his teeth marks would go from neck to neck along the generations, from father to son, until a Van Helsing – *a philosopher and metaphysician, one of the most advanced scientists of his day* – drove a stake through the heart of the beast. Was that why he had included Adam Phillips in his story – a man who could explain things to him?

What would happen if he *did* find what he was looking for? What would be the consequences? Would he survive his own descent into the cave of the seven wells, in the foothills of paradise? What if his father was in there, still alive, his teeth gleaming in the subdued limestone light? Would he, Duxie, run out again, would he retreat down the mountain, shaking uncontrollably? What if his father came to the mouth of the cave and looked down at him? Would he follow Duxie, run after him? Duxie would shout up, maybe. He would say, in his shaky voice: *Come on then Dad. I've put a very long story between you and me, a very long trail of words. Look at all the paragraphs. Look at all the sentences. Look at all the words and letters between you and me.* And his father would have to step on ever single letter, as if he were crossing stones in a very wide river, before he got to him, and Duxie would be ready for him then, he would be ready to face him then.

Would he tell her all this? Olly sitting by his side in the here and now, would she understand? Yes, sure she would. He would rush out and get some petrol, he would fire up the van and they would drive onwards, towards the prism.]

Did you get anywhere with his memory? Was he able to recall anything?
No, not at any stage. I asked him if he'd tried tastes and smells. He'd had a clear recollection once, with chocolate...
Best to leave it alone. Why play with fire? The past is the past, we can never remember it properly anyway.
How do you mean?
The past is a hologram. Your memories aren't neat little packages in a drawer, or video clips. They're a collection of chemicals which merely reflect your chemical and emotional state at the time. So don't expect the truth – just a jumbled-up version of your emotional state many years ago.

You mean he wouldn't be able to remember it all anyway?

Afraid not. Look at it this way. Imagine yourself as a little girl, lying on the ground, shining a torch into the sky at night. You twirl it around, pointing your beam at the moon and the stars. In a way you're sending out a message, a beam into the future. If you did the same tonight, if you twirled your torch around, pointed it at the moon and the stars, maybe the two beams would meet again – the beam from the little girl and the beam from you now – that would be a memory...

I think that's enough for today. I wouldn't worry too much if I were you. I come across the Duxies of this world all the time. Millions have gone through the same thing. There's nothing special about him.

Oh no, you're wrong there. Duxie was unique.

In what way?

He was different. There were things about him which were remarkable, things I'd never seen in anyone else.

Such as?

He could read my mind, almost.

That's not so rare – very common in people who've had a bad childhood, they learnt early on how important it was to detect their parents' moods.

And there was his dancing...

He won Celebrity Come Dancing, did he?

I thought you professionals weren't allowed to be sarcastic?

Very sorry. Truly. Please continue – his special abilities.

All right. You can believe me or disbelieve me, but whenever he danced people either laughed or cried. It was a definite gift. I saw him dance three times and every single person laughed or cried, every time. Honestly.

Give me an example.

OK. I remember the first time, no problem. Stefano was getting ready to close up for the night. The Gimp was putting the chairs upside-down on the tables and whistling loudly to irritate us. Stefano snuffed the kitchen lights and got his coat. The atmosphere became suddenly tense. So Duxie got up and strolled over to the jukebox, selected a number. I can't remember what it was. When the music came on – it was quite sad – Duxie started to dance in the centre aisle, moving up and down the café on the newspapers which the Gimp had put down on the floor he'd just washed. Well, you probably won't believe this, but within minutes he had us all laughing or crying. Some were laughing at him, others were crying with laughter, and there were others who were crying over the sheer pathos of his movements. No kidding. Stefano and the Gimp stopped what they were doing and sat down to look at him too. Stefano was the happiest man I'd ever met, always a smile on his face – but by the end of that dance he was wiping away tears of pure sorrow. The Gimp, on the other hand, was in pleats of laughter. That's the effect that Duxie had whenever he danced.

[Duxie would offer to walk her home, when the café closed. Would she go back for a coffee? He'd want to ask her about the magic in his dreams. Dr John Dee. The Harries mob at Cwrt-y-Cadno. What was all that about? He *thought* he knew, but he wasn't sure. Wasn't childhood supposed to be magical? But the fact that his father had been an amateur magician had muddied the waters. The whole thing was very complicated.

'Run it past me again,' she'd say as they stepped out on the pavement. 'Don't worry if it doesn't make complete sense. Just give me an idea.'

They would start up the hill, walking close together.

'Well,' he'd start hesitantly, 'it has something to do with alchemy. When you have a child it's a bit of magic, because it's all beyond comprehension. This thing comes out, and it's wonderful. Unbelievable. You've waved your magic wand (and here she'd blush a little perhaps, and cough, but he'd continue) and you perform the only magic trick you're ever going to perform. And then you want the best for it. The best you can manage, anyway. You want eternal life for it. You want to be seen as a magician in the child's eyes.'

He'd have to pause in the doorway of the gents' barbershop because talking and walking uphill would make him breathless. 'Understand me so far?'

And she'd nod, lean against the shop-front and light a cigarette. He would follow the little red dot in her hand with his eyes.

'But what if you get it wrong right at the beginning?' he'd say, now that his breath had returned.

'What if you start with gold but you make a mistake: you mix the wrong components together, you mess it all up and you end up with base metal. You're not making the grade as a parent. You get frustrated, hot and bothered. Try as you might, the base metal you've created refuses to turn back into gold. You get into a temper. You shout at the people around you. They look at you accusingly – they gave you gold but you're giving them base metal in return. That's the way I see it. Frustration. That's the main component. When a man gets it wrong and he can't get it right again he digs a bigger and bigger hole for himself, turns himself into a demon instead of a wizard.'

'I understand that completely,' she'd say, and he'd be relieved.

'It's like that with my own father – he gets it wrong, then he gets in a mood and starts shouting. But if you take that sort of shit once you end up taking it for ever. It's downhill all the way, Duxie.'

It would be the first time she'd called him by his name, and he'd feel good about it.

'Parents are like magicians,' he'd said. 'Almost all of them, 99 per cent of them are Harry Potters, but one per cent are Voldermorts. Agree?'

And she'd say: 'Yes of course I do, Duxie.'

They'd stand around for a while, then she'd say:

'Listen Duxie, about your father. I think we've got to move him from the football field. It's not the best place for him. I've got an idea...'

He'd look at her, quizzically. Would she know something he didn't? Were they going to build houses on the football pitch?

'He can still get at you down there, can't he? In fact, he's still getting at you, isn't he?'

Duxie would have to admit that he was. Wouldn't he always – for ever?

'Look,' she'd say, staring at him with those beautiful eyes of hers.

'We need to put him somewhere absolutely safe. Foolproof. And I know just the place. Somewhere in the Old World, some- where tried and tested. Up in Snowdonia, in the hills. Trust me.'

Trust her? Of course he trusted her.

'The picnic,' she'd say with a smile. 'You picnic in the snow. It's a great idea. Let's do it!'

Duxie would be over the moon. He would see towers and steeples of uncontaminated white drifting in curtains across the ravines, snowflakes rotating in *paso doble* twirls; he could smell the iron in the snow as it covered the land, extinguishing the fires of the past.

'I'll make the picnic,' he'd say. 'My treat. OK?'

'Yes, of course, that would be wonderful,' she'd say.

'Tomorrow?' A Sunday – perfect.

'And then I'll have to return to my own world,' she'd say, as if she was about to go down a wormhole, as if she was about to disappear for ever into another dimension.

And Duxie would feel very sad.]

13
THE TIDE GOES OUT

The interview tapes (3)

You decided, then, to go into the hills with him.
Yes.
Your idea or his?
The idea was his, but I chose the place.
And what was his plan?
A picnic in the snow. He'd been having dreams about it. He mentioned some famous films. Scott of the Antarctic was one of them, the one where Captain Oates walks out into the snow. He mentioned other films, too, all of them with people walking in the snow. He thought it would be fun to have a picnic in the hills when it was snowing.
Pretty original, I have to admit. And you chose the venue. Why?
It's a place I've known for a long time. It was ideal.
A long time? You're only young…
It's a special place – a place from my childhood. It's a place in Old Wales, which is about to disappear. I agree with Duxie on that. The lake will probably vanish too.
You're being fanciful now… I can see why he was drawn to you.
Perhaps I am. But the whole universe is inside your head, remember that. It all depends on how you look at things. To me, the lake is a place where I spent a really happy day once, my birthday. To a fishing club it's a commodity. There are ruins all around it, the remains of a small community – what did the lake mean to them?

[Seven momentous days – and they'd reached the final leg of Duxie's journey. He was excited, a bit edgy and nervous. They would have much to finalise. Together they would compile a list of things for him to do, in much the same way as he'd made a mental list, alone, of all the things which frightened him: *mannequins, sudden noises, whistling, big men with hairy ears and large noses, magicians…*

But on the Sunday morning she didn't turn up. Duxie was devastated. He sat forlornly in *Stefano's*, nursing his wounded heart. Mr Cassini landed right in front of him on the table and went to sleep, but Duxie was so engrossed in his own thoughts he missed his big chance to win the competition. Little Michael played *Tainted Love* on the jukebox, over and over again, just to hurt him.

> Sometimes I feel I've got to
> Run away, I've got to
> Get away…
> Take my tears…

Duxie asked everyone he saw if they'd seen Olly. No one knew anything. The ex-copper shrugged his shoulders and whistled *The Teddy Bears' Picnic* quietly under his breath. Mrs Griffiths said *don't bother me, who cares anyway* in a sharp little voice. After sitting in the café for the whole of the morning he scoured the town. He even went to the police station, stood waiting for ages, looking at a weird collection of seashells while nothing at all happened. The policeman shrugged his shoulders. For two days Duxie searched, and then he gave up. He was utterly miserable. His friends at the snooker hall phoned his workplace to ask where he was. Harriet knocked on his door and asked him if his microwave had broken down. And then, when he'd almost given up hope, she walked into the café late one evening, smiling at everyone and saying *good evening* to the copper and Little Michael, Mrs Griffiths, the Gimp, all and sundry in a breezy way as if nothing had happened. She went straight to Duxie's table and apologised. She told him that everything was OK but she'd had to go back home to see her boyfriend. It was going to be all right. He loved her and that was all that mattered, really.

She'd come back for the picnic; she'd come back specially with her red lips and her cornflower-blue eyes to help him complete his quest. Thank God. Time was running out. He could feel the water rising up inside him; on Sunday it had filled up his legs, then on Monday it had moved up his lower torso, streaming in through underground caves, rushing through caverns, carrying all before it. The water weighed him down now, he felt much heavier. He could feel it sloshing around within him; he could hear strange noises inside him: creaking, groaning, splashes, drips, echoes...]

Could you describe his state of mind at this stage?
Troubled, I'd say, but I also got the impression that something was coming to a head.
A resolution of some sort?
Yes. He talked about a book he'd read, something to do with water-divining. He said it was about a bloke who'd found a family of interconnected wells and traced the source of the water deep underground, inside a mountain.
Water-Divining in the Foothills of Paradise?
You've heard of it!
Yes, a minor classic in its day. The author disappeared, if I remember correctly – hardly anyone believed his story. All that Separate Reality *stuff was fading anyway. Too many doubts, too many fakers. By then the kids wanted to know which walls they should write on, which acidheads they should listen to...*

Anyway, he got interested in the water-divining man. He bought himself a set of rods, went out searching for underground water. He said it was quite exciting when the rods responded – he described it as a thrill coming from the metal, up through his hands. He said it was the first time he'd felt any sensation in his left hand. He was very excited about that. He told me that his hand was completely numb. That's why he wore the glove – to avoid burning it accidentally. He singed the leather if he rested his hand on a hot surface, so the smell acted as a warning.
Why wear two gloves, if only one hand was affected?
He didn't want to draw attention to it. Wearing just one glove looks odd.
This business with water – what was it all about?
I'm fairly sure it had something to do with his emotions. He described it as a force travelling up his legs and filling him slowly, as if he were hollow... as if underground water was forcing its way up his feet through a puncture and filling him up slowly.
Did this happen often?
No, not that often. He thought he'd detected a pattern. It happened in regular cycles, every so often.
Did he say how often?

He said it happened every seven years, or so it seemed to him. And then he'd have a major bout every twenty years or so. That's the way it seemed to him.

Which explains, possibly, his obsession with the number seven.

I hadn't thought of that. Yes, it could be a possibility. Again, it sounds simplistic, but you never know.

Did he talk about it?

A little, yes. He said there was no such thing as a personal catharsis – but he thought he could feel a sense of release every time, a sort of purge taking place.

You make it sound like a toilet being flushed.

That may not be such a bad analogy, actually. With the shit being left behind sometimes.

Or always?

No, sometimes – he saw the seven-year events as positive experiences. But the twenty-year crises were far worse, apparently. He described them as major inundations, as if he'd been swept away in a flood and was nearly drowned every time. He could cope with the seven-year cycles but he couldn't cope with the big ones. That's when the terror took hold of him. He was gripped by a terrible fear and he became incapable of leading a normal life. He disintegrated... dissolved. Those major inundations nearly killed him.

He was experiencing one at that time, presumably.

Yes, he was just coming to the end of it. He was pretty shaky. Our picnic in the snow was meant to be a celebration. That's why he was so excited.

[The country was opaque: the trees were broccoli, the icy hills were mashed potatoes under clingfilm – the whole land was a dinner waiting for the sun's hot *ping.*

His first task would be to dig up his father. He would have to sneak down to the football ground in the middle of the night again, he would have to remove the turf over the centre spot, dig down, and scrabble around in the compacted soil. He would have to find that grey plastic jar, reclaim it and take it back to his council flat on the hill. Perhaps he would be interrupted during his frantic mission by a night-watchman, a lonesome black-caped whistler with a torch, the fabled PC 66 striding out from the darkness of his own imagination: a representation of society and the establishment – complicit, unwilling to act until the very last moment, when it was often too late. Nevertheless, Duxie would regain his father's ashes, and after returning the sod (ha!) over the centre spot he would struggle back to his home, wet and muddy but happy in the knowledge that his quest was coming to a fitting end. He would divest his outer clothing by the front door and carry it surreptitiously under his arm along the fireproof corridors, anodyne and correct. He would wash his boots in the sink and then he would put everything in the washing machine, his gloves too; he would stand in the kitchen naked, trembling slightly, perhaps, with a mixture of cold and fear. He would wash and dry his little flowerbox trowel and return it carefully to the right drawer. Finally, he would wash the plastic jar and put it on a radiator to dry. Then he would take a bath. Phew! Mission accomplished. He would treat himself to a bong, since he had some very decent skunk stashed away behind the toilet cistern. My, how that skunk relaxed him. He was able to have a really good think...

Duxie was tired of trying to solve the riddle. All those irresolvable questions. The past had many tits and he'd sucked them all dry. He'd been looking for an unfindable personal history. He'd rebirthed a monster so that he could slay it. He had told a story. Story-telling was an archetypal need, closely allied to dreaming. Who'd said that? And all those grey depressions he'd experienced over the years, he sort-of understood them now. Big grey marshes with mantles of grey mist hanging over them. It was his mind's way of protecting him. In creating a near-constant but manageable diversion within him his mind has taken his eyes off those monstrous footprints in the mud. His unconscious had been a fretting goalkeeper, waiting for the next attack. Cunning, the mind. *You can change childhood by deciding what not to say about it.* Adam Phillips. Clever sod.]

When was your next encounter?
Tuesday morning. It was a lovely day, clear and bright, and we met in *Stefano's*, as soon as it opened. The floor was still wet – the Gimp had a habit of putting old newspapers along the main walkway to protect it from muddy feet. I love the smell of fresh coffee. I had warm croissants and there were little flakes of pastry all over my hands and plate. I felt really happy as I sat listening to the coffee machine hissing away, and the banter of early customers. Duxie had a fit of the giggles because Mrs Griffiths

had coffee cream all over her moustache. He just sat there and giggled. Stefano and the Gimp were huddled over the radio, and the Gimp said: *Hey everybody, it's good news. That little girl in the well, the one that got trapped. They've reached her. They're bringing her up. She's alive and she's going to be OK.* And everyone felt extra happy and I had to wipe tears from my eyes.

[She'd felt a hot surge of feeling coming up through her chest, a tightness in the neck too as a jet of pure, unadulterated emotion poured through her... it felt like a hot mouse going through a boa constrictor in a ripple, a peristalsis; and then the tears arrived, emerging into daylight, blinking – celebrities leaving a rehab centre in the glare of cameras, flashes... the shimmering eyes, the public announcements.]

And Duxie – did he behave normally?
Duxie was the happiest I'd ever seen him. He had a map and he laid it out on the table, facing me so that I could follow his finger as it traced a line from the coast, up through the foothills, past hamlets and villages. His finger stopped at a crossroads – no, a T-junction – up in the hills. There was a well there. He wanted to call on the way.

[At some stage, after the croissant crumbs had been swept off the table – he would use his gloved hands as a dustpan and brush – Duxie would wonder if there was time for one last game of snooker. Perhaps the cleaners would be up among the tables, swabbing the decks with those huge mops of theirs. He would ask them if it was OK. He'd play alone, under his solitary pool of light. He'd have one last contest against the forces of evil. He would go all out, make a break of 147. And he would give his children lots of extra lives, all of them. Afterwards he and Olly would execute the first part of their plan. Duxie had told her about the satellite. It watched him every day, it kept track of him. He had to account for every mile, every movement. It was enslavement. The Machine had finally won: this was a part of the New World he wanted to reject. But how? Olly would know. She'd giggle in that winsome way of hers which flooded him with concupiscence. Sitting together in the cab of his yellow pick-up, in the snow, in a tent of misted glass. That would be wonderful.]

What happened next?
We sat in the café and dreamt up a plan. He asked me how it could be done. I said: *easy peasy lemon squeezy.*
So it was your idea. You admit to that?
Yes, it was my idea. I'm not ashamed. In fact, I'm proud of it. It was great, really exciting. Standing by the flames, looking at all those colours. It was like watching a rainbow, close up. The van was like a box of fireworks going off. It warmed us up too. There must've been some glass in one of the parcels because there was a lot of smashing going on. That van looked really good, it was like bonfire night.
I don't think the delivery firm enjoyed it quite so much.
Oh, fuck the firm. They've got plenty of money, they can buy another sodding van.
You do realise you could be prosecuted?
They can do what the fuck they like. I hate control freaks.
Can you describe what happened, right from the beginning?
With pleasure. We left the café and went to his place, up the hill, in his pick-up. Then we went in convoy, him driving the delivery van, me the pick-up, along Big Bay. The roads were quiet, it was during that lull after nine when most people have already gone to work. I remember seeing a really brilliant rainbow... one end was in the sea and the other end was miles inland somewhere. As usual, I wondered if there was a crock of gold at the end of it. We joined the expressway and travelled along the pass which winds around the mountain. When we came to a lay-by I parked up and waited for him to do the business. After waiting a while, until there was no sign of traffic in either direction, he drove on for a hundred yards and rammed the van into the wall at the side of the road.
Nobody saw him do this?
No, he'd timed it perfectly. He wasn't hurt either, thank God. I saw him get out, unscrew a petrol can and douse the van in petrol. So I started the pick-up and drove up close to him, to make it look like I'd stopped after an accident. By this time the flames were taking hold. We just stood there, watching it all happen.
Other cars had arrived by now, presumably?
They started coming when the van was almost invisible, it was a mass of flames by now. Duxie ran to one of the cars and asked them to call the emergency services. Then we got in the pick-up

and drove around the van, buggered off as fast as we could. I could see the van through the rear-view mirrors, enveloped in flames. Duxie said *Yes!* and did a wiggle with his middle fingers in the air, like he was a football star celebrating a great goal. The satellite had been blinded, he said. Like the Gorgon.

And Duxie had lost his job.

Big deal. He was glad. Elated, in fact. Freedom's worth fighting for.

[Flickering red flames in the mirrors, a ball of fire. Queues of cars clinging to the shiny wet road, mosquitoes stuck to a lizard's tongue. Goodbye to the eye in the sky. Duxie stuck a middle finger out of the window and jerked it at the glassy cloche above him. *Fuck you, Big Brother,* he screamed at a wispy little cloud.]

After that you headed inland?

No, we had to stop at a lay-by again. Duxie was having a major panic attack. He thought he'd left the plastic jar – his father's ashes – in the van.

Had he?

No. The jar was in the back of the pick-up, in a plastic carrier bag, together with his telescope. So he got out and brought them into the cab.

[His immortal remains… Duxie's father had refused to die. He had lived continuously in Duxie's thoughts and dreams. Abnormally. And that was the nature of the beast. He had remained in stasis, like Damien Hirst's shark, swimming forever in formaldehyde – neither in a natural state, alive, nor allowed to become dust, or sludge, or whatever sharks became when they died in the sea. That was what his father had been to him, throughout his life: a shark swimming in formaldehyde. In a state of suspension, in a gallery. Most parents could be buried in a normal fashion, but some bodies needed quicklime.]

No signs of emotion? Did he seem upset?

No, he seemed quite calm. But I was coming to the conclusion that he needed to let go. Draw a line under it all. I think he knew that too. It seemed like a final battle between Duxie and his father's memory. He had been unable to grieve for him, to lay him to rest. That was quite clear. All through Duxie's life his father had been swimming around inside his brain. It was time to get it sorted. He needed a bloody good cry, that's what I thought. But there was one thing I didn't understand. What's the difference between memories of a normal parent and memories of a bad parent? Why couldn't Duxie let go?

I think it's the other way round. Normal parents let you go, they just go to sleep. But abnormal parents won't lie down and die. They call on you unexpectedly, shake you in the night, wake you up. They have a strong hold. The dead can be very demanding.

[He'd look at her through the corner of his eye. Yellow hair, and eyes the colour of ceanothus in a May garden, cornflowers in a field of bleached wheat. This would be a happy, happy day. And the picnic he'd made? They'd have it there in a rucksack. Where would she take him? They would head upwards, into the foothills of Snowdonia. The foothills of paradise.

> When looked at from Anglesey, they seem to rear their lofty summits right up to the clouds... at the very top of these mountains two lakes are to be found, each of them remarkable in its own way. One has a floating island, which moves about and is often driven to the opposite side by the force of the winds. Shepherds are amazed to see the flocks that are feeding there carried off to distant parts of the lake...

And so they'd wind ever upwards, Duxie and Olly, towards Snowdon itself, looming out of the clouds. Travelling through Wales, a corner store in a supermarket age. A country – like Saki's Crete – which produced more history than could be consumed locally. He'd guide her through Ysbyty Ifan, towards the well...]

Where did you go?
First, we went to a well. He wanted to make a wish. He was like that. Superstitious. Probably the most superstitious man I've ever met. We drove through an upland valley and then he guided me onto the moors, pointing with his little brown glove. I felt very close to him that day. He touched an Elastoplast on my arm and asked me about it – he wanted to know why I was wearing it. When we got out of the cab he pretended to take an Elastoplast off his own arm and then he did a little dance, pretending it was because of the pain – you know, that sting you get when you take a plaster off your skin. It was hilarious, but then it made me very

sad and I started to cry. I've told you about his dancing already. He could make you laugh or cry, jiggling about stupidly as if he was in an old silent film, like he was Keaton or Chaplin in *Limelight*, messing around.

Sounds like he had quite a gift.

He'd have won the X-Factor for sure.

So he made a wish.

Yes, though why *there* I don't know. It's in a forlorn place, at a T-junction slap bang in the middle of nowhere. It's called Ffynnon Eidda. Strange little edifice made of stone. You couldn't drink the water, it's quite disgusting. But under the water I could see a number of coins, some of them quite new and shiny, glinting in the water. It's still used as a wishing well. *How strange*, I said to Duxie. *That people are still doing this.* He pointed to the inscription. It said '*Yf a bydd ddiolchgar* – Drink and be grateful'. He seemed a bit emotional himself at that moment, for the first time. I thought his eyes misted over. Then he fiddled about in his pocket and brought out some coins. He dropped some of them on the floor, because his gloves made it difficult for him to hold onto things properly. I picked up some coins off the ground and handed them back to him. He took them, then he gave me a fifty pence piece. He held another fifty pence himself. I said: *What a waste of money, Duxie! Give us a two pee* but he shook his head and said no. This was going to be a big wish, the biggest wish of his life, so he wanted to use fifty pences.

Why not use a pound coin, then?

He said people would notice them and take them out.

Yes, I can understand his reasoning.

Anyway, after we'd chucked our coins in the water he closed his eyes and made a wish. When we got back inside the cab I asked him what it was all about, throwing a coin in a well and making a wish. He said it went all the way back to the ancient past, when early Celts threw metal objects into lakes and rivers as a sacrifice or a tribute to the water god. Some people think they were asking for good luck, other people believe they were trying to make sure a dead person's spirit wouldn't come back to cause trouble. They thought that by throwing the dead person's metal possessions into water they wouldn't be able to bother living people ever again. Some gypsies still do it – they burn the caravan and throw the pots and pans into the nearest pond or lake. King Arthur's sword is a version of the same story. That's what he said to me, anyway. God knows if it's true.

Did you ask about the wish he made?

Yes, but he just winked at me. *Won't come true if I tell you,* he said with a big sloppy here's-lookin-at-ya-kid smile.

[They would double-back, glide towards Llyn Cwellyn and its cold blue waters. By now a huge rabbit would be squatting over the pick-up, its fur pressing down on the windows. Snow would envelop them soon: greasepaint, for the final act. They'd arrive at the Cwellyn Arms and she'd stop. She'd park, and putting her hand on his arm again, in that wonderfully endearing way of hers, she'd whisper: 'Stay here. I won't be long.'

It would clear briefly; he'd watch ravens mottle the iris of the sky above, and trees swaying in a soundless wind on the slopes of Mynydd Mawr, the elephant mountain. Then she'd return, dashing suddenly from the door of the pub. She'd hoist herself into the driving seat, her left hand holding something out to him, and he'd look at it, startled. It would be half an onion, sliced cleanly into a hemisphere and still strong enough to make her eyes smart. Dumfounded, he'd ask her what was going on, and she'd snigger.

'Just you wait,' she'd say. 'You'll need that onion later,' and he'd be filled with wonder.

They'd swing off the main road and go west, the Nantlle ridge towering above them, and they'd be dwarfed by three granite giants: Mynydd Drws-y-Coed, Trum-y-Ddysgl and Mynydd Tal-y-mignedd. They'd stop again, at a lay-by. He would look at her, wondering if there was going to be another incendiary incident, but no, she'd say *come on* and she'd shoulder her bag and slam the door, then head for a stile. He would sling his telescope under his arm and within minutes they'd be standing by the side of a lake and she'd be pointing to the middle, at a small island. A neat little bump with plenty of foliage and a rowan tree drooping its red berries over a fan of ferns.

'This is Llyn-y-Dywarchen,' she'd say. '*The Lake of the Sod.* I thought you might enjoy the joke.'

And then she'd feign impatience with him, put her hands on her hips and say: 'For God's sake, Duxie, your brain's gone to sleep again. Where are the ashes?'

And he'd have to go back, across the stile to the pick-up; he'd retrieve the grey plastic jar, take it back to the lakeside. By now she'd be sitting in one of the fishermen's boats, a nice blue one, and he'd say *are you sure that's allowed* and she'd cluck and say *just get in will you* and they'd row out to the island in the middle of the lake. He would feel nervous. What if they were caught? Bailiffs could be very stern, they could shout louder than the men who watched football matches. Duxie would be feeling extra timid right now. He'd tremble and quake. *Shows a talent for sitting alone in wet bracken,* his school report had said once. *Shows a gift for loneliness.*

They would arrive at the island and they'd disembark. She would tie the boat to a tree stump. She'd stand for a while at the water's edge, with her bag over her shoulder, and she'd hold the bit of onion in her left hand, saying: 'You forgot this, you idiot.' He'd notice, for the first time, that she was left-handed. He would stand by her side, looking back towards the other boats, hoping no one would come.

'Right then,' she'd say. 'Let's get down to business.']

You rowed out to the island in a stolen boat?
Borrowed. We only borrowed it. It nearly sank – he was so heavy by then.
Arson and theft so far.
Have it your own way. I wanted him to be free.
Free to dream his childish...
We're all children at heart. Bet you've got a little kid running around inside that big body of yours too.
Let's not talk about me. Let's talk about Duxie. Why, for instance, did he dream up a book called The Dexter Propensity?
The answer was in the gloves. Duxie hid a secret in those gloves, and *The Dexter Propensity* was a major clue.

[Duxie would daydream by the lip of the lake – a mass of liquid *nothing,* and the dark water would begin to swallow stray snowflakes: yes, the snow would begin to tumble out of the sky, into the blackness, a tumult of softness falling into a mouth agape. Snow tasted of metal and violence. She would say: 'Duxie, this is important. We've come a long way to finish this story, and I don't want to mess it up now. We've reached the journey's end. You have created a causeway of words which stretch back a week.

It has been a momentous time for you. You have introduced us to the seven rainbow messengers, PC 66, and a terrible man called Mr Cassini who has lived on in your dreams and your daydreams despite all your efforts to destroy his memory. There will be some people who will wonder why you called him Mr Cassini. I think you owe us an explanation.'

And he would deflect her questions: instead, he would tell her about all the islands in his head, beginning with Gondwanaland perhaps, moving on to Galapagos with its great flightless birds and Madagascar with its aye-ayes, pottos, lorises and lemurs; the Islands of the Blest, Conan Doyle's Lost World, and Prospero's Isle too, full of sounds and sweet airs that gave delight... but the only true island was the one inside his head. Going to real islands was too risky. Like taking drugs, the trip could be either very good or very bad (and here he'd mention Cuba with its malign Guantanamo, and the Chagos Islands with their equally repugnant airbase, Diego Garcia). Like drugs, islands could enhance or destroy reality – sometimes they were sanctuaries, sometimes hellholes.]

And how did he get his name – this Mr Cassini? So far, Duxie's explanations have sounded rather unconvincing.

Duxie did have some sort of rational explanation, but only just. He said he was a melancholic, born under the sign of Saturn. The Romans were very clever people, he told me one day. They used every stratagem they could to tame and woo the people they encountered on their way to supreme power. They discovered that some of the tribes used secret names for their deities. This empowered the tribesmen: it gave them magical authority. So the Romans invited the tribesmen to Rome and seduced them with subtle promises. They gained the secret names of the gods. Once they had relinquished their secret knowledge, the tribesmen were powerless. This process of disempowerment by gaining tribal secrets was known to the Romans as *elicio*. When Duxie learnt about *elicio* he realised that he had to use a name which gave him power.

But why Cassini? Why not Jones, or Hughes, or Davies?

Cassini's Ring is a dark and divisive region within the rings of Saturn, so he thought it was appropriate. He was into the stars. He looked through his telescope every night. There was something else, too. The Cassini mission to Saturn is a voyage of discovery, and the probe had to shimmy through Cassini's Ring at one stage

to get to the other side. Duxie saw parallels with his own life…
He wanted to get to the other side?
Yes, he wanted to make a fresh start. He said he'd had enough of
it all, the angina of the past. He quoted a man called Fernando
Pessoa – *madness isn't the failure to make sense but the attempt.* He
said the water was still seeping into him but he was almost full.
The water had reached his head. He could hardly move by now,
he was so heavy with it. Some of it was coming out of his pores.
*This has cropped up in our conversations before, hasn't it? People with
holes inside them…*
Yes, he said he could see other people around him who also had
holes inside them. He would point to someone and say *look at the
holes inside her, there's almost nothing left…*
Did he discuss this in more detail?
Not really, but he did mention a man called Castaneda. This
Castaneda bloke wrote about a Mexican wise man called don
Juan. He met him in the desert. In a certain mental state this don
Juan could *see* people in a different way.
A mystic?
Castaneda described him as a Man of Knowledge.
And how did he see people differently?
He saw people as fibres of light. He said they were like white
cobwebs, very fine threads – circulating fibres. He described
people as a luminous egg-shaped mass of fibres.
On drugs, probably.
Yes, he certainly liked a smoke.
And Duxie – was he on drugs too?
He had been in the past, I'm sure of that. He'd tried to fill those
holes inside him with lots of things – alcohol, and drugs, and food
too. But that day in the snow he was clean, I'm sure of that. He
said he wanted to do it without anything inside him.

[*Olly, I'm full up again. The twenty-one years are up. Can you make
the water come out now?* She would give him one of her inscrutable
smiles. They had reached the end of the trail. She would have to
perform one last act before they could finish the story. She would
look at him with affection and compassion. His little-boy arms,
small and white. His little brown gloves. *This won't be painless,
Duxie,* she'd say. *I'm afraid you're going to suffer a bit. Duxie, you're
going to experience a little death…*]

Take me through that last hour. What else did you talk about?
He mentioned that book, *Water-Divining in the Foothills of Paradise*. He went over it again – how the author had found interconnecting wells and then went deep into the mountain to find their source. He'd emerged a totally different man. Duxie felt that the same thing was going to happen to him. Sounds to me like a little death, I said.
Little death? I thought that was how the French describe a climax.
Yes, there are similarities. But the little death which I'm describing is different. It's almost the same as a real death but you survive – just about. If a frog becomes completely frozen it actually dies. But when the thaw comes a special mechanism kick-starts its heart again. A little death is something like that, only in the mind.
And what happens then?
You start a new life. All that stuff from the past is flushed out. You get to grieve for the past and forget it all in a few hours.
You make it sound like a faked death, or a crab shedding its shell.
In a way it is. But it's a fake death of the soul, not the body.
So how did you plan to execute this little death?
I held my hand out and gave him the onion. I told him to hold it to his eyes. He couldn't cry at will, like Gielgud. But I had to get rid of all that water inside him.
The onion was a kind of ignition key?
Yes, I wanted him to cry for real – to cry for the past. I wanted him to cry for all the interconnected griefs he hadn't cried about before. I got the impression that someone had blocked up all his tear ducts. As if a well had been blocked up with concrete...

[Olly would find a small patch of ground on which they could sit, but the area would be so small they'd have to sit up close together on the tartan rug, hip to hip, and he'd get an itchy bottom from the heather stalks. She'd shove the onion into his hand while she unpacked the sandwiches he'd made earlier. She'd put some big red apples on the grass; yes, there had to be some apples.

'What's the onion for?' he'd ask. Perhaps she was going to put some in the sandwiches.

'Just you wait and see,' she'd say. And all they'd hear as she munched her butties would be the lonely sound of a distant curlew, a bleating of phantom sheep hidden away in sphagnum mossbowls, the sound of time itself winging backwards a thousand years, for

Duxie would hear Olwen's little-girl cries on the wind, coming from long ago, coming from her birthplace among the Welsh hills.

She'd point to the snowflakes, she'd say they looked like butterflies made from icing, and they'd fly like butterflies too, wavering and changing direction in the air.

Snow as congealed water. Tears as congealed emotions. Ice patterns on the ground: beauty for nobody's eyes, beauty because it was there, never to be a commodity or an adornment. By then the snow would be spinning a cocoon of silk around them.

We're in the vortex, he'd think. *We'll be inside the prism soon. The little white room.*

'Are you ready?' she'd ask. He'd waver and stutter. But she'd hold his hand in hers.

'Duxie, just trust me. I've done this countless times before. You must become a child again.'

Singularity.

He'd try to put her off one last time. 'Can I make a wish?' And she'd hand him a gold coin, a type he'd never seen before, and he'd flip it into the lake, make the biggest wish he'd ever made in his life, even bigger than the wish at Ffynnon Eidda.

She'd say: 'Duxie, can we get on with it now?'

And he'd hold the onion right up to his eyes, as the snow drifted and swirled around them, he'd hold it close to both his eyes, rub his eyelids with the stinging white flesh, but it wouldn't work.]

You tried to make him cry with an onion?
Yes.
What happened? Did it work?
No. Nothing at all happened. The onion failed to make him cry. I urged him on, told him that many brave men – even Scott of the Antarctic himself – were quick to cry. But nothing worked. He was still full of water; it was still oozing out of his skin.

So we sat there together and we had our picnic in the snow. That's not quite correct. I had a picnic in the snow. He was unable to eat by now. Too full. And by the time I'd finished my sandwiches there was a new urgency. Duxie needed to get to the end of the story. Completion. It may have been the light – that orangey smoulder before big snow – or it may have been tiredness, but it seemed to me right then that he was beginning to change shape.

14
THE TIDE COMES IN

The interview tapes (4)

I'd like you to carry on with the story. Can you describe how it ended?
I think we both entered an enchanted state. In reality we were sitting on a small island in a tiny Welsh lake, but in our cocoon of snow, sitting in perfect silence, each of us lost in thought, we were living – briefly – in a magical land. We were children again.
I suppose you saw the similarity to Afallon – it's almost too obvious to mention.
Yes, clearly. But he told me also about a former paradise on Earth called Hyperborea, at the very centre of the Arctic Circle. I've looked it up since. In Greek mythology it was a country of rich soils, soft azure skies, gentle breezes, prolific animals, and trees which bore fruit all the year, even in winter. Discord and sorrow were unknown. The inhabitants were the earliest members of the human race and they lived for a thousand years. They were a happy race, compassionate and contemplative. They died, eventually, by diving off a certain rock into the sea after full and happy lives. In some legends it was a land where white feathers fell continuously from the sky.
It was still snowing on your little island?
No, it had stopped by then. The clouds had cleared suddenly and we found ourselves in a wonderland of blue skies and gleaming snow, crisp and absolutely white.

[It was an island of dazzling fantasy. The snow was uncontaminated, not even a bird's footprint had marked it yet. When the sun shone in the Arctic, polar bears were known to lie on their backs with their limbs in the air, drinking in the yellow spirit. Duxie would feel like doing that now. Yes, he would do just that.

His breath would frost the chilly air; it would become a white balloon drag-anchored to his mouth, a cartoon bubble waiting for the right words to form in it – the words he'd want for this moment. Another balloon would float above Olly's mouth and he'd think of Salomon Andrée, a Swedish explorer whose balloon had come down in the Arctic ice-pack, condemning him to a rare death: the polar bear meat he ate in a vain bid to survive had contained a tiny parasitic worm, which had eaten him alive from within – a disease called trichinosis. Andrée's remains – a pair of legs and part of a torso, without the head, were found propped up against a rock on White Island, 200 miles east of Spitsbergen, 33 years later. Duxie would wonder if he too had worms riddling his insides, slaloming along his silvery viscera. Perhaps the worms would bore through his skin soon and he could join the circus as the Rainbow Man; fine jets of spray, tinged with all the colours of the rainbow, would arc all over his body. The water slopping around inside him would be released. He could see the headlines now:

> RAINBOW MAN FEELS A HOLE LOT BETTER
> WATER DIFFERENCE A DAY MAKES
> CIRCUS FREAK WORMS HIS WAY TO THE TOP

Yes, he'd be famous.

Then he'd almost go to sleep, a little polar bear with his paws in the air. The earth would lie underneath him still, exactly the same in form and content, yet it would have disappeared completely. Just like his childhood. He would feel its bumps and hollows pressing and yielding underneath him. Righting himself, he'd wiggle a hole with a finger through the snow between his legs: yes, he would see again the coarse grass and soft rushes of the uplands, pressed flat to the ground. A hint of sadness would creep into him; his body would have made a little hole of destruction in the snowscape already.

His mind would wander.

A Himalayan panorama, scrimshawed in carved ice, would open up in his mind's eye and a few garbled sentences from the *Tibetan Book of the Dead* would come to mind:

> O nobly-born, thy breathing is about to cease; and now all things are like the void and cloudless sky, and the naked, spotless intellect is like a transparent vacuum without circumference or centre. At this

moment know thyself and abide in that state. Thine own consciousness – shining, void, and inseparable from the Great Body of
Radiance, hath no birth nor death at this moment. Sounds, lights
and rays are experienced. These awe, frighten and terrify, and cause
much fatigue…

Olly would smile and flick her fingers with a sharp fillip because
she would have a wonderful surprise for him: seven figures would
appear over the brow of their little island and form a circle
around them. The seven Rainbow Messengers! Of course! They
would be there to witness the end of the story. They would be
frolicsome, in festive spirits, pushing and jostling each other playfully. They would be dressed in their best garb: shoes fashioned
from the finest Cordovan leather, with gold buckles; shimmering
tunics in all the colours of the rainbow. They would each represent a component of memory: sight, sound, touch, taste, smell.
Tears and laughter too. One of them – Orange, perhaps – would
tease him, saying:

*Duxie fellah, you've poked around in the earth, with your holes
and your wells. You've even dabbled with fire on the top of Pumlumon
Arwystli, but you haven't once mentioned wind,* and he'd blow with
all his might, and a strong wind would come swirling down
around them, scattering snow in their eyes, and Orange would
laugh until Olly said *that's enough now Rainbow Messengers, behave
yourselves…*

The seven Rainbow Messengers would clap and titter; one of
them might produce a Bible and read:

They went across the lake to the region of the Gerasenes. When
Jesus got out of the boat, a man with an evil spirit came from the
tombs to meet him. This man lived in the tombs, and no one could
bind him any more, not even with a chain. For he had often been
chained hand and foot, but he tore the chains apart and broke the
irons on his feet. No one was strong enough to subdue him. Night
and day among the tombs and in the hills he would cry and cut
himself with stones.

When he saw Jesus from a distance, he ran and fell on his knees
in front of him. He shouted at the top of his voice, 'What do you
want with me Jesus, Son of the Most High God? Swear to God that
you won't torture me!'

For Jesus had said to him, 'Come out of this man, you evil spirit!'
Then Jesus asked him, 'What is your name?'

'My name is Legion,' he replied, 'for we are many.' And he begged Jesus again and again not to send them out of the area.

A large herd of pigs were feeding on the nearby hillside. The demons begged Jesus, 'Send us among the pigs; allow us to go into them.' He gave them permission, and the evil spirits came out and went into the pigs. The herd, about two thousand in number, rushed down the steep bank into the lake and were drowned...

Duxie would thank the reader, and he would remember that the Mr Cassini of his dreams was possessed by demons, and had a pig living in his back garden. A hush would come upon them. The Rainbow Messengers would cease their chatter and Olly would look serious. She would point towards the way they came, across the water, towards the coast. She would say: Look at our wake. What do you think this means?]

What happened next?
Nothing happened for a while. We were frozen, too amazed to do anything.
The cold was getting to you?
No, it wasn't that. It was something else – something marvellous, more beautiful than anything I've ever seen. The ground glittered with colours – reds, and blues, and violets, and greens... we were suddenly in the middle of an extraordinary, fantastic display of lights, flashing and gleaming.
An optical illusion?
It was an illusion of some kind, perhaps, but I think maybe it was caused by the sun playing on the snow, being refracted through the ice-vanes all around us on the rocks.
Did Duxie say anything about it?
He laughed... no, he gurgled. He rolled over onto his back, pointed at the sun and gurgled like a baby.
Definitely on drugs, then?
No – as I've told you, I'm positive he was clean that day.
Why was he behaving like a baby, then?
He was stupefied by the colours – we all were. It was like being in one of those discos with a light show coming from the floor beneath your feet.
Did he talk?
Yes, he said something about the colours. He said *look, Olly, you've unwoven the rainbow.*

What did he mean?

He thought I'd separated all the colours and put them into individual bands. They were his past coming towards him, all the separate elements of his life converging at that precise spot. That's what he seemed to believe.

You've mentioned the word prism before. Was that what he meant?

Yes, that's exactly what he meant. He said he was inside the prism again. Near his white room.

White room? What did he mean?

He'd mentioned this white room before. He said he'd been in it twice before in his life. I got the impression that it was a near-death experience on both occasions.

Did he say when?

The first time was when he was a kid, the second time when he was in his late twenties.

But he didn't remember his childhood, that's what he said, isn't it?

Perhaps he wasn't telling the whole truth. Perhaps he remembered more than he cared to say. I got the impression, once or twice, that he was playing a version of the *Thousand and One Nights*, telling himself tales to keep himself alive. I simply don't know.

Did he say anything about this white room?

A little. He said it was a place with two doors. It was a place where you sat on a low white bench and you only had one decision left in life. There was only one decision left in the whole world, and it was a simple one.

[He would make a special chocolate cake, full of devious contents. But he would have no hunger left. After the water had all gone, his interior would be empty again.

> O nobly-born, when thy body and mind were separating thou must have experienced a glimpse of the Pure Truth – subtle, sparkling, dazzling, glorious and radiantly awesome, in appearance like a mirage. Be not daunted thereby, nor terrified, nor awed. That is the radiance of thine own true nature. Recognise it.

Sitting next to Olly on a small island in the middle of a lake in the middle of nowhere, he would wonder: should he ever take drugs again? Powdered or parcelled into tiny tombstones of white marble... the opiates which had kept him permanently on the threshold between two rooms. Earlier in the day, as he sat on the toilet, he would have rolled himself a supersize joint in case he became flakey during the day. But now, after rooting around for it in his shirt pocket, he would toss it into the lake. Wouldn't all this be enough in itself, without any special effects? And Olly... she would be so disappointed. She'd be looking at him and she'd be laughing, flicking the snow around her into the air, watching it cascade back to earth in small explosions of beauty. Trying to help him. She would thrust the onion into his hand and he would try again, but nothing would happen. They would sit in the snow with a ring of white water around them. Waiting for something to happen.]

This white room – I'd like to know more about it... was it a real room?
He simply described it as a small room with two doors. They could have been virtual doors because they didn't have handles, or signs on them. One led to life, the other to death. It was a very simple image, but that was the whole point, he said – at that stage nothing else meant anything at all... the entire world had disappeared. He had sat in this room in silence – the event was like a dream, but it wasn't – and then he'd made a very simple but fundamental decision.
To live or to die?
Yes, it was that simple. But it was beautiful, he said. Like being at a birth. A fundamental thing was happening, with amazing clarity.
He wanted that to happen on the island, too?
Yes, he was expecting it to happen. He said the seven colours of his life had all met again, and he wanted complete and absolute clarity for a few moments before he moved on.
You make it sound like a... a climax?
No, there was no suggestion of that. It was a feeling of supreme calm.

[He wouldn't be able to cry. But he would have to empty himself of water somehow, before it froze inside him, before it cracked him open. Ice was congealed water, tears were congealed emotions. He would look down at the hole he'd made in the snow with his finger and he'd see his whole life being carried away on a beetle's back as an insect, black and busy, snowploughed its way through a tiny terrain of snow-scree and disappeared into a hole.

He goes from place to place, he enters darkness. He falls down a steep precipice, he enters a jungle of solitude. He is pursued by karmic forces, he goes into a vast silence. He is borne away on the great ocean, he is wafted on the wind of karma. He goes where there is no certainty. He is caught in the great conflict, he is obsessed by the great affecting spirit. He is awed and terrified by the messengers of death.

The Rainbow Messengers would sing a sad lament and they would bow their heads, they would listen to the water lapping on the banks of the lake. Olly would hand out apples to all the Rainbow Messengers.

He'd tell them about the Yanomami shamans with rainbows in their hair, and he'd tell them about Merlin in the woods. He, too, wanted a vision of splendour again. A little death. When he came back to life the world would be brilliantly real. Extraordinary and beautiful. But first he would have to get rid of the water... he could hardly move.]

So there were two rooms, I think that's important, don't you?
No, he mentioned only the white room.
I think you've forgotten something.
What's that?
Well, he also mentioned a very dark room, in his dreams. Am I right?
Yes of course – there was another room, you're quite right. A very dark room, but it was getting lighter... gradually.
In his dreams?
Yes, in his dreams the room was getting lighter, he was beginning to see things inside it. He thought he was on the brink of a breakthrough of sorts.
But he never got to see what was inside the room?
No, not clearly. He thought there were people sitting in it... they were very quiet, they never moved. It all sounded weird, spooky.
A nightmare?
Close to a nightmare, yes.
Am I getting this right, then... he was between two rooms – between a very dark room from the past and a white room which... I don't know... took him into the future?
Possibly.
He was on a sort of threshold... the island was an in-between place, is that a possibility?
Yes, but you'd have to ask him yourself.

[In the bleak midwinter, frosty wind made moan; earth stood hard as iron, water like a stone... the snow would be cold and beautiful. Icing on the cake. A brief and flimsy covering for the earth. An age-old metaphor for absolution, purity, wonder and forgetfulness. He was attracted to snow because it blanked out the shadows; nothing unexpected could happen, nothing nasty could creep up on him from the darkness.

> May the Mother, she-of-white-raiment be our protector. May we be placed in the state of perfect enlightenment. May the ethereal elements not rise up as enemies. May the watery elements not rise up as enemies – may we come to see the realm of the Blue Buddha. May the earthy elements not rise up as enemies – may we come to see the realm of the Yellow Buddha. May the fiery elements not rise up as enemies – may we come to see the realm of the Red Buddha. May the airy elements not rise up as enemies – may we come to see the realm of the Green Buddha. May the elements of these rainbow colours not rise up as enemies. May it come that all the radiances will be known as one's own radiances.

The ice would be so beautiful. Icebergs were blue. Didn't the soul leave the mouth as a small blue light in Welsh folklore?

He would have to take his gloves off. It would be the only way. The onion would fail.

Olly and the seven Rainbow Messengers would fail. He would have to take his gloves off... just one more time.]

The onion failed to make him cry. Did you really think it would?
Perhaps not. But it was worth a try, wasn't it? Anything was worth a try.
Didn't work, though.
No, it was a great pity. I ran out of ideas then.
You'd finished your picnic by now?
Yes, I'd put the picnic things in my bag. There was only the rug left, a tartan thing he'd borrowed from someone. I was still sitting on it. He was still in the snow.
What next?
That was when he took his glove off. I heard the snap as he undid the popper and then I saw him peel the glove off.
And?
He had a very small hand. It was the hand of a child.
I seem to remember that he had small arms, too.

Yes, he had the arms of a child. They were puny and weak – not big enough for his body, really.

And?

I saw his right hand first.

Yes?

It was perfect, really, but very small. It could have belonged to a seven-year-old. Not a mark on it. It could have been made from porcelain. I could see his veins, they were small and blue like you see in kids. You could almost see through his hand.

[He would take his gloves off in the snow. He would reach for the little black poppers which snapped as they opened...he would peel his right glove off first. The inside of the lambswool glove would be a miniature snowscene. There would be a little warmth trapped in the wool for a while, and then the glove would lose its heat. His own heat, dispelled into the radiant air. It was a hand from a Renaissance nativity scene. Very white, with a shimmer of blue around it. Again, he thought of the *Tibetan Book of the Dead:*

> Be not attracted towards the dull blue light of the brute-world; be not weak. If thou art attracted, thou wilt fall into the brute-world, wherein stupidity predominates, and suffer the illimitable miseries of slavery and dumbness and stupidity; and it will be a very long time ere thou canst get out. Be not attracted towards it. Put thy faith in the bright dazzling radiance, vibrating and dazzling like coloured threads, flashing and transparent, glorious and awe-inspiring...

He would look at his right hand for a while, as he did every morning in bed. He would study its contours: the little hill below his thumb, the Mons Venus... the Plain of Mars; the long, delicate middle finger – his Saturn finger – with its tale of destiny... his fractured lifeline.]

Had you never seen his hands before? Surely he took his gloves off in the café, to eat?

No, never. Not to my knowledge, anyway.

Neither of them, ever?

No.

Didn't people notice? Didn't they say anything?

Little Michael was the only one who ever mentioned it... he had

a nasty streak, Little Michael. He made snide comments, like *do you wear them in bed too?*
Did Duxie ever give an explanation?
I think he said once that his hands were always sore because he was handling parcels and stuff all day – they were his driving gloves and he'd got used to wearing them. Something like that.
Were you curious, when he took his gloves off in the snow?
Yes, sure. Those gloves were part of him so I was bound to notice, wasn't I? It was like watching someone getting their clothes off before doing a streak.

[Did it snow in heaven? Of course, there was another Valhalla much closer to home – the Celtic otherworld, *Annwfn*. Below them, underneath the snow. Should he go there first? All the people down there would be speaking in a weird accent, using words he'd never heard before – they'd be talking in an ancient type of Welsh. How many words would he recognise? He would point to the snow on his boots maybe and say *eira*. Perhaps they'd look daft at him. There was one problem with going to *Annwfn*. Only seven would return – that was the tradition, wasn't it?

Annwfn – a place where sickness and old age were unknown, where there was music and a continuous supply of drink. Where they kept the cauldron of rebirth. Duxie was due a rebirth, he thought he'd earned one by now. And what would it be like, passing into the otherworld? Would there be a tinny, buzzing sound in his ears, a sharp pain in his head and the taste of blood in his mouth, all those sensations he used to get when his father banged his head against a wall? Would he be very afraid when he went to the otherworld, as afraid as he felt all those years ago when he heard the key in the lock, when he heard footsteps coming down the passageway towards him along the cracked red quarry tiles, past the black and white print on the wall with its line of pensive children? No, he would feel pretty good actually as he and Olwen and the Rainbow Messengers descended into the otherworld. But was it what he wanted? He would never be able to see the world again, never be able to go down to the café and drink coffee with his mate Stefano, never be able to score the perfect 147. He would never be able to save his children from the forces of evil...]

No, I wasn't particularly shocked when he took his other glove off. I'd felt a sort of... I'd expected something, in a way.

You expected something to be wrong with that hand?

No, not exactly. But I wasn't completely surprised either.

Why not?

I think something had warned me, inside my head. His little boy arms – they sort of said something to me. Part of him had never grown up. As if a part of his body had been frozen at a certain time in the past, like a car clock which had stopped during an accident. And I suppose there had been other hints too...all that guff about Mr Cassini's book, *The Dexter Propensity*... his hatred of left-handed people. It's easy to be wise afterwards, but we should have realised. Duxie was trying to tell us something all along.

His hand – tell me about it. Did it frighten you?

I felt nothing much, really. You get that strange sensation across your skin, don't you, like someone dropping snow down the back of your neck. Goosepimply – you know what I mean. I moved closer to him, wiggled my bum along the tartan rug, I was going to put my arm around him but I was too slow – he'd already done it.

[The click-counter would be still going in his head – *click click click click click*... everyone had one, he thought. A meter up there in the head. Every time something nice happened it went click and the number went up, every time something bad happened it went click and the number went down. He would meet his father for one last time in the otherworld and he would give him a big smile and he would hug him, hold him tight and he would be able to smell him again; that unique smell of moss, and earth, and whisky. And his father would be sober, and the click counter would go click and Duxie would read the meter in his brain, as if he were an electricity man poking around in a cupboard, and when the click-counter went click – because his father was sober – Duxie would shine his torch on the meter inside his head and it would say 1,000,000 negatives, 1,000,001 positives, and everyone would shout hurrah! They would have one hell of a party, and they would all get drunk (except his father) or spliffed out of their skulls and they would dance about in a conga, a conga that went from one end of the otherworld to the other.]

Was it disfigured?

Yes, quite badly. It had fingers and a thumb like a normal hand, but it had been burnt badly at some stage. Parts of it were a livid red, other parts were white or yellowish in a sort of cobweb pattern. It looked like a lump of meat, I suppose, with fatty bits. It had white ridges all over it, as if someone had held it under a candle and let the wax run all over it.

Did he say anything?

Yes. He held it up in the air and wiggled it at me. Then he said: 'The last bit of magic he got wrong'.

Is that all he said?

That's all he said.

Any idea what he meant?

I think he was talking about Mr Cassini – his father.

Had he been burnt deliberately?

I don't know.

I wish I could talk to him.

Yes, so do I.

[They'd be on their way down to the otherworld, and the Seven Rainbow Messengers would start singing a barbershop tune:

> We're on our way to *Annwfn*,
> We shall not be moved,
> We're on our way to *Annwfn*,
> We shall not be moved…

There would be seven wells down there in the otherworld, all them interconnected. Each well would be related to an *event* in his life… or should he say *accident*? Which word should he use? After each event – *accident* – another hole had appeared in his skin. His holes were interconnected, like the wells of *Annwfn*. Seven blemishes, which looked like fake wounds painted on a volunteer in a mock disaster staged by the emergency services. Every so often his blemishes sprung a leak and water came out of him everywhere. As if by magic. He was about to have such an occurrence now. He could barely move. Why was water so heavy? If he looked into the palm of his left hand he could see the water, moving around and glimmering under the red plastic of his skin. There were another six sites on his body: looking through them was like peering through a sheet of ice on a pond, looking at the water below: if he looked through the damaged surface of his skin, if he peeked through the old burn-marks, he could see a body of cool red water pressing up, trying to break through the surface. The Rainbow Messengers would understand everything: maybe they'd hug him, one by one, and laugh a bit and say *never mind, everything's going to be all right now...*

He would thank them all for their help. Together they would watch the afternoon fade, and he would prepare to scatter his father's ashes in *Annwfn*. The old bastard couldn't get up to any more mischief down here...he would come back to life again, as usual, but maybe they'd put him in a work party and he'd have to spend the rest of his life winding the well-buckets up and down, supplying *Annwfn* with a constant flow of fresh water. They would give Duxie a tiny bit of his father, perhaps, a bit of bone from his right hand, the slapping hand, and he could put it inside his telescope as a memento. Duxie and Olly and the seven Rainbow Messengers would sit on a little knoll and they would admire the beauty of the landscape. All those flowers, all that grass! It would be very beautiful down there in *Annwfn*. No cars, no rainbow vans, no satellites, no mechanical noises at all. The air would be busy with wings. Nature would be fresh and resplendent; they would have to shield their eyes.]

So his hand was badly disfigured. Burnt probably, or scalded.
Yes, that's what I thought too.
Did you get a close look at it?
Didn't want to, really. Anyway, I didn't get a chance to.
He put his glove back on?
No – he put his hand into the snow. Quite quickly – I hardly saw him do it.
And...?
He gave a sort of muffled scream. A cry of pain, but he tried to keep it in.
It hurt him?
A lot, I think. Then it occurred to me that he'd never felt anything in that hand before, that's what he'd told me.
Except for the feeling he'd got through the water-divining rods.
Yes, he'd felt some sort of sensation at that time, but his hand had been numb still. Now, in the snow – when he put his hand in the snow he felt real pain.

Was this a surprise to him?
No, I don't think it was. He knew exactly what he was doing.
So he could only feel pain when he put his hand in the snow?
In extreme temperatures, perhaps. I think he would have felt pain if he'd put it in a fire or in boiling water too.
What happened next?
He held it in the snow for quite a while. A few minutes – it felt like a long time.
Did he show any pain?
Yes. He started to cry.

[He would cry. Tears were fallen stars, weren't they? He would ask Olly to look through his telescope – from both ends. Look, he'd say, Mr Cassini's the same size whichever way you look at him now – from the past end of the telescope or the future end, he's the same size as a fly...]

He cried, at last?
Yes. He cried and cried. For ages. It felt like days. I was transfixed by it, couldn't move. There was water coming out of him every-where. It seemed to be coming out of his clothes, from all over his body. I've never seen anything like it. Even the lake waters seemed to rise, he cried so much.
Did he say anything?
No, nothing at all. He just wept, as if he had never cried before – as if he'd been storing it up for years. He cried like a little boy. I held him for a while. I tried to console him. We'd got rid of the satellite, I said. He could choose his own future now. He was in control. His ghosts had been laid to rest. He could be at peace.
What was his reaction?
He said *Yes Olly*, but he was miles away. It all meant nothing, really. I'd thought – hoped – that the whole thing was sorted.

[It would feel as if he had millions of gallons in there, a bottom-less aquifer. How could one small human contain so much water? It was as if he were trying to recreate a primitive ocean so that he could return to it – as if he were trying to return to an amoebic state, amniotic and protective. Finally, all the holes in his skin would seal up; he would be empty again, completely drained of water. He would feel very light, as if he were on the moon. He would look back over seven days and he would take one last look at the words he had expended, littering the ground like snowflakes. When all was said and done, words were snowflakes. They came and they covered the ground, and everything seemed magical for a while, and then they became slush, melting in dirty meltpools. And the land would be back again…

The story should end at this point, but it wouldn't. He'd be disappointed. He would stand up and flex his legs because they'd be stiff by now. His bottom would be wet. Suddenly, he would feel very tired. He would be cold too. He would rub his shoulders to warm them. His teeth would chatter. He would smile at Olwen and she would smile back at him. It would be time for him to enter the white room again… it was time to go.]

And what happened after that?
He told me not to eat any of the chocolate cake.
Pardon?
He said *don't touch the chocolate cake.*
What cake?
He'd made a cake, it was in a tin which he'd put in my bag.
Not just a normal cake, I take it.
No, obviously not.
I'm struggling… why would be say that?
I'm not entirely sure, but I think maybe he had second thoughts about something. It was like a change of plan. I think he'd intended to eat the chocolate cake and maybe offer me some too. But then he decided, somewhere along the line, not to.
Why?

[Fly agaric… poisonous, a relative of the more lethal Destroying Angel. Hallucinogenic. In Lapp societies the shaman prepared the mushroom carefully to make it safe enough to eat. During his trance he would twitch and sweat. His soul left the body as an animal and flew to the otherworld to communicate with the spirits. The shaman's urine was recycled and could pass through up to seven people, staying potent. St Catherine of Genoa used fly agaric to achieve religious ecstasy.]

He told you not to eat the chocolate cake because it was drugged, presumably.

Yes, that's the only sensible explanation.

You have no idea why?

Yes, I have an idea – but it's only a possibility, not a probability.

And that was…

He'd mentioned once that he wanted to try it without drugs.

Try what?

Moving from the dark room to the white room.

Yes, you've mentioned that already. I have a rough idea what he meant. He implied that he'd kept himself in a state of permanent suspension, on the threshold between the two rooms, I think.

Yes.

And he'd used drugs to do this.

Yes, and alcohol. Food also. He used them to fill the holes inside him, to keep the water out as long as possible and to keep himself in suspension.

Had he managed it?

Mostly, yes. Sometimes – he mentioned the twenty-year cycle – he was dragged back towards the dark room.

What happened?

He was capable of absolute terror when that happened. All his defences were broken and he became extremely scared of something.

Something?

He was never able to identify what caused his terror. But he knew it had something to do with Mr Cassini.

[Olly would be restless by now. She'd say *come on Duxie, we must get back, or we'll be here for ever.* He would see a few snowflakes gyrating in the air; it would begin to snow again. Olly would get up, shake the snow off the tartan rug, fold it carefully and put it in her bag. It would be time for them to leave the island. The snow would be melting fast. The ground would begin to appear again, rubbed into existence again by an unseen coin in an unseen hand. The Rainbow Messengers would check their apparel, rub their shoes on the grass clumps to get rid of the snow.

Shall we make a move? Olly would tell the Rainbow Messengers to go on ahead because their work was finished. They'd all hug each other and laugh or cry. One moment they'd be there on the island, then they'd have zoomed off in a brilliant, radiant, dazzling super-arc which stretched far into the distance. He'd be waving at them long after they'd gone; a rainbow tinge would remain in the air for some time afterwards.

Duxie, it's decision time, she'd say. *Look, you can stay in your make-believe world or you can come and sort things out on earth.* He'd be torn between the two options – should he stay there, or should he go back with her, to tie up all the loose ends?]

I tried to be firm with him. He'd stopped crying by then but he wanted to stay. I was bloody perished, I wanted to go home. So I tried to drag him off the island, back into the boat.

Tell me, did he put his gloves back on?

Yes, straight away. I never saw his hands again. I didn't mention the crying. I think he felt rather foolish about it. He made a joke of it, said he needed a good cry now and again. I'm just a big kid really, he said to me.

How was he at this stage?

Subdued... he looked pretty groggy and his eyes were very red. But he made me leave without him.

That must have been difficult.

Very. I thought it was crazy. But he wouldn't have it any other way.

You must have found it hard to leave him there, surely? He would have been stranded.

He was adamant. So I let him row me back to land. He got out for a bit. We sat on a tussock, looking back at the island. I tried to talk some sense into him.

What did you say?

I tried to persuade him not to dwell on the past, on his problems. I said he needed to sort things with his family, find them again. I was a bit hard on him, I suppose. I told him he needed to raise his eyes from his own petty problems. His children probably needed him right now.

[Olly would be cross with him. 'Look what *they* had to overcome to survive, all those people who came before you,' she'd say. 'Your own little problems are nothing in comparison. Your children need you...'

'But they seemed to be coping fine.'

'That's not the point, Duxie, and you know it. Maybe they need you around, that's all. One thing's for sure, you won't find out unless you get in touch. You're taking the drugs route to oblivion, and that's selfish. You know it. You're being selfish.'

He'd nod a lot, but he wouldn't say very much. He'd be occupied with something on the ground by his feet – he'd scoop it up in his hands and they'd look at what he'd found: a tiny worm, a baby worm probably, which had drowned in the melting snow water. It would look pathetic, the colour washed out of it already.]

Then he left you?
Yes, he held me tight for a long time. I could smell the earthworm on his glove. He gave me all the picnic stuff and then he got straight into the boat and rowed off. He was looking at me all the time he rowed across.
Was that the end of it all?
Pretty much. I waved to him when he landed on the island again, and he waved back. There wasn't much point standing there all afternoon so I went back to his pick-up and drove back.
And how about him – how was he getting home?
He said he'd be all right, thumbing it. So I drove home.

[He'd sit on the island and he'd see a long line of people, from one horizon to the other. There would be thousands and thousands… his ancestors on one side and his descendants on the other. His own children would be right next to him, and they would laugh and mess around. They would do the conga. *Come on Dad, do your special dance,* they'd say. So he'd do his special dance, and they'd love him again. He'd look up, and there would be a long line of people stretching into the distance, all doing the conga.

The Rainbow Messengers would have disappeared into thin air and Olly would have gone for ever. His alibi girl. He would shout out her name and it would echo back from the hills around, but there would be no response. Soon, he would be all alone. Maybe he'd get a coin from his pocket and he'd spin it into the lake. He would make a final, final, final wish. He'd hear the plop far below.

A white light would spread along the land; it would grow in strength, almost blinding him. And he would realise what it was: a mist, coming to engulf him. A cold white breath coming to enfold him. Soon, he'd be asleep in the mist and the snow would start falling again, flowing around him in the silent air, covering him in a featherweight duvet of white.]

He was going to his white room?

No, not necessarily. He was looking for it.

An igloo?

No, I don't think so.

Was it on the island?

I don't know. It could have been anywhere – I think it was a state of mind, not a place.

And the dark room – was that also a state of mind?

I don't know for sure, but I think the dark room was a real place in his past.

Would he have given you a sign if he'd reached the white room?

Again, I don't know. There was a big problem with going into the white room.

What was that?

He couldn't go into it without going into the dark room afterwards, at some stage.

Could you explain that to me?

You'd have to ask Duxie himself to get the truth.

Come on, give me some sort of idea.

Well, he said that coming out of the white room was an amazing experience.

Did he describe it?

He couldn't because it was such a personal thing. It was a feeling of ultimate happiness… complete joy, I think. The world seemed very, very beautiful. Everything seemed very simple. He said he could live happily in a single second and it would seem as if it lasted for eternity.

Sounds like an LSD trip to me.

No, that was the whole point. He'd used drugs to keep him on the threshold of the white room for a long time, but when he went into the white room the whole point of the experience was to be on nothing except fresh air.

And you believed him?

Yes. It was necessary to take the drugs route first, he said. One could achieve absolute clarity only if one had tried to reach it through drugs and failed. It was all a matter of contrast.

But I thought that every drug trip was an attempt to recreate the magic of the first trip.

Not for him, I don't think.

OK – we'll have to leave it at that, I suppose.

No, there was something else – something very important. Going into the white room was an amazing experience, but there was a downside.

Which was?

Eventually the colours faded and normal life would catch up with him again. He would start worrying about mundane things again – about bills, and having somewhere to live, and money – that sort of thing.

How long did the colour world last?

It depended on the clarity he experienced in the white room.

Go on, give us an idea.

At least six months, perhaps longer.

And then?

He would have to go into the dark room again.

But he couldn't. He said many times that he couldn't remember it clearly.

No, he couldn't remember it clearly but he could remember the fear and the dread. He could feel the horror all over again.

[Damn. He'd forget to leave a note for Harriet. She'd worry about him. She'd put a glass against the wall and listen out for the *ping*! And the boys at the snooker hall… they'd talk about nothing else, not even about motorway exits and the girls in the trailer parks. It would be snowing heavily now. The whole country would be preoccupied with this white scab, picking at it. His mind would drift to Siberia's seven time zones, the reindeer's third lung to keep it warm. He'd open his mouth and taste the snowflakes falling onto his tongue. An iron taste, like blood. He'd have a little nap, then he'd head for the white room. He'd know where it was now. Inside a snowflake, inside his head. Mr Cassini would be trapped forever in the telescope. If Duxie looked inside that cylinder Mr Cassini could be a few inches away, or he could be somewhere in deep space, or he could be a little dot moving around on the silvery moon – wherever he was, he couldn't harm anyone now. Duxie wanted a view of the truth. Galileo risked his life, everything, for the truth. Duxie would sleep for a while, then he'd wake with a start. It was dangerous to sleep in the snow – he could die. He wouldn't want to die now. He'd want to live. He'd want to go into the white room again, he'd want to see all those wonderful, brilliant colours.]

What will you do now?
I'm leaving tonight. This business has taken a lot of my time already. I was supposed to marry a month ago, but we had to delay it.
Going ahead now?
Yes, next Saturday.
You never know, it might snow. That's the forecast...
Yes, we hope it does.
I bet the photographer doesn't.
Why's that?
You're getting married in white?
Yes of course.
You won't be able to see the dress in the snow. No contrast.
Perhaps I should marry in black...
Don't think that would go down very well. In red, perhaps? That was the medieval colour wasn't it?
Funny... wasn't Mr Cassini a funeral photographer in Duxie's dreams?
That's what you said.
Are there such people?
Yes, I think so – in some religions.
Why not. Seems OK to me.
You won't have to worry about that for a while – you're still young.
True.
It's been nice meeting you. I've enjoyed it.
Well I haven't. It's been a very strange time, and I feel as if I've failed him. But there were times when I thought he was using me.
Could you explain that?
You know something – that little girl down inside the well was the only important thing to happen all week, but he was only interested in his little island of introversions. I felt like an actor, a girl in a fairy tale or a myth, just a foil for his ego trip. It's a tic of the age – a hypochondria, a pathetic need for self-diagnosis. He wasn't really interested in me as a person.
But you did everything you could.
Sure, but it didn't help much, did it?
How do you know? He could be inside his white room at this very moment. He could be about to reach the colour world again.
I don't suppose we'll ever know.
No, that's for sure. Can I offer you a lift?

Yes, that would be great.

Where to?

I wouldn't mind going to the white room myself.

Now you mention it, nor would I.

There's one last thing.

Yes?

His mobile – it rang when we were on the island.

Did he answer?

Yes, it was the nuisance caller again.

Are you sure?

Yes, I could tell. So I took it from his hand and I shouted as loud as I could at the person on the other end. I was really angry. I told him to fuck off and leave Duxie alone.

Did he answer?

No, nothing. But I could hear some music in the background, very light, the sort you get from a musical box or some sort of wind-up thing.

And?

I threw his phone into the lake. As far as I could.

He'd be almost asleep now. He would go up into the tree, he would feel as light as a snowflake, or a butterfly, in the upper branches, and he would look all around him, to all four corners of Wales. Waves would break in his head – he would miss the sea – and far below him he would see the diving rock from which the Hyperboreans made their final exit from the land, into the copious oceans from whence they came. Perhaps he would see seven swans flying along the horizon, through a rainbow. There would be an opportunity for a final imprecation to Lady Luck and good magic...

He'd feel nothing by now. His body would be anaesthetised. The numbness in his body would merge with the numbness in his hand. Quite pleasant, really. He would sleep for a while. Just a few minutes, to refresh him. The snow would mean something new to him now – a secret relationship; an eradication, a light on the truth. Perhaps he would dream again. A nice dream. There would be people on the shore, waving to him. Was that Karol Karol the Polish hairdresser he could see, and Captain Oates with Yuri Zhivago and Baron Munchausen? They would want to be there with him. But first he'd have to go to the eye of the prism.

He would see a vision of splendour. A moment of absolute clarity. All time would be there: the past, the present and the future. He would desire, now, the silence and the beauty of the prism, and then he would want to step out again, into the world… he'd want the seven colours of his existence, the seven basic plots, to meet him in the branches of this rowan tree, to fuse into a tranquil clarity; he would look down into the very earth itself, and he would see all that was below him in the ground: gemstones and crystals and agates shimmering in their myriad colours, and living creatures splendid in their earthy skins; and he would look into the sky above, at the perfections of blue and white and grey and pink. And in the exit from the prism, he would engender his own story – in the meeting of all the colours and their parting again, with the cocoon unspun, he would create his own curious refraction – another story, the eighth; his own personal version… it would start with a sheaf of white paper in a child's hand; a love letter to the world, sent in a new white envelope, unaddressed. And it would seem to him that all the many millions of words he had expended in his life would be rendered to but a few, a haiku of his own existence, or a mere verse:

> Out of whose womb came the ice?
> And the hoary frost of Heaven, who hath gendered it?
> The waters are hid as with a stone,
> And the face of the deep is frozen.

Then he would take a step forward on the tree's outstretched palm, and he would fly.

15
EPILOGUE

Arthur Jones, known to his friends as Duxie, was reported missing in February 2005. There have been no sightings of him since, and not a single message has been received from him.

Up to a quarter of a million people are reported missing in Britain every year, and although most of them are found again, or turn up safe and well, thousands disappear without trace. Duxie's family haven't given up hope of seeing him again. They believe he'll walk back into their lives one day.

Duxie left three photographs on the table by the window in his flat, overlooking the football field.

One shows a man in a fez, a magician, about to do a trick.

Another shows a rainbow over the sea with seven white swans flying through it.

The third photograph shows a picnic scene somewhere by a lake, and the hills in the background are covered in snow. A very beautiful young woman is looking into the camera. She has a happy, excited look on her face. The other person in the photograph is looking past the camera, into the distance, and he's smiling.

On the door of his flat they found an orange Post-it note with seven words written on it:

Gone for a picnic with Olly – Duxie.

Acknowledgements

I wish to thank the following: Don Waine for providing many ideas; Penny Perrin for her inspired picnics; my editor, Penny Thomas; also Dr Christine Gilbert, Patrick McGuinness, Cary Archard, Dafydd Apolloni, Derek Mahon and Brynley Jenkins.

Many thanks also to Richard C Allen for allowing me free and unlimited use of his excellent article on the Wizards of Cwrt y Cadno, which is published in the *North American Journal of Welsh Studies*, Vol 1, 2 (Summer 2001) and available on http:// spruce.flint.umich.edu/-ellisjs/Allen.PDF.

I have adapted passages from *The Tibetan Book of the Dead* for the purposes of this book. For the real thing read the *The Tibetan Book of the Dead*, edited by Evans-Wentz, W.Y. (1971), OUP, (extracts reprinted by permission of Oxford University Press, www.oup.com) or visit: http://reluctant-messenger.com/ tibetan-book-of-the-dead.htm.

Likewise, a passage in Chapter 10, written in a style similar to that of Arthur Machen, is an adaptation of a passage from *The White People* by Arthur Machen(copyright © Arthur Machen 1909). To view a proper version of *The White People* visit the website

http://gaslight.mtroyal.ab.ca/whtpeople.htm

For more information on Arthur Machen visit:

http://www.machensoc.demon.co.uk/ or read *Arthur Machen* by Mark Valentine, Seren.

The lines quoted in Chapter 10: 'Papery moths drift to the light, / Churr in a hand's cave, / Then out, out.' are from 'Early Summer' by Peter Scupham.

The passage from *The Adventures of Baron Munchausen*, by Rudolph Erich Raspe, is from http://www.authorama.com/ adventures-of-baron-munchausen-1.html

'People with bad consciences always fear the judgement of children' is a quote by Mary McCarthy.

'The Snow Party' by Derek Mahon, from *Collected Poems* (1999), is reprinted by kind permission of the author and The Gallery Press, Loughcrew, Oldcastle Country Meath, Ireland.

The following books were also consulted, and, in some cases, quoted:
The Doors of Perception, by Aldous Huxley, Vintage Classics; *The Island of the Colourblind*, by Oliver Sacks, Picador; *The Emperor's Last Island*, by Julia Blackburn, Pantheon; *A Separate Reality: A Yaqui Way of Knowledge*, by Carlos Castaneda, Arkana; *The Life of Olaudah Equiano: Or Gustavus Vassa, the African*, by Olaudah Equiano, Dover Publications; *If on a Winter's Night a Traveller*, by Italo Calvino, Martin Secker & Warburg, (extract reprinted by permission of The Random House Group Ltd); *Desert Encounter*, by Knud Holmboe, Quilliam Press; *Dancing on the Grave – Encounters with Death*, by Nigel Barley, John Murray; *Paradise Lost*, by John Milton, Oxford University Press; *Dracula*, by Bram Stoker, Penguin; *The Primary Colors*, by Alexander Theroux, Henry Holt and Co; *The Journey Through Wales*, by Gerald of Wales, Penguin Classics; *Best Walks in Southern Wales*, by Richard Sale, Constable; *Terrors and Experts*, by Adam Phillips, Faber & Faber; *Houdini's Box*, by Adam Phillips, Faber & Faber; *On Kissing, Tickling and Being Bored*, by Adam Phillips, Faber & Faber; *Winnicott*, by Adam Phillips, Collins; *Darwin's Worms*, by Adam Phillips, Faber & Faber; *Monogamy*, by Adam Phillips, Faber & Faber; *The Penguin Book of Chinese Verse*, introduced and edited by AR Davis; *The Mabinogion*, translated by Gwyn Jones and Thomas Jones, Everyman; *Celtic Heritage*, by Alwyn Rees and Brinley Rees, Thames and Hudson; *The Age of Arthur*, by John Morris, (extract reprinted by permission of Phoenix, Wiedenfeld and Nicholson, an imprint of the Orion Publishing Group); *The Ancestor's Tale*, by Richard Dawkins, Weidenfeld & Nicolson; *Voices of the Old Sea*, by Norman Lewis, Penguin; *To Run Across the Sea*, by Norman Lewis, Cape; *Arthurian Literature in the Middle Ages*, edited by Roger Sherman Loomis, OUP; *The Legend of Merlin*, by AOH Jarman, University of Wales Press; *The History of the Kings of Britain*, by Geoffrey of Monmouth,

About the Author

A former farm worker, nurse and journalist, Lloyd Jones lives on the North Wales coast. After nearly dying of alcoholism and undergoing spells in hospital and living rough, he quit drinking and walked completely around Wales – a journey of a thousand miles. In doing so he became the first Welshman to walk completely around his homeland, and his epic trek was the inspiration for his first novel, *Mr Vogel*. For *Mr Cassini* he changed tack, walking across Wales seven times in seven different directions.

Mr Vogel won the McKitterick Prize in 2005 and was shortlisted for the Bollinger Everyman Wodehouse Prize for Comic Fiction.

Praise for *Mr Vogel*

"Surely one of the most remarkable books ever written on the subject of Wales – or rather around the subject, because it is an astonishing mixture of fantasy, philosophy and travel, expressed through the medium of that endlessly figurative country."

– Jan Morris

"A rambling, redemptive mystery stuffed full of all things Welsh: rain, drink, wandering, longing, a preoccupation with death and the life that causes it. A bizarre and uncategorisable and therefore essential book." – Niall Griffiths

"The tour-guide Wales has been waiting for: warped history, throw-away erudition, sombre farce. Stop what you're doing and listen to this mongrel monologue." – Iain Sinclair.

"Mixing fact and fiction, Jones shoehorns elements of the detective novel, a great deal of mythology and some uncommon history into what must be one of the most dazzling books ever written about Wales." – *Independent on Sunday*

Mr Vogel is available from Seren, £7.99, www.seren-books.com

Overland
Richard Collins

author of *The Land as Viewed from the Sea* – shortlisted for the Whitbread First Novel Award

Home isn't a place on the map, it's a state of mind.

Sometime like 1978, somewhere like Europe, Oliver and Daniel are driving towards and away from home on a roadtrip to places that never were. Two men with very different purposes and meanings to their lives travelling, for a while, in the same direction.

Richard Collins' new novel is as vivid and atmospheric as his first, his prose both lucid and evocative. *Overland* is an exhilarating, comic, tender, crazy and ultimately moving account of two journeys towards love.

ISBN 1-85411-420-4   £7.99

Eleven
David Llewellyn

It's 9am on September 11, 2001. Just another day at the office for the twentysomethings of corporate Cardiff, as they email each other their gossip, jokes, requirements for the weekend and, occasionally, work.

At the centre of the novel's online world is 'process accountant' and would-be author Martin Davies. Martin is frustrated by his job, in denial over his break up with his girlfriend and baffled by the triviality of his life. And when, just after lunch, people start flying airliners into New York office blocks, Martin feels he is losing the plot....

Written entirely in email form, *Eleven* is required reading for anyone who has ever clicked SEND when they really should be doing something else.

ISBN 1-85411-415-8   £6.99